FRONTIER CTHULHU

ANCIENT HORRORS IN THE NEW WORLD

Call of Cthulhu® Fiction

These, and more, can be found on our catalog at
www.chaosium.com

Call of Cthulhu® Fiction

FRONTIER CTHULHU

ANCIENT HORRORS IN THE NEW WORLD

Paul Melniczek
Angeline Hawkes
Lee Clark Zumpe
Lon Prater
Stephen Mark Rainey
Durant Haire
Stewart Sternberg
William Jones
Scott Lette
Ron Shiflet
Robert J. Santa
Jason Andrew
Charles P. Zaglanis
Matthew Baugh
Tim Curran
Darrell Schweitzer

Edited by William Jones
Cover Art by Steven Gilberts

A Chaosium Book
2007

CHAOSIUM
INC.

Frontier Cthulhu is published by Chaosium, Inc.

Cover art © 2007 by Steven Gilberts; all rights reserved. Cover layout by Charlie Krank. Interior layout by Deborah Jones. Edited by William Jones; Editor-in-Chief Lynn Willis.

ACKNOWLEDGEMENTS
"Terror From Middle Island" by Stephen Mark Rainey and Durant Haire originally appeared in *Dark Wisdom* magazine (2006).

"The Rider of the Dark" by Darrell Schweitzer originally appeared in *Weird Trails: The Magazine of Supernatural Cowboy Stories* (2004).

Our website is updated frequently; see **www.chaosium.com**.

This book is printed on 100% acid-free paper.

FIRST EDITION
10 9 8 7 6 5 4 3 2 1

Chaosium Publication 6041. Published in November, 2007.

ISBN: 1-56882-219-7

Contents

It is only within the last few years that most people have stopped thinking of the West as a new land. I suppose the idea gained ground because our own especial civilisation happens to be new there; but nowadays explorers are digging beneath the surface and bringing up whole chapters of life that rose and fell among these plains and mountains before recorded history began.
—H.P. Lovecraft, "The Mound"

The Long Road Home

By Paul Melniczek

The group of warriors made their careful way up the hillside, finding it increasingly difficult to secure proper footing in the waning light. Eirik angled his neck skyward, catching glimpses of the crescent moon as it looked mournfully down on them. It bothered him, although he didn't know why. Actually, he'd felt uneasy the entire afternoon, but for no outward reason.

And that was even more troublesome . . .

He always relied on instinct above all other senses. It had saved his life more than once. Saved his men from ambush at Rijick Fjord, many seasons ago. And three moons past, it had prevented them from walking into a campsite filled with red savages. That had been close, and careless. He was determined that it wouldn't happen again. They were only eight strong, and against two or three hundred, the Gates of Valhalla would have been eager to accept them, and he was not ready for *that* journey just yet. There were still worlds to explore, like this new one. Bountiful and strange, filled with great beauty along with hidden dangers. So for now he remained alert, trying to find the source of his anxiety. He pulled his leather jacket tight against his massive frame, shaking off the cool invisible fingers which blew down from the north. The air was ripe with the stench of must, and huge runners of moss carpeted both bark and earth alike. Ahead of him, the men halted.

"What is it?"

Olaf appeared before him, his keen eyes unblinking. "The forest grows darker ahead, as if a shadow has fallen. I think a mist rises from the ground, perhaps from a bog somewhere nearby. The footing may grow soft before we reach a spot to rest."

Eirick considered for a moment. "We'll keep moving but watch for pitfalls. I want to put this side of the mountain behind us before we stop. I don't like the smell of this wood. It festers with the breath of death itself. Find us a good path and we'll camp beyond the ridge. It shouldn't be far off."

The Viking tracker nodded, retracing his way to the forefront of the group. They resumed their trek, weapons and gear rattling as they trudged along. Eirick fingered the haft of his battle axe, a subconscious motion whenever he felt a potential threat, regardless of where he was, even in the warm bed of his ancestral home. It was so far away now. They'd traveled over dangerous seas and rocky shores where waves crashed relentlessly into the land, waging an eternal battle where time meant nothing. And every day they placed more distance between themselves and their homelands. Not much further, he told himself. They would turn back soon. They had succeeded in finding new territory, but on a scale much larger than anyone had dreamed possible. The wonders they had seen . . .

The woods around him grew shrouded, and he immediately noticed the mist which lifted from the ground, seeping upward through rotting trunks, between tall grass, and from the moist earth. Several of the men drew out lanterns to help guide their way. He normally felt an unyielding confidence despite their relatively small numbers. Even against the overwhelming native savages who dwelt here, Eirick was stalwart in his belief that they would return unscathed, their fighting skills unmatched. But now, it seemed woefully insignificant beneath the low-hanging boughs, in a land which existed beyond any map or legend. It was the untamable *Unknown*, and they trespassed at their own peril.

Eirick chided himself for thinking such dismal thoughts, feeling shamed. He was their leader, and the responsibility of the mission fell upon his broad shoulders. He flung aside his grim musings, focusing on the lay of the land, or what he could make of it. The fog grew thicker while the ground continued to rise. Large rock croppings appeared at times, looming eerily out of the gloom like the feet of the mighty giants which dared to assail Asgard itself.

The company scrambled ahead, and he heard the breathing of his men heaving from exertion, steam spouting from their mouths like ephemeral wood sprites.

After long minutes of fighting the difficult terrain, Olaf whistled from somewhere in the distance, signaling a break in the rough. They had gained the ridge at last. Eirick spoke to the red-bearded Stugard, who paused directly in front of him. "Tell the men to continue. I want to find shelter on the far slope and beyond the reach of this foul breeze."

If possible, the air seemed worse here, as if the forest behind them was making a final effort to push them forward and out of its ancient grasp. The ground proved to be level for a while as they made better progress. At times one of his men would turn around, peering into the woods nervously. Eirick realized he wasn't alone with his apprehension. They felt it as well. The warriors were valiant, and would follow him into a dragon's den if he so asked it. But they were weary and homesick. He saw it in their eyes when they spoke. Fierce to the bone, they also had wives, children, and family waiting for them. Several would never return, their bodies consumed by a burial flame, victim to one of the many hazards which had faced them on the long journey. He mourned for those who had left this world, and knew they waited for him in the golden halls of Valhalla.

After several minutes they crossed the high point of the ridge and were now descending. Tall pine trees surrounded them, and a few other hardwoods which were of some strange species. The land seemed to go on forever. He already knew that they would never find the end of it. They might travel for weeks, even months, and still tread upon earth that was home to only the wild beasts and savages that lived here. It was time to return, retrace their route and rendezvous with the ship. His decision would not be questioned. The warriors were ready. Eirick nodded to himself. The new morning would be a time of hope and relief. The beginning of the journey back.

But first he had to find proper shelter for the night. A pile of fallen trees and some soft needles for the Vikings to lay upon. He gazed about with a sense of urgency, knowing that with each step forward, it only made their return trip another pace farther away. Why wait for a better place to halt when his mind was already made up?

And at that moment, as he raised his arm, ready to shout the command, the mist vanished and the forest opened up, revealing the clear sky above as tendrils of milky whiteness illuminated the landscape. It was as if he'd been given a sign. Eirick smiled, looking up.

But the smile melted from his face, relinquishing itself to an expression of confusion, and then surprise.

And shortly, to one of utter disbelief.

For the sky itself had *changed.*

❅ ❅ ❅

"Odin's blood . . ."

Someone else noticed it as well.

The Vikings huddled together, mumbling oaths, pointing, and questioning each other. Eirick strode forward, slowly shaking his grizzled head back and forth. "It cannot be, yet it is."

It was the stars.

They were . . . *wrong.*

It was as if they had unknowingly set foot in another world, for what he now saw had no part of his. Clusters of lights hung frighteningly low over their heads, twinkling—no, pulsing—as if they held a living, breathing heart within their celestial bodies. A few appeared familiar, except they were out of place somehow, realigned in the sky. There could be no mistake. These men had long ago discovered how to use the heavens in their travels about the world. Without such knowledge of direction, they were lost. And so by following these signs in the sky, they had been successful in crossing the great sea, guided along the way. But now, it was like the stars had been moved around, rearranged by some vast, demented mind. Or . . .

A horrible thought came to Eirick then. What if *they* were the ones who had been moved and somehow taken to this foreign land, where the stars had always been like they were right now? And then he realized something equally horrific—the moon itself had vanished.

Olaf moved ahead of the group, his head craned upward. "Such wonder I have never seen. Methinks we have gone too far, even to the ends of the world."

The others came forward, milling about, some hefting their weapons, but most of them simply staring at the landscape with looks of astonishment on their faces. But the brothers Beigarth and Fridgeir were the first to see it . . .

Looming in the distance, faintly illuminated by the night sky, was an enormous trunk erupting from the land, its girth far wider than even the largest of Viking warships. The earth was cracked and blemished around it as if the soil had refused to contain it any longer, vomiting it up from the bowels of the earth. The branches hung impossibly high above their heads, plunging straight into the sky as if reaching for the flawed stars. It was a tree, if it could be called such. It looked older than time, a monolith which seemed to climb into the very abyss of space. If the warriors had been daunted by the bizarre landscape, nothing compared to what they now laid their eyes upon.

"Do we dare to stand in the shadow of mighty Yggdrasil itself?" Fridgeir was the second youngest of the group, and he knelt down on one knee, shielding his eyes fearfully with his right hand.

"If that be true, then we *have* passed from the bounds of our own world. But into which other realm have we entered?" Olaf took a few steps forward, but then stopped.

Eirick was too stunned to offer any explanation. His mouth hung open, but he could find no words to describe what they were seeing, and he had nothing of comfort to add. He tried to find any rationalization for their predicament, but everything fell well short. For the first time in his long years of leadership, facing disease and starvation, with death as a constant companion, he now felt his confidence melting, giving way to deep uncertainty, bringing him dangerously close to panic itself. This was an assault on the very essence of who and what he was, and this feeling of inadequacy shook him to the very bone. He was terrified, but also angry that his emotions were taking over. His men needed him, and he must not falter. They looked to him for answers, and if his eyes betrayed him, they would all be lost . . . Several of them stared back at him, and he avoided their gaze as he fought his own inner demons, trying to salvage his pride and restore his confidence.

The entire landscape was hushed about them. No cry of animal, song of bird, or chittering of even an insect, reached their ears. The wind had died as well, although Eirick didn't remember the last time it had brushed against his face. It seemed hours had passed since then.

"Eirick, what do you make of this monstrous tree?"

Stil came forward from his position at rear guard. Of the company, he alone seemed to have kept his senses. And well he might.

As a *berserker*, he welcomed strife and chaos, and might as well be now looking down upon a grazing herd of cattle instead of what could possibly be the *World Tree* itself, the incomparable Yggdrasil, which was said to be the pillar of the very universe, sustaining it and linking all the realms of existence. Stil had stripped off his armor, placing a bear skin about himself in preparation for battle. Eirick watched as the man swallowed something cupped in his palm, and he knew it was the mushrooms he consumed before a fight. As with all the *berserkers*, he could be unpredictable at times, but always ferocious in confrontation. But Stil had been with his war party long enough for Eirick to realize more about the man—that he possessed an uncanny ability to foresee a conflict when it approached. Perhaps it was an effect of the mushrooms he ate, or due to some other heightened sense of awareness. Eirick did not know. He only knew that the man's instincts were rarely wrong. Danger was nearby. Hadn't Eirick himself felt the unknown threat as they made their way toward the ridge? And here it was. Although how this tree was a menace, he couldn't tell. If it indeed was Yggdrasil, then the implications were staggering. He breathed deeply, steadying himself, attempting to clear his racing mind, focus on what he *did* know—that they'd somehow entered into this strange land easily, so all they needed to do was retrace their steps and find the ridge.

He turned, looking at the direction from where they'd come from, but on every side was only blackness, a pitch-hued blanket of oblivion. There was no indication of where they had entered, and the horizon was in perpetual twilight, neither here nor there, only a continuation of the same, except for the monstrous tree waiting before them.

But when the first scream echoed, he realized too late that it wasn't a tree . . .

Bleigar was the first to be swept away as a massive tentacle burst forth from the attacker, taking him in its grasp like a colossal kraken emerging angrily from the sea searching for prey. Slime oozed from its passing, and along its length were small openings like tiny mouths, all of them clicking hungrily like the beaks of young birds waiting for their mother to bring them food.

At the same time the brothers Beigarth and Fridgeir were also hoisted away, everything happening so quickly that neither of them had time to raise their weapon, the tree/creature moving with amazing speed and agility despite its hulking mass. Eirick, stunned like the others, felt an overwhelming sense of rage and shame boiling inside. Three of his men snatched away in an instant while he did nothing!

"Back!" Eirick roared, turning his indecision into action. His battle axe in hand, he grabbed Olaf's tunic, shoving the man behind him while the Vikings rallied, some yelling oaths, others too shocked to find words. Mighty warriors all, nothing in their experience had prepared them for this . . .

Eirick backed up, never taking his eyes from where the assault had come from. What they had mistaken for huge tree limbs were appendages from whatever this thing was, and he saw movement from high in the air, as more tentacles waved menacingly, shuddering in agitation. They had struck swiftly, using the gloom as a cloak of secrecy. And there was no telling how far they could reach. From their vantage point, the tentacles appeared enormous. The Vikings placed as much distance between themselves and the creature as possible, although it seemed they were going nowhere. The landscape remained unchanged in every direction, and Eirick knew they were hopelessly lost. It was impossible to know from where they'd entered, and equally difficult to find any point which might lead them back. He held them together, keeping alert for any new attack while trying to think of a strategy which could give them an advantage, but he fell short of any ideas. After many minutes of flight he called for a halt, believing them long out of the creature's reach, and they huddled together on the ground. Eirick sent Stil a few paces back to act as guard. Even the *berserker* had been affected by the assault, his head snapping about as if expecting to find tentacles raining down on his helm.

"Our comrades have entered into Valhalla," said Eirick. "We'll grieve for their loss another time, and miss their company. But for now we need to understand our foe, and seek to return back to the land we left behind."

Olaf spoke up. "Eirick, perhaps there is no returning for us. What if we've been chosen for this battle?"

"Then we will fight and die like Vikings, and avenge the loss of our brothers." Eirick hoped his voice and stance were convincing, as doubt teethed eagerly at his heart. "I think we may find a way out of here yet, wherever this may be . . . And I don't believe 'tis Yggdrasil that we've set eyes upon, but something else, a creature that lurks in this foul land, waiting to ensnare its prey."

"How can you know this, Eirick?" It was Leingif who spoke now, the quietest of the group, as well as the youngest. Despite his years, he had proven himself many times over, long ago earning his place among them.

The leader shook his head. "I don't know the truth. I've listened to tales spoken to me when I was but a whelp. Strange things make their life in our world, and in others. I can't say what realm we've stumbled into, but I will follow my heart to get us all back. I like not these stars which watch us from above, their fire strange and unfriendly. Spark the lanterns and gather up all the spare wood from your packs."

The men followed his orders without question. Eirick knew he needed to keep them active. The worst thing for them would be to dwell on the horrors of the great lurker which waited behind. The dead air was cool, and the heat of a fire would warm their spirit, and perhaps lend some light to their position. They soon had a modest bonfire going, and Olaf replaced Stil as guard. Eirick forced them to eat lightly of bread and dried meats, and to sip from their ale skins. Weapons were either in hand or at their sides, and they appeared to recover somewhat from their earlier terror. He decided to wait for a time and have the warriors rest, hoping for light, or at least a diminishing of the gloom. And so they made a makeshift camp in this desolate plain which seemed to have no end, catching what sleep they could. Hours passed and they rotated the guard, but nothing changed. The stars remained fixed in their celestial positions as if they had been set that way for eternity. Eirick stayed awake, feeling no need for rest, his body and mind blazing with renewed conviction.

But his hopes were unfulfilled, and he knew after what had to be long hours, that this place hadn't changed, might never change. The only option was to keep moving. He gathered the men together and they resumed their search, trying desperately to retrace their entry point.

Unexpectedly, it was Eirick himself who sighted the change in the horizon, as something vast reared up in the distance directly ahead of them, something familiar . . .

"Impossible," he whispered. "This cannot be."

The warriors paused with him, scanning the landscape, and Eirick realized with sinking heart that it was the lurker once more.

"We could not have been so misled even by this blasted land."

Olaf thumped a gloved hand against his shield. "And yet ahead of us lies the bane of our comrades. Perhaps it is another of these things?"

Eirick didn't have an answer, only an uncomfortable feeling of inevitability. They all stared into the distance at the immense creature before them.

Then Stil broke the silence. "We look upon our destiny, to do battle with such a devil." His pupils were dilated, an after-effect of the mushrooms, and there was a terrible grin on his face. He had worked all fear and tension from his body and mind, and the release must come soon. Even Eirick couldn't restrain the Viking once the lust for battle came to a climax. But what options were available to him? To avoid the monstrous thing, hope to find an escape around it? Confused as he was with this strange territory, he knew for certain that they hadn't doubled back. They would have seen their own footsteps at the very least, since their boots surely made clear enough prints in the earth. But when he looked down to confirm this, his eyes narrowed. He moved forward a pace, and looked behind him.

Nothing.

There was no mark of his passage. It was as if he were a thing of air himself, not having the weight to make the slightest impression on the ground. The others were still focused ahead, oblivious of this new, unpleasant discovery.

But the Vikings were all surprised when a tremendous *crack* echoed across the horizon, as if a thousand claps of thunder had erupted all at once. The men cowered beneath this startling event, several of them falling flat to the earth. Stil yelled an oath, raging into a battle frenzy, daring the denizens of this frightening world to come forward and stand against him.

And to the horror of all, the monstrous tree creature *moved*, its massive trunk twisting, heaving itself free from the ground, and somehow sliding and shifting toward them, balanced by a combination of its own bulky stem and the tentacles, hundreds of them waving madly in the twilight. They'd seen remarkable things since entering this forbidden land, terrible and wondrous, but the sight of this abomination coming after them drowned everything else in comparison.

Eirick guessed the creature would be on them within the span of a few minutes. It wasn't moving fast, but surprisingly quick for something of such phenomenal girth and height. He looked up, and the deadly tentacles seemed to reach right into the heavens, at home with the stars above. Maybe they were, he thought. In this strange land, anything was possible, it seemed. Earlier, he'd thought they had stumbled into a world somehow removed from their own, but maybe not the lands of Viking legend. Now, he wondered whether they were actually standing in Midgard, facing the guardian of the worlds itself. He took out his mighty bow of ash, drawing an arrow forth, which he lit with his own lantern. The flame looked frail against such a behemoth. Face grim, he turned to his men.

"We make a stand here as Vikings, and fight to our last breath. Are you worthy of entering Valhalla? I think I know that answer. We'll show the great ones in Asgard the kind of valour that only our people possess."

The monster came closer, and Stil burst forth, too far gone to do anything but soothe his blood-thirst. With a flaming brand in one hand, he charged directly at the creature, screaming in fury. Eirick held his men back. Stil's was a rash move, one that only a *berserker* would commit. Eirick knew what the outcome would be, and he hoped to build a better strategy other than rushing headlong to his death along with his warriors. Instead, he signaled them to move slowly forward in formation with shields held firm by Olaf and Leingif, while himself and Stugard were ready with their flaming shafts.

To tell himself he wasn't frightened would have been a lie. The fear ran cold through his veins and along his skin beneath his protective gear. But a strong feeling of pride overwhelmed him. He looked straight into the eyes of death without flinching, and he was deeply proud of his comrades. This is what they lived for. And yes, what they died for as well. But their reward would be great, earning an eternal place in the hallowed halls of the afterlife among the bravest warriors of history. Even knowing the certainty of his own ending failed to diminish Eirick's determination.

They were Vikings to the bone, and even if none would ever sing praise about their last stand against the demon from another world, this battle, this moment of courage, would last until the end of time itself, and *that* was all that mattered.

Scores of yards before them, Stil encountered the first assault as a trio of tentacles raged toward his head. The *berserker* actually laughed at his peril, taunting the deadly limbs with his long sword.

He dove to one side, narrowly missing what would have been a decapitation as one of the appendages swept right above him, the mouths clicking in agitation. He scored it with his brand, and the tentacle whipped backward, clearly injured by the fire.

"See! The creature is wary of the flame."

The small group moved steadily forward, and the ground shook as the bulk of the creature tore its lumberous way across the land, drawing ever closer. Stil dodged and pranced about in a wild state, at one point singing an old hymn to Thor in his epic battle against the cunning giants. *Berserkers* were unpredictable and dangerous, not only to their enemies, but themselves and even their comrades due to their frenzied state. But he served as a distraction, keeping the tentacles away from Eirick and his warriors. Dozens of them came for Stil, and he slashed at them, marking a few, but he was grossly overmatched, and any second could spell his death.

The Viking leader wondered what world could breathe life into such a monster, and if this were indeed Yggdrasil, then the stories were terribly wrong about it. The distance between the combatants narrowed with each moment, and Eirick was in awe of its vastness. Tentacles showered the air in every direction. Some helped the trunk of the monster move, others harassed Stil, and more came toward his group, and it took a tremendous effort for them to avoid being swiped away. As they drew nearer, Eirick caught a glimpse of an odd-shaped mark on the creature's trunk, almost a round symbol of some type. It was several moments later when he realized it was an opening, like some enormous mouth. Even in the gloom he made out the razor teeth which lined the maw. There had to be thousands of them. The great mouth rippled with anticipation, a terrible stench issuing forth from the aperture unlike anything Eirick had imagined, as if a harbor load of fish had decayed for weeks beneath the high summer sun. The warriors faltered, beaten back by the foul odor.

"Hold fast. If we attack the mouth, perhaps it will retreat from us for good."

A slim hope, but there was nothing else to grab onto. Leingif coughed, and Eirick shouted words of encouragement to the youngest of them. They pushed ahead, Stugard and himself firing volleys, trying to make the creature hesitate, if nothing else. Stil was only a few dozen yards from the monster's trunk when he made a fatal mistake. He lunged right into a tentacle that was much thinner than the rest. The warrior had failed to see the danger in time, concentrating on the heavier appendages. The coil wrapped itself unmercifully about his waist and the *berserker* screamed in agony. Eirick shouted in anger but there was nothing they could do but watch in horror as the man was pulled into the gaping maw and swallowed whole.

The other tentacles paused for a moment as the creature digested its prey. Eirick knew it was their only chance.

"Now!"

He launched an arrow straight into the monstrous opening and the brand disappeared into the black depths. Stugard did the same, both of them deadly accurate with their shots, but to their dismay it had no effect on the monster, and the tentacles whipped about with renewed fury. Olaf was then clubbed to the ground by one of the thinner limbs, metal and bone cracking horribly in the gloom. It was enough to disrupt the fragile formation, and the three men scattered. Eirick tried to fire another arrow, but his bow was knocked from his grip and he rolled against the earth, his chest heaving from exertion. He lost sight of the others as he tried to save himself from certain death as several limbs focused on him now. After tense moments, he regained his footing, looking about for his comrades.

Olaf was nowhere to be seen, and Eirick feared that his body had already been consumed. He spotted Leingif, desperately fending off a pair of limbs, and his situation looked dire. Stugard was in the clutches of a massive tentacle, and he slashed down on it with his knife. Eirick tried to find a path toward him, but there were too many appendages for him to get anywhere close. In seconds Stugard was thrust headlong into the mouth, and the tentacles trembled as if savoring a feast.

They were only two now, and Eirick used every remaining ounce of his strength to reach his comrade's side. Tentacles thrashed everywhere, and the pair of warriors had a moment of respite as the limbs backed off unexpectedly for a moment. The leader fired two more volleys, both of them vanishing into the mouth, but he knew it would be to no avail. The thing was too powerful and huge to be overcome by flesh and blood, iron or flame. Their time here was short, and soon they would be joining their companions.

"Well fought, my friend," he rasped. "The halls of our fathers call to us now. May our end be quick."

As Eirick spoke, there was a blinding flash of light overhead, and a sound as of something enormous being ripped to shreds, like a curtain vast enough to contain the very stars in the heavens.

Now they saw the reason why the creature had stopped its assault. A shadow fell upon them, larger than even the monster. It spread out around the landscape, encompassing their adversary and passing over their own heads. They stumbled to the ground, too weary and beaten to question yet another unthinkable event, but to their amazement, the monstrous creature was hoisted away, disappearing into the sky, even the stars blackened out by the immense intruder. Eirick was stunned, unable to speak, and the only thought that came to him was the image of something like an enormous *hand* bearing down on them and taking the creature with it.

Eirick then noticed a shimmering dozens of yards to their right, tendrils of mist seeping through. He grabbed his companion, pushing him forward. "Look, the air opens. Move swiftly 'lest we're trapped here forever." They pushed weary limbs to their limits, striving to find a way out of the barren land, back to their own world . . .

In moments they plunged into the fog, and Eirick welcomed its invisible grasp, his skin tingling. And things changed in an instant . . .

He smelled the forest again—must, rotting leaves, and he felt the dampness on his skin. The mist dissipated, and overhead the air grew brighter. The sky wavered for a moment, and then in the blink of an eye, all was normal. The stars had returned to their proper resting points, and even the moon was there again, leering down at them from the night sky.

The pair of warriors slowly stood, almost reverently. They'd been drained of emotion, and nothing could surprise them anymore.

Leingif's voice shook when he spoke. "I never thought to see such simple pleasures before. Are we really back?"

Eirick clapped him on the shoulder, nodding. "I think so, although I don't believe it either."

The younger man collapsed on the forest floor, leaning against an old stump. They were both silent for a time, savoring the sights, sounds, and aromas surrounding them, but keenly felt the loss of their companions.

Finally, Leingif broke the reverie. "Eirick. What we saw back there . . . Was that the hand of Odin himself which saved us from the monster?"

Eirick didn't answer for long moments. There were no answers to be found, he realized. They'd thought the wonders of the New World would be unsurpassed, as they were the first men to venture into these undiscovered lands. What tales they would bring back to their people, returning as conquerors who followed the sun and stars to whatever path they would lead. But he understood now that it was all folly . . . They'd witnessed too much, walked beneath the forbidden twilight where men were not meant to trespass. Experienced events that no Viking, or any other man, had ever seen or even dreamed possible. Incredible things beyond mortal comprehension. And no, he couldn't say as to what it was that had saved them.

The only thing he knew for certain was that there existed other frontiers beyond man's limited vision—vast and strange, inhabited by great and terrible things—that they would never begin to understand.

In Waters Black the Lost Ones Sleep

By Angeline Hawkes

Eleanor watched as the ship sailed over the horizon, a smudge of black swallowed by blue skies. She pulled her cape tight, struggling with the gusting winds that kicked up over the rocky shoreline tugging at her skirts. Her eyes strained, hoping for one more glimpse of the ship that carried her father back to England, anxious feelings seizing her heart. He promised he'd be back within three months with the supplies needed for winter. Even if he returned when he planned, they'd be deep into November and blustery Old Man Winter would be upon them. Hesitantly, she turned away from the white-capped waves of the Atlantic, and made her way back toward the ringing of hammers. The men were hard at work on repairing the settlement.

The babe stirred in her arm beneath the heavy wool of her winter cape, and she lifted the fabric to look within. The little white face greeted her with a yawn and a curious expression that Eleanor had not yet learned how to read. Her daughter was just nine days old, and already a brave adventurer. Eleanor laughed at the thought.

"Are you hungry poppet?" she asked and cooed at the sleepy girl. She picked up her skirts with her free hand and stepped quickly to the dwelling Ananias had secured for them. Because she was John White's daughter, their house was a little larger, which, really, didn't matter that much as they also had to share the lodging with two sisters and their uncle. The five of them made for a tight squeeze.

Ananias was hard at work slapping mortar between the falling stones of the fireplace when she crossed the threshold seeking a place to feed Virginia. Molly and Katherine, the sisters, had managed to string a makeshift bed and were busy stuffing a mattress with dry grasses. Molly smiled at her as she sat on the newly hewn bench and slipped Virginia's flailing body beneath her apron.

"She's growin' already, that one!" Molly said with gusto. She had a child once. On the voyage over, Molly had told Eleanor a sad tale of losing her husband and her son to a fever. Nothing more to lose, Molly had joined the colony.

"As much as she eats, she'll be as big as her father within the week!" Eleanor laughed. "How's the mattress coming along?"

"Slowly," Katherine said, a grimace on her tired face. "Everything is coming along slowly."

"Patience, dear Katherine. The Lord will give us strength." Eleanor sighed, and surveyed the cramped quarters. "Once the baby is asleep, I'll help."

"I need help with the mortar first," Ananias said, until now content listening in on the conversation. "We need heat before we need comfort."

Eleanor nodded. "Yes, husband." She looked beneath her apron at Virginia who was nursing steadily slower at her breast. Loud voices erupted outside of the wood wall.

Ananias glanced toward the door. "What are they about, I wonder?"

Eleanor listened to the voices of John Gibbs and Tom Durrant, apparently heavy in argument. "I know not, but you should see if you can help."

Ananias scowled. As assistant to his father-in-law, the governor, his position required a great deal of leadership while the governor was away. So far, those duties had consisted of a lot of petty disputes in need of judgment. He set his bucket on the hearth and wiped his hands on his apron.

Pushing open the heavy door, Ananias greeted both men, who paused from their quarrel long enough to acknowledge his presence. "What is the matter?"

John Gibbs frowned. "I've told the others that White will not be able to return in time for winter. Even if he does return when he says he will, the supplies we have won't last longer than two weeks.

Too much has spoiled."

Tom Durrant interrupted. "Gibbs wants to trade with the Croatoans, but I've told him that trade with the savages is completely out of the question since White's men mistakenly attacked them instead of the Powhatans."

Ananias nodded. "Things with the Croatoans are very delicate right now."

"Right now?" Tom asked. "I don't expect the situation will improve anytime in the near future, if ever; and right now we need to concentrate on restocking our food supplies."

"That's why it's essential that we open trade negotiations with the Croatoans once again. Surely, we must have something in the storerooms that will interest them enough to push aside their grudge," John said.

"I wouldn't be too sure about that, but we must do something. Water has damaged nearly everything. Even the armor is beginning to rust. I think Tom has a point. The Croatoans aren't going to easily forgive White's indiscretion, regardless if it were an accident or not." Ananias shut the door behind him, leaning closer to the men so that the women couldn't hear. "We should consider exploring the forests around the settlement. Maybe go out in parties of four or five to hunt. We have one-hundred sixteen people to feed here."

"117, the Harvie's had a child last night," John said.

"Well, thank G   od the infants have food." Ananias thought of his daughter inside, nestled in Eleanor's arms.

"Only if the mothers are fed," Tom pointed out.

"Right you are, man, and that's precisely why we need to explore the surrounding region and see what nature can offer us. Set traps. There must be small game nearby and perhaps larger deer in the forests." Ananias cleared his throat. "Whatever we do, we need to do it soon. When the rest of the colonists discover how low the food supply is, there is bound to be panic. We don't have the means to control 90 panicked men."

"Agreed." Tom nodded. "Should I call a meeting tonight to organize the exploration parties? I think we can pull it off without revealing the dire need just yet."

"Spread the word. There's a bountiful harvest waiting in those lush forests, and we're going to restock the pantries if it's the last thing we do," Ananias said with a laugh.

John Gibbs frowned. "If we don't, our attempt just might be the *last* thing we do, Ananias."

The men parted in solemn spirits. Ananias returned to his bucket and resumed his repairs.

2.

Eleanor slung the wet shirt on the stone, and rubbed it with a handful of sand. Sand. The one thing that was plentiful in Roanoke was sand. She reserved the soap for what the sand couldn't remove. The soap was not plentiful and weeks had passed since her father had left for England, and many more weeks would pass before he'd return. She needed to conserve the soap.

A lovely sweet voice wafted over the breeze. Eleanor turned an ear in the direction of the song. The words were not English, nor were they Spanish or French. She listened carefully, not wanting to make a sound lest she catch the attention of the singer. The singing was just over a small sand dune, surrounded by a clump of trees, near the edge of the forest. Eleanor lifted one wet foot from the water and padded across the beach. Crouching, she peered between the low branches of the trees trying to see the woman who was singing.

A lone Indian woman sat on the beach, a small fire burning, and a rabbit turning on a makeshift spit. Nearby a birch-bark boat was run aground.

Eleanor watched in curiosity. *What was the woman doing?*

Studying the singer, she noted the beads around her neck and remembered beaded necklaces her father had shown her and identified as Croatoan. The woman must be Croatoan, but why was she here, so close to Roanoke, after all that had happened?

Eleanor gathered the laundry and her basket of bread and walked into the sight of the woman. She stood there waiting for a reaction.

The woman continued to sing, barely acknowledging Eleanor's presence; so, Eleanor walked closer. Finally, she sat outside of the ring of stones that the Indian woman had placed around herself and her fire. Eleanor retrieved a loaf of bread from her basket and broke the hard lump into two halves. She held out one half.

The woman stopped singing long enough to take the bread and sniff it. Then she stuck her tongue out, tasting it. Approving, she crunched a mouthful from the end. Eleanor chewed her own bread in silence. The Indian ripped a hindquarter from the roasting rabbit and handed it to Eleanor in exchange. Grateful for meat, Eleanor ravished it. The men hadn't been successful in trapping animals of any kind and fishing had also proven fruitless. The drought of the summer had parched the surrounding wildlife and berries and nuts were scarce. The Indian's eyebrows rose in surprise at Eleanor's apparent hunger.

"You no meat?" the woman asked, shocking Eleanor with the English words.

Recovering from her startled amazement, she shook her head. "No. Our supplies are gone. The men haven't caught any game. They go to fish, and don't even get a nibble. This bread is from the last of the flour." Eleanor held up the last bites of her bread.

"No fish. Waters bad. He sleeps in black water."

Eleanor smiled. Indian superstitions. She evaded the issue. "You speak English?"

The Indian woman rocked herself in a silent song. "Many moons ago, a white man came and was friend to my people. I learn such talk then."

"Is there something that I could trade you for food? I know that your people are many. Surely, you must hunt, or farm."

"What do you know of my people, girl from across the big water?"

"My father has told me much of your people. They are a great people." Eleanor remembered that her father had told her that the Indians were easily flattered.

Again the Indian woman seemed unimpressed. "Hmm."

"I know that the Croatoans are not pleased with us English presently, but, perhaps, you and I could trade something for food, just for my family?"

"Not all of the white faces?"

"No. Just for my house. I won't tell anyone. Not even my husband."

The Indian woman swayed some more, faster in her silent crescendo. "What do you have for Singing Woman?"

"Singing Woman? Is that your name?" Eleanor said, excitedly. "My name is Eleanor."

"My nai-m?"

"What you are called. How you are known." Eleanor explained.

"Hmm," she said again. "Croatan know me as Singing Woman."

"Because you like to sing?"

"Because I sing for *him*." Singing Woman made a sign in the air and her face took on a look of reverence.

Eleanor didn't care whom she sang for. She could stand on the beach and sing for the gulls if she wanted. All Eleanor cared about was obtaining food for Ananias and the others in her house. "What do you want in exchange for food? What can I give you?"

Singing Woman frowned. She looked Eleanor from head to foot, her gaze stopping at Eleanor's neck

Eleanor grabbed the gold necklace hanging there. "This? Do you want my necklace?"

Singing Woman shrugged, not very interested.

"What do you have with you now?" Eleanor knew that Singing Woman was a few hours from Croatan lands, but must have come with something to eat in her bag.

Singing Woman pulled out a bag of nuts, some sort of ground meal, and a larger bag of dried meats. Eleanor's eyes lit up in happiness. She took off the gold necklace and held it out for Singing Woman. The Indian grunted, but took the necklace, handing over the foodstuffs. "Will you come back?"

"Why would Singing Woman come back here? I come to sing for *him*. I don't sing here always."

"If you come back every four suns . . ." Eleanor didn't know if *every four suns* made sense, but she'd heard the strange way that tribes told time, and hoped that Singing Woman would understand. From the expression on her face, she did. "If you come back, every four suns. I'll bring things for you to pay for the food. Trade. I'll trade for food."

"Iron?"

"You want iron? I can bring iron—pots? Tools?"

Singing Woman nodded. "All of these."

"Yes. Yes. I can bring those things. We'll meet here then? In four suns?"

Again, Singing Woman nodded. "Eleanor alone."

"Eleanor alone."

The Indian seemed pleased with the arrangement, gathered her belongings and shoved her small boat into the ocean waves. Eleanor watched the strange woman paddle away, excited by her clandestine arrangement to trade for food.

3.

From a small leather bag, Eleanor measured out ground corn, mixing it with water to form a paste-like dough. The two rabbits, she skinned and prepared, dropping the pieces into a boiling pot of water hanging over the fire. It wasn't much food, but enough for a weak soup and corn bread of sorts.

Ananias watched her from across the small room. He worked on whittling wooden pegs to use in place of nails, observing his wife darting around the small cooking area. "You say you trapped those rabbits yourself?"

Eleanor jumped, startled out of her thoughts. "Yes. Yes, I did. In the woods near the farthest dune."

"I'm not too sure it's safe for you to be venturing out alone."

"Oh, it's not too far." Eleanor pushed the small leather bag into the pocket of her skirts, out of view from Ananias's curious eyes. "Father showed me how to set the traps."

"Hmm. Well, he should've shown the rest of us then, because every trap we set up in this area, stays empty."

Eleanor knew that Singing Woman wasn't trapping near here. She brought the meat in her birch boat, from Croatan lands, an island not very far away. "Well, practice makes perfect. Maybe a few more tries will yield some animals."

"The men are starting to grumble about the inequality of my house having food where theirs goes without."

She frowned. "There's hardly enough here to share. If the others worked harder, maybe their labor would produce more to eat. I never see Sarah or Rachel looking for nuts or berries in the woods. I never see Morgan or Wesley fishing. There are many more who could be doing their part."

"You don't have to convince me. There's just the natural assumption that we have more because you're the Governor's daughter."

"That's ridiculous! My father left us in the same state that he left everyone else. Foolish rot!" Eleanor stirred the pot with the wooden ladle.

"Hmm. Well, maybe I'll come with you the next time you go out trapping. It seems I have more to learn." Ananias smiled. "I'm going to go check on how the men are doing on the palisade. The fortifications aren't much, but something is better than no protection at all."

Eleanor watched him leave, and then breathed deeply. Guilt panged her. She lied to her husband frequently now, to avoid discovery. If the others knew she was trading with a lone Croatoan woman solely to feed her own household, there would be great repercussions. Surely God would forgive her untruths, all of which were necessary for her to put meager rations in the bellies of those in her house. She also had the safety of Singing Woman to consider. If the others learned of their trading relationship, they might feel threatened. There were many unpleasant consequences of this precarious partnership.

4.

The next morning was her meeting day with Singing Woman. Eleanor carefully folded the length of red fabric into a square, tucking it into the waist of her petticoat. She also placed a handful of metal nails, a precious commodity, into her berry basket, and picked up Virginia for the walk to the little cove.

Ananias lingered near the fence as he watched his wife take a narrow path into the woods, toward the beach. Darting between trees, he followed her, undetected, suspicious as to her destination.

In the cove, on the sandy beach, a woman, clad only in a breach cloth and a bead necklace, sat near a small bark-covered boat. Her glossy black hair hung in heavy braids and beaded earrings swung from stretched earlobes. Around her were an assortment of small baskets and bags, and she looked to be busily starting a fire.

Eleanor trekked closer, waving to the seated Indian. Ananias scowled. It was apparent that the two women were very familiar with each other. Even more so, when he watched his wife hand their daughter to the half-naked stranger while she hiked up her skirt and withdrew a length of red fabric. So, Eleanor was not only lying to him, but she was stealing from the common storehouse to bankroll her trading. Disappointed, he shook his head.

"Yesterday, four men went out in one of the small boats to try to fish." He heard his wife saying.

"He sleeps there. No fish." The Indian woman frowned as she spoke.

"The boat capsized in the waves. Two of the men were drowned."

"Hmm," the Indian woman said. "You should not fish. Rabbits, squirrels, birds. These are good meat. White man boats disturb He

Who Sleeps."

Ananias watched his wife scowl. *What the devil was the Indian jabbering on about?* Whatever it was, Eleanor reacted with disbelief or disinterest, he couldn't tell which.

Eleanor and Indian made their trades, talked in their shared way, and then went their separate ways. Ananias was careful to sneak back to the settlement undetected. He loathed having to confront his wife about her activities, but if the rest of the colonists discovered her secret trade partner, there would be hell to pay.

5.

Ananias was sitting on the bench, before the fire, when Eleanor and Virginia arrived. Eleanor was caught off-guard by her husband's presence. He should be helping with the palisade.

"Husband? Are you well?" she asked, laying Virginia into her cradle. Eleanor walked toward Ananias.

He sighed. "My heart is sick."

Shock spread across Eleanor's face. "Is something wrong? What's happened?"

"Maybe you should tell me these things, for my heart sickness comes because of your actions."

"What?" Eleanor stepped backward, confusion contorting her expression. "What are you talking about?"

"Today I followed you when you went into the woods. And, when you went to the beach. *And* . . ." Ananias felt his brows knitting in disapproval. "When you met with the savage and traded stolen goods from the common storehouse for food."

Eleanor covered her mouth with her hand. "You *followed* me?"

"You left me little choice. I checked the woods around the settlement. There are no traps save the ones myself and the men have left, and those remain empty."

"But, you *followed* me?" The distrust on her husband's part overwhelmed her.

"Eleanor, you have food for every meal. The others in the colony exist on broth and little more than crusts of bread. I asked myself how it was that my wife could create something out of nothing. I determined that you've been obtaining food from outside of the area. Somehow."

"Is it a sin to feed one's family?" she asked, her voice barely above a whisper.

"No, my love. But, it *is* a sin to lie to one's husband, to steal from your people, and to take food for your own when others starve."

Eleanor wiped tears from her eyes. "It's not my fault that father's men ruined relations with the Indians. My child shouldn't starve and die because of the actions of rash men."

Ananias sighed. "You must talk with these savages and insist that they trade with all in the colony."

"What?"

"I must tell the others of your actions, and when I do, they will insist that you serve as our mouthpiece and speak with the savages about trading for food."

"But, I only know Singing Woman. I've never seen any others," Eleanor said.

"When does she come again?"

"Every four suns." Eleanor untied the bags from beneath her skirts and placed the food in a wood box under the table.

"Four suns?"

"Every four days." Eleanor stood. "But, I cannot ask her to trade with all of us, that was our arrangement. She'll only trade with me for my family alone."

"That will change." Ananias went to the door. "In four days, you'll meet with this Singing Woman and tell her what will be. We'll need to speak with the chief." He opened the door, stepping over the threshold. "I must go help with the fortifications. Last night Gibbs claims to have spotted something in the waters, from the watchtower. It could be those bedeviled Spaniards coming up the coast looking for the colony."

Eleanor watched him leave. Singing Woman would never agree to trade with the entire colony.

6.

Four suns came and Eleanor tread her usual path to Singing Woman. In the woods, men lurked, watching her unaware. Eleanor spoke with Singing Woman who, as Eleanor suspected, refused to trade with anyone other than Eleanor for anyone other than Eleanor's household, and was angry over the insult to the arrangement that Eleanor made by asking.

Singing Woman hurried the trade, and left without a farewell. Cupping her eyes from the sun, Eleanor watched her boat shove off into the murky waters. With a sigh, she returned to the colony.

In the woods, the men watched the Indian woman leave, and then using two boats they had built in the Indian fashion, slid into the water following the savage. They would go to the tribe and ask to trade instead of relying on one disagreeable old woman.

7.

Shouts filled the air. Eleanor bolted from her bed, as Ananias pulled on his breeches. He fumbled for his boots in the darkness while Eleanor struggled to light a lamp. Their front door burst open and whooping Indians descended upon them. Many warriors overcame Ananias, as Eleanor and Virginia, and the other residents of the house were rounded up, and shoved outside into the center of the settlement.

The moon shone brightly, lighting the center yard. Indians, Croatoans, were everywhere, swarming like bees. Angry expressions greeted Eleanor at every turn. Arms and hands pushed her, clutching her baby, into a group of women and children. The men were forced toward the beach, to a long line of birch-bark boats.

"Where are they taking them?" Eleanor shouted above the wails of the children. The women anxiously peered over the shoulders of their captors trying to see through the commotion. Ringed by Indians, jostled by curious women, it was hard to see anything at all.

"I cannot see. I can't see a thing," Katherine whispered, fear and cold chattering her teeth.

Eleanor stooped low, peering between two of their guards. She saw the men being led to the canoes, kneeling, and falling. A pair of Croatoans would then lift the motionless man and lay him in the nearest boat.

"No!" she whispered, a hand over her heart.

"What is it?" Molly hissed in the darkness, somewhere near Eleanor's elbow.

Eleanor felt a stab biting through her chest as her brain sorted the images her eyes fed it. She knew what she saw; she just wanted to believe it wasn't true. She stood straight, gripping Virginia tighter.

"What is it that you saw, Eleanor?" Katherine grabbed her arm, tugging urgently.

"They're killing the men," she croaked. "Killing them and stacking their bodies into boats like cords of wood."

Katherine and Molly gasped. Virginia began to cry. Then, abruptly, the savage captors herded the women and children to another line of boats, indicating they should get in.

Black ebbing water lapped at the sides of the narrow boats as Eleanor watched the lights from their fires shrink the farther they floated, until, at last, darkness swallowed the settlement. She looked ahead, praying frantically to God for deliverance.

8.

Seventeen women and eleven children crawled from the small boats, stiff, wet, cold, and completely unaccustomed to such means of travel. The Croatoans roughly herded them into a central yard where a bonfire blazed. A ring of bark-covered longhouses circled the fire while bronze faces stared from every direction.

Eleanor caught a glimpse of Singing Woman and her heart leapt. A friend! An ally! "Singing Woman!" she called toward the old woman.

Singing Woman walked to her, earrings bobbing from her lobes. She stood hands on hips, scowling the way she normally did whenever Eleanor spoke with her.

"What has happened? Why are they doing this?"

Singing Woman glanced around at the Croatoan warriors. "White men follow me to Croatan. They want to trade. Talked with He-Who-Walks-With-Kro." She bristled at the mention of this odd name. "Blood was shed."

"*What*? When?"

"After I left you on the beach. He-Who-Walks-With-Kro will take no more. He says white faces have angered Kro."

"Who's this *Kro*, and who is this *He-Who-Walks* person?"

Singing Woman frowned so deeply that her brows became one. She gripped Eleanor's arm hard, nails biting through her thin nightgown. "Ssh." She leaned near Eleanor's ear. "Kro is guardian of The Old One Who Sleeps."

"*Who*?" Eleanor felt like she was having a bad dream from which she could not wake.

"Kro is guardian of *Kro-Atan Ga*."

"I don't understand what you're talking about. Is Kro here? Is it possible that I could speak with him? I think the men have been killed." A flash of Ananias's smiling face shot through her brain, and a pang cut her heart. There was no time for tears or sorrow now. Virginia's life depended on her actions, and she must preserve her daughter at all costs.

Singing Woman nodded her head slowly, affirming Eleanor's beliefs. "Kro wills it."

"Where is this Kro?"

The old Indian pointed toward the dark water around the island. Despite a brisk wind, the water was still as glass. Not a shimmer or a ripple broke the blackness. "Kro is no man, white face girl."

Eleanor shuddered. She saw the warriors talking amongst themselves and then shouts began. There was a dispute. She looked at Singing Woman questioningly. "What are they about?"

"They want to separate the women. Women who have known men, there." She pointed. "Women who are pure, there."

"What of the children?"

"Go with mothers."

Eleanor frowned. "Will they let *you* keep Virginia?" She was terrified to be parted from her daughter; her last connection to her beloved Ananias, but reason gripped her, steadying her emotions. The savages might kill her, but if one of their own claimed the baby, Virginia might live. Her arms circled her baby girl tighter, not wanting to let go, not wanting to believe that anything that had happened this night was real. Her heart thundered in her chest.

Singing Woman's face softened. "They will." She held out her hands for the sleeping baby. "I will care for the child. You have the word of Singing Woman."

Eleanor kissed Virginia's head softly, as her eyes drank in the sleeping visage of her baby. It took every fiber of her being to will her arms to let go and pass the infant into Singing Woman's arms. "Mother loves you," she whispered. Singing Woman clasped the baby to her own chest and backed away from the shouting warriors.

Eleanor watched the old woman shuffle into the crowd. Tears coursed over her dirty cheeks. Molly realized what the young mother had done, and slipped an arm around her comfortingly. An Indian warrior seized Katherine by the arm and dragged her screaming toward the second group of unmarried women. Together, Molly and Eleanor quaked in each other's arms, overcome by fear and sorrow.

The savages led the two groups in two different directions, ensconcing Eleanor's little group in a longhouse near the beach. The exhausted women soon collapsed in huddled bunches surrounding the children and slept restlessly. Eleanor lay on her stomach, listening to the sound of her own blood crash through her ears. A pinpoint of light caught her attention near the floor. She crawled on her belly toward it, realizing there was a chink out of the bark covering the exterior wall. Peering through the hole she witnessed a group of savages gathered around a heap of something, and a large stone altar near the ocean. The waves, once serenely still, now tumbled and leaped, spraying the altar. Moonlight cascaded over the unfolding events, as Eleanor held her breath in dreaded anticipation.

A long knife rose and fell over the altar stones, and warriors walked back and forth from the altar to the hungry waves. Her mind sorted the images. As the blur melted away, she made out arms and legs, then a body being dragged, and flung onto the altar.

An Indian severed the arms and legs from bloody torsos, tossing the dismembered pieces into the raging ocean. A steady drum beat throughout the night, followed by a low chant that never seemed to rest.

Eleanor fell asleep watching the horrific scene repeat itself over and over again. She stopped counting at fifty.

9.

An old man sat on a bench in the door that was partially obscured by a stiff hide. Eleanor sat in the dirt observing him. It had been three, maybe four days, since the women had been separated. She hadn't seen Singing Woman since the night she gave her Virginia. Her heart ached for her daughter. She found herself skimming the passing people, hoping, yearning for just the tiniest glimpse of that small downy head.

Leaning against the doorframe, she pushed back the hide. The old man turned, staring disapprovingly.

"It's too hot in here with the hide closed," Eleanor said, not expecting the man to understand her. "We need to leave it open to let the air in."

"I cannot. He-Who-Walks-With-Kro has forbid it."

Eleanor was surprised. Apparently more Croatoans than just Singing Woman understood English. "You speak my tongue?"

"Windmover learned 'white tongue' before."

"Windmover? That's your name?" Eleanor asked.

"Yes. You go back inside."

"How did you learn English: 'white tongue'?" she persisted.

He grunted and shrugged. "Many moons ago white men were caught like animals by Powhatans. Croatans took white men away."

"When was this? How many men?"

Windmover held up both hands, then one hand again.

"Fifteen?" Eleanor's eyebrows arched inquisitively. Fifteen former colonists had gone missing before her father had arrived with the present settlers. "What happened to those white men?"

"Kro demanded them."

"This Kro, he's the guardian of The Old One? Did the Old One want the men?" Eleanor still had no idea what anyone was talking about in reference to this Old One or this Kro, but she hoped to glean something that would enable her to understand.

Windmover's face registered surprise at her comment. "The Old One Who Sleeps."

"Yes, yes, that's the name."

"The Old One Who Sleeps never wakens. It is Kro, the guardian of *Kro-Atan Ga* who *is* The Old One Who Sleeps, who demands the blood of life." Windmover chewed on a stick and studied Eleanor.

Slowly she began to put the names together. These imaginary creatures must be the gods of these savage people. From what Windmover just said, she had little to fear from this *Kro-Atan Ga*. It was this other being, this Kro, who was the true decision maker. "The night we came. The men from our colony . . . I saw them being cut apart on your altar."

"You should not see these things."

"Did Kro demand these killings? Were the men from Roanoke sacrificed to Kro?" Eleanor listened to the words coming from her mouth, but they seemed surreal, something from an old Greek myth, or a fanciful tale of horror meant to scare disobedient children. "Is that why they were chopped up and slung into the ocean?"

Windmover's body went rigid. His eyes narrowed into black squints . "You should not speak of these things. To do so is to be punished."

"By Kro?"

"By He-Who-Walks-With-Kro."

Ah! Eleanor thought. So, He-Who-Walks-With-Kro, was the real creature to be feared; and he was just a *man.* A very clever man, from what she could tell. He was the one issuing all of the mandates on who died and who lived in the name of Kro, and this *Kro-Atan Ga*, who apparently, just lay around under the ocean, sleeping. "It was He-Who-Walks-With-Kro that killed the white men?"

Windmover nodded his head and began to reply, when a hush fell over the crowded area outside. Children scurried away, followed by many others. Indians hurried to their dwellings, disappearing behind hides. Windmover prostrated himself onto the ground, a monotonic chant muttering from his shriveled lips. Eleanor jumped nervously at the unexpected motion, and clung to the wood of the doorframe.

A bent, twisted man walked into the central yard of the village. A crown-like string of shells was drawn tightly around his forehead. Earrings of strung shells hung low from his ears, and a long strand of the same pink-white shells reached nearly to his naked navel, shaking musically with each step. It wasn't his manner of dress, which was much like the rest of the males of the tribe that caught Eleanor's attention. It was the hardened glare of his black eyes that gripped her heart like a cold fist, squeezing it . Involuntarily, she gasped for breath as if the very life was being crushed from her. She couldn't tell if he was a young man or an old one, for it was as if his face was fluid, changing, shimmering, blurring from one expression to the next in an unnatural way. Eleanor stepped sideways into the dwelling, hoping the man didn't notice her standing in the shadows.

The man stopped before Windmover and rattled a long scepter-like stick with a turtle-shell over the prone elderly man. Windmover continued his furious chant, never faltering.

"Windmover?" the diabolical-looking man said Windmover's name in a strangely inflected language, but to Eleanor's mind, she heard English. Her ears registered foreign words, while her eyes witnessed the man's lips forming unfamiliar syllables, but it was her own tongue that she recognized.

Windmover rose to his knees, head still lowered. "Yes, He-Who-Walks-With-Kro?" Again, Eleanor realized the Croatoan language, but understood the words as clearly as if he'd spoken English.

Then this shaman, this human liaison for this monster of the deep that the Croatoans worshipped, said nothing more, but turned and made three circles around the central fire, shook his turtle shell stick, and left the same way he came. Through this entire spectacle, Windmover remained kneeling, staring at the dirt, and Eleanor huddled beside the door, peering through a chink in the exterior bark. When He-Who-Walks-With-Kro had gone, Windmover drew himself to standing in a daze, and then resumed his spot on the bench in silence.

Eleanor let her breath escape her in a loud gasp. "What did he want?"

"It begins."

A shudder crept over her flesh at Windmover's words. She didn't know what it was, but the way in which Windmover said the words; she knew that something evil, something terrible was going to happen. Windmover stared ahead in a trance. *Was he afraid too?* She wanted to ask him, but knew she shouldn't, and didn't. Instead, she asked her next question. "Am I in danger? Am I going to die? Like the men?"

Windmover turned his wrinkled, bronze face to her. "All that lives must die. All must die so he can live."

She frowned. "Certainly, you're not in danger. You're Croatoan."

"Kro cares not the blood that flows. Kro only demands that there be blood."

Eleanor understood now. They had to make sacrifices to this Kro, and it was better to kill and deliver enemies, then it was to kill and offer their own. *What manner of god was this that demanded such extreme devotion?* Eleanor rubbed her arms within her dirty nightgown. The longhouse grew suddenly colder. She closed the hide, listening to the wind howl outside.

10.

The moon was a huge pearl hanging heavy in the ebony sky, a shiny ball of white illuminating the stone altar as He-Who-Walks-With-Kro danced wildly around it, turtle shell shaking, drums beating in rhythm with her pounding heart. Eleanor lay on her belly, peering seaward, watching the primitive ceremony through the crack in the wall.

Around and around He-Who-Walks-With-Kro spun, shrill voice cutting through the silence of the night. His maniac chants were coupled with a woman's shrieks and Eleanor strained to see who was tied to the altar. The women and children huddled, entwined together in fear, as Eleanor, alone, was the only one possessing enough courage to behold the slaughter.

This was the fourth night in a row that someone had died beneath He-Who-Walks-With-Kro's knife. The Croatoans were sacrificing the pure women, the unmarried maids to their god first.

"Please! Please!" the woman begged, and Eleanor finally recognized the voice as belonging to Mary Dunne, a former scullery maid in London, who'd come to Roanoke in hopes of finding a husband and a new life after her parents had succumbed to an illness.

The knife flashed silver and silence fell over the island, save for the sniffling and weeping of the women and children in the dwelling. Eleanor forced herself to watch the drawn out process of poor Mary's body being thrown into the roaring waves one piece at a time. There was only one maid left, soon the Indians would be coming for the ones here: the children, and mothers. A sinking feeling washed over her as she realized, they were all doomed. Doomed to die gruesomely by the hands of these deranged savages.

11.

From the scratches she etched onto the support beams in the dwelling, Eleanor estimated that a year had gone by. Only she and two sunken-eyed women were left to await the coming of their turn on the altar. The horrors they'd been through left one woman mute, and the other stark raving mad. They had to keep her tied up so she wouldn't yank her own hair out, or gouge her eyes. Eleanor alone remained strong. She lived for the day that she'd be reunited with Virginia. Prayed daily for deliverance. She knew that her father must have returned from England by now and most possibly was searching for her and the lost colonists. She prayed that he'd find her before it was too late.

Everyday Eleanor looked for Singing Woman, who seemed to purposely evade the longhouse and hadn't been seen since the night she was given Virginia. Eleanor hoped and prayed they were alive. In the dark hours of the night her imagination would spark with terrible images of Singing Woman and Virginia being cut up and tossed into the sea. She awoke awash in her own sweat, chills and tremors overtaking her.

One morning, while Windmover was allowing her to bathe in a small inlet, she spotted Singing Woman talking with the monster that was He-Who-Walks-With-Kro. Fear overcame her, as she thought that perhaps Singing Woman had an alliance with the shaman. *Had Virginia met her death in the black depths of the Atlantic?* Where was her daughter? Her heart crashed in her chest, bile rose from her stomach and she fought the urge to panic, to scream out, demand her child. No, no, that wasn't the way. She must talk with Singing Woman. They were friends of a sort at one time, maybe that friendship continued. Windmover returned her to the longhouse.

On a stiff, stinking hide, Eleanor rocked herself, her nightgown just tatters now, wet from being washed, and clinging to her rail-thin body. She must speak with Singing Woman. Windmover was in his normal place on the bench. As weak as the women were, Eleanor didn't see how they could escape on their own and they needed little guarding. She crossed to the doorway. The hide was tied to the side to allow in the air.

"Windmover?" she asked.

"Hmm," he said, eyes closed, head resting against the exterior wall of the longhouse.

"Could I speak with Singing Woman?"

"Hmm," he said again. "Maybe she not come."

"Would you ask?"

Windmover opened his eyes and stared at Eleanor. "Wait here. Stay inside."

Eleanor was shocked that Windmover would leave his post and a brief thought of escape pricked her mind. She didn't want to risk not seeing Virginia ever again though, *if* she were still alive.

The minutes crept by slowly. Eleanor's shoulders drooped in disappointment. Singing Woman must not be willing to come. She sat in the dirt near the door and waited, hoping.

She heard the lilting, honey-sweet song of Singing Woman drifting toward the longhouse and leapt from the ground. Struggling, she restrained herself from running to Singing Woman and Windmover. But, when she looked at the approaching couple, she noticed that Virginia was not with them.

Singing Woman came to the door and clasped hands with Eleanor. "Old friend," she said.

"Virginia? How is she? Is she safe? Is she well? She must be so big by now!" Eleanor asked the questions rapidly.

"She's safe and she's well."

Singing Woman looked Eleanor over. "You look like bones."

Eleanor touched her own gaunt face, smiling weakly. "They don't feed us much."

"I will bring food."

"Will you bring Virginia?"

"I will bring food." Singing Woman wore her familiar stern expression.

"I need you to take me back to Roanoke," the words burst from

Eleanor's mouth before her brain fully comprehended what she was saying. "My father might be there waiting for me. You have to help me get away."

Singing Woman scowled. "I bring more food." And, she turned, and walked away, leaving Eleanor, gaping, and in tears.

12.

A few days later, Windmover and Eleanor were scraping hides outside of the longhouse. The other women were too weak and too insane to be of much help with anything anymore. Across the yard, shouting erupted and Eleanor tried to see who was arguing.

It was Singing Woman and He-Who-Walks-With-Kro.

"Go in," Windmover said to Eleanor. Eleanor laid her scraping tool beside Windmover and did as she was told. She watched as Windmover crossed the yard to where Singing Woman was shouting at He-Who-Walks-With-Kro, and then he flung himself into the dirt in supplication.

Eleanor listened closely trying to catch the words. Windmover returned to the hides and sat quietly, watching Singing Woman who stomped away at the end of the argument with the twisted shaman.

"What were they shouting about?" Eleanor whispered from the door of the longhouse.

"He-Who-Walks-With-Kro wants Singing Woman's child."

Singing Woman's child? *Her* child, her Virginia! She gasped. "What did Singing Woman say?"

"Singing Woman tell He-Who-Walks-With-Kro that she gave him her son, he cannot have her girl child too."

Eleanor breathed a sigh of relief. "Why doesn't Singing Woman lay in the dirt like the rest of the tribe when she speaks to He-Who-Walks-With-Kro?"

"She is his sister."

Eleanor was shocked.

"Singing Woman say she give son to *Kro-Atan Ga*, and she was rewarded with the girl. She will not give the girl to Kro. He-Who-Walks-With-Kro is angry."

"Will you tell Singing Woman I need to talk with her?"

Windmover shrugged. "Soon."

13.

Singing Woman came two days later to see what Eleanor wanted.

"I know you don't want to help me escape, but Walter Kendall left knives and other iron tools buried in a secret spot at Roanoke. I can show you these things and you can give them to He-Who-Walks-With-Kro. Maybe he'll forget about Virginia if he has all these useful things," Eleanor said.

The old woman's eyes looked hopeful. It was clear to Eleanor that Singing Woman was concerned for Virginia's safety as well. "I will think on it."

Eleanor thanked her.

That night, Eleanor was awakened with a start. A calloused hand slid over her mouth to stifle any scream that might utter forth. In the pale moonlight, Eleanor made out the face of Singing Woman. The old woman leaned close to her ear and hissed, "Say no words. Come."

Eleanor followed behind Singing Woman. They hurried toward the sandy beach away from the stone altar, and into a forested cove.

"Come," Singing Woman said, pulling Eleanor behind her. Eleanor bumped into the woman's back, and felt a sleeping child tied there. No cradleboard, just a hide bag. The bag stirred.

"Virginia?" she asked.

"Ssh, no words!" Singing Woman dug around in the brush until she uncovered a rope, which she followed. It was tied to a birch-bark boat. Together she and Eleanor pushed it into the water. "In."

Eleanor did as she was told and Singing Woman handed Virginia to her. Virginia's sleeping face was angelic in the moonlight and Eleanor resisted the urge to shower her with kisses lest she wake.

"She'll sleep," Singing Woman said, paddling the boat from the island. Eleanor deduced that the old woman must have given Virginia a sleeping draught.

"Are we going to Roanoke?"

"Yes. Tonight the other women in the longhouse go to sleep with *Kro-Atan Ga.* Kro has demanded it."

"And me?"

Singing Woman grimaced. "He-Who-Walks-With-Kro also send you to sleep with Kro."

"Is that why we're going to Roanoke?"

The old woman switched hands and continued to oar. "Kro also wants Virginia."

"No!"

"Kro will not have Virginia. You say white man at Roanoke?" Singing Woman looked hopeful.

"I don't know. My father, the governor, was supposed to return with supplies. He should be there by now. He should be searching for us." Eleanor held Virginia protectively. "Have you been back to Roanoke since we were taken?"

"No. My brother, He-Who-Walks-With-Kro forbids it."

Eleanor watched the waters ripple beneath the stealthy boat. "Will he hurt you, Singing Woman? If Virginia and I get away?"

"Singing Woman not returning to Croatan. Kro has demanded that you, the child, *and* Singing Woman sleep with *Kro-Atan Ga* for my defiance."

Eleanor shook her head. "But, you're He-Who-Walks-With-Kro's sister!"

"Kro cares not. Kro only cares for blood. The blood is life. The deep one must sleep and to sleep he must have the blood that is life."

Eleanor felt confused. "Won't Kro be angry when the three of us are missing?"

"I don't think Kro will know where Singing Woman and white faces go."

Eleanor shuddered. Singing Woman didn't sound too convinced. She watched the shoreline, sandy, rocky, tree-lined. It shifted and changed rapidly as they approached Roanoke. No fires illuminated the settlement. No lights shone over the black waters. Hope sunk within Eleanor's heart as she realized that if her father had been back, he wasn't there now.

Singing Woman saw the same thing. "No fire."

"No fire," Eleanor said, sorrow heavy in her voice. "Maybe they've made camp elsewhere. New settlers can be fearful and superstitious. Maybe when they found us missing, they wouldn't stay in the old settlement."

Singing Woman looked doubtful. "Maybe your father not come back."

Eleanor considered that momentarily. "Maybe not."

The canoe ran aground on the sand of the beach and they waded into the water, pulling the boat behind. Occasionally, Virginia stirred in Eleanor's arms. "She's so big," she said.

Singing Woman smiled. "Good baby."

"Yes, she always was." Eleanor plodded through the sinking sand toward the drier beach, Singing Woman close on her heels. When they walked the path through the forest and into the settlement, it was clear to Eleanor that no one had been here since the night the Croatoans had killed and abducted the colonists. What had kept her father from returning? The thought that he too had perished at sea or in England was too painful to bear. Without him, she and Virginia were totally alone.

"No white faces," Singing Woman proclaimed, hands on her hips, looking around at the deserted settlement.

A door swung on its hinges, banging loudly open and closed. Eleanor twitched and jumped in constant alertness and fear. "We must go somewhere else. Somewhere that your brother won't look, or can't find us."

Singing Woman nodded. "We will find supplies here."

Eleanor went from house to house. The dirt floors were overgrown with grass and weeds. Everywhere vegetation had crept, in some places obliterating what had been there before. The tall palisade that had been useless to defend against the attacking Croatoans stood unmolested, still frozen in the process of repair. Eleanor laid Virginia onto a soft grassy spot and picked up a rusty knife she found. She began etching, chopping the word CROATOAN on a wood post of the fort.

"What is the word that talks?" Singing Woman watched; her head cocked to one side.

"*Croatoan.* I'm telling my father that we are with your tribe. Or were. By the time he searches for us, *if* he returns at all, there will be none of us to be found." Eleanor sighed, but continued chopping the word into the post.

Singing Woman picked up the hide bag containing the sleeping Virginia and slung it onto her back. "You carry supplies. I take Virginia."

Eleanor dropped the knife into the bundle of supplies, wanting to protest, but realized that what Singing Woman proposed made sense. She was stronger; Singing Woman was old and would tire easily. Even in her weakened state from lack of food, Eleanor would last longer than the old woman. Eleanor heaved the bundle of goods onto her back. Singing Woman walked toward the beach, back to the boat.

A loud rumbling thundered through the night air. Eleanor looked around them, toward the sky, into the swaying trees. The ground quaked, trembling beneath their feet, sending them sprawling onto the ground. Eleanor struggled to stand, her knees buckling with her every attempt. She reached for a tree stump to brace herself, but narrowly missed it before being thrown into the sand once again.

Virginia awoke, screams of terror engulfing her. The baby flailed within the brown hide; one small hand waving from the opening. Singing Woman held tightly to the strap on the bag. Dirt and sand sprayed as deep crevices split the earth. Eleanor let the bundle drop and scurried in a frantic dive toward her child.

The sandy dunes around them sank and bubbled, waves spilling inland. The trees shook, giant trunks falling, wrenched from the earth, ancient roots clawing the air like skeletal hands. A dark monstrosity rose from the depths of the water hovering above the three cowering figures. Huge, bulging eyes stared down on them: eyes that were black and piercing just like the eyes of He-Who-Walks-With-Kro. Glassy and twitching, the orbs rolled in their sockets surveying all before this monstrosity of the deep.

Singing Woman shrieked in her own tongue and clung to Virginia. "Kro!" she screamed and stood, trying to run, trying to climb the sifting sand that poured into the sea faster than she could scoop, dig, and cling to the dry dunes.

The creature from the hellish depths of the black sea stretched out a grotesquely scaled, webbed hand—surprisingly human—clutching at the air toward Eleanor.

With a primal shout of maternal rage, Eleanor struggled to get to her daughter, struggled to evade the dripping grasp of the ancient demon of the sea, but for every inch she managed to gain, she slid backward another foot. The sand beneath her was collapsing into the black waters of the Atlantic.

Tentacles, gray and black, wet and glistening, slapped the sand around them, spraying gold into the ebony sky. Eleanor's screams rent her throat, tearing from her gut, bursting into the air. The sounds of her daughter wailing and of Singing Woman shrieking ripped her ears.

A great roar rumbled, and pain engulfed her. Eleanor covered her ears with her hands instinctively and in the process slid farther into the watery sand. She struggled to climb, to crawl . . . and saw Singing Woman doing the same.

Behind the old Indian woman, Virginia slung on her back, the abomination rose still higher from the churning sea, swooped down and in a gurgled hiss enveloped them. A wake of foam and debris washed from where they once stood, shattered tree limbs and swirling sand churning out to sea.

"Virginia!" Eleanor screamed, clamoring to get to her daughter.

But there was no daughter to get to ... the bulbous monstrosity turned its massive head in her direction and bashed the sand around her furiously with enormous tentacled arms. Tilting its misshapen skull skyward, repulsive, flapping lips let loose another nerve-shattering shriek.

Eleanor found a root protruding from the diminishing shore, and using it, heaved herself upward, out of the sinking sand. She ran across the beach, toward the settlement, the roaring ancient guardian destroying all in her wake.

A tentacle grasped her ankle, cutting her, leaving crimson ribbons where once was white flesh. Eleanor spotted a knife stuck in a stump near the fortified walls. She ran to it, yanking the blade from the wood.

The monster bellowed behind her, breath reeking of rot and fish—a powerful gust that knocked her into a nearby tree. Tentacles whipped her body, seizing her legs. The scaly hands grabbed hold, sliding, slipping; raking flesh from her legs. Wrapping her arm around the tree, she lashed with the knife, blindly stabbing whatever the rusty blade made contact with.

Kro thundered around her, above her: the beast was everywhere. She would die in a watery grave. She knew she would soon sleep with the deep one *Kro-Atan Ga* and her daughter. Eleanor slashed with the knife, furious that her father would never know her fate. With her last efforts, she turned and chopped the letters *Cro* into the tree.

"I have named my killer!" she shouted toward the tentacled beast, its great mouth gaping, black eyes rolling. "And now, *I* will be *yours!*" Eleanor launched herself toward the guardian, knife plunging deep into his eye, black ooze bursting like a volcanic eruption. The guardian squeezed her body with the strength of a gale wind, and Eleanor felt life choking from her.

Kro slid into the dark waters, black blood bubbling, as Eleanor felt the cold Atlantic swallow her, delivering her to *Kro-Atan Ga* to sleep in his embrace forever.

Where Men Had Seldom Trod

By Lee Clark Zumpe

1.

Frontier Massacre!

COLONEL BENJAMIN WADDEL:

It is with utmost earnestness that I appeal to your compassion and entreat your consideration in a matter of gravest concern amongst the loyal tenants of this province. A spate of aggression hitherto unseen in the westernmost hinterlands has resulted in the destruction or abandonment of several strategic outposts and considerable loss of life. Standing militias have been unsuccessful in quelling this vicious uprising and there is a growing belief that the violence may spread eastward toward the coast. As acting colonial governor, I humbly request your support in subduing this insurrection.

—Zephaniah Pettyford
April, 1760

The mephitic putrescence corrupting the secluded cove confirmed their worst fears even before Elijah Greenheath and William Haley reached the remote site. An uncanny silence engulfed the steep-walled valley still thick with hemlock and poplar stands.

"This savagery is a grim omen considering the burden we bear,"

Greenheath said, inspecting the breadth of the butchery. On the face of it, the episode showed marked signs implicating the Cherokee; still, clouds of doubt had already formed in both men's minds. In a world riddled with enduring enigmas, the most plausible explanations often ceded to the extraordinary.

Greenheath knelt amidst a field of charred debris that had been the modest foothills settlement of Rowan. No stranger to the highlands, he had visited the outpost often during the decade since its founding and counted among its denizens more than one friend. News of its plunder traveled east along the Cherokee Path, obliging the travelers to make a portentous and unexpected detour.

No building had been spared the torch; no settler had been granted mercy. The dead lay where they had fallen, victims of a savage massacre. Their wounds varied in implementation but not in severity: Some had been shot while others had been butchered by tomahawk. Men, women and children had faced the same grim fate.

"Five or six days at most have passed since this took place. Much blood has been shed needlessly," said Haley, Greenheath's senior colleague. "The Cherokee are still on the warpath. I hesitate to think what has become of all the settlements and trading posts between Ninety-Six and Fort Prince George to the south." Once again, the uncomfortable peace between the colonists and the Cherokee had shattered, leaving a string of remote villages at increased risk. The presiding governor alleged French intrigue, but the catalyst behind the current hostilities more likely stemmed from an ill-fated Virginia expedition against the Ohio Shawnee in which a provincial regiment had abandoned their Cherokee allies without provisions. The regional magistrate, when reviewing legitimate grievances brought forward by the tribe's chief, yielded to ethnocentricity and refused to admit any misconduct in the matter. "Next," Haley continued, "the British will undoubtedly send troops into the Keowee valley in hopes of restoring order."

"The restoration of order would be better left to those who have grown accustomed to the ways of the Cherokee. If not for sporadic intervention by British authorities, provincial troops and a handful of deceitful frontier administrators who today disregard the very treaties they forged yesterday, there would be no animosity, no distrust and no need for war." Born to a patrician family, Greenheath had a far greater affinity for the pioneer than he had for the landed gentry. His father instilled in him both admiration for the common man and deep-seated dissatisfaction with the haut monde. "The British, as you say, may dispatch a contingent of unqualified, ill-equipped regulars to protect their interests in the southern marches; but, I suspect, their continuing campaign against the French and their Algonquin and Huron supporters in the north will keep them from fielding any formidable force."

Though much inclined to forsake the trappings of his aristo-cratic heritage, Greenheath had availed himself of an education only ample wealth could guarantee. His parents had voluntarily relocated from Staffordshire, England, to Charles Town, eventually settling in coastal Smithville in the early 1720s. Fearing banish-ment due to his undiscovered but unflinching support of Francis Atterbury and his efforts to place James Francis Edward Stuart on the throne of England, his father left behind much of his fortune as well as the ancestral estate of West Wardour Abbey, not far from Shugborough Hall.

Greenheath's father recouped a great deal of his lost prosperity by establishing a trade and export business in struggling Smithville, a small seaport established not far from where the swarthy floods of the Kaldetseenee River empty into the Atlantic. The primary commodities channeled through his growing concern were pel-tries—mostly deerskins—for which there persisted a substantial European demand in the manufacture of breeches, gloves and hats. While brother Ernest embraced the responsibilities of managing the enterprise upon their father's death, Elijah—eager to escape the insipid complacency of city life and explore the wilderness—trav-eled to the far ends of the frontier to meet with trappers, traders, colonists and trailblazers, securing new contracts and solidifying old agreements.

Occasionally, inherited commitments compelled him into ac-cepting supplementary chores.

For five years he had crisscrossed the piedmont, surveyed the borderlands and traded with the inhabitants of the Overhill settle-ments strewn along the Unaka Mountains. In both the scattered colonial settlements and the remote Cherokee villages, Greenheath had become a familiar and welcome caller. His prowess as an es-tablished frontiersman had come to rival his skills as an executor and negotiator.

Likewise, he developed a capacity for handling covert operations for his late father's established English patrons—an avant-garde, orphic fraternity of academicians and literati known only as Sodalitas Invictus.

"Have you ever known such wanton savageness from your former Indian friends?" Haley nodded toward the corpse of a colonist, partially burned and ruthlessly mutilated. His face, limbs and torso had been stripped bare of flesh, his eyes plucked from their sockets. His lower jaw dangled askew from the skull as if frozen in a final shriek of agony, the white of his teeth conspicuous against the crimson backdrop of exposed muscle. "Bearing in mind the information we are privy to in our current undertaking, I cannot help but wonder if the doom that came to Rowan sprang from a more degenerate source than what we are prone to first imagine. What injustice could inspire such malice and malignity?"

"In all my years dealing with them, I have never known the Cherokee to be capable of such atrocities as this," Greenheath said, more closely inspecting the remains of the victims. Again and again, he found the bodies disfigured, dismembered and defaced. The absence of animal tracks allowed him to eliminate the possibility of foraging scavengers affecting the gruesome wounds posthumously. A pattern of disproportionate injury materialized suggesting that the episode had been something more than a simple vengeful exploit or an aggressive act war. "These people suffered significant tortures before they were slain."

"Their anguish cannot be likened to any physical torment imaginable . . ." An old man staggered from the underbrush, his tattered garments soiled with blood and mud. His own injuries, though less severe than those of his fellow villagers, would bring about his death in little time. A deep gash scored his right shoulder leaving a nub of protruding bone and a swathe of swollen, purple flesh. Horror, grief and disbelief mingled in his vacant stare and bleak expression. "But for all the misery they endured, I mourn more for those the wicked ones spirited away."

"Sit and rest, good sir," Haley said, even as the colonist collapsed to the ground. Both men charged to his aid, together propping him against a mossy log along the edge of the forest. The survivor gratefully accepted a drink from Haley's copper canteen. "What can you tell us of this massacre?"

"The devils fell upon us in the middle of the night following the last Sabbath. The sentries never barked a cry of warning, their throats no doubt slit before they could raise a voice."

"Remain still," Greenheath said grasping the man's wounded shoulder. From his medicine bag he gathered a mix of bruised alder, crushed scarlet buckeye nuts and other ingredients to produce a poultice. Though he realized no care could ward off imminent death, he hoped that treating the injury might afford the victim some relief from pain in is final moments. "Those who attacked you," Greenheath said, "Can you describe them? Were they Cherokee warriors?"

"There were Cherokee in their ranks," the man said. He winced as Greenheath applied the poultice. "But this was no common war party. I recognized amongst them mainly renegades and fugitives. This small army consisted of runaway slaves, exiled Cherokee and Creek warriors and assorted British and French deserters running from the conflict in the north." Tears streamed from the survivor's eyes as he recounted the carnage he had witnessed. "They slaughtered everyone, chased children into the forest and hunted them like game animals. Even dawn could not curtail the bloodshed. When they finally sheathed their weapons, they collected a handful of carefully chosen maidens, bound and gagged them and made for the mountains to the north with their spoils. Those are the ones I pity most, those five young women destined to suffer acts of perversion and debauchery in the savages' camp until death liberates them."

"Not if we can find them first," Haley promised, already scanning the surrounding woods for signs of recent passage. For the first time, he recognized from the man's torn vesture he had served as an itinerant preacher, traveling the borderlands delivering sermons and seeking converts. Though Haley summarily rejected organized religion, he respected those who chose to lead a missionary life, admiring both their faith and their fearlessness. "I'll swear to secure their emancipation or suffer death in doing so."

"If you possess the courage, then, cross the Odawadeesga Branch at Wayah Ford." Blood trickled out of the corner of the man's mouth. He shuddered with spasms as he coughed violently, fluids filling his chest. "Pick up their trail there—they do not need to cover their tracks. Their callousness and contemptible cruelty make the likelihood of pursuit almost unthinkable."

"We will find them and hold them accountable for this bloodbath." Greenheath gazed at his longtime friend, estimating the degree of his determination. For any two common men, no matter the profundity of their valor and frontier experience, such a vow would have amounted to no more than a fool's errand against insurmountable odds. Haley, though, showed no trace of fear. Greenheath reflected his resolve as he nodded, wordlessly expressing concurrence with Haley's oath. "Justice will be done."

"May God watch over you," the preacher said, a stillness settling over him as death neared. His eyelids fluttered and closed. "I came to this land as an evangelist, to bring the gospel to those whose circumstances had left them living in darkness for so long. After a lifetime of work, I die seeing that the shadows here are too rampant to scatter with benign sermons and urbane goodwill."

"Rest, now," Greenheath said. "Your work here is done."

2.
The Spanish Blockhouse

"For the few who survived the foredoomed expedition of 1509-1510, the preoccupation with exploration, adventure and the beguiling search for wealth in the New World forever lost its allure. No promise of fame or gold could transcend the terrible memories of gore, grief and turmoil suffered at the hands of bestial and degenerate primitives. The stigma of that discomfiture devastated the reputation of conquistador Diego Hernández de Salzedo and arrested further penetration into the region for half a century."
                                    —*La odisea de Diego Hernández*,
                          Francisco Velázquez de Andagoya, 1675

Elijah Greenheath watched as twilight yielded to the approaching day. The subtle glow of morning's first light spread steadily across the eastern horizon, staining the receding dusk and snuffing out sparkling stars one by one.

Surrounded by pines, mountain laurel and oaks, he and William Haley camped along the crest of a ridge that extended northeastward from the valley where they had discovered the ransacked settlement two days earlier. The intricate network of serpentine roots securing the trees to the windswept cliffs made for uncomfortable bedding, but the benefit of opting for defensible ground eclipsed all shortcomings. As company on the brief respite, ferns sprouted from unlikely fractures in the stone and lichen stretched across the gray faces of scattered boulders.

Greenheath had skirted the edges of the highlands in the past, traveled along both established trading routes and lesser-used game trails, spent months in the wilderness living off the land where he regularly divested himself of all the fixtures and fittings of civilization. Still, he had never roamed so far into these mountains. Most settlers still shunned the region, where parallel ranges stretched for countless miles, punctuated by long, deep troughs carved by churning rivers. Even the Cherokee balked at building permanent villages beyond the Odawadeesga, their fears rooted in legends and myths passed from generation to generation and rarely shared with outsiders.

Greenheath knew the stories all too well, and had learned to pay them the respect they deserved. Each primitive legend, no matter how far-fetched, sprang from some long-forgotten seed of truth.

"There are places on this earth not meant for man." Greenheath offered his companion a hand. Morning mist met in darkened hollows beneath the mountains reluctant to yield to the dawn. Likewise, umbrageous sanctuaries the world over excluded illumination, clinging to primeval gloom to shield the last surviving vestiges of a protohistoric race. "These abominations of nature—the things which built citadels and cities long before the earliest nations of man matured—their intransience threatens our own fruition."

"The Great Old Ones endure, lingering in Stygian gloom, content to manipulate the flora and fauna of the waking world as it suits them." Haley had encountered such beings in his long years of service to Sodalitas Invictus, fought against them and their pathetic worshippers. "Though their sway is formidable, resistance is not wasted."

"I know," Greenheath said, still waiting for his first opportunity to face such a creature. "Ultimately, though, can our defiance keep them from reawakening?" The longstanding war remained deadlocked with neither party able to claim the smallest victory. Sodalitas Invictus, unwavering in its vow to rid the world of this blight, barely managed to contain the influence of the latent godlings. "Perhaps it is best not to ponder such abstract matters when we have a specific undertaking before us."

"Do you think we will find them in time?" Haley inspected his smoothbore musket, an old and trusted companion. He scratched his scalp before repositioning his black tricorne. Less inclined to eschew his aristocratic pedigree, his manner of dress distinguished him from Greenheath. He wore buckskin narrow-fall knee breeches, knit hose and soft leather buskins. Having slept in the final hours before morning, he gathered his tailored coat, belt, cartridge box and axe before slaking his thirst with water from his canteen. "It is possible that they have already been sacrificed."

"From the information enclosed in the dossier from the Duke of Newcastle-upon-Tyne, we must presuppose the alleged cultists we seek are unlikely to inflict injury upon their captives before the prescribed date of the ritual." Though Greenheath had spared the dying preacher details of their present assignment, the incident at Rowan had shed all his previous doubts about the legitimacy of recurring reports of slayings in outlying settlements and among villages of the region's indigenous people. At the start, he deemed the testimony no more than exaggerated accounts of conventional frontier raids and skirmishes, regrettable but routine occurrences. Even when the sporadic tales began to echo elements of Chero- kee legends, Greenheath discounted the similarities. Over several months, both the abundance and the indecency of the stories made them increasingly difficult to dismiss. Somewhere in the uncharted back country, an apocryphal group of zealots had reemerged from longstanding dormancy. "The misplaced fanaticism that drives this cluster of miscreants should make them adhere to the principles of the ceremony they intend to perform. As long as we can locate their lair before the autumnal equinox, we should find all their captives unharmed."

"That leaves us little time," Haley said. "The season will change in only two days time."

"Let us trust that their method of reckoning time is as accurate as our own."

Upon receiving cryptic instructions from his secretive bene- factors in England, Greenheath found himself obliged to further investigate the matter—to "handle the situation with equal parts discretion and determination." As a private abettor acting on behalf of the clandestine London-based cabal, Greenheath now understood this assignment could only end in violence. The profile the duke had provided left no prospect for either compromise or clemency. Though the reputed history of the mountain-dwelling sect remained as ambiguous as it was implausible, the extermination of the group could not be deferred.

"Judging by their tracks, we are within a day's reach of them now,"

Haley said, eager to rejoin the hunt. Taking a few steps, he glanced over his shoulder. Greenheath stood passively, frozen in contemplation, stoic as the soaring spruce beneath which he reflected. "Is something vexing you?"

"We are perhaps hours away from a confrontation that will certainly end in chaos and indiscriminate killing." Greenheath patted his Kaintuck rifle, acknowledging its willingness to serve. He treated his weapon with reverence and fidelity. He preferred its accuracy to the outmoded imprecision of his partner's Brown Bess. Its sleek custom design—from its long octagonal barrel and small bore, to its stock made from tiger maple—lent it a quality of audaciousness. "Though the motivation is clear and the intended outcome is amenable, the righteousness of the act makes it no more palatable to me."

"We have worked together for many years, Elijah. Once, you considered me a mentor. In truth, I have gleaned as much knowledge from you as I have imparted to you." Haley regarded his former apprentice with the pride of a satisfied taskmaster. Realizing his son's potential significance, Greenheath's father had paired the two intentionally. Haley's guidance helped enhance Greenheath's intellectual propensity and reinforced his extraordinary perceptive skills. "We two are different from the common man. We are privy to things few could imagine. We are aware of confidential details of state that could incite revolution and topple governments. We are apprised of all the undisclosed facets of history that cause kings and queens to suffer sleepless nights." The secret society to which both men had sworn their allegiance harkened back to an epoch when civilization dissociated itself from the pursuit of knowledge, when wisdom which might have been forever lost had to be cached and concealed. "Even with the dawning of this age of enlightenment, the burden of confronting these dark legacies may always fall upon our shoulders—and upon the shoulders of those who follow in our footsteps."

"I sometimes wonder if this birthmark was more a curse than a blessing." Greenheath pulled back the self-fringed sleeve of his buckskin wamus to reveal a curious star-shaped blemish. At its center, an eye appeared to contain a tiny flame. His father had understood its meaning, recognized and explained its assurance of extraordinary mental capacity, amplified insightfulness, imposing physical strength and dexterity and unconventional longevity. Along with the boon, though, came custodianship. "Despite all the inborn traits this mark guarantees, I regret that I was denied the choice of living a more ordinary existence."

"Even a Sentinel has the right of choice, Elijah." A hundred years earlier, Haley had struggled with his destiny, too. "I elected to serve the brotherhood, to do what had to be done to allow civilization to flourish." The elder Sentinel empathized with his younger partner's trepidation. Never before had Greenheath faced such a treacherous task. Never before had he met a foe so tainted by the darkest elements of the cosmos. "I know that compared to our past endeavors, this assignment must seem particularly disconcerting—and I will not deny that what lies ahead will surpass your innermost fears. You would be a fool not be concerned—but your resolve is not diminished because of it. You have already made your choice, years ago. The characteristics that lend us strength may be inherited, but our will is all our own."

Shrugging off his momentary disinclination, Greenheath returned to the task at hand.

※ ※ ※

Shortly before sunset, the men discerned a slender ribbon of smoke climbing into the evening sky amidst the laurel slicks of a broad valley. Standing on a blue-gray, slate-like promontory surrounded by a clump of blooming monk's hood, they beheld a deep gorge that stretched far toward a distant ridgeline, a sizable basin already half-bathed in the shadows of dusk. At the center of lowland, a peculiar granite dome swelled from the gently rolling forested floor.

With daylight quickly abating, the men began a wary but swift descent, passing along a dry wash choked with boulders and through a rhododendron tunnel. On the steep slope, Greenheath and Haley roved through stands of sand myrtle clutching the bare rock, continuously aware that though civilized men had seldom trod this remote hollow, the odds of encountering hostile entities increased with each passing moment.

Tracking the source of the smoke, Greenheath soon stumbled upon the smoldering remnants of what must have been a copious bonfire blazing through the previous night. At the center of the fire pit, the men identified three charred skulls. Surrounding the scene, scattered amidst a low understory of purple-berried pokeweeds, a macabre collection of bones on rancid entrails confirmed the disgraceful degeneracy of wanton cannibalism.

"This inhumanity leaves little doubt that those we pursue were accurately identified and described." Haley recalled with angst the portrayal of their quarry as detailed in the dossier channeled through Sodalitas Invictus. Its tradition, the Duke of Newcastle-upon-Tyne claimed, went back thousands of years to a time before recorded history. Its disciples originally consisted strictly of various indigenous peoples—expatriated natives coerced into ceremonial worship. More recently, the brotherhood believed their ranks had been augmented by discontented Europeans and various pariahs. "It is one matter for isolated indigenes to exhibit what must be deemed barbaric attributes. What I cannot fathom is how cultured men born of civilization can adopt and embrace such brutishness."

"Neither refinement nor edification confirms a capacity for morality or magnanimity," Greenheath said. Leaving his companion to pick through the bones of the cult's most recent victims, Greenheath discovered the silhouette of an unexpected edifice skulking in the darkness. There, amidst a tangle of briars and dog-hobble, an old, dilapidated Spanish blockhouse squatted on a small plateau overlooking the valley floor. "Follow me," he whispered, beckoning Haley. "I may have found their lair."

Both men sensed straining eyes mindful of their cautious approach, eyes anxiously watching them from an embrasure in the blockhouse. The quadrangular fortification had been ravaged by the callous elements of slowly passing years, subjected to the varying extremes of an ever-changing climate and the stubborn and steady repossession by the omnipresent wilderness.

The building's primitive construct offered further evidence of its considerable age. The vine-covered walls of the wooden palisades, interrupted by sporadic loopholes for musketry, showed signs of both an immemorial and a more recent siege. From his studies, Greenhealth immediately recognized it as a vestige from one of two noted Spanish excursions in the area, both predating the English colony at Roanoke Island by many years—both episodes only marginally recorded by history and destined to be ultimately forgotten. Each adventure had ended in tragedy: Captain Juan Pardo lost all his troops to a native uprising in 1568; earlier, conquistador Diego Hernández de Salzedo's expedition set out to survey the mountains and abruptly vanished. Intermittent accounts gleaned from purported survivors of the 1510 campaign bore striking similarities to the many Cherokee legends which now seemed increasingly credible.

"A rather slapdash attempt at constructing a frontier garrison—its original occupants must have found their way to the grave long ago." Signaling Greenheath to take a defensive position, Haley crouched behind a black cherry tree. Continuing in a whisper, he added "It is not large enough to house the numbers I would expect to find participating in the clan we seek. The rogues may use the blockhouse as a sentry point, though, to warn the others of an incursion."

"Do we attack?"

"No—we wait. The sound of battle would only serve to draw in additional combatants." Though Haley remained confident that their combined ingenuity and agility would prevail against an enemy benefited by large numbers, he saw no logic in hastening the looming mêlée. A deft strategist, he planned to stalk the eremitic cultists from the shadows, eliminating as many as possible before conducting a decisive raid on their retreat. "If they know we are in their territory, they will come to us."

Silence lingered as stars began to fill the heavens, aligning themselves in predetermined patterns forming familiar constellations. Rifle in hand, Greenheath pressed his back against the mossy trunk of a birch, his attention briefly beguiled by the mesmerizing display of stellar grandeur. Beyond the thin canopy of the forest, beyond the sparse wispy clouds and the invariable orbit of earth's subordinate moon, the boundless universe sprawled endlessly, content knowing that even in the expanse of eternity only a fraction of its mysteries could be unlocked.

Greenhealth knew that science might ultimately take future generations to the far-flung stars. Having studied legends asserting the existence of extraterrestrial spawn locked in earthly exile—bound, caged, imprisoned or withdrawn—he knew, too, such explorers along that grim perimeter would face countless horrors in a noble but fundamentally futile effort to conquer the unknown.

Little time had elapsed when the soft sound of inconsolable sorrow drifted from the blockhouse. Staggered weeping and muffled voices gradually filled the darkened stockade, echoing amidst the rafters.

"Friend or foe?"

The query reverberated only a short distance in the thick, rugged woods.

"Friend," Haley responded, recognizing both the accent and the undeniable mark of civility in the man's hail. Instinct afforded him the luxury of provisional trust, and he lowered his musket.

"Approach—but be quick about it."

Inside, Greenheath and Haley found the vestiges of a British expeditionary force apparently sent into the mountains to suppress the warring Cherokee. A contingent of 124 men under the command of Colonel Benjamin Waddel had stumbled upon the valley even as the cold-blooded cultists returned from their recent raid on Rowan.

"Not men—they were like animals." A rank-and-file soldier, identifying himself as Erastus Peters, described the ensuing skirmish. "They had at their disposal every manner of firearm, yet they favored crude hatchets and spears and rocks. They came at us with such fury that we had time for but one fusillade. Our bullets rained down on them like leaden hail, but they attacked nonetheless."

"This is all that remain?" Greenheath looked into the faces of the four men cowering in the blockhouse. Fear had kept them from full retreat, shackled them into the false security offered by the old fortification.

"There were seven of us—last night, they claimed the other three." The soldier trembled as he spoke. His companions shrank in silence, too frightened to interject any personal observations. "One moment they were here, among us—the next, they were gone. We don't know how the monsters carried them off without disturbing us." Peters cringed as he recalled the long night. "We heard their unbearable screams resonate through the darkness, heard their pleas for either deliverance or prompt death. Upon hearing such excruciating torment, no man could hope to summon courage. We dared not leave this shelter lest we share their fate."

"How many attacked you?"

"Dozens—Cherokee and Creek and Choctaw fighting right alongside French and British and Spanish." He paused, rubbed his eyes as if trying to expel a particular image from his mind. "Some of them were different, though, I swear it. Some were beasts or devils. The man who claimed to be their leader called them his Uquedaligeesdee, his Servitors of Chaos."

"Who commands them?" Greenheath recognized the Cherokee word from recitations of old legends. In his studies of medieval grimoires, he had also come across repeated references to the cryptic Servitors of Chaos. Spread throughout the pages of assorted rare occult treatises in diverse citations, these pagans were categorized as worshipers of a single, subterranean deity and were notorious for their enactment of a particularly hideous communal ceremony. Originally concentrated within some antediluvian society lost to history, they dispersed into smaller tribes during one of the violent cataclysms dividing the great ages of man. In nomadic clans, they spread to the farthest reaches of the world where they went into hibernation. "Who called them by that name?"

"Their leader—a dark-skinned man who speaks fluent English. He calls himself Zhaig." Peters paused, turned toward a nearby loophole. Reluctantly, he peered out the breach and scanned the murky darkness rife with nebulous shadow. "He will be here soon enough. He will come to taunt as he did last night. He will come to claim us, to loose his savages on us. By God, we will all beg for the succor of expeditious death before this night is finished."

As if invoked by Peters' confession of fear, the bloodcurdling howls of prowling cultists, actively stalking the wild darkness outside the blockhouse, shattered the relative silence leaving no one unaware of the forthcoming struggle for survival.

3.
The Valley of Uquedaligeesdee

"Regarding sacrifice, the consequence of human suffering has no significant bearing upon the deliberation of primitive man. Amongst all established instances of ritualistic violence, the most prominent models may be found in those still practiced at the Beltane fires in the highlands of Scotland; amidst the high-volcanic atolls that form the Andaman Islands and within certain inaccessible jungle villages of Malaysia; and inside the ancient stone temples atop the wind-swept Shan Plateau in northern Burma. In remote corners of Europe and in regions completely isolated from foreign influence, pagans have sustained their old heathenism. Therefore, one should expect to find widespread religious aberrations in the New World."
—*Culto Cattivo*, Raymundus of Capua, 1685.

No strangers to the enmity of the cloistered delinquents and zeal-ous disciples, William Haley and Elijah Greenheath instinctively readied themselves for pitched battle. The raw recruits they found cowering within the centuries-old Spanish blockhouse, however, had been immobilized by fear having witnessed the slaughter of their fellow soldiers. Their trepidation vastly overshadowed any impulse for endurance. In order to enlist their active support, the veterans would have to project both confidence and courage.

An upheaval of unnerving shouts, grunts and growls filled the woods, rising from the lungs of unseen foes, vented in grim fervor. In that instant, the younger conscripts believed that the demons of hell had possessed themselves of the surrounding shadows and that they voiced their hellish spite in wolfish howls.

"No ordinary man could utter such detestable sounds!" The inexperienced Erastus Peters fretfully joined the other soldiers huddled in a corner around a flickering oil lantern, waiting feebly for capture or death. "We are defenseless against them."

"Like hell," Greenheath said. He positioned himself on the side of the blockhouse overlooking the valley, thrust the barrel of his Kaintuck rifle through the loophole and fired. Haley joined him instantly, and together their bravery gradually persuaded the surviving British troops to shelve their apprehension and join in the fray. An angst-ridden wail arose in the twilight shortly, evidence that at least one bullet had found its mark. "See," Greenheath said. "They are men of flesh no different than we. Once their noses are bloodied, they will not be so eager to approach."

The caliginous woodlands erupted with bright flashes and the sharp crack of rifle fire as the cultists attempted to forge on with their stalled offensive. With six assertive shootists now defending the stronghold, the rogues soon arrested their advance and scattered in retreat.

"You fight with new-found poise and skill." The voice sounded through the darkness, inhibiting the now erratic howls of the attackers. Inside the stronghold, Haley wordlessly implored silence from his companions. Peters offered a nod in an unspoken confirmation that the man addressing them was the one called Zhaig. "Had such resistance been presented last night, I would have been forced to sup on rancid squirrel instead of enjoying a delectable banquet of freshly carved man-meat." The revelation of cannibalism visibly shook the young men-at-arms. Even in their most abysmal musings, the concept had clearly not entered into their thoughts. "Still, it is only a matter of time before you share their fate."

"Zhaig, if I might be so presumptuous as to cut short your deliberate harassment ... " Haley searched the shadows for movement,
expecting a small raiding party to use the diversion of dialogue to
screen their foray. In Zhaig, he recognized the voice of an old nem-
esis, one he believed had perished more than 30 years earlier when
plague visited Masuria. "I believe we are acquainted; although, I am
unfamiliar with the appellation you have adopted in your present
incarnation as chief of this ancient tribe."

"Impossible ... I am Z-Zhaig," he stammered. "I am—I am now
the presiding high priest of Yghol, born unto the Uquedaligeesdee
upon their most recent awakening." Zhaig's dithering betrayed his
sudden insecurity. "I am an avatar of the Great Old Ones, emissary
of Ach'Maz and anointed herald of the inevitable cosmic trans-
mogrification."

"An impressive compilation of assumed designations, each of
which I am certain you are well-equipped to retain." Haley's sus-
picion quickly evolved into certainty upon hearing Zhaig's inven-
tory of titles, harvested directly from one of two pertinent esoteric
manuscripts and delivered verbatim from the memorized text. "I
suspect, however, you formerly were known as Albrecht von Tschirnhaus, distinguished Prussian mathematician and accomplished
student of cabalistic arts and hermetic magic. Your aversion to death
leads you down corridors not meant for mortal men. This obses-
sion has diminished your genius leaving you writhing in infectious
madness."

"Is it madness to seek to make a pact that will ensure unequaled
longevity? Is it madness to align myself with the Servitors of Chaos—those the indigenes know only as the Uquedaligeesdee? Many
have survived thousands of years in loyal serfdom." That the migrant
Prussian had managed to install himself as high priest of the clan
came as no surprise to Haley. His intimate knowledge of arcane lore
coupled with his radical theories in unconventional geometry would
have made him almost godlike. "I find I am at a disadvantage: While
you have identified me, I do not recognize your voice. No matter—I
can deduce your affiliation with Sodalitas Invictus, or some similar
fraternity of priggish prodigies."

Haley's familiarity with Zhaig provided little comfort. Years
before Greenheath had even been born, Haley hounded the self-
proclaimed magus and consort of Things Which in Dark Quarters
Dwell, gathering information on the renegade hermeticist's vari-

ous political intrigues and exploits at the behest of his patrons. To Sodalitas Invictus, he personified the dark designs of primordial chaos and put at risk the measured progress of civilization. Had he not been perceived to be among the dead buried in mass graves dug in the wake of plague, Haley surely would have been directed to stem his nefarious penchant.

"We serve different principles," Haley said, finally spotting the expected incursion all but secreted beneath the cloak of utter darkness. He signaled their approach to Greenheath who in turn relayed the information to the other soldiers. Waiting for Haley's word, each man carefully tracked the stealthy advance of the cultists as they drew closer to the blockhouse. "While you extol the virtues of indentured servitude to your professed god, you disregard the repercussions of your actions. I seek only to maintain the longstanding armistice which has allowed the fruition of a new society."

Haley's quick nod supplied the only necessary command. Following a flash of musketry within the redoubt, a volley of leaden messengers traversed the darkened woods conveying prompt fatalities amongst the advancing raiding party. Abandoning their dead, the survivors recoiled uneasily, unaccustomed to such staunch resistance.

"Very well," Zhaig shouted into the night, perceptibly angered by the failure of his heathens to deliver a decisive blow to the embattled warriors. Inside the blockhouse, Haley, Greenheath and the soldiers had proven their skills clearly superior, their position readily defensible and their resolve less likely to be degraded by derision and fear. With the autumnal equinox upon them, Zhaig knew preparations for the ceremony could no longer be delayed. "We will withdraw and find a less palatable meal foraging for game deeper in the valley." Neither Greenhealth nor Haley believed that Zhaig would leave the stronghold unguarded. Still, the men had no intention of searching for the cultists' lair until morning illuminated the wooded basin. "I urge you to leave this place at dawn. Tomorrow night, if I find you lingering here, no show of force will keep me from cutting your throats."

The balance of the night crawled along endlessly while Greenheath and Haley took turns scanning the shadows for signs of an impending ambush. The rank-and-file soldiers endured intermittent intervals of slumber interspersed with nightmares and fits of uncontrolled sobbing. The acts of butchery they had seen and the horror Zhaig's Servitors of Chaos had inspired in them left them emotionally and spiritually crippled. Fortunately, no further challenges emerged during the long, hellish night.

"With or without these men, we must carry out the will of Sodalitas Invictus." Greenheath glanced at the sleeping soldiers as he whispered to his mentor. Though he had no personal experience with the man Haley knew as Albrecht von Tschirnhaus, he had read enough about him to consider him a dangerous adversary. The fulfillment of the planned sacrifice would, according to all available literature regarding the Servitors of Chaos, entitle Zhaig to near immortality. The servitors were said to sleep for eons, stirring only four times every thousand years to make sacrifices and increase their fold. "We cannot allow the ceremony to succeed."

"The acquirement of such a powerful and knowledgeable individual as von Tschirnhaus would enhance the influence of the Great Old Ones. As a member of the Servitors of Chaos, he could single-handedly accelerate their resurrection."

"At all cost, then, we eliminate the risk he and this isolated cult represent," Greenheath said, "for the sake of civilization."

4.
The Guardian of Yghol

"Though caged and confined, their elemental influence must not be misjudged; though quiescent in induced languor, their dark designs must not be disregarded."
—*De Vermis Mysteriis*, Ludvig Prinn, 1542.

Morning delivered an anticipated sanctuary, overwhelming the omnipresent shadows and offering evidence that those who besieged the Spanish blockhouse in darkness had completely withdrawn on the authority of their newfound leader, Zhaig. Elijah Greenheath and William Haley, able frontiersman and Sentinels acting under the mandate of the secretive Sodalitas Invictus, left the stronghold and struck out into the valley after instructing the four surviving British soldiers to flee southwestward along the ridgeline. They warned them that the Cherokee, no doubt similarly victimized by Zhaig's murderous Uquedaligeesdee, would not be peaceable if encountered in the wilderness and should therefore be avoided.

Greenheath estimated their chances for survival alone in the wilderness without escort only marginally better than if they stayed and faced Zhaig's disciples.

"Your prior history with this Prussian—Zhaig or von Tschirnhaus—gives you an insight into his deportment that should prove valuable." Greenheath kept his voice low as they penetrated the thick hardwood forest dominating the lowlands encircled by steep, rugged cliffs. "Have you any theories on how he arrived here, so far from his last known residence?"

"In fact, I suspect his intentions lay in this direction long ago. During the period I was asked to monitor his studies, he displayed growing interest in Spanish conquistadors; particularly Cortés, Pizarro, de Orellana, de Salzedo and Pardo. At the time, I believed his curiosity to be no more than academic."

"You think he was looking for evidence of the lost tribes, the Servitors of Chaos?"

"Precisely." The scraggly woods periodically obscured the slate gray dome of the colossal granite monolith centered in the valley. Its gigantic scale, though, overshadowed the environment even at times when the forest kept it from direct view. Through massive tangles of branches and vines, they descended into a ravine thick with hickory, pine and sassafras. Both men had already guessed their destination lay at the base of the immense rock. "He found what he was looking for in the lost expedition of de Salzedo. He used the Masurian plague to cover his departure for some Mediterranean port where he must have gained passage to the New World. Passing through Charles Town, he probably used his guile to attract the attention of refugees and fugitives who could help him retrace de Salzedo's course."

"Once he found this place, though, how did he keep from being butchered by the Uquedaligeesdee?"

"He arrived during a period of hibernation," Haley said. Greenheath remembered that Servitors of Chaos only awoke every 250 years. "He prepared for them, learned indigenous languages, studied the environment they had chosen for their long periods of rest. When they stirred, he used his charisma to convince them of his ascendancy."

At the heart of the ravine Greenheath and Haley found a rippling creek, its course flowing across mossy steps in its plodding retreat from the encircling cliffs. Strewn along the shallow streambed, countless human skulls rested alongside polished stones and a mix of jewelweed, woodnettle and jack-in-the-pulpit. The somber remains offered irrefutable evidence of long-standing abominations in the area, of unappeasable bloodthirstiness that had perhaps impeded the advancement of nearby cultures and resulted in enduring fear among the Cherokee as manifested in their disturbing legends. Having been witness to wars, famines and pestilence, even Haley found himself unnerved by the unforeseen scope of brutality and by the pervasiveness of death.

"The Servitors of Chaos that dwell here have long been known to my Cherokee friends." Greenheath spoke in a tentative whisper, still startled to find the nightmarish legends rooted in the repugnant reality of prehistoric evil. "In their story cycles, handed down from generation to generation, they are the Uquedaligeesdee—outcasts from an ancient race that existed even before Grandfather Buzzard formed these mountains with the flapping of his wings. Shunned by the grace of benevolent gods, they sought consolation from some unnamed spawn of the abyss. They earn their uncanny longevity through acts of cruelty and carnality and are known for their infamous appetite for flesh."

The scattered bones offered silent testimony substantiating the tale. If ever the unsettled dead had reason to linger pending the execution of vengeance, the ghosts in this valley could justifiably claim that right.

Following the weaving trail upstream, Greenheath and Haley felt the shadowy eyes of slaughtered victims scrutinizing their progress. Even as the wind mimicked the whispers of ghosts pleading for a settling of scores, the dense woodland abruptly gave way, opening onto a weedy field littered with old, charred stumps and further remains of tortured victims. Directly in front of them, the grim, gray dome lumbered in pastoral stillness, its ashen hide stippled with sparse vegetation.

Taking a few steps, Haley felt his leather buskins sink into muddy ground.

"Watch your footing," Greenheath said. Along the forest's edge, the stream dispersed greatly creating a strip of swampy land. "Let us survey the field before risking detection."

"There," Haley said, pointing toward a murky pocket where the granite mound met the meadow floor. Into its depths the remnants of the creek vanished. "The mouth of a cave leading beneath the rock, beneath the valley floor itself—that is where they must secrete themselves during their long periods of slumber."

"No guards posted? No traps set?" Warily, Greenheath scanned the vicinity. "It seems foolish to think fortune would be so friendly as to smile on us thusly."

A volley of distant shots shattered uneasy silence. The war cries of pitched battle followed promptly as two armies clashed beneath the azure skies. Their attention drawn to the distant southern ridge of the valley, the Sentinels discovered unexpected allies. Fate had favored them after all: The balance of Zhaig's heathen Uquedaligees-dee had been effectively diverted, sidetracked in fending off an attacking Cherokee war party.

"Their reckless raiding and murderous scavenging has made them more enemies than they could have anticipated," Greenheath said, wondering how long the Cherokee warriors could occupy them. "Let us not waste this fortuity."

"Agreed."

With swift but deliberate progress, they traversed the marshy patch and sped across the meadow toward the lumbering mass of stone. Haley first detected the slender ribbon of smoke drifting from the mouth of the cave. Only when the two drew close did he recognize the aberration of its movement . . . only when their impetuous footfalls set them dangerously close to the dome's gently sloping bulk did the Sentinel discern the unmistakable pattern of rhythmic breathing.

The mountain moved.

"It lives," Haley said, but the realization came a moment too late. Thick tangles of entwined vines slithered down the side of the beast as it stirred from its lethargy. A jumble of asymmetrically positioned eyes opened simultaneously all across its stony face. Its cold, rank breath surged from the mouth of the cave as it lifted its body from the valley floor revealing a network of interlaced, monolithic stones forming a vast floor. "Back to the woods," Haley said, grabbing Greenheath by the shoulder. Even as they forged their retreat, he marveled at the ancient monument concealed beneath the animated granite protector. Cryptic symbols had been painstakingly carved into each block in a spiraling configuration leading toward a central aperture. "We've got to find cover."

Wormlike, the Guardian of Yghol towered over the valley as it gave chase. Its shadow engulfed the Sentinels as they retreated. Clusters of vines, as functional as they were fatal, lashed at the ground like leafy tentacles as it sought to smash the trespassers in their tracks.

"I can get a clean shot if we can make it back to the forest," Greenheath said, relying only on reflex and instinct to guide him in his flight.

"No use—it would be like shooting a mountainside." The things lower appendages now swept the valley floor, hurling boulders, bones and logs with the force of cannon-fire. "Once we've reached the tree line, skirt the border and remain visible, heading toward the northwest."

"We would find safer refuge deeper in the woods."

"I do not seek to hide from it," Haley said. "We must slow its progress for a few moments."

Employing their athletic prowess and enhanced sensory abilities, Haley and Greenheath avoided the Guardian's attacks and reached the forest quickly. Aggravated by their escape, the thing continued its pursuit, its mountainous bulk scarring the earth as it pressed on. Its passage along the valley floor produced a roar of thunder more terrible than any storm nature had ever bred. Its blazing eyes now moved in appalling disharmony, twitching and darting, obsessively seeking its prey. Only as it neared the forest did its swiftness and tenacity begin to falter.

"Target one of its eyes," Haley said, knowing Greenheath's aim to be truer than his own.

"You said it would not affect an injury ..."

"Most likely, it will not—but it will get its attention again."

The Kaintuck rifle which had never failed him lived up to expectations once more. The ball struck the Guardian in one of its many eyes resulting in an eruption of orange slime and white pus. As a stray knot of vines reflexively clawed at the ruptured organ, the thing vented an appalling wail. If Zhaig and his Uquedaligeesdee had not yet taken notice of the situation, the cry of the Guardian would no doubt alert them.

The Guardian wavered, its colossal form momentarily confounded by unfamiliar pain. Like a wounded predator, though, its hesitance dissipated promptly. Its remaining eyes quickly fixed on Greenheath and Haley.

With newfound animosity, the thing lunged at the Sentinels as Haley had expected, plunging into the soggy ground where the forest stream met the grassy meadow.

"Now," Haley said, bolting out of the woods. Together, the men crossed the fen and the field while the Guardian struggled to keep itself from sinking into the mud. Its incensed howls made the earth tremble. Haley ignored the commotion, focusing instead on what lay before them. "In the stone floor there is an opening—race for it. That is what the Guardian shelters—that is the entrance to the refuge of the Servitors of Chaos."

By the time the Guardian of Yghol had freed itself from the mire, Greenheath and Haley had descended into the shadowy, subterranean temple beneath the Valley of Uquedaligeesdee.

5.

To Shadows Betrothed

"A Priest seeking communion with Yghol should select as an offering only those which are virgin, these being more suitable unto Yghol, rendering Him more amenable. Further gifts of blood and flesh may be expected."

—*Andere Götter*, Heinrich Niemann, 1496.

A ring of blazing torches encircled the underground lair segregating the shadows without banishing them entirely. Their frozen flames flickered unnaturally, burning far too slowly as if they existed outside the dominion of time. The temple's design aped the great shrines of antiquity, echoing the architectural manners of Sumer and Egypt and Rome and Greece. Still, something in either their outline or their execution deviated from any known style—the form relied too zealously upon unsettling angles and distressing patterns and plans. Lines intersected which should have remained parallel while in distant corners darkness huddled in deep swathes so profound that stars may have swarmed within them unseen.

"We walk a narrow path few dare follow," Haley said. "Veer off the course and the abyss will claim you."

"It is so close?" As a Sentinel, Greenheath understood that forces existed capable of bending time, warping space and maligning the laws of nature. Even as civilization's emerging scientific renaissance produced physicists, natural philosophers and mathematicians eager to categorize and clarify the composition of the universe, he had gleaned from forbidden tomes arcane wisdom which surpassed the most innovative theories of his age. "There is an unnatural thickness to the air, a heaviness afflicting my bones."

"Here, gravity ebbs and flows as the fabric of reality oscillates." Haley ventured deeper into the vast underground chamber, soon approaching the center of the shrine where twin pillars supported a fragile bulge in the granite ceiling. Beyond the columns, seven steps led down into a recess containing accumulated plunder and timeworn treasures. Jewels, gems, and priceless works of early art unmatched in any museum or private collection lay in musty abandon. Here, too, were collected manuscripts written in forgotten languages, predating the pyramids of Giza and the oldest sanctuaries of the Orient. "As in the crypts of kings, here rests the relics of some culture that waxed and waned before the Flood."

"That, and more ..." Greenheath gestured toward a group of women situated around a vast pit. In all, he counted 20 maidens meant to be sacrificed to the slumbering Great Old One known to its adherents as Yghol. Once completed, the ceremony would assure Zhaig both near immortality as well as ascendancy over the Servitors of Chaos. "There are more than I anticipated, more than the old man said had been taken from Rowan."

"They come from separate villages and settlements, differ in origin and circumstances yet share this same tribulation." Haley walked amongst the shimmering gold and silver cache taking particular notice of a wealth of strange instruments and implements that suggested a level of innovation and invention far beyond that of any nation presently in existence. The Sentinel also saw the stream, now rerouted through a series of deftly crafted channels in the floor of the temple. The cataracts reunited toward the rear of the cavern, the watercourse coming together to wind its way ever onward through the meandering subterranean labyrinth. "They appear unharmed and untouched aside from the cords which bind them. Let us gather them quickly—Zhaig will be returning soon."

As they crossed the chamber to free the captives, the cavern shuddered. A deafening sound rumbled through the very earth. Pebbles dislodged from the benighted ceiling rained down over the floor.

"The Guardian has returned," Greenheath said. He tended to the first woman, loosening her bonds. "Even if we can untie and awake them all before Zhaig returns, I do not see how we will evade that horror when we depart."

"I have already considered that and I am formulating a stratagem."

Before Greenheath could question his comrade further, the woman he had released regained consciousness and demanded his immediate attention. He knelt beside her, brushed the hair from her eyes. Initially, he perceived a mix of distress and relief in her sullen expression. The speed with which her expected gratitude soured into contempt and derision stunned both men.

"Blasphemers. Nonbelievers." She stood, pulling away from her would be saviors. Her declaration lacked passion and intensity—the words rolled across her lips in an emotionless chant, as if discharged from memory and devoid of spirit. "Yghol offers purpose and fulfillment. Yghol is my redeemer."

Driven by a counterfeit embedded zeal, she allowed the charisma of Zhaig to govern her will. His beguiling enticements, his magnetic charm had undermined her reason and her identity, leaving her no more than a pawn in his ruthless sport. Though both Greenheath and Haley tried to keep her from self-sacrifice, she flung herself over the edge of the precipice, plummeting into the depths of the pit where Yghol slept.

From the shadowed nadir, her screams never ceased. Instead, they faded beneath a distant growl that gradually increased in timbre until the very floor of the cavern reverberated to its unholy pitch.

"It begins!" Zhaig's voice called across the immeasurable chamber where both time and space seemed distended and distorted. Fresh from battle with the Cherokee, the high priest led his Uquedaligees-dee—their numbers noticeably fewer—toward the Pit of Yghol. Streamed across the darkened lair, racing toward their stirring god, the Servitors of Chaos drew their weapons as they prepared to make additional sacrifices of the Sentinels. "Rise, chaste daughters of the earth. The time has come to offer yourselves—show these skeptics the scope of your fervor!"

One by one, the women stood, staring at the dark crater with haunting indifference. Haley and Greenheath tried to rouse them from their stupor, tried to curtail their suicidal impulses. One by one, though, their frail bodies plunged into darkness and into the horror of the abyss.

"It is done, then," Haley said, turning to Greenheath. Zhaig and his followers advanced swiftly and would soon fall upon them. The Uquedaligeesdee would offer no quarter, and the ordeals and agonies which lie ahead would prove to be legendary. The distant drone of

Yghol pulsed through the cavern—the Great Old One, still in repose, acknowledged a welcome offering. "Go!" Haley raced up the stairs, positioned himself between the pillars. Greenheath, prepared to die alongside his colleague, stood firm. "Go," Haley repeated, pointing toward the back of the chamber. "Follow the river through the cavern—swim if you must, but hurry …"

"I will not leave you!"

"My time is spent. You have more challenges to face, more shadows to dispel." For the first time, both Sentinels noticed a lone survivor. Coiled up in the darkness, she alone had managed to overcome Zhaig's influence. Now, she cringed at the looming madness of battle. Greenheath recognized her as a daughter of a merchant of Rowan. "Take her," Haley said. "Take her and go!"

Without another word, Greenheath swept the woman into his arms and sped down the darkened tunnel, following the course of the underground river—hoping it would eventually deliver them both to freedom.

Haley towered above Zhaig and his Uquedaligeesdee before the Pit of Yghol.

"We will find them," Zhaig promised. He stayed his heathens for the moment. "They will not find their way without light—the darkness is demon in the depths."

"My friend is resourceful. I have faith in him."

"What else do you have faith in, man of Sodalitas Invictus?" Zhaig's features had grown hard and harsh. His tanned flesh and long gray hair, his ragged beard and jagged nails all confirmed his fall from civilization and his descent into madness. "Do you believe in a struggle between good and evil, light and darkness, order and chaos? Do you predict an eventual victory over those elements you deem evil?" In torchlight, the Servitors of Chaos revealed themselves. Once human, the taint of the abyss now corrupted them. Their bargain with Yghol provided them a protracted lifespan but failed to protect them from the common afflictions of humanity. Festering wounds centuries old lingered … lost appendages regenerated, but in hideous, inhuman form … all aspects of refinement and sophistication and culture withered beneath the cultivation of the bestial savage beneath the surface. "Do you contend that mankind can deny its inherent malignancy indefinitely?"

"Far more renounce the inclination toward the dark side than embrace it," Haley said, each arm now resting on the cold, polished stone of the ancient columns. "My faith is in the capacity of humanity to do good. In my long lifetime, I have seen ample evidence of this." Summoning all his might, the Sentinel stretched his arms, pushing outward against the supporting pillars. With unearthly force, Haley's burst of energy shattered the stone. "Now, let me die with the Servitors of Chaos who would seek only to spread shadows amidst civilization."

Down came the temple on the high priest and all the Uquedaligeesdee; down came the cavern, sealing off the Pit of Yghol, further isolating the Great Old One and entombing his disciples. Above ground, on the valley floor, the Guardian's eyes opened one last time as fractures raced across its stony hide. It shuddered once before disintegrating into a mundane mound of boulders.

※ ※ ※

Hours later and miles away, Greenheath emerged from an underground labyrinth, the stream at his feet cascading over a rocky ledge and tumbling through jumbles of rocks into an unfamiliar valley some distance below. A difficult but passable trail twisted and turned down the mountainside through flame azalea and blooming dogwoods.

In the morning sun, the Sentinel recognized blood tinting the water washing over his buskins.

"I want to go home," the woman of Rowan said, not realizing her home no longer existed. "I want to get away from this awful place, go somewhere clean and proper and safe from all the horrible things plaguing this land."

"We will head east toward the coast, ma'am," Greenheath said. "I have acquaintances in Charles Towne. You will be safe there."

In his heart, Greenheath knew that comfortable dwelling places protected by palisades and buttresses and hawkeyed sentries offered only limited sanctuary in a weary world fouled by the shadows of its former keepers.

SOMETHING TO HOLD THE DOOR CLOSED

BY LON PRATER

John Reed stared at the lump of yellow metal his son Conrad dropped on the hard packed farmhouse floor. Young George and Elizabeth ran in behind him, eyes wide, while Henry and John Junior lugged in a bucket with a few fish tails hanging over the edge and shut the plank door behind them. It swung open again almost as soon as John Junior stepped away, his fishing poles rattling.

Conrad, strong for his thirteen years, flexed his arms as if he'd been carrying a great weight but the thing was no bigger than one of Sarah's smoothing irons. "What is it, Vater?" he asked switching into German in his excitement. The other children followed his lead until their babble was louder than both the crackling hearth and the pot of boiling potatoes within it.

Sarah shushed them all from her rocking chair, careful not to disturb baby Catherine, who was already getting fretful on the teat. "English, Conrad," she reminded him, and John Reed, once long ago the Hessian deserter Johannes Reidt, nodded his agreement.

"Is it gold?" petite Frances said from the table, her wild onion chopping forgotten for the moment. She was a year or so from marrying age and on Sundays Reverend Love liked to tease her that she still looked like she was ten.

"I'm not sure what it is, but it doesn't look like gold to me. Where was it, Conrad?"

"In Little Meadow Creek. We was fishing—" he looked at his brothers before correcting himself. "They was fishing and I was chasing toads. Then I saw this glinting up at me from the wide part so I went in after it."

"It's real heavy," Henry said.

Conrad agreed. "It was like the thing was fighting me to stay out there under the mud. I like to never pulled it out."

"And we caught some fish, too," John Junior piped in, eager for a share of the attention. He slapped a trio of perch onto the wooden table.

Sarah adjusted a rough woolen blanket around the baby. "Put that bucket back in front of the door, John Junior. I hate it when you boys go fishing and take my doorstop. There's been a draft in here all day."

It was springtime, gloriously so, and today had been the first rainless Sunday in weeks for the hills of Upper Mecklenburg County, North Carolina—newly renamed Cabarrus County—and this change of names was proving no easier to get used to than his own, even after all these years since he'd run off from von Porbeck's regiment in Savannah. He'd given in to the urge to dodge church and spent the day outside sharpening the plow and attending to a dozen other little tasks that had until now eluded him.

With the bucket in place, the door would still creep open for a strong enough wind, though, which set John to thinking.

"How heavy?"

"At least twenty-two pounds, Father!"

John bent down and picked it up, the skepticism on his face disappearing almost at once. "More like fifteen or sixteen, but it'll work."

"For what, Father?"

John didn't answer at first. He stared instead at the clammy yellow rock in his hands. He did not know his letters, but he knew what normal letters looked like and the markings feathered across this lump of mineral were utterly unlike any of them he had ever seen. Maybe the Reverend would recognize them. More likely, he'd just laugh at John and make a comment about the devil throwing out distractions to reward those who failed to keep the Sabbath.

John shook his head, flaring out his nostrils. The room smelled of blood, of the insides of animals on slaughtering day. He shoved the lustrous lump in front of the door. "For keeping out the draft," he said. "And what is that smell?"

Frances jumped up from the table and opened the hearth's baking door. "My breads!" she cried out, and the smell of entrails was replaced by waves of billowing smoke as she hurried the blackening loaves onto the table with a pair of long handled tongs.

The baby woke up at that and began to cry. She fussed all night, and while she did, John dreamed of being Johannes again, dodging the Negroes and Indians that made up the so-called Tory Militia back in the summer of 1782, as he slunk away from all the fighting, and out into the night.

※ ※ ※

In August, when the year's cycle of farm work finally allowed it, John took Henry and Conrad and the yellow door stopper to Concord. When their buying and selling was complete, the three of them stopped at the home of acquaintance William Atkinson, who passed for the county silversmith when he wasn't overly drunk. He told them in no uncertain terms that the mineral was most likely not gold, and furthermore that he couldn't identify it as silver either. Beyond that, he had no idea what kind of rock Conrad had dug out of Little Meadow Creek.

On the ride back, Conrad kept a firm grip on the door stopper, even when it was his turn to hold the reins and cluck at the horses. John Reed couldn't quite figure out why the look in that boy's eyes worried him so.

※ ※ ※

Baby Catherine nearly died of dysentery, Frances began mooning after one of the Phifer boys, and a hill country 1799 Christmas faded into a sunny new century that was already bustling along with the spectacle of Representative Colonel Dempsey Burges' surprise death and funeral in Shiloh and sermons a-plenty on the ill fate reserved for sinners and Federalists.

Reverend Love made it out to the farm nearly two years later for Frances' wedding dinner. He slathered his corn with fresh butter but only ate half of it, staring at the yellow hunk of metal that John Reed made Conrad lug over.

"Those aren't any letters I've ever studied, if they even are letters. Could be just the way the running water ate at it. But are you sure that metal ain't gold?"

"Bill Atkinson says it's not."

"Bill Atkinson barely knows silver, unless it's buying him whiskey. You take it in to Fayetteville?"

"Hadn't planned to."

Reverend Love stared him down.

"But I could, in August. Once the planting is all done."

"You do that, John. Somebody in that town can tell you for sure one way or the other . . . But imagine if it was gold, right here in North Carolina!"

Sarah cleared her throat from across the room. "Your oldest daughter is going to be leaving us for the other side of the valley tonight, and maybe you should wish her well before she goes." She put a hand to the bulge of pregnancy beneath her apron. "If you are all done talking about eyes of needles and ways to heaven with our preacher, husband."

John grinned at the reverend, who grinned back. "I reckon she's right, John. If the Lord meant us to talk about gold today, surely he meant it to be your Frances' lovely long hair."

John got up and kissed Sarah once on each cheek then stepped out to see his daughter off, careful not to trip over Little Polly. Conrad stayed inside, by the kitchen door and his rock.

※ ※ ※

In August of 1803, John and Conrad fought bitterly when John came back from Fayetteville with three dollars and fifty cents and no door stopper, which the French jeweler had said was solid gold. When the fighting was over, Conrad slammed the loose door like a thunderclap, nearly ripping it from its joints. All the other boys breathed a sigh of relief at the absence of their quarrelsome brother and John Reed slept easy for the first time in years, even with Sarah being as cold to him as she was.

She thawed some when Conrad came back the next day with her brother Frederick Kiser, Reverend Love and Martin Phifer, Jr., who owned about twenty times as much land as the seventy acres the government had granted John not too long after he'd been declared a citizen.

"They have a plan, Father. Listen."

Martin Phifer was a paunchy man with too much red in his eyebrows for someone with such gray hair. "Your boy tells us the man in Fayetteville bought a seventeen pound lump of gold from you for three and fifty, John."

"That is so. He gave me what I asked for it."

"Did he say it was pure? That much pure gold would be worth more like two, three, maybe even four THOUSAND dollars."

John's cheeks were hot with embarrassment, which always made his hands itch for the old regiment rifle he still kept wrapped in oilcloth under the bed. He saw a glint in Conrad's eyes as well. Like two fires burning. "He said he fluxed it to make it pure as he could get it—the lines that look like letters kept coming back up on edges of it—and asked me what I'd take for it. I didn't know how much to ask, but three fifty buys a lot." He stopped. "Was it really worth three thousands?"

Frederick nodded sadly. Sarah gave a little cry and grabbed Catherine and Polly up in a hug. Reverend Love cleared his throat.

"I'm afraid so. But the good Lord doesn't take away without providing. In this case, *us*."

"What do you mean?"

Martin Phifer took the lead and began explaining how gold is often found near other gold and so that meant that there could well be more in Little Meadow Creek for the taking. With he, Reverend Love and brother-in-law Frederick offering up two slaves each and equipment to hunt gold on John's land, any precious metal found would be split four ways after it got sold off to the mint in Phillydelphia. After much deliberating and explaining, and not a few mugs of ale, John agreed, slipping into German as he did so. "Ja, we have a deal, but only when the farming work is all done. This is still a farm, and we can't count on gold to feed us. We start in August once the planting's done."

Conrad, now a wiry spit of sixteen, had been listening attentively all night, and hardly touching the ale, which was unusual for him. When the men had all left, John tried to engage him in conversation, but his son seemed eaten up with some strange fever.

No, that wasn't it at all. The boy seemed to be finally getting past seasons of mounting arrogance and anger. John Reed hoped it would last. He slept that night even better than the last, dreaming of taking his old regiment rifle to Fayetteville for Hessian-style reparations from the jeweler who had taken advantage of him, and of gold that kept bursting up from the ground like cornstalks. The gold in his dreams lacked any of those softly etched symbols. Instead, they kept writhing just below the surface of the jeweler's ruined face.

✳ ✳ ✳

It was the Reverend's slave Peter who found the first near boulder of gold, a foul-smelling twenty eight pound wonder that had been hiding just six inches below the surface of Little Meadow Creek for who knew how long.

"Washed out by alluvial deposits," Martin Phifer said, wrinkling his nose from a comfortable spot on the bank. "That's probably what the smell is."

The reverend was so pleased with Peter he half-jokingly offered the slave a walnut-sized knot off one clammy end of the gold, but the slave would have to break it off himself. "Only got my dinner fork, and I don't want to be breaking it. Besides, something about that rock makes a man feel, I don't know—like he needs to wash up a hundred times before he'll be clean again. But I thanks you anyhow, sir."

The white men all laughed it off as slave superstition, and sent them back to work. By the end of the month, the deep section of Little Meadow Creek had earned the name "the Potato Patch" because of all the gold that kept turning up from beneath its muddy bottom. Though none quite matched in size what Peter found, by early September they had found enough of the yellow rocks for one of the children to build a shimmering little pyramid with them.

In the late summer heat, it seemed to John that the odd erosion lines on one rock mated up perfectly with those on the next, no matter where he looked. It reminded him of the night he'd nearly been caught, of the way all the different hairs on that Tory Militia Indian's collection of scalps ran together, so Johannes couldn't tell which hair came from which deserter's head flesh. He had stared at those scalps as the Indian approached him unawares, and when the red man was close enough, Johannes had used his bayonet more viciously and instinctively than ever before. Von Porbeck was not kind to deserters, and the Tory Militia were well known for allowing their prey a quick death and afterward taking the deserter's scalp to trade for payment.

Shaken by the memory, John was more than ready to see the little mountain of gold on its way north to be melted into coins, and to see himself handed back a share of them. What he was not prepared for was to find the golden rocks replaced by a mess of trampled, tumbled, marshy wet earth in a ring of lye-white grass. And Conrad, whose turn it had been to skip church that day and watch over it, was nowhere to be found.

※ ※ ※

"That boy of yours took it and run off!" Reverend Love declared when he heard, and though Frederick defended Conrad and John did all he could not to curse the preacher in front of Sarah or the children, he had to admit it was probably the truth. Who else but Conrad felt like they were owed a piece of it, and who else couldn't spend any time on chores without going out of his way to Little Meadow Creek to stare and touch the growing pile? For all he knew it had been Conrad who built it up into that pointy little mountain.

Martin Phifer, ever the diplomat, called out every free hand in the county to search for John Reed's missing boy, presumed taken by wild animals, and made sure there was a table laid for lunch and dinner every day for the next three days for any who would help find him. Phifer never once mentioned the gold, and the others followed suit.

After three days of searching and fitful, dreamless nights, John woke up to Elizabeth screaming. He rolled from the bed and jerked his regiment rifle from beneath it without thinking, hoping the powder in his horns was still fresh and cursing himself for the lack of patches for his shot.

Elizabeth was not in the farmhouse. The sun was just starting to rise over the hill when he burst through the loose door (he really ought to fix it one day) to see his daughter halfway between the privy and the farmhouse, her long woolen gown bunched in her fists out of habit to keep it from dragging in the mud. She was still screaming.

John rushed up to her. He heard the boys stumbling out into the cool dawn behind him.

"What is it, daughter?"

She pointed across the shadowed grass at the torn earth where the gold had last been seen. Her mouth opened, but only a pitiful whine came out. Then more tears.

"*Vas ist?*" one of the boys shouted.

A soft wind stirred the tall grass and the brushes Sarah kept growing around the privy. They did not help the smell.

"There's nothing there, daughter."

Her lips quavered and she seemed on the verge of another explosion of tears, but she straightened her back in a way that made John proud. "A troll, Vater. There was a troll digging and sniffing. He had on a white shirt."

John laughed and regretted it. "A troll in a white shirt? Surely you were dreaming, Elizabeth?"

In answer, she drew her sleeve across her cheeks to dry them and marched stiffly over to the place she had pointed, holding his hand and pulling him along with her. Her steps slowed more and more the closer they came.

John wished he had grabbed a knife, even his old jack, and felt silly for it. If his nine-year-old girl could stifle her fear enough to go over, surely he could do no less. But then she stopped and would go no farther, leaving him with nothing but the feel of his unpacked musket's scrolled stock to accompany him the rest of the way.

The ground had already been torn and turned over, but now it looked as if some animal had been digging a burrow there. Fresh, loamy soil lay strewn in dozens of clumps just past the original disturbance. There was a jagged crater about two feet wide and nearly the same depth gouged into the land. Something glinted in the loose earth. John stretched out a hand to pick it up, but it would not budge.

The boys were behind him now and even Elizabeth had crept closer. Sarah called to him from the house. "Is all well?"

John grunted. The thing wouldn't move, and he knew that it shouldn't be what it was, and his words were failing him. Something was very wrong.

"John? Is all well?"

He looked up at her, nodded. Something about the way he looked must have scared her. She called the curious younger ones inside.

"Get the shovel," he said to John Junior. The boy bolted. While he did that, John began priming his musket automatically, his hands eager for something to do to calm his nerves. He remembered the fear he felt every time the battles began, how he could stand no longer the senselessness of it all. *Measure, pour, patch, ball, prime.* None of it seemed to matter. If he were to lose his life to keep some American colony under control, what difference would it make? So he had run, because he was afraid of dying for no good reason. Hardly German of him, he knew, but there it was.

John Junior was back with the shovel. John took it and thrust the musket into the boy's hands. It was the first time he had been allowed to touch it and the boy's mouth hung open in disbelief.

"You're not shooting it today, just holding it," John said, sternly as he could manage. His son's lips pressed together without a word.

John set to work with the shovel and was at it for nearly five minutes, time enough to be certain he actually was uncovering what he thought. All that dirty etched gold had somehow begun merging together and digging itself into the earth and there was something else there, something John didn't want to believe he saw. When he glanced up to tell John Junior to ride for Frederick Kiser and Reverend Love *immediately*, the boy wasn't looking at him. He held the rifle up in shaking hands, sighting it and licking his lips.

"Boy!" John said, but that was all he had time to.

A horrible sound like a breeching mare came from his son's throat and John felt his face go cold.

One of the other children was screaming now and over it he heard Elizabeth, not screaming, but shouting: "The Troll, Vater! The Troll!"

John turned to see a figure he barely recognized charging toward him, chipped teeth flashing and a golden light in its eyes. It was not Conrad.

It was the jeweler from Fayetteville, but only barely so. The man before him now was in such disarray he would have been unrecognizable if not for the prominent French nose and those deep set eyes. His clothes were all torn and filthy with mud and blood. His bare stomach shone whitely and a tremendous growth or boil protruded from it. Worst was the frenzied way he wrung his hands, every nail broken and bleeding.

He bore down on John like an American officer's horse had once bore down on Johannes Reidt, bowling him over. The man choked out a series of guttural cries in no language John could understand, if language it was at all.

John Junior shot the musket well over the crazed jeweler's head and yelled. The weapon clattered to the ground in a haze of bluish smoke. The boy cradled his right arm as if it were broken.

John went sideways, letting the jeweler's momentum carry them both against one side of the growing hole. A sharp corner of one of the gold rocks ripped his nightshirt. He could feel the cool damp metal chilling the warm blood as it poured from his back.

John Junior whimpered, but grabbed the musket by its barrel

and began beating on the jeweler's back. John could smell the man's breath, raw meat and something awful beneath that. He punched the man for all he had, twice in the face, wishing John Junior hadn't wasted the shot, or that he'd taught the boy before now how to load and shoot. But none of that would help him now, and he had his back against the missing gold and something he refused to acknowledge and the man was on top of him, golden flickers in his eyes and that bulge tearing, ripping at his stomach, pressing harder and harder against John, like it was trying to get out of that man and into the pit—going through John in the process.

He got a sick feeling at the same time he heard a sound like a slit sow's belly, and felt the cold metal pushing against him and all the man's blood cascading from the ruptured torso onto John, onto the loose soil. The man rolled off of him but the red lump of fluxed gold—*how had it gotten into the man's stomach, how in Gott's name, How?*—kept pressing against him, pushing through him with the force of a cannonade and it was all he could do to gasp at John Junior.

"Get it off."

The boy hastened to obey, but the weight wouldn't budge with just the boy's left arm and John's efforts. He wished Henry were here, but his eldest was too far away now, with fields of his own to plow. "Call your mother, call the others, get the shovel. Quick boy, or I'm damned!"

John Junior yelled for all he was worth, wincing as he tried to use his right arm as well. Then Sarah was there then, in his face, and stronger looking than ever he'd seen her.

"Help get this off of me," John begged. "The shovel." The pressure against his own stomach was far too great for it to be the simple weight of this seventeen pound lump of gold trying to tunnel through his gut and spine.

Sarah grabbed one end of the shovel and forced it under the bloody rock, doing her level best to ignore the fresh cadaver next to her husband. *She doesn't even know what's under me.*

The blade of the shovel bit into John's flesh and he shouted out hoarsely. Spots began to form at the edges of his vision. *I will not die for this gold.* With one final ounce of stubborn Hessian resolve, he grabbed the shovel's shaft and began turning it at the same time as he forced himself to roll into the jeweler's gore-soaked shirt.

The stone clanked against its fellows with a sound like the gates of Heaven clanging shut before an unworthy soul and John lay there on top of the dead man, breathing hard.

Sarah loomed over him, her mouth working silently. He knew what she was looking at. What he'd seen and not wanted to believe. A young man's hand, clutching a knob of blood-caked, dirt smeared gold.

Sarah looked at him and he heard her say it without ever seeing her lips move.

Conrad.

He nodded.

She turned and walked back to the house, leaving the children to tend to themselves and to help their father up. Had the boy seen the bewitched gold start growing together and tried to stop it? Had he been pulled down with it because he could not stand to let it go? Not just buried alive, but dragged beneath the surface like a burrower's dinner? John stood, shaking the thoughts from his head. He tugged the mess of jeweler several yards away from the gold and his lost son, then picked up the shovel. The children had all seen the hand, had inferred from their mother's reaction what it meant, and most of them wept. But not Elizabeth.

John tossed her the shovel. "Help me bury your brother."

John Junior looked up at him, his arm no longer so sore that it required cradling. "But what of the gold, Vater?"

John thought back to the day he'd arrived in the Upper Mecklenburg, his German name already surrendered. He thought of the night he'd had to kill that Indian, and of how easily he'd done it—and worse—all in the name of escaping the game of kill-or-be-killed. He felt sick at his throbbing stomach, but he did not feel cowardly.

The sun was already climbing and nearly the whole family still outside in their nightclothes. One son had been lost to an unholy pile of metal like no other on earth, if it was even *of* this earth. Who ever heard of metal that could join together with its own kind like that? Or that somehow dug itself back into the earth when a man dared to pull it into the daylight? And no kind of metal should be able to make a man swallow it in lumps and lug it back to Little Meadow Creek all heavy and bulging in his stomach like some freakish child of sin.

John Reed turned his back on the jeweler's open-bellied corpse and gazed down the valley at his fields. Some were fallow, some nearly ready for the harvest.

"There are many things in this life we need to get by, son. Good food, fresh water. A strong family. Something to stop the door from blowing open." He picked up his rifle, decided to clean it later, after he himself got himself and some other things taken care of.

"We Reeds come from good stock, boy. Remember that. Why do we need gold when this land already gives us so much?"

Elizabeth dug the shovel in as deep as her nine-year-old arms could drive it and let fresh unbloodied dirt shower down on what remained of her brother. John Junior got up to take the tool from her, but she wouldn't let him.

John Reed felt tears beginning to seep from the corners of his eyes as he turned from the two of them. Later, he would need to explain these things to his partners. But for now, fixing that swinging door would have to be enough.

※ ※ ※

AUTHOR'S NOTE: The events of this story prior to Conrad's disappearance are drawn as closely as possible from the documented history of the North Carolina Gold Rush (which preceded California's miner 49ers by nearly a half century.) John Reed really did sell the gold doorstopper for $3.50, but went back later and managed to make the opportunistic jeweler pay him $1200 more. Though no one ever found a larger piece of gold in North Carolina than the Reverend's slave Peter (who was never freed), the Reed Gold Mine remained in contentious operation well into the 1900s.

TERROR FROM MIDDLE ISLAND

BY STEPHEN MARK RAINEY
& DURANT HAIRE

May, 1854
Territory of Wyoming

"Ibaptize thee in the name of the Father, the Son, and the Holy Spirit."

The boy felt his body being lifted from the frigid river, and when his water-filled eyes were able to distinguish shapes amid the crystalline sparkles of afternoon sunlight, they saw Reverend Wolfe's full-moon face beaming proudly back at him. He wiped his face and gulped refreshing air as his feet sought and finally found purchase on the gritty river bottom.

"Now go in peace and may the blessings of the Lord go with you," the minister said, patting Tom Mayworth fondly on the shoulder. Tom splashed his way to the bank, where his mother and father waited for him with expressions of ecstasy, as if his baptism represented their own personal raptures. Of course, they were thrilled to see this day come, and even he was happy enough to be confirmed as a child of God; now that he had turned 12, though, his most fervent hope was that Miss Anne Cheshire, age 15, would no longer consider him a child at all.

He stumbled onto dry land, heedless of the water sloshing onto his mother's flowing linen skirt, and anxiously scanned the crowd gathered on the banks for a sign of his heart's desire. There—a dozen yards or so away, half-hidden behind her father, her eyes fixed firmly on the river, where her cousin, Peter Stewart, was wading toward Reverend Wolfe, who waited with arms outstretched. Tom focused on Anne and desperately willed her to turn her face toward his, only to find frustration when his father's bear-like frame shuffled thoughtlessly into his line of sight.

"I'm very proud of you, son," said Daniel Mayworth, his bearded face bright with uncustomary warmth. "You're becoming a most virtuous young man."

"Thank you, Father," Tom said distractedly, leaning around the giant body to peer at the beautiful, white-clad lily on the upper bank.

Look my way, Anne. Please look at me.

Then—wonder of wonders—she did! The eyes beneath the gleaming chestnut hair slowly turned toward his, cool and disinterested; then, very gradually, warmth crept into the hazel irises, and one corner of her mouth turned up slightly, transforming her face into a brilliant star that shone on him and *only* him.

It took several moments for Tom to comprehend the sudden blurring motion and the change in Anne's smile, which became a kind of confused gawk, as if she had spied Tom with a finger up his nose. Then he realized that a crimson stain was spreading down the front of her dress, and a long, feathered black shaft had sprouted from just above her left breast. With a weary sigh, she collapsed at her father's feet, and Milton Cheshire unleashed a cry that sounded like a cougar whose tail had been set alight.

"Dakota!" came Daniel Mayworth's voice. "It's Dakota!"

Tom's eyes somehow tore themselves from the white-clad heap at Mr. Cheshire's feet and followed his father's pointing finger. Amid the tall pines that lined the banks of a long island in the middle of the river, a dozen inhuman-looking figures stood like devilish statues, their hair in ponytails, their faces painted crimson with bands of black across their eyes. Even motionless, their bodies blazed with energy, like coiled snakes preparing to strike. One of them slowly raised a bow and released an arrow, which arced over the river like a shooting star and ended its trajectory with a nauseating *thump* right in the neck of young Peter Stewart, who pitched backward, his limbs flailing uselessly. As the river swallowed his twitching body, the water slowly changed from emerald green to thick, rusty red.

A strange, screeching cry split the air, and the bronze-skinned creatures leaped from the island into the river—or, rather, *onto* the river, for their feet barely disturbed the smooth, sparkling surface. Like dark wraiths, they sped toward the baptismal party, their eyes shining unnaturally, as if blood-red lanterns blazed fiercely within their skulls. Those without bows and arrows brandished gleaming, stiletto-like knives, and at least one of them had a rifle slung over his shoulder.

Tom had never seen an actual raiding party. For some reason, after years of relatively peaceful coexistence, the Dakota—the *Pte Oyate,* as they called themselves—had begun turning against the settlers along the Oregon Trail. As he watched the approaching red men, the fact that he might truly be in danger simply failed to register. This was a rare spectacle, a once-in-a-lifetime event, which he would someday relate excitedly to his children.

But they had killed Anne! The love of his life was dead!

An arrow zinged past his ear, so close he could hear the hiss of its spinning fletching. His father shouted his name, and his mother uttered a low, shocked moan, but his feet would not move. He could only watch in awe as one of the red men loomed before Reverend Wolfe, the blade of the rising knife flashing in the sun like a hypnotic jewel.

"Stop!" Wolfe cried defiantly. "This place has been consecrated to the Lord. You shall not defile it! Begone! Leave these people in peace. I command it! God himself commands it!"

As if he understood, the Indian paused and cocked his head uncertainly, his eyes boring curiously into the minister's. Wolfe seemed to draw himself up, and the beginning of a smile appeared on his lips. But then the warrior grinned, exposing white, shark-like teeth, and Tom saw that his hesitation had been a cruel ruse. The knife slashed quickly down and across, laying open Reverend Wolfe's throat, and a great gush of blood poured over his collar and black coat; then his body toppled into the river and disappeared without so much as a gurgle or whisper.

The Indian's predatory gaze slowly swiveled until it fell upon Tom, and the bloodless lips spread in a wildcat's smile. Now, Tom's muscles found their motivation, and with a cry, he spun around and ran, neither knowing nor caring which direction he was heading. He saw his father a dozen feet ahead of him, his feet kicking up dust; then came another hiss and a flash, and an arrow thudded into

Daniel Mayworth's back, hurling him into Tom's fleeing mother, who collapsed beneath her husband's weight. She cried out as something materialized from the trees directly in front of her; another flash of silver quickly silenced her voice.

Tom spun again, his heart pounding, his mind beyond comprehending the horror unfolding around him. He could hear a man's voice screaming, and numerous figures were hurtling through the nearby trees. Behind him, the river was red and churning like a fountain. Two bodies floated facedown, their arms thrown wide as if to grasp a lifeline from the shore. To his left, something exploded into motion, and his shocked eyes turned in time to see a long, barbed shaft arcing toward him like a bolt of lightning. Pain such as he had never known suddenly clutched his body in a vise-like grip, and his legs buckled like twigs beneath his weight. As if in a dream, he saw the sky whirling overhead and the trees spinning like tall, green dervishes.

The cold touch of the water shocked him back to momentary lucidity. A red-tipped arrow protruded from his breastbone, and fingers of pain clawed at his heart. As if a misty curtain had been drawn across his eyes, his vision grew disturbingly dim; but it cleared, long enough for him to witness something that filled his soul with greater fear of eternal damnation than the most vitriolic sermon ever spat by the zealous Reverend Wolfe.

The Indians faced the forested island in the river, growling some kind of weird chant—a sound more animalistic than human. The trees themselves appeared to sway with the cadence of the voices, and to Tom's horror, the blood-red water began to lap like an obscene tongue at the island's banks, first slowly and tentatively, then more vigorously. Crimson streamers began to flow *up* the incline to the woods, and Tom saw the bloody tendrils caress the trunks of the trees, almost lovingly, passionately, and then slowly dissolve into the bark.

Then the trees exulted, their branches spreading in supplication to the heavens, their trunks bending like the bodies of lanky giants throwing back their heads to bellow at the sky. The sound that joined in harmony with the voices of the Dakota exceeded anything in his worst nightmares: an endless, hissing, screeching, blaring *shriek* that bored into his eardrums and pierced his brain like the tip of the arrow that had found his heart.

Something in the water struck him, and for a moment, he

thought one of the living trees had reached into the river to clutch him with savage, skeletal fingers. But his fading vision briefly glimpsed the countenance of Reverend Wolfe, again close to him and staring, this time with eyes of blue ice, the gash in his throat leaking streamers of thin, purple blood. The pastor's face seemed to shrivel into a contemptuous frown, and then the body sank beneath the surface, the eyes continuing to stare blankly at him until they were all Tom could see.

When at last the light shrank to a dying ember and cold hands closed around him to carry him away from all he had known, Tom Mayworth accepted their caress with a whimper of welcome and relief.

May, 1887
Territory of Wyoming
As yet unsullied by the relentless westward advance of white men, the countless tributaries of the Platte River wound like questing tendrils through the endless miles of silver-black pines, which glowered in silent disdain at the antlike humans that occasionally passed beneath their boughs. Now and again, as if in an act of cleansing, one or more of the trees would release a shower of delicate, dead needles into the glimmering water, which carried them slowly away to rot in stagnant coves that hid along the banks at infrequent intervals.

In the middle of one broad expanse of river, a long, pine-studded island protruded from the water like the head of a huge black bear breeching after having caught its fill of fish. The water surrounding the protuberance offered a bounty to aspiring anglers; yet, while settlers often congregated like geese on the banks of nearby tributaries, they unfailingly avoided Middle Island, which it was commonly called, as if it straddled the gate of Hell itself. Regardless of the sun's position in the sky, the dense pine forest seemed to swallow its every brilliant ray, so that a perpetual mass of shadow hovered about the island, and even on the warmest day of the year, the water gurgling around the banks barely rose above freezing. Worst of all, in the spring, strange, murky red clouds gathered in the river and refused to be dispersed even by the seasonal rains, which turned the lazy current into a rushing cataract.

In his youth, Reverend William Wolfe had frequently heard the story of the Middle Island Massacre, which had claimed the life of his grandfather, and more recently, the accounts of travelers on the

Oregon Trail who swore they had heard strange, inhuman cries that both beckoned and terrified them. Whether he actually believed such tales, he could not say with certainty; but the people of Gaynor, the small settlement at a fork in the river not five miles north of Middle Island, obviously did, and they refused to so much as drop a canoe in the water within sight of its banks. If anything strange was going on along that stretch of river, Wolfe thought, the blame lay squarely at the feet some local Sioux tribe—the Shoshone or Dakota—who considered the white men interlopers and wished to discourage them from settling without resorting to open warfare. After years of savage fighting, the Indians and the whites in that region had established something akin to peaceful relations, and neither side wished to be the one to ignite a new conflict.

In the summer of 1886, Reverend Wolfe had embarked westward from Missouri to spread the gospel to all who would listen, as had his grandfather before him. He lingered at many farms and settlements along the way, especially on the dusty prairies of Oklahoma and Nebraska; but he had long ago decided on the Platte River basin as his final destination, so that he might view firsthand the place where his grandfather had met his end—and, most importantly, discover the truth behind the legend of Middle Island. And so, eventually, he found himself in Gaynor, which was named for the scout from the American Fur Company who had first made camp on the site in the year 1812. It was a close-knit, God-fearing community, and Wolfe spent several days there ministering to its people before mentioning his intention to visit Middle Island. When he did, it was to invite a hardy trapper named Paul Stewart to accompany him on a fishing excursion. To Wolfe's surprise, the face of the stalwart, silver-haired outdoorsman turned to chalk at the very mention of the place.

"Sorry, Reverend, but that's not a hospitable place," Stewart told him. "Go on out to Golden Shoals, a mile or so farther down. The fishing better there, that's for certain."

"It seems a sweet enough place," Wolfe replied, bemused. "In my canoe, we can be out there in less than half an hour's time."

With an almost melodramatic air, Stewart refused again. "Reverend Wolfe, it's your business if you want to venture out there. But that place doesn't sit right with men of the Lord, and they don't sit right with it."

Thoroughly nonplused, Wolfe pressed Stewart to explain himself, but the trapper simply shook his head and bid him a half-hearted good day. "I shall look forward to your sermon next Sunday, Reverend."

His invitation to Henri DuPont, the local blacksmith, netted a similar cryptic response. So, now more eager than ever to explore, on a pleasant Friday afternoon, Wolfe set out in the canoe he had purchased and paddled downriver from the settlement to Middle Island, packing stores for two days, his fishing gear, and the well-used, walnut walking stick that his father had carved for him. By the time he drew near to the island, the sky, which had been clear most of the day, assumed a grim, indigo hue, as if storm clouds were marshaling somewhere in the distance. Beneath the ominous canopy, the jagged silhouettes of the pines on the island gave it the appearance of a hunk of crudely sculpted onyx, the shadows around it deep and foreboding. Upon reaching the bank, he slipped out of the canoe, grabbed the gunwale, and shoved the bow into the narrow cove, where he secured his towline to the nearest sturdy tree. Then he carefully gathered his equipment and clambered up the reedy bank until he stood on a broad outcropping of rock, which offered a panoramic view of the southern stretch of river. The current here was slow, although at the farthest reaches of his vision, he could see a white sheen above the water that certainly indicated rapids. The surrounding hills, draped in silver-green pine, rose like sentient monoliths above the water, and it was easy to imagine the eyes of the Shoshone or Dakota peering curiously down at him, wondering about his motivation, debating whether to simply ignore him or discreetly do away with him, leaving those who knew him to ponder his fate. There would be no witnesses here; no one to help him in case he found himself in trouble.

Where exactly, he wondered, had the massacre of legend actually happened? Probably over there, he thought, glancing across the river at the densely wooded eastern banks. Did restless ghosts truly haunt the forest, calling like sirens to those who entered their dark domain? Would they deign to acknowledge him—perhaps recognize that he was descended from one of the dead?

But Wolfe did not believe in ghosts. Departed souls had but two possible destinations, neither of which gave them leave to revisit the land of the living. Still, his ears seemed almost preternaturally sensitive, as if he *expected* to hear a voice, not entirely human, singing enticingly to him. A disagreeable shudder passed through his body and he turned away from the far bank with a grunt of contempt for his own foolishness.

The afternoon air felt heavy, and from far in the distance, a low peal of thunder rumbled up the river basin. When he took a step, his foot struck some loose shale, and he bent to pick up a chunk of the sharp-edged stone. On a whim, he wound up and hurled the piece as far as he could into the river, where it disappeared with a soft *kerplunk.*

At first, he thought the dim afternoon light was playing tricks on his eyes, for a dark cloud seemed to be gushing slowly from the depths where the stone had broken the jade green surface. But it wasn't his eyes; sure enough, a dense, roiling splotch had begun to spread over the water like a spill of crimson oil. When the leading edge of the murk touched the muddy bank, it did not stop but continued to ooze forward like a vast, scarlet amoeba, making a soft, liquid *squishing* sound as it moved, like a snake slithering through mud. Viscous tendrils glided up the bank toward the nearest tree root and took hold of it in pulsing, curling fists, as if seeking to pull the trailing mass onto dry land. Instead, the bloody fingers began to seep slowly into the bark, as if the wood were a thirsty sponge.

Wolfe watched the unfolding spectacle first with detached curiosity, then with mounting disquiet as more and more of the fluid vanished into the exposed tree roots. Clutching his walking stick as if it were a bludgeon, he nervously shuffled back a few feet, but after another minute or so, the substance in the water had vanished, seemingly absorbed by bloodthirsty roots. Then the afternoon began to grow perceptibly darker, and the brooding pines around him assumed an oppressive, vaguely hostile aspect, as if they concealed strange eyes that glared at him with unfathomable purpose.

Unable to suppress a shiver, Wolfe took a few steps toward the shadowed interior of the island, for the prospect of standing close to the water now gave him the chills; the knowledge that he would have to get back into his canoe to make his escape was not something to think about just now. Yet the dense trees offered a scarcely more comforting alternative, for their vigilant silence seemed as unnatural as the bloody cloud in the river. He briefly prayed that the Lord's eye might watch over him, knowing in his heart that, whatever strangeness existed here, its strength surely paled next to the omnipotent hand of God.

Then, just beyond the nearest trees, something moved. A slow, crunching tread, he thought; too heavy for a coon or a muskrat, too cumbersome for a deer or a bobcat. He tightened his grip on his walking stick and took a few more steps into the trees, curiosity getting the better of his judgment. Might someone else actually be on the island? It seemed unlikely, given the local population's eccentric prejudice against the place. However . . .

A handful of Indians could have concealed themselves on the island. Were they perhaps stalking him even now?

He pushed his way through some low-hanging branches and found himself facing a small lagoon formed by a narrow arm of the river that had bored through the mud and foliage of the northernmost bank. A few sickly sunbeams dribbled through the canopy, creating shifting, amber-colored speckles on the dark water, and a musty-smelling breeze sent a few brittle needles raining down on his head. After a time, his mind registered a vague, almost imperceptible change in the appearance of the trees. At first, they all seemed to be leaning slightly forward, as if bowing over the lagoon; but now they stood tall and erect, and some of them actually seemed to arc away from the open area—as if to expose him to some watchful eye above.

He heard the low crunching sounds again, and now something moved in his field of vision. Peering into the dark depths beyond the lagoon, his eyes descried a black figure, intermittently visible as if it were creeping stealthily from tree to tree, possibly trying to avoid being seen.

"Hello!" Wolfe called, hoping that someone might actually answer him and break the cold, uncomfortable spell of his isolation. But no voice replied, and now, his nerves beginning to feel raw, he took up his stick and strode into the pines, determined to find some answers no matter the consequences. "I said hello! Who is that? Answer me!"

And then the half-seen figure began to move. With astonishing speed, the shape hurtled through the trees, at first straight toward him but then breaking to his left, its obviously heavy footsteps somehow strangely muted, as if the dry needles beneath its feet were balls of cotton.

"Wait!" Wolfe cried, but then his voice died in his throat. The dark figure, as it whisked past him perhaps a dozen feet away, revealed itself as nothing more than an ambiguous, *almost* human-shaped swirl of seemingly solid shadow; a mere break in the bands of visible light that moved with the unmistakable bearing of something alive. A distant, *whooshing* sound reached Wolfe's ears, almost like ocean breakers, first waxing and then waning, and a barely perceptible but certainly human scream suddenly issued from the woods. To Wolfe's horror, pine boughs that had bobbled lazily in the afternoon breeze suddenly became animated and spread themselves wide, like the claws of a cat, as if to strike at the moving shadow. Just as the shape began to pass beyond his range of vision, *something* shot forth with a clattering, scraping noise, and the vague echo of a scream rose to a shrill whistle.

The shadow dissolved with utter finality into the darkness of the pines, but the movement around him did not cease. Eyes wide with dread and disbelief, Wolfe hastily scanned the nearest trees as he realized with chilling clarity that he had just witnessed a murder. No; the *remembrance* of a murder. Echoes from the past were reverberating through the cool air, but these were not the sounds and images of any age-old *human* violence. There was something more here, something darker—and far *bigger*—than a mere conflict among men.

My God, what is happening in this place?

A rustling from behind caught his attention, and he spun around in time to see the gnarled limbs of a great pine disentangle themselves and extend toward him like the arms of a giant praying mantis, barbed, crooked, and menacing. He stumbled backward and his feet came down on slippery stone; with a cry, he crashed into the cold water, his breath exploding from his lungs with a harsh croaking sound, and then he felt himself being dragged downward, his ankles on fire, as if thorny cords encircled them.

Down he went, deeper and deeper, far deeper than the relatively shallow bottom of the lagoon should have allowed. His arms smashed against stone and his forehead struck a jagged rock, which nearly caused him to gasp. But somehow, the knowledge that certain death awaited him if he opened his mouth overrode his instincts, and he kept his jaws clamped against a fatal intrusion of water into his lungs. Daylight faded around him, and he felt himself moving with ever-increasing speed through the frigid water—on and on, impossible fathoms deep. This must be the end, he thought. If he felt compelled to make his peace with the Lord, now must surely be the time to make it.

Then his head broke the surface, and his mouth involuntarily opened to gulp the precious air. His feet flailed desperately to find purchase, but the water was too deep, and wherever he was, there was no light. Utterly blind, he propelled himself in a random direction, hoping to find solid ground before his strength gave out.

He expected at any moment some dreadful death to descend upon him like the very wrath of God; but if death were in store for him, why had he not already been killed? Something had intentionally brought him here, something with a grip like steel. Surely, he was not meant to simply drown in this never-ending darkness! But as he kicked himself on through the seemingly endless expanse of water, any hope of returning to daylight and his comfortable, ordinary reality seemed more and more remote.

Then one foot cracked painfully against stone, and he realized his eyes were no longer totally blind. A dim glow rose around him, vaguely illuminating walls that at first he thought were sculpted into some sort of grotesque, abstract bas-relief; then he realized they were adorned with the bizarrely intertwined skeletons of creatures that might have been animals or men—or something else altogether. The ancient remains appeared to have melded with the living rock, creating obscene, organic figures that screamed their agony in dreary silence and gaped with hollow eye sockets at one another in everlasting horror. The light, Wolfe realized, came from glowing crystals that studded the walls like super-heated quartz and cast a sickly orange hue over the entire chamber.

He dragged himself from the water onto a narrow shelf of rock that surrounded the underground pool. Something metallic glittered before his eyes, and when he automatically reached for it, his fingers touched cold metal; a comforting, familiar sensation, for it was an object from the world of men.

A crucifix.

The tiny gold treasure sent a comforting, reassuring thrill of hope through his terror-numbed mind. But as his eyes lifted and roved the horrific, ossified walls, he saw that, from the bony neck of a crumbling body, the tattered, yellowed remains of a clerical collar hung like a sagging noose. The bearer of the little cross had come to a tragic end in this place and been made into a mere bit of ghastly ornamentation.

My God.

Of course, he thought; these must be the victims of the Middle Island Massacre!

Which meant that the dead cleric could be but one man.

Jeremiah Wolfe. His own grandfather.

"No. No!" he groaned, his breath all but stolen by the impact of the terrible realization. What in God's name could have done this? But surely *he* could not be meant to share such a perverted, ignominious fate as this . . . ?

"Choose."

The voice sounded like the growl of lion that had acquired the power of speech. Wolfe's eyes frantically searched the sepulcher for a sign of the speaker, but by all indications he was alone. Then, at the very edge of his hearing, he heard a low rustling sound, which grew quickly louder, heavier. Amid the tangled limbs in the farthest corner of the chamber, something began to move: a dark, shapeless mass, or so it seemed at first. As it pulled itself free of its grotesque berth, Wolfe saw that the thing appeared somewhat manlike but with a black, misshapen head that was much too large for an ordinary human's. A dark, spindly limb stretched toward him, at least four feet long, ending in a spidery, fleshless hand whose fingers each had four knuckles.

"Choose."

The thing looked like the roots of an ancient oak that had become anthropomorphic and burrowed its way through stone and bone to reach the dimly glowing chamber.

"What do you want of me?" Wolfe whispered, his fingers tightening on the gold cross until one of its tips punctured his skin. He did not feel the pain.

A pale green light shone from a hollow in the bulbous head and focused on him like the headlight of a train that threatened to lurch into sudden motion and crush him to atoms. The glare drilled into his brain with a force that shocked him, and he suddenly saw a series of shapes moving slowly and ambiguously, not within the chamber but inside his head. Like the bizarre shadow he had seen in the woods, these figures passed insubstantially through his mind, each image laden with meaning: sorrow, fear, pain, sadness . . .

He saw people dying; men, women, children—and yes, his grandfather!—all attacked without warning, slaughtered like animals, their blood offered to the thing that lived in the rocks and trees, lurking silently and inimically as its land was little by little devastated by the usurping settlers. The Indians had known it; they had revered and served it, and it had provided for them and protected them—until the sheer weight of the alien humanity had driven it to earth, leaving it only scant few retreats in remote, scattered places. And now, after all these centuries, it seethed in endless hatred and anger, occasionally snaring someone such as Wolfe, who could never have begun to believe or understand the terrible secret that hid in the darkness of Middle Island.

"Choose," came the voice again. The single luminous eye seared his brain.

He shook his head, still not comprehending, unable to grasp the will of the awful thing confronting him. "There is nothing to choose," he whispered in desperation. "There is only the Lord Jesus, my savior. I choose only His will. Begone, you thing of Satan."

He thought he heard strange laughter somewhere in the distance, a low, rumbling stutter that conveyed only spiteful, cruel mirth. The walls then seemed to shift, and several bones clattered to the rocky floor as a black opening appeared amid the glowing, jewel-encrusted stones. The black, spidery arms of the thing in the corner began to work their way toward him, and he then realized what was about to happen.

Mortal terror suddenly seized him, crowding out the comforting voice of the Lord, its chilling hands loosing God's warm embrace, which he had known all his life. Something grasped his shoulders, and he felt himself being dragged toward the opening in the wall. Around him, the vacant, hollow eyes of countless skulls glared at him in frigid welcome to an eternity unlike any he had ever dreamed of, one so utterly horrifying that an unexpected, unbidden shriek burst from his lips. With his remaining strength, he hurled the tiny crucifix at the black figure that was slowly pulling him forward.

"No!" he cried. "No!"

The thing took no notice of the impotent projectile. Wolfe felt a sharp, shooting pain in his chest, as if his breastbone had been rent by a scythe. Ice in his brain, his vision began to fade as the approaching shadowy horror seemed to lose its solidity and waft toward him like a living thundercloud. A rumbling in his ears slowly grew louder and more powerful, and eventually, he understood the words that were reverberating in his brain.

"Your choice is . . . accepted."

※ ※ ※

"I baptize thee in the name of the Father, the Son, and the Holy Spirit."

Reverend William Wolfe let the water from his cupped palm drip upon the child's head, and the slight shock caused the baby to squirm restlessly in his arms. The little boy offered a few indignant chirps, but thankfully he did not begin to cry in earnest.

With a stern smile, Wolfe carefully passed the baby back to its mother, who beamed proudly at her son. The father, looking on in abject approval, ran a hand over the baby's head to brush away a few lingering drops of water. Wolfe lifted his arms to present the family and their newly christened son to his congregation.

His demeanor remained as impassive as ever, yet his heart quavered with the guilt of his hypocrisy. But he knew it would pass; he had been assured it would pass. He served a new master now, one whose power he had felt, whose countenance he had seen. Unlike with his previous faith, there was no great mystery, no shadow of doubt of the veracity of the one he served. He no longer faced the threat of some nebulous punishment for his sins in an unimaginable afterlife; now the punishment for disobedience was clear, for it had been laid out before him in stark relief—in the mosaic of rotting bones in the jeweled glow of the underground catacomb.

For hundreds of years, the Indians had served their hidden god, bringing it blood to nourish its wrath as the white man ran roughshod over the sacred earth. Perhaps one day it would reclaim its rightful place—perhaps even in his own lifetime. With *his* help.

I shall start with these, he thought, solemnly regarding the young couple and their infant son. *Tonight, they shall partake of a wholly different sort of communion.*

Wolfe's eyes fell upon the silver cross atop the altar of the new little Gaynor church, but he quickly averted his gaze and returned to the pulpit as the three-man, four-woman choir began to sing, a little off-key. Although he still felt a measure of discomfort, the guilt—as had been promised him—was beginning to fade. Free of the shackles he had worn all his life, he now faced an entirely new existence, one free of the trappings of a religion far less ancient yet more antiquated than the one to which he now subscribed. Now he would know the meaning of power—something his old God had never deigned to show him.

Still. He could never forget the reason he was standing where he was now.

Fear.

Power and fear from now on would be one. He controlled

the destiny of the mortals around him, he thought with some satisfaction. As long as he offered others in his own place, he would be safe. That was the thing's promise to him.

Out of years of habit, before he rose to address the congregation, his eyes again flickered to the cross. All the old reassurance it gave him was gone. But he could not bring himself to apologize or to indulge in regret. He had done what he had done so that he might survive. He would *never,* he had vowed, suffer the fate of those miserable, wretched beings imprisoned beneath the earth, whose voices still screamed in silent torment from the belly of their malefactor.

That will never be me.

Then, for one brief instant, he heard a voice. Not the voice of his god in the catacomb, but the *old* voice, the one that had once greeted him with the rising of every sun and whispered him to sleep with the falling of every night.

"*I* am the sole keeper of promises," it said.

It was the last time that voice ever spoke to him.

Children of the Mountain

By Stewart Sternberg

They set the rendezvous in a valley by the Green River. There, the mountain men and the Indians would arrive throughout July to sell beaver pelts and stock up for the coming year. After a difficult spring in the Tetons, the flat expanse of grass running between the river and dense wood suited Morgan Fisher and gave him a sense of security. The warm grasslands seemed far removed from the dark rock of the Wind River Range visible to the north, remote and unwelcoming with its chilling winds and hostile terrain.

He hitched his belt and stood slowly, the morning's breakfast still making him lazy. A bowl of sweet Virginian tobacco would be just the thing to aid digestion. Searching his pockets, he found his clay pipe and savored the smell of the leaf while packing the bowl.

Someone coughed and said: "Mr. Fisher?"

Standing with huge hands stroking a thick gray beard, a trapper peered anxiously at him. The man's eyes were black and deep-set above a nose that looked as though it had been broken several times. Dirty buckskins hung from his shoulders like rags from a scarecrow.

Fisher threw his arms around the man in a bearhug.

"Amos, I was starting to think we weren't going to see you," he said. The other man shifted about, looking uncomfortable in the embrace. When released, Amos Caldwell removed his otter skin hat. Red rimmed eyes buried in ruddy flesh regarded Fisher.

"You look sickly," said Fisher.

"I ain't been sleeping much."

Taking seats on one of the logs circling the fire pit, the two men silently studied one another. "Take a pull," Fisher said, reaching for a keg. Caldwell nodded and drank deeply, wiping his mouth with a forearm.

"You got any food?" asked Caldwell. "I'm hungry."

"Sure, we have some ham and here's cornbread."

Caldwell thanked him and sat down while his friend brought him a plate heaped with food. He ate like a dog expecting to be challenged for its kill, attacking the plate and shoveling food into his mouth. When Caldwell finished, he started on a second helping, consuming the food with no sign of contentment.

Fisher watched him, amazed that this was the same man who had trapped with him at Jackson's Hole two years ago. That Amos Caldwell had been a husky giant, with a thick chest and powerful arms. The man before him now looked more like a cadaver than that explosive brawler.

A few other men came about the fire-pit. Fisher introduced them to his old friend. "Did you have a good spring?" asked Fisher.

Shifting his eyes from side to side as though listening to an inner voice, Caldwell answered slowly. "I got one litter high with two hundred beaver skins and one with somethin' else," he said.

"Not bad."

Caldwell shook his head, sopping the surface of the plate with a finger. "I'm done," he said. "After I settle accounts here, I'm goin' back East. Kentucky. Maybe I'll turn farmer. I'm done with the mountains."

"He's done with the mountains," said Fisher with a loud laugh that lured smiles from the other men.

"I can't do it anymore," said Caldwell. His voice quavered when he spoke. Looking back at Fisher he clenched his jaw and shrugged with embarrassment. Any expression of emotion from Caldwell aside from anger or disgust was a rarity; it was one of the reasons the man had been unable to trap with a team.

"We can talk about that tomorrow or the next day," said Fisher.

Whisky trailed through Caldwell's beard as he took another drink.

"I got somethin' to show you," he said.

Rising and waiting until Fisher followed, Caldwell strode toward the mules and ponies. A couple of Arapaho standing there, admiring the number of pelts, looked up and gave respectful greeting.

"Get away from my pelts!" Caldwell roared, lurching forward and shaking a fist.

Fisher grabbed the rangy man by the shoulder, pulling him back with some effort.

"They aren't Sioux," said Fisher.

"They ain't white," said Caldwell.

Hostilities between the Sioux and the trappers had been increasing over the last year, but Fisher knew it wasn't just that. Caldwell hated all Indians.

"Ain't nothin' but animals," he had once said. "They don't have no respect for what those pelts mean to others."

Caldwell wasn't alone in his resentment. Indians were paid less than whites and that drove down the amounts other trappers received for their efforts, a value already deflated by the ridiculous mark up on goods brought by the bosses. The trappers took it because they had little choice.

"Show me what you were going to show me," said Fisher.

Caldwell had regained his composure, but still glared at the Indians. The group's leader, a brave with a strong jaw and dark skin, glowered back with contempt.

The mountain-man stepped to the last litter and tugging at a couple knots, whipped back a buffalo skin and revealed the carcass of a strange beast. Almost humanoid in shape and covered with thick, purple-black fur, the thing had a lean, emaciated look. Shiny wings emerged from its shoulder blades. Small in comparison with the rest of its body, its head had a huge sloping brow and non-existent chin. Small razor teeth poked through yellow gums. The stench should have been unbearable, but instead the corpse smelled of the fall in the high forests.

"I killed it two months ago," said Caldwell.

Uneasiness gripped Fisher as he moved a hand forward to touch the shaggy coat. Cold as ice. Wiggling his fingers, he turned back to Caldwell.

"There's no rot," he said. "It's still fresh."

"I killed it two months ago."

One of Fisher's men, a short Georgian named Perry, let out a low whistle. "What is it?" he asked, his voice filled with respect. "Is it an angel?"

A few more passersbys stopped to gawk at the beast.

Fisher grinned at Perry. "If that's an angel, then we're all damned," he said.

"It's my angel," said Caldwell. The statement sounded like a challenge. The smaller man held his ground. The tension passed and Caldwell turned to address Fisher: "No one's ever seen the likes of this. Never. They'll pay big money. With what I got saved and with this year's profit, I'll be able to go back East."

"Where did you find this horror?" asked Fisher. Although the creature appeared dead, he wanted to take his knife and stab it. Caldwell eyed him and leaned down to cover the carcass again.

"The Tetons, up by a place I call Marla Peak," said Caldwell.

Marla had been Caldwell's bride some fifteen years ago. Fisher remembered a picture of her that the trapper still carried.

"I was travelin' along an ice field, headin' toward Stewart's Lake. You know the spot. I camped for the night and woke to singin'."

A few other men had gathered. Some sniggered, but the others listened raptly.

"Only it wasn't singin' exactly, it was more like the wind." Caldwell seemed to be reliving the experience. "I should have stayed where I was hunkered down, but you never heard the likes of it. It was such a sad sound."

Knowing looks passed among the Indians.

"Then what?" asked Fisher, thinking his friend might end his story there.

"I went to find its source. I had to move on the ice and there they were, creepin' along and lookin' like bats. Maybe a dozen. They were draggin' things with them."

Fisher turned away and scoured the heavens, watching the clouds trying to block the sun. The mountain ridge visible over the hills to the north darkened.

"That's when the fog began movin' in," said Caldwell. "There shouldn't have been a fog, but there was. I looked up, but I could only see two stars in the night sky, set close together like eyes. When I looked back down the creatures were scatterin' and the things they had been draggin' were gone."

Caldwell stopped and licked his lips. "I got out of there fast," he said. "I hurried back to my camp, but before I knew it one of those creatures attacked me. Thank God I only had to deal with one of them. I had my gun out and shot it in the chest."

Whispers ran through the gathering crowd. The Indians shook their heads. "You must take this back to the mountain," said their leader. "It is one of the mountain's children. If you do not, Ithaqua will be angry."

Clenching his jaw until the corners of his mouth twitched, Caldwell answered by fingering the pistols hanging from his belt.

"Ithaqua?" asked Fisher. "Is that one of your Gods?"

"He is not one of our gods. He is of the Others."

"Indians have a god for every day of the week," said Perry, clapping a friendly hand to the Arapaho's shoulder.

"You saw him feed," said the Arapaho. "If he had touched you, you would have become like his children. You would have shared his hunger."

"You shut up," said Caldwell. "I catch you anywhere near that litter and I'll kill you."

Muscles tensing in his arms and neck, The Indian started forward. Hoping to avert disaster, Fisher grabbed Caldwell's arm. Perry spoke in a placating tone to the Arapahos, moving between the would-be combatants.

"Whoa. Everyone step down," said Fisher. "There's no need for this. We're all friends."

The Indian made a sign with his finger: a circle within a circle. "Return it to the mountain," he said. "Even in death it has power by being here. It upsets the balance."

Making a last sign, the Arapaho turned and moved toward a group of wagons coming out of the east. The others followed their leader. With a jerk, Caldwell pulled free and glared at the Indians' backs.

Fisher stepped in front of Caldwell and smiled. "I don't know how lucky or unlucky that thing is, but that kind of ugly is sure bound to be worth money."

The muscles in Caldwell's neck appeared to relax.

Biting on the stem of his pipe, Fisher nodded with amusement. "The bosses don't pay much of anything for beaver these days, but they'll pay for something like this."

"There's nothin' like it," said Caldwell. A breeze from the north touched them and the mountain man, appearing at last mollified, turned to tying down his prize.

※ ※ ※

The trappers spent the rest of the day socializing with friends not seen in the last few years. Some of Fisher's camp became melancholy. Others looked forward to the nights' activities. There would be a high stakes card game later and a series of strength and agility contests. Word spread that a new wagon of whores, mostly women from the south, had arrived.

Making sure his men were content occupied most of Fisher's time. He played mother and father to some; older brother to others. A portion of cash vouchers went into a safe place so that earnings weren't squandered or targeted by skillful confidence men. Coming to the rendezvous needed to be a healing experience where the men could take a break from the loneliness and frustration of the wilderness.

Throughout the evening he also kept an eye on Caldwell. The man sulked and stayed close to the fire-pit. At dinner, Caldwell again ate like an animal, stuffing food into his mouth so quickly that Fisher became concerned that he might choke. Not knowing what to say, Fisher said nothing.

As quiet reigned over the campsite, Caldwell rose and went to again check his prize. He passed two Arapaho deep in conversation with a Shoshone and made comments that again threatened to break the peace.

Perry pulled Fisher aside after that. "Your friend's gonna get himself killed," he said. "The Indians think he's been 'kissed by a demon'. That's what they keep saying. I'm not sure I can disagree."

"I'll talk to him," said Fisher.

"You be careful," said Perry.

"Maybe Amos is sick, but he's always been a good man. He's saved my life and I've saved him."

"Maybe that's not the same man."

Midnight found the temperature dropping. Using an old blanket for warmth, Fisher settled in by the fire and lit a last pipe. A stream of blue smoke curled up and vanished with the breeze. No stars were visible above and the moon only a path of light behind the clouds. A few of his men were unaccounted for, but that wasn't unusual, they were most likely passed out by someone else's fire. Snuggling deeper into his blanket, Fisher glanced over at Caldwell, gratified to see him drowsing.

Sleep came and only seemed to last a short while before Caldwell shook him awake. The sky showed at least three of four hours had passed, but he felt drained and his head hurt when sitting up.

"What's wrong?" asked Fisher.

"They took my trophy," said Caldwell, his voice filled with venom.

Fisher looked around. "Who did?"

"The Indians. Arapaho. The ones talkin' about takin' the thing back to the mountains."

If the Arapaho wanted the carcass, they would have tried buying it. Good and bad people could be found in any folk. Maybe stealing the carcass had been someone's idea of punishing Caldwell for earlier behavior, or maybe it wasn't anything more than a stupid prank.

"Thieves, every Redskin," said Caldwell.

"Not every one, Amos."

A glint appeared in Caldwell's eye. "I'm goin' to track 'em. They can't have gone too far. If they're on their way to the Tetons, we can catch 'em."

"What makes you think it wasn't one of the other trappers? I've seen some shady characters here. I don't think you'll accomplish much by running off without knowing for sure who might have done what."

"I'm packin' up and goin'."

"You'll get yourself killed, Amos. You shoot a brave or two and you can cause real trouble for the rest of us. The Arapaho have been as good a neighbor as you could wish for."

"I'm goin'" said Caldwell. He started to rise but stopped and gripped Fisher's shoulder. His grip hurt. "You come, too."

"I'm not chasing after Indians."

"Come with me. I don't have anyone else, Morgan. You tolerate me."

"I'm your friend. I'm telling you not to do this."

Caldwell scratched the back of his neck. His eyes drifted toward the dark still gathered over the mountains. "Best way to make sure I don't kill one of them savages is to come along. You do and I promise I won't start shootin' unless we know for sure they took it."

In this state, Caldwell's tendency toward violence might be extreme enough to endanger them all. Considering this and the unlikelihood that anyone at the rendezvous had taken the carcass, Caldwell's assertions almost sounded credible. He wracked his brain to think who might have shown interest last night, but drew a blank.

Most regarded the thing with loathing and several scoffed at the idea that anyone would pay anything for the abomination.

He walked to where the mules were tied and knelt beside the litter. Caldwell stood over him. Leaning close to the ground, Fisher studied the few footprints there. Some were Indian, but those could just as easily have been left from earlier. He picked up the rope that had been tied across the monster and ran a finger tip over the frayed edges.

This didn't make sense.

"Amos, why can't this wait till after everyone's up and around?" asked Fisher. "We'll ask and see if anybody has information."

"If we leave now, the Indians are only a few hours ahead of us," said Caldwell. He had thrown a blanket across his pony's back and was now slipping the tack over its head. "The longer we wait, the harder it's gonna be to catch up."

"That's assuming they're trying to cover their tracks."

Pulling a strip of jerky from his pocket, Caldwell gnawed on it. He stopped chewing and squinted toward the sky, dropping his voice into the weary tone of a man speaking to his own loneliness.

"I'm goin' with you or without you, Morgan. I'd rather go with you. We can catch 'em by late afternoon. Settle it, one way or another. Be back by midnight, or take our time and return by mornin.'"

Fisher kicked the ground and made up his mind to try and keep Caldwell from doing something stupid. In his heart he knew the Indians hadn't taken the thing. He decided to take a few men along and those that left behind could circulate through the camp and ask around about the missing carcass.

Fisher went back and roused four men. While three of them readied their horses, Fisher took Perry aside. "I want you to stay behind."

The younger man protested, but Fisher quieted him with a gesture.

"Talk to the Indians about this and see if they know anything," said Fisher. "Have some of the other men circulate through the camp and ask questions."

"The Indians didn't take that thing," said Perry. "They don't want trouble any more than we do. They're worried about your friend more than they're worried about some dead monster."

"I know."

"So why are you wasting your time going off with Caldwell?"

"I owe him."

"You watch yourself, Morgan. He's dangerous."

"Always has been," said Fisher.

A short time later, five riders headed North along the river.

※ ※ ※

Caldwell squatted and grazed the ground with his fingertips. Fisher let go a low whistle. "I don't see it," he said. "I know what a tracker you are, Amos, but I don't see it."

Standing now, Fisher walked to the narrow river fed from the headwaters. He dipped a handkerchief into the water and wiped his face with it. Icy rivulets streamed down his face and into his mustache and beard.

"They been this way, I can smell 'em," said Caldwell.

"Land's awfully flat here; you would think we'd see them."

"They had at least four hours on us. Maybe more."

"Still."

Purple and white, the mountains rose above the somber green of pine forests to the north. Their search would soon take them into that tree line. Working through the wood would be tougher going than a leisurely pace across flat grasslands. One day and one night, then back to the rendezvous. If Caldwell wouldn't follow, then he would have to be left behind. The men weren't pressing one way or another, but Fisher guessed they weren't keen on following a fool into peril.

They spent the next few hours riding toward the mountains. Without much cloud cover, the sun beat down and made the ride wearisome. Relief came in the form of a sparsely wooded area where the temperature eased slightly in the shadow of the trees. Fisher seriously doubted that they were still following any trail.

Toward late afternoon, later than Fisher had intended, the party stopped and prepared for dinner. Caldwell, who had been snacking throughout the day, slid down against a tree, dropping his head and letting out a deep, mournful sigh.

Fisher slid down next to him and closed his eyes. The smell of a small campfire made him realize he hadn't eaten all day. Caldwell's head came up.

"We ain't goin' any further, are we?" he asked.

Surprised by a deep weariness, Fisher shut his eyes. "You can if you want, Amos. I don't see the point of it. I came this far because I respect you and you're a friend. I haven't seen anything to show me the Arapaho came this way. I can't see them going into the mountains. Not to return a corpse, at any rate."

Caldwell ran rough hands against the legs of his buckskins and exhaled slowly.

"I'm still goin'," he said.

"I know."

"Tomorrow. First light."

"It's a mistake. You're not going to find any Arapaho. At least not the ones you're looking for."

Tilting his head to one side, Caldwell turned his face toward the breeze. "I still got my mules down at the rendezvous. Like I told you before, I got two hundred and twenty-five beaver pelts. I expect to be back down within a week. If I'm not, will you sell them and hold onto the money?"

"I will."

That seemed to satisfy Caldwell. Fisher couldn't help feeling tremendous affection and sadness for the man.

The party settled in for the evening and the mood lightened with the knowledge that by tomorrow morning they would be heading back. The men talked business and shared experiences. Caldwell ate and as the moon rose relaxed and become more sociable, even offering humorous stories about his time together with Fisher. The whiskey began to circulate and in time the laughter became more raucous.

Putting his head back and closing his eyes, Fisher stepped into memories. He dreamed of winter and heard the sound of the wind blowing dry powder across the ice. His fingers hurt, a sure sign of frostbite. He awoke with a start, instantly orienting himself to where he was.

"You never did judge no one," said Caldwell, leaning so close that Fisher could feel the other man's beard against his cheek. The man's eyes reminded him of polished onyx.

"You were always fair. You were always ready to give people a chance," continued Caldwell. "And you were right about them Indians. They never took that thing from my litter. No, Sir. That thing left on its own accord."

Something sharp kept Fisher pinioned to the ground. He moved his head. Two claws rested on his shoulders. Black eyes blinked rapidly at him. A bit of spittle hit his forehead as thing's tongue darted in and out of its mouth with each panting breath.

Caldwell nodded toward the small cooking fire. Something moved there. Fisher saw shiny black fur and moonlight reflected off those terrible wings. Another one gently hit the ground and scrambled sideways. From where he lay, Fisher counted six of them.

"I'm so hungry," said Caldwell.

The growing fear made it difficult for Fisher to organize his thoughts. Caldwell shrugged and said: "I had to get some of you away from the rendezvous, don't you see? There was no help for it. Up in the hills they'll call Him for his gift and He'll feed. And when He feeds he'll take away our hunger. My horrible hunger."

Licking his lips, Caldwell lifted a face toward the moon, partially obscured by overhead branches. His shoulders began to shake and soon he wailed. When he turned back, his cheeks were moist.

"It ain't just the hunger," he said. "It's somethin' else. When He comes upon us, we're children again."

Caldwell groaned with pleasure. The creature holding Fisher down chattered at Caldwell, a sound made more horrible by the mountain-man's apparent understanding of the thing.

A scream cut through the darkness. Two of the beasts were hissing and making clicking sounds as they slashed at something on the ground. Caldwell's eyes rolled with excitement and he spun around.

"Don't kill him," cried Caldwell in a panic.

The thing above Fisher whined and lifted up for a second; he took advantage of the distraction to roll sharply to one side. Gun out of reach, his fingers clawed for a weapon. He frantically clutched the hilt of a knife and slashed out. The creature dodged. He feigned to the left and came back in, the blade cutting the side of the monster's face. Wings beat madly at the air. An arm clubbed Fisher, dropping him to one knee. Too strong, too fast. The thing would overpower him in seconds.

Rodent eyes burned into his and he could see from the way its legs tensed that the thing was about to go on the offensive. Lips pulled back from razor teeth. Without much hope, Fisher readied for the attack.

An arrow came out of the darkness to bury itself in the black fur of its neck. Another arrow followed, this time piercing a wing.

Fisher jumped, stabbing the thing in the chest. The monster

screamed and beat its wings, going airborne for a moment before returning hard to the ground. Still alive, it melted into the darkness, no longer an immediate threat.

A rifle sounded. Fisher caught a glimpse of Perry running between the trees, keeping low as he fired a second time. Several Indians moved with him, many of them with guns. Another of those creatures screamed out and stumbled backward. It grabbed its abdomen and fell.

Fisher turned in time to see Caldwell charging and tried to meet the other man by setting a defensive posture. Caldwell brushed aside his knife arm and tackled him to the soft earth. Fingers closed on his neck, cutting off oxygen. Panic shot through Fisher, but staying focused, he slashed toward Caldwell and felt the knife cut through the man's skin. Another slash and the jugular opened.

Time slowed. Caldwell's eyes rolled back, lips red with blood. A spasm shook him and he fell to the side in shock.

Crawling forward on his elbows, Fisher laid a hand on Caldwell's cheek. He lay there for some time before being helped up by Perry.

Signs of carnage illuminated by the moon startled Fisher. Three of the winged things lay dead on the ground, along with two of his own men. Fisher shook his head and had to be steadied by Perry.

An Indian approached. "Let us make a fire and burn the dead of Ithaqua," he said.

Fisher looked to Perry, who nodded. The Indian called out instructions.

"We lost good men," said Perry.

"I had to follow Caldwell. I had to try," said Fisher.

Perry shrugged.

"You did right, Morgan. You thought he was your friend, but he was more one of those things than he was Amos Caldwell."

Fisher watched as his old partner was dragged across the ground toward where the Indians were setting their fire.

"It could have been any of us," he said to himself. Nodding, Perry walked away.

THEY WHO DWELL BELOW

BY WILLIAM JONES

They referred to them as "those people," "the old people," or "they who dwell below," and appeared to hold them in too great a frightened veneration to talk much about them.

—"The Mound," H.P. Lovecraft

HE COULD SENSE THEM shifting and pattering in the darkness, pallid, bleached things, always beyond the splash of the torchlight. Henry Kane saw them in his mind. In the black tunnels, they crouched waiting. Simply waiting.

His hand tightened around the grip of his Colt. Desperately he wanted to shoot, but the last few hours in the endless maze of tunnels had taught him otherwise. *They're waiting for you to use all your shots,* he thought. *Then they'll come.* Only he knew what they were. *A man's sins always came back to haunt him.*

"I believe this might take us in the proper direction," Milroy Beck said, holding a torch high, peering at the black walls. He was straggly as a worn blanket, and as thin as one too. "A man of science" was how he'd introduced himself to Kane back in Cheyenne.

"If I'm correct," Beck continued, "these markings refer to Yig and a ritual of some sort." He slid a hand across the graven surface. "And this ritual was performed in an open area."

"That's great," said Frank Wilcox gruffly. "What's a yig, and how do we know that *open area* isn't just one of those big rooms we've already come across?"

Beck sidled along the wall, eyes shifting up and down as though he were listening to the glyphs and agreeing with them. Kane stepped forward, revolver pointed. As the torchlight melted the darkness, things scurried away. Occasionally, Kane thought he heard the flapping of wings. That gave him hope, because he knew if there were bats in these tunnels, a way out must be near.

"These hieroglyphs are not referring to a *big room*," Beck said mockingly. For a slip of a man, Beck took privileges most others wouldn't. Kane suspected things would change once they were above ground again.

Frank Wilcox was a barrel-chested man who had trouble working his way around a solid thought. But he was good with a gun, and sometimes fast to use it. Being a bit slow on the draw, so to speak, men like Beck always rubbed Wilcox the wrong way. Kane knew he wouldn't tolerate much more. *A man could only take so much of anything*, Kane thought. *Only so much.*

Kane had known Wilcox since back in sixty-five, the last year of the war. The burly man had been a Confederate prisoner, one who'd witnessed the "cruelties of war," as General Sherman had termed it. As best as Kane could figure, like so many veterans, Wilcox had tumbled west after the war—maybe hiding from the past, maybe looking for a new life. The two ended up in Cheyenne, spending most of their time avoiding each other. It had been Milroy Beck who'd brought them together with the promise of riches.

"That's dandy, Beck," said Wilcox. "Do any of these scribblings make mention of the gold?"

Beck sighed heavily. "Most of what is here means nothing to me. However, if it did, I'd venture it *wouldn't* include directions for grave robbers. That is the sort of sport one does without guidance."

Wilcox spat and hiked the torch in one hand and revolver in another, lighting the way behind. "This weren't my idea in the first place. I didn't know you planned to burrow into the earth like some prairie dog."

The three men had arrived at Binger, Oklahoma, looking for an Indian burial mound filled with gold—at least that was how Milroy Beck had spun it originally. After nearly a month of searching outside of town, they'd found a capstone leading into an unwholesome labyrinth. On the first day, Kane suspected the expedition might be light on gold, and heavy with treasures for "a man of science." The three had found golden trinkets and strange coins along the way, but those were far from a treasure, and not worth the sleepless hours spent in the dark folds of the earth.

In a day and a half, they'd slipped, crawled, and walked through narrow passages, gigantic tunnels, and vast, vaulted rooms so high that there appeared to be no ceiling. Everywhere were monstrous carvings and shapes that caught in the mind and stayed. No one had slept more than a few hours that first night, and the foulness of the place quickly eroded any rugged exteriors a man might have.

"Kane," Wilcox called. "What do you figure is out there?" He waved the torch at the darkness. "Some kind of lizard or such? They been dogging us the entire time."

"Don't know," Kane said. *They're not lizards*, he thought. *And they're not human.* "Our shooting makes them keep a distance. I reckon that's all that matters."

"I'd like to get me one just to see," Wilcox said as he tromped down the tunnel. "An albino lizard hide has got to be worth something."

"Get back here!" Kane yelled. "You'll get lost-"

The roar of a pistol cut Kane's words short. Wilcox's torch darted about in the distant blackness. Two more shots reverberated off the black walls.

Just as Kane started after Wilcox, the man came trotting back. "Damn things are fast," Wilcox said. "What are they, Beck?"

Kane moved in. Beneath the hiss of the torches, he heard a wet, ragged breathing.

The looming darkness reminded Kane of the nights he'd spent in Georgia during the war. It was called Sherman's March, but it was plain butchery. He'd been young then, and did things a man ought not to do. Things that haunted him every day of his life. Now it felt as though all those years of nightmares had come together and were prowling in the darkness.

"They are adapted animals," Beck said, approaching Wilcox.

"And that's supposed to mean something to me?"

"If you believe Darwin's theory, they have evolved to live underground." Beck squinted into the shadows, his dark eyes seemingly reading the gloom beyond.

"You're makin' less sense now than before," Wilcox said. "How much farther?"

Beck pulled a journal from his bag, flipping through its pages. Kane had seen him studying it many times. Once or twice, when Beck was gazing to some far away place, Kane sneaked a peek. He was a fine reader, but the writing on the pages looked like they were made by a chicken with ink on its toes.

"I think it's another six or eight hours this way." Beck pointed in the direction they'd been heading.

"You're crazy," Wilcox said. "There ain't that much underground to walk. That way there keeps going down. It can't do that for another eight hours. It has to turn up and probably lead out."

"I admire your naiveté, Mr. Wilcox," Beck said. "Nonetheless, this is the direction." Beck stood, stuffing the journal into the bag slung over his shoulder.

"Right now anywhere seems better than here," Kane said. Turning to Wilcox, he added, "Don't go wanderin' off again."

A coarse laugh escaped Wilcox. "You goin' to string me up and set me afire like you did those in Atlanta? You're not the coward I took you for, Kane." He pushed to his feet. "I figured you only killed unarmed folk. Guess I was wrong."

"Mr. Wilcox," Beck said. "If you please."

"I told you 'fore, Beck. I don't trust this lowdown dog. He ain't changed since the war. He's the kind who'll kill you sleepin'."

Kane remained silent, thinking Wilcox was right. Men don't change. Sure, they get older, haggard and worn out from use. But the stone they're cut from is the stone they're made of, and that never changes.

"Unless your share of the profits is too great a burden for you, I urge you to take the lead, and stop this talk."

For a moment, Wilcox seemed to consider the proposition. Then he spat, and said, "Fine."

※ ※ ※

Six hours of hard walking brought them into a sprawling cavern. Pools spotted the rugged surface, and water ceaselessly dripped from the limestone ceilings.

Beck took account of their location, thumbing through his journal, and finally announced that they'd make camp in the cavern. They used an open oil lamp as a fire, chewing jerky and drinking whiskey for dinner. With the ease of a man without a conscience,

Wilcox dropped off to sleep. His hat covered his face, but did little to mute the snoring.

Kane sat on a blanket, leaning against his pack. A small, yellow flame danced before him, painting shadows on Beck's face as he scribbled and studied his journal.

"Who made this place?" Kane asked, his voice echoing in the stony chamber. "It sure wasn't Indians."

Beck's dark eyes peered up. A fine, white stubble had sprouted on his chin and cheeks, making him look as gaunt as a dead man.

"Some of the Indians call them the 'Old Ones,'" Beck said. "Others named them 'They who dwell below.' They lived here long ago, even before the Indians, before humans walked the earth." His voice was somber, quickly swallowed by the darkness.

"Don't see how that's possible. But you're the man with the book." Kane cocked his head, following the shifting shadows above. Water dripped from limestone teeth. "The place seems empty to me. Unless there's spirits or ghosts or such down here."

A thin smile formed on Beck's visage. "These tunnels lead to another place, to their world—a vast land inside the earth." He waved a hand dismissively. "What's lurking beyond our lights are sentries that once protected these forgotten passages. There are no spirits here."

"Maybe this place is like the Caddo Reservation," Kane said. He remembered passing the territory when riding to Binger. Crowds of empty faces staring at the three of them as they passed. "Indians say a reservation is where those who have stopped living go. Could be this place is a reservation for others."

Memories of Atlanta flicked through his mind. Houses burning, and the countless dead—the stench of decay. The same fetid odor drifted in the tunnels and caverns.

"Superstitions," Beck said. "Myths created by humans to torture themselves. Ghosts don't haunt this world. A man's lack of strength is what stalks him in the reaches of the night."

Kane peered at Wilcox, sprawled and snoring. "He must be very strong."

Beck flipped through the haggard book resting on his knees. "There were many entrances to this underworld at one time." He pointed upward. "These chambers have complex vents to purge the fumes of fires. But in time, the tunnels to the surface were sealed. Mankind lost many dreams when that happened." Snapping the book shut, Beck leaned forward, eyes wide. "Their cities are made of gold. They are immortal. They speak with their thoughts. *So many marvels.* There is no excess, they even animate the dead as servants."

"You mean slaves? Dead men as slaves?" Kane asked.

"No. No. These are mindless bodies continuing to serve. It is a utopia, Mr. Kane. Everyone is of the same stock—perfect specimens each. Mr. Bulwer-Lytton's writings were not so far off."

"Don't know him," Kane said. He scanned the cavern. He still sensed them lurking out there. Shifting about. Waiting.

"You'll see," Beck said, his enthusiasm fading. He returned the journal to his knees, opening it. "Why don't you rest? I'll keep watch as I read."

"Don't think I'll rest much. But I'll try." He shifted on the blanket, closing his eyes, feeling the ghosts stir in his mind.

※ ※ ※

In his dreams, Kane had returned to a burning city. Houses, shops, schools, everything blazed in hellish flames. People fled the madness while groups of Union soldiers pillaged and hunted down men dressed as civilians. They were called cowards for removing their Confederate uniforms. Finding them was easy. It seemed as though Kane could read their thoughts on their faces. Killing them was easy, too. A rage surged through him—hatred swelled in his mind. The men were shot in the streets, beneath a churning black sky...

A hideous howl pulled Kane from the nightmare.

He sprung to his feet, Colt in hand. In the pale light of the lamp, he saw Wilcox twist about, revolver pointing this way and that. Beck dug frantically through a pack, pulling a resin torch free.

"What in tarnation was that?" Wilcox growled.

"They're angry," Kane said.

"How would *you* know?" Wilcox snapped.

Anemic light stretched across the cavern floor, holding back the shadows by only a few feet. In a flicker of motion, Kane glimpsed a creature with milky flesh, vanishing as suddenly as it appeared.

"He's correct," Beck said, lighting a torch, raising it high. The darkness retreated a few more feet. "They are guardians. Their hatred of us keeps them near. But now their hate is being fueled. Like throwing dry wood on a fire."

Kane's dream flashed through his mind. He remembered what Beck had said about speaking with thoughts. *Can they hear my thoughts?*

"Yes," Beck said. "I suspect they were threatened by your dreams."

Kane spun on the man. "How . . .?"

"Some people are sensitive to the thoughts of others," Beck said. "Most," he nodded toward Wilcox, "are too thick-headed. I found you because you aren't. It wasn't chance we met. My abilities are too weak. I needed an interpreter for my expedition."

A guttural rumbling came from the blackness. Kane felt the loathing twist through his mind.

Wilcox fired his pistol. "I say we head back. I ain't seen enough gold to keep at this."

Beck pulled another torch from his pack, igniting it from the first. "Your dream lingers in their minds," he said to Kane.

"Mine too," Kane said. "It's like gawking in a mirror and finding something ugly peering back at you." He inclined his head. "Hang a pack over my shoulder. I'm with Wilcox on this."

"We can't do that," Beck exclaimed. "We are near. Think of the riches . . . the marvels!"

Kane forced himself to remain calm. A flurry of thoughts whirled through his head as if he heard the creatures whispering. Cold fear chilled his bones.

Wilcox edged toward the slanting entrance, a revolver in both hands. "I can hear 'em gettin' closer. Beck, if you want to stay, you're welcome to it."

"He has to guide us," Kane said. Flashes of the dream gnawed at him, awakening memories long buried. *What do they want me to do?*

Then Beck's face turned ashen. "We'll go," he said, as though he'd heard a whisper as well. But his words seemed as they were aimed to someone else.

Coming alongside Kane, Beck said in a hoarse whisper, "Move quickly." The clandestine tone was razor sharp.

"Pick it up, Wilcox," Kane called. Out the corner of his eye, Kane noticed Beck stiffen. Things started to piece together. *He's offering Wilcox as a sacrifice.* Without the promise of gold, Wilcox and Kane got along like a flame and a hay bale. Even so, Kane wasn't going leave the man behind just to gain a few steps.

They trudged up the steep slope; Wilcox nearly stumbled several times, trying to move his bulk backward and uphill. "Don't plan on leavin' me," he yelled.

As Kane turned to speak, a white shape leaped from the shadows, toppling Wilcox. It snarled with a vicious fury, clawing at the man's face and throat, a cruel maw snapping loudly, lined with small, pointed teeth.

For a moment, Kane stood in silent terror, watching as Wilcox flailed helplessly, claws raking across his flesh. The urge to flee washed over him.

From behind, he heard Beck scrambling up the slope. *Do something you fool*, Kane chided himself.

He turned to follow Beck, but stopped. Instead, he took aim at the creature, cocking the revolver. Suddenly the thing froze, statue still, as thought it recognized the sound. Or maybe Kane's thought.

Its head lifted; eyes large and black fixed on him. An misshapen head, sallow and lumpy seemed impossibly delicate. It almost looked human.

Seconds passed without measure. The hiss and snarl of the creature faded. Kane squeezed the trigger.

In an instant, the world exploded. The report of the Colt and the howl of the creature filled the tunnel as the thing vanished into the blackness.

Bleeding, Wilcox stumbled to his feet, swaying like a drunk.

Kane kept watch as Wilcox ambled toward him. "I would have left you," Wilcox said, gulping the darkness with rattling breaths.

"Me too," Kane said dully.

"Where the hell did Beck go?"

"Seems he thinks like us."

Wilcox limped forward. "Come on. There's no way we're getting out of here without him."

Time slipped by without measure. Kane and Wilcox stalked through the tunnels, pausing often to tend to Wilcox's wounds. The stony earth prevented them from tracking Beck. And each time they paused, snarling echoed from behind.

Still, they trudged on, following Kane's lead. It was a chain of hunches and guesses, feelings that urged him one way or the other through the confusing passages. He reasoned that if Beck *could* read his thoughts, it might work the other way around.

"This is pointless," Wilcox groused. "I'd tell you to go on without me, but if we're gonna die in here, we might as well do it together."

In the sickly torchlight, Kane watched as Wilcox hobbled over to a wall, dropping his weight against it.

"We'll take a rest," Kane said. "I'm not ready to quit yet."

"Beck swindled us. We ain't gonna find him, and we ain't gonna find a way out." He spat, sliding down the wall, his vest and belt scraping the stone as he went. A harsh laugh sounded when he landed. "Just like a bluebelly coward. I ran away without my guns."

"You're never going to let the war die, are you?"

"Some things die. Some things don't." Wilcox grinned through the bloodied scrape of cloth he held against his face. "I guess you know which side we land on."

A strange wisdom lurked in Wilcox's words, Kane thought. *The horrors of the world never die. They are as persistent as the sun and the moon. Only the people facing them die.* He'd seen it over and over again, horror living, surviving on the faces of the dead. Sometimes he'd brought the horror.

Kane shrugged off his pack. "You're right," he said. "So let's celebrate. There's whiskey in there."

Without hesitation, Wilcox prowled through the bag. "I'm up for that." He yanked out a bottle, pulling the cork free with his teeth. "Here's to *not* seeing your ugly face in the future."

As Wilcox tipped the bottle, a *clanking* came from ahead, followed by someone yelling.

"That's Beck," Kane said, moving toward the sound.

"I'd rather stay here and poison the bastards with my drunken corpse."

Kane grabbed Wilcox by the arms, hefting him up.

"You're wasting your time," Wilcox said. "We're on our last torch. Maybe Beck has one or two more, but that ain't gonna get us out of here."

"Have you seen anything else down here except those creatures?" Kane asked.

"No." Wilcox shifted his weight to one leg. "That mean somethin'?"

"They have to eat. My guess is they're the ghosts people claim to see in these parts. That means there is more than one way out."

"They probably eat each other," Wilcox said, taking a swig of whiskey. "I'll stay here."

As though to punctuate the statement, a low growl slipped from the shrouded passage—a sonorous rumble.

No doubt Kane would move quicker without Wilcox. But he saw in his mind Wilcox's fate if left alone. And buried in the gruesome thoughts was a deep hunger. *There is only so much a man can take,* Kane thought. *And I've had a bellyful of death in my lifetime.*

"You're coming with me." Kane braced Wilcox on his shoulder.

"No! You are a damnable fool. Don't try to use me to make up for your sins. I'd just as soon see you in Hell." He took another swig of the whiskey.

"We're already in Hell, and that's why you're coming with me."

Kane stepped forward, supporting Wilcox. Ahead the hammering and yelling continued.

"Stop," Wilcox said. He flipped the bottle over his shoulder, letting it shatter on the rocky surface. "Light that. It'll give 'em somethin' to think about."

They hobbled sideways, and Kane ignited the whiskey with the torch. Flames whooshed, clawing at the low, smooth ceiling.

"Damn shame," Wilcox muttered.

The men trundled down the passage.

They trailed the noise for several minutes. With each step, the clatter became more distinct. To Kane it sounded like someone hammering with a shovel. A flat ringing followed each strike. Occasionally a foul word or two echoed above the noise. The hard walls made it seem as though the clamor were coming from everywhere. Only in the cross passages was Kane able to focus on a direction. Still, the sounds sometimes seemed closer and other times distant.

"We're goin' in circles," Wilcox snapped. "We'll wear ourselves out before we find that fool."

"Rest a bit," Kane said, letting Wilcox lower to the ground.

The clanging continued, bouncing off the walls, echoing from every path.

"What's he doin'?" Wilcox said.

Without a word, Kane slipped the gun belt from his waist, letting it coil into Wilcox's lap.

"You've always been a coward," Wilcox said, anger twisting his face.

Kane stepped into the intersection, torch in hand. Closing his eyes, blocking the world around him. Lights danced across his eyelids; his labored breathing covered all sounds except for the persistent drumming of his heart. Inhaling deeply, he let his mind drift like a compass searching for its bearing.

The sensation was faint at first. In the depths of his mind, he felt a faint tug, a tenuous thread stretched taut, ready to snap. He concentrated on the feeling, slowing his breathing. Again, came a wispy touch like that of butterfly's wings.

Droning in the back of his consciousness was Wilcox's yelling. Kane ignored the men, following the pull of his thoughts. He charged forward.

The hammering grew louder.

With each step, Kane's boots slapped against the solid earth. When he hit a slope, his pace quickened until he was running simply to remain upright, racing downward.

He spotted the glow of light ahead, and heard the sound of steel against stone.

Unable to stop, Kane dropped the torch, stampeding forward. He collided with Milroy Beck, toppling the lanky man. The two rolled and tumbled. The shovel rattled to the ground. Kane slammed into a wall.

With the speed of a snake, Beck sprung to his feet, retrieving the shovel and preparing to strike.

"Hold on," Kane said, puffing. "I'm not here to kill you."

Sharp, dark eyes studied Kane for a moment. Slowly, Beck lowered the tool. "I didn't want to leave you," he said. "But Wilcox was slowing us down. I tried–"

"Stop," Kane interrupted, climbing to his feet. "I reckon we're all three suited for each other. We can sort the *if*'s and *why*'s out later. Right now I just want out of here."

Beck let the shovel fall; the blade hit the rock with a dull ring. He paced toward one of the torches, grabbing it. "That may be possible," he said calmly. "I think there is a concealed doorway here." He shifted to the spot where he'd obviously been hammering. "I suspect this is one of the many paths to the surface. But I don't know how to open it."

"Could those creatures open it?" Kane asked.

"If it were triggered by weight or pressure, I suppose."

"You'd said that there used to be many tunnels out of here. I think those creatures still use them. They must eat something, and there's nothing down here but rock. I can't fathom them tromping back the way we came in every time they're hungry."

Beck seemed to consider the point. "You may be right," he said after a moment.

"Why do you think this a door?" Kane motioned at the marred stone. Like every flat surface in the tunnels, it had mysterious markings across it.

"If I'm correct," Beck said, squinting at the script, "this series of markings indicates 'surface.' I'm certain the opening above is well concealed, but if we could reach it . . ."

"We're not going without Wilcox," Kane cut him short.

Beck gazed at him in astonishment. "You brought him with you," he said slowly as the realization came to him. "Leaving him in the tunnels will slow them down. He's our best chance of getting out of here alive. Their minds are bent on one purpose, and that is to kill us."

Cut from the same stone from start to finish, Kane thought.

"He wouldn't hesitate to leave you," Beck added quickly.

"Neither would you. Besides, I know where he is. So I'll fetch him, while you keep brooding on this *door*. I imagine we'll have company following."

"An offering might pacify the them, maybe garner us passage. Imagine the secrets we'd discover, the riches. If we found this hidden land, it would be a new frontier opened to the world."

Kane shook his head. "I won't do that. You said they locked themselves inside the earth to keep away from us. And they put these creatures here to make sure no one snuck in. The way I see it, there wouldn't be a welcome wagon when we arrived on their border." Kane brushed past Beck, retrieving his torch. "You keep at this, 'cause I'm not going any deeper into this place."

Kane stalked down the tunnel, increasing his pace with every step. All the while he felt Beck's burning gaze. Kane had known plenty of rotten men, but one thing he'd learned was the men like Beck were the most dangerous because they were always willing to spend the lives of others on some great dream.

While retracing his steps, Kane wondered where his life had gone. His youth had been given to the Federal Army and the War Between the States. He'd joined searching an escape from his hometown, to become a hero, to earn medals and glory. All the war did was make him hollow and resentful.

The *crack* of the Colt rolled down the corridor like thunder. A second shot followed, and a third. Kane pushed aside the dark memories and bolted forward, calling as he ran.

In moments he came upon Wilcox, the roar of the revolver and the muzzle flash revealing his location in the gloom.

"It's me," Kane said. "Don't shoot."

"Why the hell not? You left me here to die."

Kane eased forward, the yellow light from the torch forming a circle around the men. Snarling and snapping sounded from beyond. *They hate me*, Kane realized. He felt their raw anger in his mind. *I remind them of their past—of their purpose.*

"You're as crazy as a raccoon in the daylight," Wilcox said. "Too much a coward to stay. And too much a coward to leave."

"Beck has a way out." *Maybe*, Kane thought but did not utter. "We need to meet up with him."

"And stupid to boot," Wilcox blared. "I can't walk, and these critters –" he pointed the revolver at the black curtain surrounding them –"don't seem too forgivin'."

"Keep the Colt and hold them off while I carry you."

Wilcox flipped the Colt's chamber open, replacing the spent cartridges. "When I'm done reloadin', I'm gone to shoot that melon of a head on your shoulders. Whether you want to admit it or not, I'm twice the man you are, in *every* way. There ain't no way you're goin' to haul me 'round."

Suddenly, a shape slipped from the blackness, landing on Kane. He dropped the torch, locking his hands around the creature's head. Through the thin flesh stretched over its skull he felt the soggy bones. Fanged teeth snapped; sharp claws burrowed into his back. Kane stumbled backward, landing against a wall. The Colt boomed, followed by the whine of a ricochet dancing from one surface to the next.

"Hold still," Wilcox yelled.

An empty sound filled Kane's throat. He'd thought about dying many times. But this didn't seem right.

The white face lurched back, jerking from side to side, trying to pull free of Kane's grasp. Rancid breath ushered from it in ferocious bursts. Its raging hatred spilled over Kane's mind, nearly overwhelming him.

In an instant, a claw released from his shoulder and swiped at his face. Kane carried the creature across the corridor, slamming its sickly soft form against the wall, pinning it.

It snarled with impotent fury, unable to move.

For a brief moment, its malevolent, black eyes held the horror and misery of every person Kane had ever killed. Icy terror seized him. He pulled back, letting the *thing* drop. A split second later, Wilcox put a hole in its head. Kane never heard the Colt fire.

A black syrup oozed from the creature's pallid head.

Kane's body felt numb. Still, there was a tingling at the back of his mind. *Are they trying to speak to me?* he wondered.

". . . don't get movin', I'll shoot you where you stand." Wilcox's voice slowly pierced the fog filling his head.

"Let's go! Breakin' my neck can't be any worse than wrestlin' with these varmints."

A chorus of billowing howls filled the tunnel. Kane sensed them. They were gathering. No longer waiting.

"You are the most useless, lowdown, dirty . . ."

Kane stepped forward. "Put the belt around your neck," he said. "You might have to reload. I can't move quick with a bag of manure on my shoulder, so I reckon you'll have to shoot to keep them off our tail."

Kane yanked Wilcox up with a grunt. His legs already felt as though they were about to buckle.

"Best hurry," Wilcox said. "They're gettin' bolder."

Balancing himself, Kane took a step, then another, increasing his pace.

"The torch, Kane! We're gonna need that."

"I can find Beck without it."

Wilcox mumbled under his breath as they moved down the tunnel.

When Kane spotted the flicker of Beck's torch, he called out, warning of their approach. From behind, the snarling continued.

Each step was a struggle, and the slope forced Kane to unwillingly quicken his gait.

"Slow down," Wilcox called. "If we fall here, I'm on the losin' side."

His muscles burned; his heart pounding with such fury that it seemed like it would burst from his chest. Finally he reached Beck, letting Wilcox slip to the ground.

"Did you figure it out?" Kane said, gasping.

The hammer of the Colt *clicked*. "I ought to shoot you, Beck," Wilcox said.

Frantically, Beck shifted his eyes from Kane to Wilcox and back again.

"We need him alive," Kane said, his breathing still ragged.

"For now," Wilcox answered.

"I did what any man would do," Beck snapped. "Both of you would have sacrificed me to save yourselves."

Wilcox spat. "Yep, we're alike in that regard. 'Cept, I'd shoot you for doin' it."

"Did you find a way to open the door?" Kane asked, standing straight to catch his breath.

Beck looked at Kane as though considering whether or not to answer.

"We might not need him afterall," Wilcox said.

"I did," Beck stammered. "But I can't open it."

A series of desolate wails filled the tunnels. Kane turned to see countless gray-white faces creeping closer. The sheer number prevented them from remaining in the shadows.

Bitter loathing flooded Kane's head—a timeless, remorseless hatred of all life, of *their* lives. A chill slithered along his neck as he recognized the feeling. He struggled to push the thoughts aside.

"How . . .?" he asked Beck, although the solitary word took great effort.

"They use their minds to speak," Beck said. "The key seems to be in a thought. Actually, I would guess something closer to an emotion. I don't believe these creatures are capable of thought as we know it."

"You're worthless," Wilcox exclaimed. "We have to *think* our way out of here? Is that it?"

"Not you," Beck said sharply.

Kane lowered himself to the ground, dropping against the cold stone. "I can do it," he said.

"This is foolishness," Wilcox said. "You're going to think the door open?"

"I reckon," Kane said. His throat tightened and his head ached.

The snarling grew louder. Hunched shapes scurried from the tunnels in every direction.

"Do it!" Beck said hysterically. "Open the door!"

Wilcox fixed Kane with a hard stare. "You've always been stupid."

"Cut from the same stone, start to finish," Kane replied. Then he closed his eyes, letting the darkness swallow him.

Rage poured through his body like a fiery river. A flaring pain shot through his head as every buried memory clawed its way to the surface. The countenance of every person he'd killed blazed. He was no different from the men he despised, from the creatures that despised him. As though he were an empty soul, the creatures poured into him a foulness, an abhorrence for life, until he was overflowing with a profound blackness.

Miles away, he heard the grating stone, of shifting rock, of the doorway opening. Leather boots shuffled against stone. He sensed Wilcox and Beck climbing upward, back to the surface.

Before him were pale faces—inhuman, tortured things, eyes feverish with anger and insanity. Something worse than pain pulsed through his body, biting, gnawing at his soul. It was then that he realized life may be the most miraculous of things. Dreams, hopes, ideas, all manner of wonders filled it to the point of bursting. And he'd squandered it, losing everything along the way. Everything.

WAGON TRAIN FOR THE STAR

BY SCOTT LETTE

Jake Elsworth had spent the night standing and staring at the solid wall of his cell, unable to focus on much else thanks to the liquor he'd drank and the powerful blows that had rained upon him from Tom Smith's hands.

"There's no hard feelings," Jake said to Bear River Tom from his side of the bars that next morning. "I'd have handed over my guns if given the chance."

"That ain't the truth," Tom said. "I made it clear as day, all firearms were to be deposited with the saloon proprietor. I'd be giving you another round if it wasn't for your early morning visitor."

Jake turned on the weight of his heels to face Tom Smith, to see the approach of his employer Joseph McCoy. McCoy seemed fine as creamy gravy in comparison, his slouch hat sitting straighter than a penitent man on Sunday.

McCoy patted the marshal on the back. "Don't worry, Tom. I just want a few minutes alone with the man."

Tom obliged and soon the pair was alone.

"I told you I was done with your cattle drives," Jake said with conviction. "I've worn out my welcome and it's time to move on."

"On that we can agree Elsworth. No, I'm here to ask you to help me out with a little problem. You saw those settlers and their wagons last night?"

"I did and much perplexed I was by their words and presence," Jake said. "I thought those folks kept further to the North?"

"These folk have arrived all the way from Red River station. I've spoken to their leader, Alfarr Odinsson. He seems a good Christian."

"I might delight more in the man's spiritual temperament," Jake said as he paused to rasp the dryness from his palette, "If I became convinced your tale would come to a charitable end."

"The man has made to me considerable payment," McCoy continued undeterred. "I'm prepared to part with some of it if you'll help this preacher find a home for their flock. Have you heard of Pilgrim's Peak?"

"That miserable place? It's a far cry from the mountains of Montana or Manitoba," Jake said. "But if that be where the man and his flock wish to settle, I'll not be one to get between them and their God."

"I thought you'd see it that way," McCoy said as he drew his pipe with intent to smoke. "You leave as soon as you're able to ride."

There was a silence as the marshal returned Jake's guns. Although the Bear stood almost two hands higher than the cowboy, Jake had given him considerable trouble before last night's subdual. There was little lazy fat on Jake Elsworth; he had a fiery temperament to match his flaming red hair and a dogged endurance earned through many months upon trail and saddle.

"Much obliged Tom," Jake said with a matter-of-fact tone.

"Don't be coming back to make us go another round," Tom said, sizing up Elsworth one final time with wary gray-blue eyes.

"Once I'm done I'm heading further north," Jake said as he walked out of the jail. "You're seeing the back of me for the last time, Tom Brown."

※ ※ ※

Abilene woke to the sounds of breakfast, cowhands moved subdued from the merriment of the night before while more bright-eyed folk went about the start to their day among the turned earth and bulldust. Jake Elsworth walked down Texas Street with a nod and the occasional cheer from his compadres, fellow trailblazers who had survived another night of furious drink.

"I should probably tell the boys that I'm leaving town," Jake said to himself as he walked. "But better that I don't."

He continued to walk out along Texas Street toward the Smoky Hill River to the north, where he could see the wagons of the Icelanders had gathered in anticipation of leaving. Their numbers were great, Jake estimated some two-hundred head of settlers among their rank although they seemed woefully short on livestock. Other hired men made preparations for the journey among them, Jake at once recognized the man upon a pale horse in Union blues with a modified Sharps rifle held to his side.

"Bob Taylor, I had hoped we wouldn't cross paths again," Jake said as he drew close enough to grab the Captain's reins.

"That makes two of us Elsworth," said Robert Taylor. "But here we are, both trying to make a living."

Jake Elsworth did not like Captain Robert Taylor, a man to whom the ways of war had never ended. After the end of the war in sixty-five, Taylor had been stationed at Fort Gibson, whereupon and under dubious circumstances he had been discharged with full recompense. Elsworth heard ugly rumors about the "good Captain" through the other townsfolk, a story of unrequited love, a rancher's daughter and a bevy of murdered suitors.

Their shared history however was a much more personal and straightforward affair. Jake had insulted and slighted Taylor in front of his commanding officer at Fort Gibson when he had brought to the Army's attention a certain "levy" Taylor had extracted from folk to ensure their safe passage.

"You are to keep within my sight at all times," Robert Taylor insisted. "Don't have mind now to wander off, only the good Lord knows then if my aim would be true."

"I've given my word to McCoy," said Jake Elsworth as he looked for the group's preaching leader. "If it's good enough for McCoy I reckon it's good enough for you."

"You and I both know I'm here to make sure you keep your word," Taylor said. "If we both do our jobs these settlers will get to where they're going and we'll both see our pay."

Among the crowd, Jake Elsworth noticed a tall woman with long blond hair, leading his tamed mustang Tucker toward them. The air between Jake and Taylor fell silent as she walked among them, without a word being spoken she gently handed Elsworth the reins of Tucker before walking slowly and almost dreamlike away from the pair.

"That's Freydis, the preacher's daughter," said Taylor with regained composure. "She's not one for talking."

Taylor cursed as he struggled to control his horse. "Just make sure to get us to Phantom Hill before sundown."

✳ ✳ ✳

Although it was no more than ten miles from the outskirts of Abilene to the Post on Clear Fork of the Brazos, or Phantom Hill as the locals called it, the first day's journey was one of constant shakeouts. At least three of the wagons threw a wheel in crossing the ford near the river; Jake spent two and some hours retrieving contents from the flowing water and reassuring their occupants. Captain Taylor lost his patience, screaming to Elsworth to make as much haste as God himself could muster.

The settler's poor grasp of English was already a problem. While Jake had worked before with Mexican and even Indian cowhands, gaining understanding with these Icelanders was proving more difficult than he had anticipated. There was more than just a language barrier to it, there was a general reluctance of direct contact between the settlers and outsiders. Their eyes looked first to their leader the Reverend Alfarr Odinsson before they'd act. The preacher spoke little to Elsworth that first day, speaking more with Captain Taylor in quiet words said between horseback and the side of his wagon.

The settlers had also hired on a small but experienced band of teamsters, led by Jamie Mitchell. Elsworth made eyes at Mitchell a few times during the day; the necessities of their work, however, precluded interaction during the daylight hours. And so it was on their first night out from Abilene that Jake Elsworth approached the campfire around which Jamie Mitchell and his fellow teamsters were enjoying chuck wagon chicken with a whiskey chaser.

"It's me, Jamie. Longhorn Jake." Elsworth spoke as he stepped from the darkness around their fire to join them. Due to their numbers, the settlers had camped within sight of the Fort itself; Mitchell had made his own camp for the teamsters in turn within sight of the settlers.

"I heard the Bear had knocked you into next week!" Mitchell said and handed Jake a plate. "I'm surprised you could join us this early."

"I'm mighty appreciative of the food," Elsworth said. "I didn't have the chance to provision my own."

"Bloody Taylor mentioned it when he was talking down to me," remarked Mitchell.

"Better not let him hear you use that name," Jake Elsworth said. "That man isn't known for his temperance."

The other teamsters murmured among themselves as they all sat and ate upon the events of the day. In particular, talk began to focus upon the availability of Odinson's daughter Freydis.

"Healthy, silent, with child bearin' hips and a beauty not seen in these parts outside a cathouse," said one of Mitchell's men emboldened by liquor. "Sign me up for their religion!"

"What is their faith, anyway?" asked Jamie Mitchell. "I ain't seen much in the ways or signs of a cross."

"With some protestant faiths," Jake Elsworth said, "It's considered sacrilegious to display religious icons."

"That could be it," said Mitchell. "Don't make a lick of sense but that could be it."

After their meals Mitchell broke out whiskey and cider to celebrate the beginning of the long journey ahead. Pilgrim's Peak was a great distance away in North Dakota, several hundred miles as the crow flies and certainly a few months away given the practicalities of traveling the trails at this time of year.

"Don't it strike you as odd they're not approaching it from the north?" asked Mitchell in time.

"It did," said Jake Elsworth from the bottom of his cup. "But I'm in no mood or position to question more than what is before me. I'll do my job, earn my pay and find somewhere else to roam. I'm done with Kansas."

As the pair continued to talk into the night, music could be heard coming from the settlers. To Jake Elsworth their folk instruments had a haunting quality with wooden pipes, drums and a curiously melodic chant perplexing yet alluring to his ears. The men sat and sang songs of their own. Jake lay staring at the majesty of the night sky as Jamie Mitchell struck a harmonica tune.

"These stars, they are for you and me," Jake said.

※ ※ ※

They travelled west for a week, they followed the trails northward through the last few counties before crossing the line to the territories of Nebraska and the Dakotas. They would not see a major settlement again until Ogallala once they left Kansas, that town met this trail, a stop for the recently finished continental railroad and the Pony Express. The land along the way was even and lush, bountiful with the fruits of labor the farmers produced. Healthy crops of corn, grapes and watermelon populated the roadside along the wide and well-worn trail, their campgrounds often among low rises and depressions in the otherwise flat earth with even trees and long grass.

Each passing year Jake Elsworth had noticed the trails becoming more like macadam roads, reaching as veins across the states in which they traversed. "Soon," he had said to Mitchell on one such evening, "there will come a day where men and women will travel freely. And on that day my friend, you and I will be looking for a new line of work."

"I think your time in the saddle has made you a dreamer," Mitchell replied from around the campfire.

The next week saw their wagon train continue along the Great Plains of Nebraska. Mostly oblivious to the possibility of Indian or other raiders attacking, the settlers continued with their daily chores and journey unabated in spirit.

It was a different matter for Jake Elsworth and Captain Robert Taylor. The pair, despite their dislike of one another, had taken to frequent conferrals and discussions on horseback, organizing Mitchell's men into an impromptu milita.

It was in this atmosphere of tension that once again Taylor and Elsworth discussed matters of security the next Friday morning.

"I don't like this," said Captain Taylor. "Those tall grasses, that ridge and those trees ahead are positioned just right for a dry gulch to the road."

"Maybe we should just burn it all down," Jake Elsworth said in nervous jest. The men paused and exchanged glances for a while before Elsworth again spoke. "You're right, we should send someone ahead."

"Appreciate you volunteering, Jake," said the disreputable Captain. "Godspeed and good luck."

Jake made his way to stand beside his horse and made ready for his approach. "I'm sorry boy," he told Tucker as he checked the loads and barrel of his two revolvers. "I'll be back as soon I can be."

Jake had originally purchased a single firearm and only under duress and ridicule from his fellows. The Remington .36 calibre Beals Navy revolver had saved his life on a few occasions since.

Admittedly only in one instance he had to fire the weapon. The other .44 Army service revolver he received as a parting gift from a former cowhand and good friend Lee Adams, a man some fifteen years his senior who'd passed away from cholera soon after Jake's thirty-fifth birthday.

"Confound it," Jake said under his breath as he soft-footed it low, along the ridge to the right. "I pray I don't have to shoot a man again. Or an Indian."

The trees provided better cover than Jake had hoped for, he made his way around the top of the ridge peering down from the top of the rise. After taking a few minutes for his senses to adjust, he noticed a lone Indian crouched low, facing the suspect straight of the road.

"He's not alone," said Elsworth to himself. "There's bound to be more."

Jake peered across the distant road and to the other rise to the side, seeing much to his surprise a large bundled pile of tree timber, held back by a series of ropes controlled by several more Indians.

"I'll be damned," said Jake after noting their positions. "I've never heard of their kind using such a tactic before."

The mystery deepened further when Jake spotted a taller man, dressed much as the Vaqueros did in Texas. This man conferred with the Indians in what Jake took to be English, one Indian in particular nodding and speaking softly with animated hands.

"I'd better get back to Taylor," said Jake. "And quick!"

As Jake stood and turned he almost bumped into a tall man dressed in black, who cried aloud with surprise, falling back onto the seat of his pants. Jake surprised himself as he drew the gun and pointed it directly toward the startled Monsignor.

"Father!" cried out the Mexican man from the other ridge.

With a whoop and a holler the remaining Indians sprang into action, the one nearest to Jake running toward him with tomahawk at the ready. A single shot rang out but not from Jake's weapon. Captain Taylor revealed his position on the far side of the ridge as he felled another Indian with his Sharps. Jake fired as the Indian leapt toward him, his hesitation to shoot swept aside by the look he saw in his opponent's eyes. The bullet struck the charging Indian in the chest, Elsworth stepped to the side and discharged another round into his attacker's back.

Still the man pressed, screaming at Elsworth as he corrected his path and leapt onto the cowboy. The pair went to the ground, the Indian possessed by a violent savagery as he beat Jake's face with fist and wood. Jake screamed as he wrestled with the Indian. The cowboy struggled to shoot again, unable to raise his .36 pistol as the Indian pinned both arms with his knees. Only another ring from Taylor's rifle ended the matter, the round caught Jake's attacker in the throat and knocked the fight from him.

Jake Elsworth pushed the dead Indian from atop him, his eyes meeting those of the narrow-eyed priest still nearby.

"May God forgive you," said the priest in accented English. "For you know not what you do."

"Don't move, Father," said Jake as he stood. "I'm no religious man so I ain't losing sleep over anything that might happen."

"More that you would," said the priest. Before any words could be uttered the priest charged Jake much as the Indian previously had with a swiftness that took the trail rider by surprise. Jake had just enough time to utter a single curse as he was struck hard on the back of the head, unable to bring his pistol to bear upon a man of God.

Monsignor Gregoire Laurent stood over the felled Elsworth, unable to bring a killing blow. "This man knows not our struggle, Father," he said. "Forgive us our trespasses."

※ ※ ※

Jake Elsworth awoke sometime after the end of the battle. Unknown to him, Captain Taylor had taken command of the twelve or so teamsters, and armed they had taken to the left ridge. By the time Elsworth revealed himself on the right, Taylor took decisive action and gave the order to open fire. In the heat of the battle some six Indians were killed with the far-traveling Vaquero and the Monsignor escaping prosecution. Taylor presumed the pair had been the instigators of the ambush and at once began to formulate in his mind reasons for the skulduggery.

"Clearly," he thought, "these men are deserters or Mexican spies. Perhaps the disguise of a priest was part of their plan?"

The casualties among his own men had been light, only two injuries. As a result of shooting from just one man. It was that Vaquero, a marksman as well as a mastermind.

"Where's Elsworth?" Captain Taylor cried from horseback. "I last saw him on the far ridge!"

Jamie Mitchell nodded and ordered his men to fan out across the area and search for him. By the time they found Elsworth he had already awoken, he sat and cradled his sore head next to the dead Indian.

"About time you boys got here," Jake said. "As soon as my world stops spinning I'll be right as rain."

Two of Mitchell's men helped Elsworth to his feet, with the search concluded, preparations were made for the wagon train to resume its journey.

❋ ❋ ❋

The next few weeks were a nervous time as the wagon train continued farther north across Nebraska. Emboldened by their military-like encounter, Captain Robert Taylor took on the role of a tyrant. He frequently gave orders to Mitchell's men, often without consulting Jamie Mitchell directly as he had done before the incident.

This change of relationship did not sit well with Jamie Mitchell.

"Do we look like Union soldiers?" Mitchell said to Jake as the pair sat alone around their fire. "I'm doing this as a favor to McCoy, I'm headed to Deadwood once we're done with this."

"Not so loud!" Jake said as he cradled his head in his arms. "My head still aches and I'm not sure how I'd feel with it parted from my shoulders."

"Have you tried talking to those settlers?" said Mitchell. "I've had some of the strangest conversations and none of them ain't been too theological."

"I've kept my distance," said Jake. "I just figure it's smarter that way."

Jamie Mitchell adjusted his position to sit closer to the fire, his strong and broad shoulders shivering. "Something just ain't right with these folk Jake," he said. "And I'll be damned if I don't put my finger on it."

Later that night, Jamie Mitchell decided to go speak with their leader about the budding situation with Taylor. Jake Elsworth decided that he'd be better off with a full-night's sleep and left the talking to those keen to engage in it.

The next morning Jamie Mitchell was strangely silent, his eyes distant as if transfixed upon things that he alone could see.

"I don't want to talk about it," he said to Elsworth when taxed on the matter. "Suffice to say the sooner we get to Dakota, the sooner I'm out of here."

※ ※ ※

Their journey across the plains of Nebraska was for the most part uneventful. Their supplies were holding out much as expected; already the camp rations at night had shifted away from salted meats and toward beans and corn.

Now and again, Jake would discover what could only be described as sabotage. An unbraced wagon wheel here, untethered cattle threatening to wander there, suspicions of night time visitors despite Taylor's effort to organize armed patrols and sentries. On two separate occasions Jake found curious tracks within shooting distance of their camp, tracks that could have come from some sort of snake or from ropes being dragged.

"I'll be damned if I can make sense of it," Jake said on the third occasion he observed the tracks. "What kind of animal makes these sorts of tracks?"

Rumor had already begun to work its social poison among the men. Jake began to hear stories from the other teamsters, of secret meetings among the settlers with strange lights and golden masks whenever a grove of trees was nearby. Jake rediscovered his passion for drinking, joining a mostly silent and sullen Mitchell in an impromptu tradition of late night soakings.

Autumn threatened to give way to winter as they hit the Dakota territories. The verdant plains slowly transformed into a dustier and colder clime as the wagon train wound its way toward the badlands.

"As I told you before," Jake said to Captain Taylor one frosty Monday morning, "this is a bad time of year to be heading through White River. If we had come at another time . . ."

"And as I said last time Elsworth," said Taylor with roused displeasure, "I don't give a damn for ifs. Take your place and scout ahead."

"All right, but I'm telling Saint Peter to cross you off the list if I get there first," Jake Elsworth said.

Even in the times before settlement, most Indian tribes had shunned this landscape. To this day some Sioux and Lakota made homes in isolated pockets, living on what few remaining Bison could be found. Taylor had prepared for such an eventuality, issuing extra ammunition and arms to the teamsters as well as some of the traveling settlers. "Don't shoot until I give the order," Taylor shouted. "Unless you see the whites of their eyes."

Jake paid Captain Taylor's trigger-happy attitudes little heed, the memories of that dead savage still upon his mind. "Take me out of my paleface clothes," he muttered to Tucker as they rode together between the buttes, "and even you wouldn't mull over the difference."

At the juncture of the Green and White rivers, there was much excitement as their wagon train came across another encampment. Jake noted right away that their tents were more military than teepee.

"I see Indians," said Captain Taylor in haste. "Ready your guns, best not to take our chances!"

"You might want to hold your horses," said Elsworth with a smile. "I'm seeing a bald man dressed in too fine a suit and those others certainly aren't Sioux."

The initial apprehension between them dispelled; the wagon train and encampment shared a night in common together.

Their leader among their group was a Professor Marsh, who invited some of their number to join them for drink, pipe and conversation.

"We're on an expedition from Yale," he explained. "We're headed back east once we're finished here."

"What kind of work are you in, Professor?" Jake asked.

"Palaeontology," said Marsh. "I dig things from the earth and make sense of them. Pray tell, where is your flock headed?"

"We're headed north to a place not far from Turtle Mountain," Jake said. "But we're not part of their flock, just hired help to get them there."

The Reverend Odinsson had refused the invitation to join Marsh's group politely, sending his regards through Elsworth. Curiously, it was only one of the few times the pair had spoken directly.

"I guess a man of God and a man of Science can sometimes stove their disagreements," Professor Marsh said. "Still, give my best to Father Odinsson when you next see him."

"I'd not bother," said Captain Taylor as he stood to take his leave for the evening. "He's a man of few words and limited understanding. Don't be too late now, Elsworth."

The embers around the expedition fire grew dim as Jake and the Professor spoke on into the night. Professor Marsh had taken to drawing in the earth with a stick, doing his best to recreate what Jake had described to him.

"Like that, you say?" Professor Marsh said.

"No, these marks were wider and straighter than that," Jake said rising with some effort. "They were more wider on one end and as if there was some sort of bulk being dragged."

"I've not heard of any such animal that makes such tracks," Marsh said. "If you manage to capture or kill one, I'm sure the University would be very interested."

After more drink and conversation Jake Elsworth returned to his own camp nearby, his mind already beginning to formulate a plan.

"I want you to help me catch it," Jake said to Jamie Mitchell that next night around their fire. "That Yale fellah said that there's good money in it."

"Enough with your words," Jamie Mitchell said with an uncommon vehemence. "Stop this foolish talk now before you get us all killed!"

"If it's Taylor that you're worried about," said Jake, "I'm sure we can come to some sort of arrangement."

"I'll have no part of this," Jamie said as if settling the matter. "And if you know what's good for you, you'll get this foolish notion out of your head!"

※ ※ ※

Jake started to see things more clearly over the next few days as they continued through the badlands. He'd seen it by accident that next morning while preparing his saddle, a mark like a brand or tattoo on the arm of his friend Jamie Mitchell. It reminded Jake of the writings of the Chinese as much as it did the pictures he had seen of an Indian tribe. Jake did not recall seeing this on Mitchell before, who had not served in the Army during the War. Jake began to see this mark upon a good portion of the settlers and even the Preacher's own daughter Freydis now that he looked.

"What queer religion do these settlers revere?" Jake found himself asking. "And why has Mitchell and some of his men joined their number?"

Then there were the birds and other animals that seemed to fall silent within the presence of the wagon train. Even the vultures and eagles gave their band a wide berth overhead, signs and portents that Jake only wished he had paid attention to before.

"This be no mere religion these folks embrace," he said to Tucker ahead of their number later that afternoon. "This is the Devil's brood!" His horse had been nervous and quiet for most of the trip, Jake had previously attributed that behavior to the delicate matter of Tucker's growing age.

"I'm sorry I didn't listen to you boy," Jake said as an apology. "But I'm going to make all of this right."

❋ ❋ ❋

On orders from the Captain, Jake had ridden ahead to choose the camping spot and make the necessary arrangements. That night the wagon train drew to a halt in between two buttes, making camp by a small creek that flowed there by the trailside with a nearby grove. Captain Taylor gave the order to offload the wagons early; their camp was well and truly established before nightfall.

"I feel the fool for agreeing to this," said Robert Taylor as he and Jake met after supper. "But I'd be lying if I said I too hadn't noticed those tracks."

"I've given thought to this Rob," said Jake as his wheels turned. "And I've got us a plan to catch this beast."

"You're quite the ranny," said Captain Taylor. "If anyone can bring this thing to bear, it's Longhorn Jake."

"Has the good father Odinsson turned in for the night?" asked Jake.

"I've one of Mitchell's men watching him," Taylor said. "One that don't sport any tattoos."

"Good," said Jake as he made the final preparations. "We're ready."

❋ ❋ ❋

"It's time," said Captain Taylor as he awoke Jake Elsworth.

"I barely slept a wink," Jake said. "Has the good father gone out then?"

"He has," said Captain Taylor as he loaded his Sharps and toyed with his belt. "Word is that he and several of his followers made out to that grove of trees yonder, like you reckoned."

"I'll gather the men," said Jake as he loaded both of his pistols. "It's time we sort ourselves some bad eggs."

The pair crept in near silence, signaling to the six other loyal teamsters. Each of them carried a gun of some sort, four pistols and two single-barrel shotguns as well as the weighted rope. Jake's own lariat was a matter of reputation; he'd earned his name as one of the greatest Longhorn wranglers Kansas had ever seen.

Each came at the lone grove of trees equidistant to one another, careful not to alert the Reverend and his men.

Jake Elsworth could not believe his eyes as their group crept upon the clearing, a sight that he could not have imagined even in his most moonstruck moments.

At first Jake had mistaken it for a tree in the clearing, for the way in which the two limbs moved about like whips. Odinsson's daughter lay at the foot of the thing naked, playing wooden pipes to which the other settlers danced in an ecstatic sway.

"Now!" cried Jake Elsworth as he gave the signal and threw his lasso. The other men cast their own lariats, none were as deft as Jake in finding their marks.

The thing howled with rage, opening a mouth on its head-like appendage and shrieking louder than any animal they had ever heard. They managed to bind around one of its two arms and legs with the ropes, Jake's own lariat growing tighter around what must have been its head.

"Pull harder, get it under control!" Jake ordered as he struggled to control his rope.

The thing lashed with its remaining free whip-like arm, striking one of Mitchell's men by the brainpan with its end. He let out a terrible cry as his scalp was knocked clean off with his hat, eyes gone wild as he passed from the sudden violence.

Stirrings were heard from the wagon camp, men and women gathering what they could in their hands and heading as a mob in the grove's direction.

"They're coming!" cried Captain Taylor who already shot in their direction and felled a few followers. "Get that thing under control!"

Jake did his best to direct his men; however, they lacked the experience to do the job properly.

"Where's the preacher?" Jake hollered as he stepped in to tie the beast. "Tell him we'll kill his pet unless he calls the flock off!"

"Beware," cried a hoarse and loathsome voice. "I shall feast upon your souls!"

Jake watched with horror as the leathery thing began to shrink in size; he struggled to maintain his lasso around the creature's neck. What had once been as tall as a wagon shrank down to a man, adopting the features of the preacher Odinsson!

"I shall strip the flesh from your bones, Jake Elsworth," said Odinsson. "How dare you oppose my will!"

Jake gave his answer in bullets, drawing both pistols and shooting the Icelandic preacher where he stood. Freydis leapt to her father's defence, two of the bullets piercing her breast. Jake stopped firing at once and raced to her side.

"What have you done?" Odinsson shrieked and transformed again, losing the cowboy's rope around his neck to rise up beside Jake. "It was not her time!"

Jake's eyes were on Freydis as he held her. She struggled to speak but could not. As the bullets took their toll, Freydis looked upon Jake Elsworth with a relief and died.

Jake arose with a fury of his own, spinning on his heels to see an even more terrible sight. The mob had reached the grove; they beat, grasped and rendered at the remaining teamsters. The free men fought back, their own morale browbeaten as the settlers charged them unfazed by the smell of gunpowder and the death of their comrades.

Jamie Mitchell was among the mob, his eyes dulled and distant with tears as he smote with an axe.

"Retreat!" Captain Taylor enacted his own back-down as he rode from the scene, his horse sure-footed as they disappeared beyond the corner of the butte.

Jake closed his eyes as he heard the last of the screams from his fellows. He sat upon a knee and shook; he held the limp body of Freydis and felt something sharp whip his right shoulder and yank him to the ground.

Jake had little time to cry out as he felt the brand of the creature scorched upon his arm. He now saw a harsh and yellowing mark upon it.

"You are now my cattle!" the monstrous preacher bellowed. "You too shall serve my purpose."

Jake Elsworth screamed, his rage-fuelled mind already battling the mystic pull of that yellowing sign. Not yet beaten Jake stood and ran, whistling for his horse.

He swung his fists to and fro, striking those who crossed his path. Tucker's mane and reins soon fell into Jake's grasp. He faded to unconsciousness as his horse assailants rode into the night.

※ ※ ※

The sun struggled to warm the earth; the chill of an early winter gripped the heart of the badlands. Tucker nudged the dying Jake Elsworth where he lay. Jake wasn't sure as to how many days had passed without food or water.

"I'm dying," Jake said weakly to his horse. "Go on and be free." The lone cowboy drifted between these lands and the next, seeing with inner and outer eye lands and places beyond description.

By night, Jake was sure he was to breathe his last. The call of that mark grew in his mind, a fervent devil that weakened his will and colored his soul.

Jake did not even stir when he saw a pair of figures standing above him like angels.

"Have you lost anything, my son?" Monsignor Laurent bent his knee.

"My soul, father. I fear I am losing my soul." Jake's words were soft in comparison to the harshness of his wind burnt face and his cracked lips.

"Drink this my friend," said the second man, the Vaquero. "My name is Santiago Bandera. We have ridden for many months from Carcosa, my home destroyed by that blasphemous thing who wears a man's skin."

Jake did his best to sit up, feeling something that tasted much like honey poured down his throat.

"Rest now, we will break camp in the morn," said Monsignor Laurent. "Then we ride. God's work still needs to be done."

"I swear to you now, Father," said Jake as he felt the Monsignor's concoction take effect. "I will see that monstrous thing rent from the earth but not before I teach it that Dominion was not something that God said in jest!"

Incident at Dagon Wells

By Ron Shiflet

Lonnie Otwell looked over his shoulder, keeping a close watch on the Comanche war party that had for two days been trailing him and his weary companions. Turning in the saddle, he looked at Tom Hawkins and said, "It's the damnedest thing I ever saw."

The red-bearded man took to whom Otwell spoke, took off his hat and fanned himself, saying, "Yeah, they could've taken us at any time during the past two days. Think they're just toying with us?"

"Who knows how those fucking savages think?" interrupted the perpetually hoarse voice of Jamie "Frog" Jenkins.

Otwell smiled and said, "My God, he lives and breathes!"

Hawkins joined in. "That's the first word I've heard him speak since that Comanche bullet took off a piece of his ear."

"Well," said Otwell, "he may have said nothing but he sure left a wet, stinky trail for those bastards to follow."

Frog spat on the ground in disgust. "You're awfully chipper for a couple of dead men. You two go right on making sport of me. It warms my heart to know that I've made your final hours more pleasant."

Otwell wiped his grimy face with a stained bandana and smiled at Frog. "Why not laugh?" he asked. "If we're fated to die then I expect there's not much in hell we can do about it. Might as well laugh."

"Sure," Hawkins agreed. "I don't figure there'll be much of that where we're going."

"Speak for yourself," Frog replied, peering back at the barely perceptible Indians in the distance.

No one said anything for the next several moments, each man lost in his own inscrutable thoughts, perhaps wondering how they had found themselves in such terrible circumstances. Things had been carefree back in Ft. Worth just a few days earlier. But that had been before the fateful evening when the three of them had engaged in a drunken shootout at the White Elephant Saloon with some cowhands from Waco. The culmination of that evening had left three men and a woman dead. One of the dead men had been a town constable and the deceased woman had been a very popular saloon hostess named Big Nell.

Following this deadly event, the three had lit out of town and had been riding west ever since. There had been talk of laying low in New Mexico but nothing had been decided except for the need to keep moving. Otwell was certain that any posse after them was half-heartedly into their work at best—the town constable not being particularly well liked by the citizens of Cowtown—and were only going through the motions because Big Nell had made some influential friends during her stay in town.

But the Comanche, they were another story entirely. The three men should've been dead by now, based on precedent but for some unexplained reason the Indians seemed to be herding them and not making a concerted effort to overtake and kill them. It was damn strange business.

Tom squinted his steely blue eyes and looked to the west. "Looks like a dust storm's going to blow in."

Frog noted the hazy red horizon ahead and said, "Maybe we can lose those Injuns in it."

"Yeah," Otwell answered, "or find ourselves smack dab in the middle of them."

Frowning, Frog retorted, "You got a better idea?"

Hawkins looked expectantly at Otwell, more than just a little bit interested in his partner's answer.

Otwell removed his sweat-stained hat and wiped his brow. "Not much of one," he said. "But better than wandering around in all that blowing sand that's coming."

"Well, let's hear it then!" Hawkins exclaimed, willing to grasp at whatever straw might be available."

Otwell remained silent for a moment, frowned and said, "You boys ever hear of Dagon Wells?"

The question drew a blank look from Frog but the cheeks—at least the part of them not concealed by Tom's red bushy beard—turned fish belly white. Frog caught his pal's expression, frowned and said, "What? Someone care to tell me why Tom's all of a sudden got piss running down his leg?"

Hawkins ignored Frog's jibe. He turned to Otwell and said, "Damn you, you ain't serious are you?"

Otwell glared at him and replied. "It's the closest shelter we're likely to find in these parts. We're just a hop and a skip from it, if memory serves."

Hawkins spat tobacco juice onto the rocky ground. "That's an idea you'd do well to forget."

"Just a minute!" Frog protested. "What's this Dagon Wells that's got Tom so spooked?"

"No shame in wanting to stay clear of that place," Hawkins whispered. "It's just good sense."

Otwell rolled his eyes and smiled at Frog. "You want to hear what it *was* or what some *claim* it to be?"

"What I *want* is to get somewhere's safe," he answered. "Our horses need rest and I'm not feeling any too spry myself."

"Somewhere's safe?" Hawkins mumbled.

"What?" Frog snapped.

Shaking his head no, Hawkins said, "Then you want to steer clear of that place."

Frog started to cut loose with a stream of invective but was forestalled by Otwell's explanation.

"Dagon Wells," Otwell said, "was part of the stage line. It was a way station like any other such place."

"Only . . ." Hawkins interrupted.

"*Only*," Otwell sighed, "some bad things supposedly happened there."

"Supposedly my ass," grunted Hawkins, shifting his weight as his horse grew restless.

"You want to tell this?" Otwell asked.

"Somebody better do it soon," Frog croaked, glancing over his shoulder. "Those Comanche are getting closer."

"Anyway," Otwell continued, "some bad things happened at the way station and now people use the place to spook gullible old women like Tom here."

Hawkins shot Otwell a poisonous look.

"Damn it, what sort of bad things?" Frog asked, his impatience growing.

"Does it matter?" Otwell asked. "It's just an abandoned old way station. That's all it is."

"Abandoned old slaughterhouse," Hawkins stated.

Frog looked at Otwell, still waiting for an answer.

"Someone went crazy there and murdered some folks," said Otwell in frustration. "Ain't that pretty much how it went, Tom?"

It was Hawkins' turn to smile. "I reckon that's it . . . up to a point."

"Jesus Diddly Christ!" blurted Frog. "Just tell me what the hell happened before I die of old age."

"Not much chance of *that*," said Otwell and Hawkins in unison as the first blast of red sand blew in and the Indians picked up their pace.

"Stay close," Otwell urged. "The wells are just a short ride ahead."

"Damn you!" Hawkins yelled. "You've been leading us there all along."

"I didn't see that we had much choice," Otwell yelled in reply, struggling to be heard over the howling wind.

"Damn you to hell!" Hawkins answered, his voice unheard behind the scarf he had lowered over his mouth.

The three riders led their horses through where a large gate once stood, the only entrance into the adobe-walled way station. The sun was a crimson, all but obscured orb that like a whore seemed to promise much but deliver little in the way of comfort. "This place is like a goddamned fort!" Frog exclaimed, getting down from his mare.

"Any sign of those Comanche?" Hawkins asked nervously, pulling free his rifle as he hit the ground.

"Who can tell?" Frog asked. "I can't see shit through this blowing sand."

Otwell dismounted and cursed the grit that stung his face. He walked to his two partners and grinned. "No need to worry about those Injuns while we're here. They're more afraid of this place than Tom is."

"I always said they were savages," Hawkins replied. "I never said they was stupid."

"Let's get these horses some water and then get out of this blowing hell," Frog offered. "This place looks to be in pretty good shape to be abandoned."

"I don't see no damn well," Hawkins groused, surveying the immediate area."

"Other side of the building," Otwell answered.

He saw Frog and Hawkins give him an odd look and quickly continued. "I've been here before, you idiots. That's why I knew how to get here. Tom, check out the inside and see how it looks . . . and watch out for snakes."

Hawkins appeared reluctant and Frog said, "Go water our horses and fill the canteens. I'll take a look-see inside."

Hawkins smiled gratefully and led his and Frog's horses to the other side of the way station. He found a well, protected from the elements by three adobe walls and roof. He watched Otwell approach and grinned at him.

"Well, sonofabitch," Hawkins said, happy for a brief respite from the wind and sand.

"Now ain't this a damn sight better than dealing with those Injuns?" Otwell asked.

Hawkins grinned sheepishly and said, "I reckon so, but I thought it was Dagon *Wells* not Well."

"There's a second one over there," Otwell replied, pointing to a square, rock lined well house. "Somebody's covered the opening with sandstone slabs and painted some crazy symbols on it."

"Probably those damn savages," Hawkins said.

"Could be," Otwell replied.

The two men watered and fed the horses, making small talk while finishing the mundane but essential chores. When finished, they had a smoke in the shelter of the adobe walls surrounding the well and wondered how Frog would find the condition of the main building. They soon received an answer when their companion sauntered up with an odd expression on his face.

"I thought you said this place was abandoned, Lonnie," he yelled, straining to be heard over the wind.

"Someone's living here?" Hawkins asked.

"Someone *was*," Frog answered, joining them in the relative shelter of the three walls.

Otwell frowned, nervously drumming his fingers on the butt of his holstered Army Colt. "What's *that* supposed to mean?"

Frog finished rolling a smoke of his own and said, "There *was* somebody living here."

"But not now?" Hawkins asked.

"No, definitely not now," Frog croaked. "The inside is in good shape and pretty clean . . . considering."

"Considering what?" Otwell asked, his impatience growing.

"Considering the owner hanged himself several months ago by the look of things."

Hawkins turned pale.

"He still inside?" Otwell asked.

"Yep, just sort of hanging around I guess," Frog chuckled.

"That ain't funny, Frog," Hawkins said.

Otwell sighed and said, "I guess we better go have a look."

"Yeah," Hawkins grunted, "seeing as how this hell hole is living up to its reputation."

"Just shut up with that nonsense!" Otwell snapped. "Who knows why a fellow would do something like that? Probably just some crazy old hermit."

The deceased occupant of Dagon Wells was not the typical old hermit that Otwell had expected to find. The corpse was dressed well—considering the environs—and was a fairly well educated man if his taste in reading material was any indication. There were books on astronomy, mythology and several others written in languages that none of the three cowboys recognized. The corpse itself was little more than dried skin stretched over bones—the dry arid climate beginning a mummification process—and the noxious smell one would normally associate with death had all but dissipated over the weeks.

The cowboys had passed through a large sparsely furnished main room to get to the smaller one that was obviously what the dead man had utilized as his sleeping quarters.

"Frog," Otwell said, "climb up on that stool there and cut him down."

"I *found* him," Frog replied. "You or Tom should do the honors."

"For Christ's sake!" Otwell exclaimed, "I'm riding with a couple of old women."

"You're free to part company and clear on out," Hawkins growled, surprising even himself with the outburst. "I don't need no nursemaid."

Stunned, Frog's eyes grew wider as he shot a glance at Otwell. Any fool could read the look of danger on the man's face and it was usually a prelude to violence. He watched Hawkins inch his hand toward his holster and decided to act. Stepping between the two men, he grasped Hawkins by the shoulder and said, "Take it easy Old Hoss, Lonnie didn't mean nothing by it." He shot a glare at Otwell and said, "Did you Lonnie?"

Otwell remained silent for a moment but Frog could see his muscles relax slightly. "It's just those damn Injuns and this storm. Hell, it's got us all on edge."

"Yeah," Lonnie replied, his answer seeming to mollify Hawkins.

Hawkins started to speak but Lonnie interrupted, saying, "Frog's right, we just need to rest a spell. Frog, how about we both get this *thing* out of here? There's a storage building out back we can put him in until the weather eases up enough for us to plant him."

"Good idea," Frog said, thankful that the crisis had been averted. "Tom, why don't you see if this fellow's got any identifying papers around here while me and Lonnie take him out back?"

"Sure," Hawkins answered. "I'll see what I can find in the other room."

Hawkins went to begin his search as Otwell and Frog lowered the corpse to the floor and wrapped it in a gritty blanket from the bed. With that completed, they hauled the dead man outside and placed him in the small out building.

"Thank God *that's* taken care of," Frog said as he and Otwell slammed the front door and barred it behind them.

Otwell brushed at his clothes and watched red sandy granules fall to the floor. "Hell yeah," he replied. "My tongue's got enough topsoil on it to plow."

Frog beat at his clothing and stomped his boots on the floor. Glancing at Hawkins, he asked, "Did you turn up anything of interest?"

Hawkins remained seated at a rough-hewn table in the center of the room and pointed to a book. The wind continued to howl as he picked up the object and opened it. Grinning, he said, "Lonnie was right. The old fellow was crazier than a shithouse rat."

"You got *that* just from reading a book?" Frog asked.

Otwell smiled at his partner's ignorance but said nothing.

"It's a journal," Hawkins answered. "Looks like he just started it a few days before killing himself. I looked for others but didn't find nothing."

"So," Otwell asked, "did he write down what had him so worked up?"

Hawkins slid the book across the table and pointed to the last entry. He watched Lonnie look closely at it and frown. "You were dead on about the sonofabitch being crazy."

Lonnie moved his lips silently as he read the words in the crabbed writing.

There is no recourse left to me except ending my life. The THINGS are at the roof again and I hear others burrowing in the soil below. My few pathetic defenses against them are ultimately inadequate and I prefer a clean death to their hellish and blasphemous touch . . . I still shudder when recalling what they did to the mules. Thankfully the well remains sealed against one greater than those who assail me. The sky has changed again and I no longer know if there will be a return to normalcy . . . the noises are growing louder and my terror increases . . . God forgive me but I can hesitate no longer . . .

Frog read over Otwell's shoulder and frowned. "Is he writing about Injuns?"

Otwell shook his head in bemusement. "I don't *think* so. Never heard of them burrowing and they damn sure wouldn't kill the mules."

"Kill the mules?" Hawkins asked.

"Something got the man's mules," Frog replied.

"Besides," Otwell said, "that crazy talk about sealing the well against *one greater* proves the man was loco."

Looking worried, Hawkins asked, "Reckon someone better watch the horses?"

"You volunteering for the job?" Frog countered.

"Uh . . . no, just that stuff about the mules sort of got me to thinking."

"Believe me boys," Otwell said, "those Comanche wouldn't be caught dead near this place. The horses will be all right but we'll keep an eye on 'em if this storm blows over."

"Hey," Frog said, "I saw a sack of coffee over there. Tom, get that stove going and we'll be all set."

"You betcha," Hawkins replied, turning from the table.

The three cowboys drank coffee and rolled smokes for a while, none of them addressing the problem of their Comanche pursuers. It seemed enough to be relatively safe for the moment and drowsiness came quickly to the fatigued men. They had their bedrolls and each found a place on the floor of the big room, none of the three showing any inclination to use the dead man's bed.

The banshee wind continued to howl but the horses had been secured and sheltered as much as possible. Only a short time passed after extinguishing the coal oil lantern before the three men were asleep.

Hawkins woke a little after midnight and heard his companions snoring loudly. The wind was still blowing but seemed to have lessened in intensity. Feeling uneasy, Hawkins struggled to remember the strange nightmare he'd been having moments earlier. It was the damnedest thing because it didn't consist of the usual day to day imagery that normally filled his slumber. There were no mundane scenes of riding, herding cattle or card playing in some saloon. No, the dream had been filled with bizarre and monstrous creatures, massive and oddly designed structures and a nighted sky filled with constellations never viewed by him during his many nights on the open prairie. Hawkins shuddered at the recollection and listened closely as a low rumbling emanated from far away. Immediately upon its cessation, the wind died suddenly and completely as an ominous silence reigned over the area.

"What the hell?" he whispered, getting silently to his feet.

He moved quietly to the door and lifted the thick wooden bar. He heard someone stirring to his left and then the voice of Otwell asking, "Anything wrong?"

"Nothing Lonnie," he whispered. "The wind's stopped blowing and I need some air."

"Sure thing," Otwell answered. "Check on the horses while you're out there."

"Will do," Hawkins answered, leaving the way station and shutting the door gently behind him.

He knew that everything was wrong the second he looked around the area. "Sonofabitch," he gasped, staring in disbelief at the three moons in the midnight sky.

They were of varying size and color but none looked like the familiar one he had known since childhood. Hawkins pinched himself, thinking that he was perhaps still dreaming but the three eerie satellites remained in the sky. One of the orbs was a sickly yellow, another an unwholesome looking gray and the third was a pale hue of red. The moons floated in a sea of unfamiliar constellations.

In shock, Hawkins looked for other changes and was relieved to see the familiar adobe walls bordering the way station. His eyes scanned the perimeter and his heart sank as he realized that the horses were missing. "Got to tell the others," he mumbled, his heart pounding.

He started to cry out but his attention was drawn to what had been in the east. Dark flapping shapes moved erratically across the skyline, far too large for any birds with which he was familiar. He didn't know what the things were and liked the idea of their approach even less.

"Lonnie . . . Frog!" he yelled. "Get out here on the double!" He started to holler a second time but the door soon opened and Lonnie—with Frog on his heels—emerged into the eerily-illuminated night.

"Jesus Christ!" Frog exclaimed, taking in the changes that had been wrought while he slept.

Otwell's gaping mouth and bulging eyes communicated his feelings sufficiently without the need for words.

A loud discordant piping blasted forth from the sealed well, drawing the attention of the men. They stared in dismay as a violet beam of light shot from a small crack in the well-house and into the heavens.

"Good Lord!" Otwell gasped. "What has happened here?"

"Don't know," Hawkins replied. "What's making that awful music?"

"It's coming from the well," Frog offered.

"Thanks," Otwell answered. "You want to mosey over there and see what it is?"

"Not really," Frog said, trying to decide whether to focus on the well or the large flapping things in the sky.

It was decided by Hawkins who pointed a finger at the sky and said, "Them things are getting closer and they're bigger than hell."

"What's that one carrying?" Frog asked, focusing on the nearest one.

"Don't know," Otwell replied, raising his Winchester. "But I plan to bring the sonofabitch down."

He aimed but before he could fire, a shrill squawk echoed across the sky and his attention was diverted by another winged thing flying in from the north.

"Damn!" Hawkins exclaimed. "There's more of them."

Otwell and Frog looked to the north about the time Hawkins screamed, "Look out!" as he spied the plummeting object only seconds from impact.

The object landed about ten feet from Otwell with a horrendous splat, sending blood and gore flying in the immediate area. Frog retched as Otwell screamed, "That's my goddamn horse!"

Hawkins aimed his pistol at the dark flapping creature and fired two ineffectual shots, one miraculously striking the monster's massive orange beak and ricocheting harmlessly away.

"Jesus!" Otwell yelled. "Look at the size of that bastard."

"That ain't like no kind of bird I ever saw," Hawkins said, staring in disgust at the bits of flesh and bone that stuck to Otwell's clothing.

The men watched the monstrous winged creatures fly over, mindful that two other horses were gone as well. Nothing else dropped from the sky but something had caught Frog's notice and he failed to hear his companions speaking to him.

"Frog!" Otwell shouted, slapping him on the shoulder.

"Look at *that*," Frog whispered, pointing to the west.

Hawkins and Otwell turned their gaze and stared in disbelief. A huge structure comprised of cyclopean stone blocks had appeared on the plain while the men had been distracted by the flying creatures and the light and music from the sealed well.

"It looks like a pyramid," Hawkins stated.

"A what?" Otwell asked.

Hawkins looked at Otwell and sighed. "Like in them Bible stories. The Pharaohs had 'em built by slaves."

"Guess I missed that one," Otwell replied, wiping a hunk of horseflesh from his pants leg. "I don't reckon seeing it here is a *good* thing."

"This ain't good at all," Frog said. He started to continue when a low rumbling came from beneath the ground, causing it to shake and tremble. The slabs of sandstone covering the well crumbled into tiny pieces and dropped into the shaft. Much of the adobe wall surrounding the way station cracked and collapsed as well while many deep fissures appeared in the ground.

The three cowboys struggled to remain on their feet as fear coursed through their bodies. Soon the rumbling ended and their attention was again drawn to the until recently sealed well. A phosphorescent mist belched from the opening and hung in the air. The strange piping sounds no longer issued from the shaft but the sound of water lapping against the sides of the well was quite audible.

"What's thrashing around in there?" Hawkins asked, gripping the butt of his pistol.

"Something *damn* big," Frog said, stepping back toward the way station.

Otwell lunged forward and grabbed him by the arm. "Watch your damn step," he warned, pointing behind Frog.

Frog looked to his rear and Hawkins said, "You almost fell in it."

Frog stared at the gaping crack he had barely escaped falling into and mumbled, "Thanks."

"It ain't very wide," Otwell said, "but I can't see the bottom of it."

"Shit!" Hawkins cried. "What the hell's going on here?"

"Bad things," Frog answered, staring at Otwell. "Are these the sort of *bad things* that happened in those old tales about Dagon Wells?"

"Are you loco?" Otwell replied. "Have you ever heard stories about anything like *this*?"

"Sure," Hawkins snorted. "Three moons, giant birds, a musical well and one of them pyramids . . . seems pretty common to me."

"Go to hell!" Otwell growled, stepping toward Hawkins.

"Pardon me all to hell, Lonnie," Hawkins shot back. "Ain't this right where *you* wanted us to be?"

"Come on fellows," Frog pleaded. "Don't start this shit now. I say we get back inside and study on things from there."

He watched Otwell's eyes widen and then jerk his pistol as Hawkins looked on in horror. He started to yell but instead screamed in pain as something bit into his ankle, severing boot leather and cutting to the bone. Looking down, he saw a massive orange claw around his ankle and blood pouring from the wound. The claw was attached to a scaly, lengthy appendage about the width of his arm.

"Lonnie, do something!" he screamed, fumbling ineffectually

for his pistol.

Otwell fired two quick shots, one missing and the second ricocheting harmlessly off the claw's tough covering. "Oh shit!" he yelled as two lengthy eye-stalks rose up from the fissure and other crab-like creatures struggled to emerge from the jagged rift in the earth.

Hawkins came to life and began emptying his Colt at the large unnatural crustaceans. His face was pale as Frog's rasping shrieks cut through the night. A second creature latched onto Frog's arm and severed it with a sickening snap. Blood spurted from the severed limb and Frog's eyes rolled up in his head as he lost consciousness and collapsed.

Hawkins turned his gaze to Otwell who stood transfixed in shock. "Lonnie!" Hawkins screamed. "Let's get the hell inside!"

Otwell stared blankly at him, still mindlessly squeezing the trigger of his empty gun.

"Lonnie!" Hawkins yelled. "Move your ass!"

He watched Otwell take a step back as if he had all the time in the world. The crab-like creatures were still struggling over each other in an effort to leave the deep crack in the ground. Cursing, Hawkins holstered his pistol and rushed forward to pull Otwell away from the snapping claws just out of reach. He heard a loud flapping sound and tried to block it out as he reached for Otwell. Finally, his fingers grasped the dazed cowboy by the shirt sleeve and he was pulling him away when a loud shriek followed by the appearance of monstrous talons signaled the return of the hellish winged things they had seen earlier. There was a loud rip and Hawkins was left holding only a tattered piece of fabric as Otwell was carried into the unrecognizable sky.

"Jesus!" Hawkins moaned, turning to make a dash for the adobe building. He traveled only a few feet before tripping over a smaller crack in the shifting ground. He struggled to rise but stopped as another massive rumbling shook the area. The phosphorescent mist was now belching from the second well and to the west, the pyramidal structure was glowing brightly as if containing the sun.

Half-blind, Hawkins looked back in time to avoid a claw that missed him only by inches. He lurched to his feet and staggered to the partially open door of the way station. As Hawkins reached it, a noise—as if the clang of a loud gong—echoed across the flat land in all directions. The stone well-housing cracked sharply and collapsed outward as a wet and humongous webbed claw and scaly arm emerged slowly from the mist-spewing shaft.

"Oh Jesus!" Hawkins screamed, entering the way station and slamming the door behind him. The glow from the pyramid had turned the night into day and lit the inside of the building with its strange light.

He nearly collapsed as he stared into the withered and mummified face of the building's former occupant.

"Dagon comes," said the lich, somehow managing to speak without the presence of breath and functioning lungs. "Dagon comes . . . Dagon comes . . . "

Panicked, Hawkins smashed the empty pistol across the dead man's skull, causing it to crack. A hoard of small writhing insects fell to the floor and scurried to the shadows of the room. The mummy fell to the floor and lay still.

"Dagon comes?" Hawkins whispered, having no desire to meet the one for whom the wells were named. He walked aimlessly in circles, clutching his ears to block out the cacophonous sounds from outside. Claws raked along the cracked adobe exterior and perverse squawks sounded above the roof. Something hit the building with a loud thud and through the cracked window coverings the impossible stench of rotting flesh and stagnant water filled the room.

Hawkins gagged, leaning against the barred door and wondering what to do. Spying the discarded journal, he laughed hysterically and slammed it onto the table. He clutched a fountain pen and using the tiny amount of remaining ink, he began to write.

There ain't nothing for it but to kill myself. Them damned winged THINGS are on the roof and I hear claws tearing at the walls . . . I get sick when remembering what they did to my partners . . . the well is no longer sealed and Dagon comes . . . God forgive me but I can wait no longer . . .

One Year Later

The short, weasel-faced man got down from his horse. Squinting against the blowing sand, he yelled at his mounted companion. "They ain't following are they?"

"Don't see hide nor hair of any Injuns," answered the hawk-faced figure with the slouch hat.

"I told you! I told you!" the first man gleefully sang. "Them superstitious savages wouldn't be caught dead around here."

"Why's that Buster?" The second man asked, getting down from his horse.

"Well Wylie," Buster answered, "seems they think this area belongs to some ancient god and is cursed. Who knows? It's all a bunch of twaddle."

"What kind of curse," Wylie asked, straining to be heard over the howling wind.

"You know," Buster replied, opening the door to the abandoned way station. "A mess of bad things supposedly happened around here."

Wylie frowned. "You *sure* we're safe here?"

"Safer than we'd be with those Injuns," he answered, walking inside. "Besides, look how clean this place is. I'd say we don't have a thing to worry about."

"I hope you're right," Wylie answered. "I surely hope you're right.

AHIGA AND THE MACHINE

BY ROBERT J. SANTA

Sunrise bathed the river in soft shadows. The canyon sparkled with reflections, from the stone chips in the red walls, from the gently flowing water, from the sky itself. Ahiga relished in it as he splashed water on his face and chest. The warrior's fast was a difficult spiritual journey, but mornings such as the one that greeted his all-night prayers made it far easier.

His painted horse sleepily wandered through the scrub grass, eating with automatic ease. Ahiga's stomach prodded him for attention. Gone was the growling of the first day's denial, and it was a small matter for Ahiga to ignore the dull aches. He cupped his hands and scooped more water onto his face, letting his open mouth receive some of it. The water chilled his throat and belly and quieted its urgency, if only for a few moments.

Years earlier, when Ahiga left his family for the vision quest, the valley had seemed a place of fearful desolation. At thirteen summers, shadows jumped with invisible big cats and worse creatures of a boy's frightful imagination. At twenty and two, his warrior's heart loved the canyon for the same reason that caused him a week's worth of nightmares before.

He stood and dressed. Then he fitted the bit into the horse's mouth, which accepted it with dull complaint. With a great shock of mane in one hand and his weapons in the other, Ahiga leapt onto the horse's back. It nickered and came fully awake, protesting his weight as it had every time. But it was a good horse, strong and capable even after five years of bearing him, and let itself be guided by his knees and the reins. Together they walked upriver.

Ahiga rode in quiet contemplation, letting the horse lead him. They both startled as they stumbled upon a quail's nest. It squawked, transforming from camouflaged invisibility to flapping, fleeing chaos in an instant. Ahiga looked down and saw three eggs in the depression. His stomach shouted, lusting after both the eggs and their mother. Two more days, he told his belly. Two more and you will have your fill. Until then, be still and enjoy the canyon's peace.

Wind howled, high-pitched screeching as it sped between tight pillars and cracks in the walls. Ahiga felt nothing on his skin, his unbound hair not so much as fluttering. He wondered if a tornado had developed and craned around. The sky, a brilliant cloudless slate, was fast losing its orange and turning blue. No green, no clouds. It could not be a tornado. Yet the wind-whipping sound only became louder. Ahiga's shoulders tensed at whatever it was that approached.

The crash shattered the canyon's silence. Small animals, hidden in the shadows and rocks, dashed aside. Ahiga's horse tried to rear, but he leaned his weight forward to bring it back. He whispered calm words to it. The horse settled, even while the horrific crashing escalated and neared. It seemed to be coming from the top of the canyon, though the echoes made it difficult to tell.

A massive shadow fell upon him. At the canyon's lip, a great object sat upon the edge and blocked out the rising sun. Stone debris sprayed out, splashing into the river below, larger pieces bounding off the walls. The object teetered. It paused as if waiting for Ahiga to acknowledge its presence, then tipped and slid over the edge. It smashed into the canyon floor with much breaking of stone and rending of metal and stood on its side.

It was as large as a village and obviously a manufactured object. Very little of the natural world seemed to make up its outside, like the rifle Ahiga had taken from the soldiers the year before. It was shaped like the great, round leaves of the prairie cactus, the kind that flowered purple tufts. The thing was undoubtedly a machine, probably a transport like the railroad trains. But there were no tracks nearby; this machine must be able to move without them.

Who was inside, and did they survive the fall from the cliff? Ahiga urged his horse into the water. They swam, the current pushing them downstream several hundred yards away from the machine.

From the new angle, Ahiga could see the machine was badly damaged. A great gash tore through its side, like a rabbit with its guts removed and ready for the fire. Pieces of the machine hung from a broken section and smoldered. As he neared, he heard the hiss and crackle of fire, though he couldn't see it. The machine was ruined.

His horse shook its head and whinnied. It snorted hard three times, and Ahiga tried to smooth its quivering skin with his hands. There was much to be nervous about, even for a warrior. He dismounted and let the horse trot off downriver. It stopped by a succulent patch of greenery further on from where they crossed. He would reunite with it later, once he examined the destroyed machine.

Several paces away, he felt heat. The fire must be on the inside, for the metal skin of the machine radiated with it. But on the outside were long burn scars. It looked as if the machine were no more than a log that had been thrown into the bonfire and quickly removed. Ahiga walked around the machine and found that it was noticeably cooler, almost cold. He touched it with the tip of his spear; it clicked with the sound of metal on metal. When he pressed his palm to it, he felt the cold strength of steel.

The broken section behind the leaning machine made a sort of ramp, one with jagged edges and strange pieces hanging or sticking out. Ahiga could climb it, but he would need both hands. He leaned his rifle and spear against a great rock, touched the knife on his belt, and moved up the slope. Twice his hands closed on a sharp edge. The cuts were not severe, easy to ignore.

At the top of the climb, Ahiga stalled. There didn't seem to be a grip, and he would need to jump into the opening. He looked down upon a drop of at least six times his height, steeled the tightening in his loins, and leapt.

Ahiga landed with puma-like grace on a steeply-angled surface. He stayed upright but scrambled for something to halt his slide. He came up hard against a straight wall of metal and leaned against it. That's all there seemed to be for him to explore.

A section of the wall vanished, like morning mist touched by sunlight. A long, artificially-square tunnel ran down and away from him. At the base was a horrible thing, climbing up.

Ahiga scrambled back toward the outside slope. He rushed down, heedless of the jagged edges that caught his forearms and hands and once his thigh, that opened with flaring protest. He tripped and fell the last distance. The riverbed banks were soft, worn sand, and he landed on his belly with an outpouring of air that paralyzed him. A large stone was too near his head; had he landed a hand's length closer, his brains would be splattered all over it. Gasping for air that wouldn't come, distracted by the throbbing of his leg, spitting the taste of dirt from his mouth, Ahiga rolled over and looked back up the metal slope.

In the darkened tunnel, the monstrous thing was only a nightmare. Out in the quickly brightening day, Ahiga tried to blink to make the vision disappear. Surely such a creature as this offended the many gods, that they would never permit such a thing to exist.

He was first reminded of a spider, in that the thing had many legs that gripped the edges of the tunnel and opening. Yet they were flexible legs that seemed to have no bones. The thing's body began as a great, round shape, ending in a fluke-like tail. Centered in the body, surrounded by the flailing tentacles, a slavering maw dripped. It seemed to examine the world beyond the damaged machine, though it had no eyes. It turned its grotesque face toward Ahiga and seemed to stare at him. A limb emerged holding a shining ball of metal about the size of Ahiga's head. It sparkled with reflected sunlight, and then Ahiga realized the sun was behind the creature.

Like silent lightning, a beam of light shot straight down from the metal ball. Ahiga rolled to avoid it. The light struck the ground an arm's length from him. But unlike lightning, the light stayed. The thing moved the ball, and the light traced the ground, following Ahiga. Everywhere the light touch, the sand smoldered and scorched. He had no doubt that if the light touched him, it would burn through his flesh.

Ahiga raised himself onto hands and knees then dove for his weapons. His hand closed on the upper stock of his rifle. He tumbled, saw the light out of the corner of his eye, and raised the gun, pulling the trigger almost immediately. When the gunshot sounded, the thing reacted as if it had been struck, but Ahiga couldn't be certain for he aimed by instinct alone. It had such a large body—like a buffalo—and one bullet didn't seem like enough. Yet the thing's tentacles drooped, as if it were a quickly-wilting plant. The body rolled forward, tore open on the jagged metal of the slope, and dropped wetly to the ground.

He held the rifle aimed at the thing. He looked to see if it was breathing; all that its body did was settle. From the gashes, a sunset-purple liquid oozed. The tips of its limbs quivered with obvious death rattling. Ahiga stood and lowered the rifle.

Flopping motion sounded above him. He looked up and saw masses of tentacles at the top of the ramp. Two bodies poked out, mouths questing.

Ahiga ran underneath the metal machine. The ground tore apart, thunderous rifle shots coming from overhead. The two other things didn't bother with a fancy weapon that threw sunlight. They used guns. Ahiga knew about guns.

With his back pressed against the crashed machine, Ahiga considered his options. The two creatures were probably still up the ramp. Their skin was as delicate as his, so they would need time to get down the slope. He could run from the machine to the cover of the rock pile beside the river, then attack them with the rifle. The first shot was clearly a fortunate one. The rock pile was surrounded by open riverbed. If he had to retreat from it, he would be fully exposed.

But waiting any longer to decide was out of the question.

He ran, straight for the heavy boulders that had obviously once been part of the cliff face. Without looking back, he dove behind them, curled quickly, and sat behind their comforting protection.

Ahiga raised his eyes around the border. The two things climbed gingerly down the metal slope. They used their tentacle limbs more as arms than legs, holding on and lowering their weight. His bowels quivered as he watched. These strange, frightening creatures made him feel like a boy clinging to his mother's breast, afraid of the coming night, and he felt no shame in it.

The things took position on either side of the slope. They moved cautiously, flexing their tails so that their bodies rippled forward, aided by wide-spread limbs. It seemed as if they believed him to be hiding behind the machine, for they moved together in that direction one slow pace at a time.

He chambered a round, lifted the rifle into place. Where to aim on these things that had no heads? He positioned the sight just a bit over the nearest creature's mouth and squeezed the trigger.

The creature jumped. He knew the bullet flew true, and Ahiga levered the rifle ready again. The thing seemed wounded, for it wobbled and flailed its tentacles. He sighted again and fired into the thing's center. It collapsed, dead.

The second creature appeared suddenly, propelled quickly over the sand by the many, strong tentacles. Ahiga's head and shoulders were still exposed when it fired upon him. The stone flew apart. Chips stung his scalp and tore his ear. He fell to the ground and slapped a hand over the side of his head. When he drew it away, it was smeared with blood. He searched again with his fingers and found the upper third of his ear gone, a vicious—but shallow—cut on his scalp above.

Ahiga readied the rifle. He raised himself up quickly, fired almost blind, and dropped. The bullet struck the machine and ricocheted loudly. In the afterimage, Ahiga saw that the green thing was nowhere to be seen.

The stone cover was inadequate. If there was just the one creature, Ahiga and it would be unable to do anything until one of them moved. If there was even one more inside the machine, the two of them could keep him pinned down until they moved for a clear shot. Ahiga had to get away. He looked around. It was twice as far as he could throw a stone to the next rocky protection. All that open riverbed sand looked like death to him.

Noise deafened Ahiga. Heat and flame swept the rocks aside. He blinked, found himself in the air above the river. Pain stabbed his back and arms, but all was erased when he hit the water. The cold slapped him so savagely he gasped, taking water into his mouth before he knew what he was doing. It was hardly a quick-flowing river; Ahiga could easily get to the surface.

But what of the creature? It could be standing at the river's edge, ready to gun him down when he broke the surface. There could be a partner, or more. No, Ahiga knew better than to reach for the air so close by. He dove, found the rocky bottom, and crawled with the current.

Ahiga loved the water. As a boy, he often swam and did so now whenever he could. Like an otter, he could hold his breath for what seemed like an impossible time. Yet, following the bright flash, he hadn't been given the chance to take in a good lungful. The sick air inside him longed for release. It pounded on his chest. Many times he caught it in his throat and swallowed it back. There was plenty of light reaching him in the relatively shallow water, but it faded at the edges until all he could see was a bright spot. Surely he had gone far enough. He steeled his impulse to get more air and crawled all the harder.

A long moment later, Ahiga needed air or he would die. He

turned onto his back, pushed air out of him in a long stream of bubbles, and raised his head so that only his mouth and nose broke the surface. Air filled his lungs. Desperate for more, he lowered himself under the surface and traveled further downstream.

His willpower gave out much sooner. Ahiga brought himself to the shallows and lifted his eyes above the surface. The horse's head was level with his, lifeless eyes staring out, long tongue lolling in the water.

A green thing inspected the horse's carcass with its tentacles.

Ahiga burst from the water. The creature was clearly surprised, for it flinched back, tentacles stiff with inaction. Ahiga pounced and buried his knife to the handle in the space above the thing's open mouth.

It flinched again and tried to push him away with suddenly ineffective limbs. Ahiga withdrew the blade and stabbed again, six times through the thing's flesh that was stiff like tanning leather but as rubbery as river clams. A tentacle wrapped around his thigh and squeezed weakly. The great mouth opened and closed but in no way threatened him; his horse had had a more vicious bite. The thing quivered as Ahiga pressed down on the knife. With a gasp that smelled of lavender, the thing collapsed with limbs splayed.

A metal ball with a protruding stub rolled out of one of its tentacles. It looked like a gourd though all of one color as it was fashioned from a single piece of metal. Ahiga lifted it and found it surprisingly light, the way a bird was. He twisted it and pressed, pulled at the object's stem with no result. When it occurred to him that he might be handling a weapon, he set it aside.

The creature fascinated him. It was a monster, larger than his horse which had a great chunk blasted out of its back. Four long tentacle limbs ended in tiny prickles that were supple and soft, like braids of hair. An equal number of shorter limbs lay under the mouth, ending in wide circles. Surrounded by fat lips, the mouth that was as large as Ahiga's head held flat, uniform teeth. The shape of the creature was fishlike in that it had a tail that broadened at its tip. He could find no trace of eyes on the thing and wondered how it saw.

A shot sounded. Something whined past his ear like an angry insect. He dove behind the thing's body and held himself flat. Another shot tore up the ground before his face, as did a third. Like the rock pile, a strategy of waiting was unsound. And if whatever weapon caused the rocks to fly apart was unleashed on the inadequate protection of the corpses, surely he would be killed.

Ahiga jumped to his feet and sprinted from behind the creature's body. He didn't have much of a destination, just the idea to move quickly away. He turned his angle, sped and slowed, not wanting to be like the deer that catches the bullet for moving in a single direction and at a constant speed. From the corner of his eye, he saw only one of the tentacled things. It raised a forelimb. Several shots fired in quick succession, some few coming near. Ahiga reached a field of sturdy grasses and dove into it as if it were a lake.

With legs begging to continue running, Ahiga lay as still as the rabbit when the coyote walks by. There had been only one; were there no more in the machine? If that were the truth, and if he could get to his rifle, perhaps he could live out this morning. Both were very big ifs.

A bullet screamed into the grasses not far from Ahiga's feet. Instinct told him to flee, but he knew it was a mistake. Panic tried to overwhelm reason, eventually losing the battle. Ahiga lay still and listened. Another bullet dove into the grass, this one much farther away. A third and fourth also came nowhere near him. The creature didn't know where he was and sought to flush him from his hiding place. Were he a quail, the tactic would work. Even when a fifth bullet slammed into the ground close enough to spray his face with metallic-tasting dust, he hardly flinched.

Something massive crunched on the hard grass. Behind him, out of his field of vision, the creature had moved into the field. He listened, trying not to move even his head for a look. Better to be the invisible rabbit and take the killing stroke unknowingly than to reveal his position and ask for it. Yet the sounds of trodden-upon grass came closer. Ahiga feared the thing would step on him. He thought of sunlight reflecting off the knife in his hand and gently slipped it into the soft ground.

The creature paused. Surely if it had seen him he would be dead by now. Perhaps he was, lying in the grass, awaiting the spirits to guide him into the world beyond this one. Even with that possibility, Ahiga dared not moved. It would take the spirits calling his name to get him to rise and probably more than once to convince him he didn't imagine it.

When the next shot fired—so nearby—he came as close to running as he could without actually doing it. In his mind, he saw himself sprinting out of the grass in diagonal bursts. The only movement he allowed himself was a clutching of the earth. The dirt compressed in his hands and tightened under his nails, but he stayed still.

A long while passed, long enough for the birds and insects to return to their noisemaking. An ant crawled over Ahiga's hand, followed by a second that followed in the leader's footsteps. He felt a large insect crawl from underneath his shirt and tumble down his side when he realized it was blood from the wounds on his back. Ahiga knew the creature was waiting him out, a much slyer tactic than the gunshots. Unless the ant returned with hundreds of its nest mates, he knew that he could wait all day.

His stomach growled. Ahiga swallowed hard and tightened the muscles in his belly. He knew it was only a soft grumbling, but it was more than the background sounds of the canyon. With the creature so near, how could it have not heard?

The grass crunched, one step closer. The things could be killed with a knife. Was it just another fortunate kill? Ahiga had no way of knowing. And the creature held a weapon trained in his general direction. Worse yet, he knew Ahiga was there; surprise was no longer on his side. His insides constricted, waiting for death.

The creature moved suddenly away. The first steps revealed that it had been dangerously close, so much so that Ahiga thought it impossible he was not discovered. Had the creature possessed eyes, he would have been. His motionless hiding seemed like genius, and he would brag about it to the other warriors of his tribe should he live out the day.

Ever so slowly, like the melting of ice at the springtime's first warm day, Ahiga lifted his eyes above the level of grass. The creature moved rapidly toward the machine with no apparent regard that Ahiga was behind it, for it seemed not to take any precautions. It flexed its tail and pushed with its smaller limbs much faster than Ahiga thought it could move, almost as fast as he could jog. Straight toward the machine with no variation. If it could not see, Ahiga wondered how it could so accurately aim for the broken machine.

That was undeniable; the machine was broken. If the creature was moving to the machine for protection, then it was no longer a threat. While it was in hiding, Ahiga would flee. But if it intended to find another weapon or something that could seek him out of camouflaged areas, Ahiga had a problem. Better to take action against a possible threat than suppose victory and die in ignorance.

Ahiga stood. In a crouch, he ran for the cover of bushes and rocks, all the while keeping his eyes on the retreating creature. It ignored him, even as he stood taller and ran faster. When it ran underneath the fallen machine, Ahiga sprinted to the blasted rock pile. He gained his rifle as the thing finished its climb and disappeared into the machine.

With sights trained on the top of the metal slope, Ahiga waited. The creature did not emerge. Ahiga waited for so long he contemplated running off, further contemplated climbing into the machine to hunt it down, and returned to running off. The rifle became intolerably heavy. His arms shook for keeping them upright, and he had to lower them or lose his ability to aim altogether.

The instant the rifle came down, the creature appeared. Only its very front edged out of the machine's opening, and a tentacle lobbed a small object at Ahiga. Even though it was barely the size of his closed fist, Ahiga knew he had to get away from it. He ran to the side, away from the spot where the object would land. Out of the corner of his eye, he saw that the creature had ducked back inside the machine.

Six long steps later, the Sun roared onto the riverbed in all his hot, bright anger. He pushed Ahiga to the ground and breathed fire onto him. Ahiga's already injured back blazed with fresh agony all the way down to his calves. Despite this, Ahiga rose and ran for the shelter of the lee side of the machine. Once there he turned to look back at the Sun, but he had already returned to the sky. How the creature had called the Sun to the ground baffled Ahiga. He knew for certain, though, that he wouldn't allow it to do it again.

He aimed the rifle. With sliding steps, he angled around so he could see the top of the metal slope. Not so much as a flicker of movement gave him any hint the creature was still up there. He moved across the space he had been before, noted how warm the sand was, that a circle of charred earth spread around where the object must have landed. Ahiga leaned over the great rock and saw what he was looking for. He moved to its opposite side, knelt, and lowered the rifle to the ground.

The creature appeared again, but Ahiga took his eyes from it. His right hand closed around the wooden haft. He stood and stepped forward, launched the spear. It flew as straight as the edge of a knife and pierced the thing's body through its open mouth. The creature stiffened and relaxed. A fist-sized object fell from its grasp and landed at the top of the metal slope.

Ahiga turned and ran again, up the riverbed. He glanced over his shoulder and saw a bright flash, much brighter than the Sun. The roar of it shook his ears. The creature and the top of the metal slope evaporated into tiny pieces. A great crack formed in the machine, and it lost its ability to prop up against the canyon wall. Scraping with the agony of a tortured animal, the machine slid and crashed on the riverbed. Ahiga considered stopping then heard the rumbling complaint of the canyon itself. He continued to run, not looking back, as the avalanche started.

His feet tried to slip out from under him, so fiercely the ground shook. He felt like a bee trapped in a little boy's hands, being shaken in a game of don't-be-stung. Twice he stumbled, yet he recovered and kept running. He thought he was far enough away when a rock the size of his head tumbled to his right. Dust followed, and he ran until the noise behind him settled to a whisper.

When he turned, he saw the entire cliff face had fallen. His entire village would have fit at the top of the plateau; now it lay in a heap on the riverbed. Much of the stone had settled in the water, creating a dam. Already the river worked its way around—as water always did—up along the bed and through the cracks between the rocks. Of the machine, nothing was visible.

By the time he walked all the way back to the village and returned, animals would probably have stripped the dead creatures of their meat, leaving little evidence. Unless he could convince his fellow warriors to help move the rubble, the machine would lay underneath the stone forever. Perhaps it was wisest to not speak of his adventure in the canyon for fear of seeming a braggart and a liar.

Ahiga sighed deeply and began the two-day walk back to his village. He passed his dead horse and took the reins from its open mouth. The metal ball with the stud went into the middle of the river. He stared hard at the dead thing, already attracting insects.

His stomach rumbled violently. Ahiga patted his belly. Then he looked again at the dead thing and took out his knife. It seemed silly to walk all the way back home hungry.

Much later, when he told his grandchildren a wild story about a young warrior and the things that came out of the fallen machine, he would add that the tentacled creatures tasted like buffalo liver.

The Dead Man's Hand

By Jason Andrew

On the steamship voyage from San Francisco to Seattle, Finneas Bagley won three thousand dollars in a poker game while sipping his customary olive martini. He had planned to spend a quiet, leisurely trip on the upper passenger deck. He might have resisted the temptation to gamble if a young lad had not overheard his name mentioned by the concierge. The boy gingerly approached Finneas holding a weathered copy of a dime novel titled *Wild West Stories*. "Are you Finneas Bagley?"

Finneas had not been considered young in several decades, but his eyes still gleamed with boyish charm. He had gained a small pooch in his belly, but he was still an impressive figure clad in velvet. "I have that dubious honor, son."

"Is it true that you saw Wild Bill draw the Dead Man's Hand?"

The old man rolled his eyes and then wiped his brow. "I did indeed witness that unfortunately tragedy."

After that, various passengers constantly harangued him to recall the dreadful night. Of course, he told the popularized version of the evening's events. If he had told them the truth, he would be labeled a madman. It was quite arduous, but then he never had to pay for a single meal or drink. Several men wanted to play poker with one of the men that had been playing poker when Wild Bill Hickok drew the infamous aces and eights in black and was murdered by Jack McCall.

Finneas was careful to avoid winning too much. Professional gamblers sometimes paid scouts to watch opponents for their tells. There was a big game in Seattle, perhaps the biggest of his career. Finneas made a strong effort to keep his winnings low, but several traveling businessmen insisted upon making colossal blunders. He prided himself on being an honest gambler and an occasional scoundrel. Many sharpers were rogues that cheated to win. Still, he could use the extra money to build his stake. He wasn't entirely certain how much money was required to enter this game. He only knew that this game would be his last chance for immortality.

As soon as the ship reached port, he hailed a carriage and passed along a note with an address. The coachman winked and Finneas suspected he was well acquainted with the destination.

The landscape of the Puget Sound was lush with vibrant colors of green and brown. Seattle was a small camp built in the middle of a series murky mudflats. The trip from the docks was quite bumpy as the driver attempted to dodge several of the potholes in the dirt road. Some of them were several feet deep and filled with foul smelling water. The carriage slid to a stop, jerking Finneas forward and knocking the bowler off his head. He glanced out of the window to see one of the only brick buildings in the camp. He stepped out, over another mud puddle, and was warmly greeted by a short boisterous woman of many curves and charms. "Finneas Bagley! It's about time you show up, you old scoundrel!"

Finneas kissed her lightly upon the cheek. "Miss Lou Graham, it is my privilege and honor to see you once again; though I am unaware that I had announced my arrival."

She grinned slyly. "I run the best brothel and gambling hall in three states. Not much happens in this town that I don't hear about in the morning over toast and coffee." Lou curtsied wryly. "And when I found out what deck they would be playing with, I knew you would be arriving soon enough."

Finneas wiggled his eyebrows and leaned closer. "As I hoped, my beautiful dove. Alas, while I have heard news of the pending game, I have not yet secured arrangements for an invitation."

Lou fluttered her eyes. "Such arrangements might be neigh on impossible. I've seen man and beast with better clothing and fatter wallets turned away." She whispered into his ear, "But it might be possible that I know of a potential benefactor for your cause."

"How much would such information cost, my ever succulent

lambchop?"

Lou's eyes narrowed. "Fifteen percent."

Finneas scoffed. "Would you take my shirt and shoes then? Five percent!"

Lou rubbed his chin with her forefinger. "Ten percent. And a free room."

Finneas took her hand and kissed it. "My dear, we have an understanding between us."

Lou's smile returned. "You want to find Lewis Borri. He's a local Jew doctor. He has a stake in the game, but doesn't play cards. I've heard that he's looking for a proxy."

Finneas rubbed his hands together eagerly. "I've heard many stories of him in other circles. Well then, Miss Lou, if you would honor my arm by escorting me to the tables?"

The gambling den smelled of sweat, tobacco, booze, and cheap perfume, which suited Finneas nicely. Lou had five poker tables, all of them busy. Customers gulped drinks at an ornate wooden bar. Several of Lou's soiled doves were plying their trade. Some were dancing for twenty-five cents a song. Others were hawking drinks or other more intimate pleasures. Lou gestured to a dark curly-haired man who appeared to be no older than twenty.

Finneas frowned. "That can not be Borri! Surely it is his son. The man should be pushing forty, if the stories are true."

"I've known him for fifteen years and he's never aged a day." Lou shrugged. "Everyone is too afraid to call him on it. He might look like a tenderfoot, but he can turn a man yellow with just a word. He's a real curly wolf that one."

Borri was a thin, frail looking man with delicate features. He was studying the various games, tracking the winners and losers. Lou tugged him toward the center of the room, amongst the tables and players. "Pick a table and we'll cash you in, Mr. Bagley. We'll have your room ready for you when you are tired." It was said loudly enough that several turned their heads from their various activities to take a look at the new player. Now, the gamblers knew that he had money, and if Lou's attentions were an indication, quite a bit of it.

Finneas closed his eyes and listened to the shuffling of the decks. The familiar rhythm of cards shuffling brought a grin to his face. He listened for a few seconds and then scowled. "Alas, Miss Lou, I regret that I can not play cards in this establishment." Several of the gamblers craned their necks to listen. He pointed at a thin, gaunt man who had been shuffling the cards. "The dealer is cheating."

The players at the table reached for their guns. Lou pulled a derringer from her garter belt and shot into the air. "Wait! Wait! My games are all clean according to Hoyle!" She glared at Finneas. "You'd best explain yourself."

Finneas held his own hands in the air, palms up. "If I may demonstrate."

Lou wagged her finger at him. "You had better be right. We take accusations of cheating dead serious around here."

Finneas winked. "What was the high card from the hand?"

"Ace of Spades," a ruffian replied. He had a small pile of chips and a peacemaker revolver in his hand and wasn't in a mood to be too particular about who he used it on.

Finneas reached across the table and scooped the deck of cards into his hands. "Let's just deal face up and see what would have happened."

He expertly dealt the players their hands, in the same order as the round would have played. *Deuce of Clubs, Five of Diamonds, Six of Hearts, and the Ace of Spades.*

The burly man with a dusty rancher's hat snarled defensively. He had the largest pile of chips at the table. "That just proves I'm lucky." He leveled his six-shooter at Finneas, but the other three players were aiming their weapons toward him.

The gaunt man cocked his pistol and stood. "You cheating, Bart? You ain't ever had a lucky streak like this!"

The dealer started sweating. He raised his hands gingerly. "That don't prove nothing."

Finneas nodded, solemnly. "That my lad, is very true. But let us continue and see what fate the cards had for these players." He quickly dealt through the rest of the deal. Bart drew the *Ace of Clubs*, the *Ace of Diamonds*, and the *Five of Hearts*. "That my friends is a handsome hand."

Lou aimed her derringer to the back of the dealer's head. "How'd he do it?"

"There is a rather unique sound to dealing from the bottom of the deck. It is a hard thump, but with the noise in this room hardly noticeable unless you were listening for it." Finneas waved his hand over the covered poker table. "That is why steamboats on the Mississippi only allow hard wood tables."

Lou cocked her derringer and patted the dealer on the shoulder.

He closed his eyes, shaking, fighting tears. "Sorry, Pete. You know the rules."

Finneas quietly sipped a martini, annoyed that there were no olives to be had in Seattle. The ruckus from the gunfight had died down and he was weary. He wanted to go to his room minus the complementary dancing girl, but he waited for Borri to approach him. He did not have to wait long.

"I've heard a great deal about you, Mr. Bagley."

Finneas nodded. "It would seem that the deeds of my youth have been wildly exaggerated."

"Lou informs me we have common business interests." He gestured to a side room. "Shall we speak in private?"

"Of course, Doctor Borri. Your reputation is well known."

Borri strode to a door on the side of the bar, opened it, and bowed.

Finneas followed entering first, secretly gripping his pistol. Borri followed and closed the door behind them, locked it, and then gestured to two comfortable looking plush chairs. "Please sit, Mr. Bagley. I am going to ensure that our conversation remains private." He removed a small beaker from his jacket pocket and pulled out the wooden cork. It was filled with a milky liquid. He dropped a few drips in front of the door and smiled. "There! That is as much privacy as I can assure."

Finneas wasn't certain what Borri had just done, but he didn't want to ask. Borri was quite infamous for his involvement in the occult. "I trust this is about the upcoming game."

Borri nodded. "You are seeking Tituba's Deck. I am seeking a proxy to play for my interests. The winner of the evening will receive Tituba's Deck. Tell me, why do you wish to procure it?"

Finneas swallowed nervously. "That damned deck of cards destroyed a great man. I've tracked it for years while learning all that I could about it. I know that it can't be destroyed, but I can prevent others from falling to its seductive charms."

"And you believe that you can resist its siren charms?" Borri asked.

"I did once before in Deadwood with Wild Bill. I caused him to draw the Dead Man's Hand." Finneas finished his martini. It felt good to admit this to someone. "If I had stayed in the game, I would have burned off the last few cards."

Borri narrowed his eyes. "If that is true, then you saw what really happened."

"I felt uneasy and didn't know why so, I folded. I ordered a drink and stepped away from the table. After Wild Bill drew the Dead Man's Hand, a thick black fog seeped forth from the cards. A dark figure reached for Wild Bill. We were all struck with panic. It laughed maliciously. McCall panicked and shot Wild Bill. Afterward, the smoke cleared and no one else there seemed to remember that part. If I hadn't folded, Wild Bill wouldn't have drawn that hand."

"Perhaps that is true. However, I believe that fate and the cards will not be denied."

"Does the Dead Man's Hand always mean death?" Finneas asked.

Borri shook his head sadly. "Not as you mean it. Tituba's Deck was made in mockery of the tarot. Spades for swords, hearts for cups, diamonds for coins, and clubs for wands. During play, if a player draws the correct combination of cards, it can summon the Black Man."

"The Lord of Witches? I had heard the legend, but hardly credited it to be true, despite what I had witnessed," Finneas protested.

Borri shrugged. "He is known by many names. In this guise, he is the lord of witches. I suspect his company would be unpleasant for you."

"Do you know where it came from?"

"I do. And if you agree to be my proxy, I shall explain all."

"What are the stakes?" Finneas asked. He didn't like playing without knowing the rewards.

"Several illuminares are quarreling over matters that do not concern you. The winner of this game will be allowed to dictate certain terms that do not concern you and yours."

"Why would they let a card game decide?" Finneas asked.

"As you know, this deck of cards is special. Unique. Some of them will consider this a form of worship." Borri shrugged his shoulders. "I can not say more until I have your word that you will be my proxy."

"What happens if I lose?" Finneas asked.

"There is no penalty for losing." Borri grinned. "Of course, the game has other dangers, of which you have witnessed, yes?"

"What would have happened if McCall hadn't shot Wild Bill?"

"The Black Man would have taken him. His life would have

been a series of unending torments. McCall unknowingly did him quite the favor."

"Forgive me for seeming rude, but why not play yourself?" Finneas asked.

Borri coughed. "Gambling is not one of my skills, Mr. Bagley. This is a game that cannot be fixed or marked. Tituba's Deck won't allow it."

Finneas spat in his hand, extending it. Borri rolled his eyes, spat in his hand, and then shook hands. "We have a compact then. I shall make the arrangements."

"It would help me win if I knew everything about Tituba's Deck."

Borri nodded. "The legend is true. Tituba's Deck was a gift from the Black Man to the witch Tituba in Salem over two hundred years ago. It has the ability to tempt those who play to lose themselves in the game."

Finneas scratched his chin. Wild Bill had played like a fiend, foregoing sleep and food. Had he been enchanted? "Why was I able to leave the game then?"

"I suspect that you view gambling as a profession, a skill. It is not mysterious, nor random to you." Borri coughed into his handkerchief. "Forgive me, I was recently poisoned and the toxin is still working its way through my system. As you might surmise, the cards have a life of their own. Madness follows Tituba's Deck everywhere. Salem is proof enough of that."

Finneas thought about it for a moment. "You seem to know quite a bit at such a young age."

Borri grinned, showing off his perfect white teeth. "I assure you that I am far older than I appear."

"If that is so, sir, then you must have found the legendary fountain of youth." Borri appeared no older than twenty years. "Would you care to share the secret?"

"Perhaps, if you win this game this evening, I shall give you a small taste."

Lou's brothel had been closed to the public around eleven that evening. It was very early end for the brothel, but the tournament promised that Lou would make up every lost cent and double an average night's profits. Finneas was pleased that the arrangements had been made so quickly, but learned that the other players had been waiting for Borri to select a proxy for several weeks. Whatever the stakes of the game, he realized that the contestants considered it very important.

Finneas bathed and shaved. He then dressed in his finest ensemble and tied his favorite cravat. If he was going to die gambling tonight, he wanted to ensure that he left a well groomed and snappily dressed corpse. He descended the stairs and was surprised to see that the layout of the gaming room had been rearranged. The overhead oil lamps had been removed and replaced with candles. The air of jovial excitement had been drained from the room; there was only anticipation, dread, and loathing. He had seen many strange things in the dark cracks of this world, but rarely had he felt the dread creeping into his stomach as it did now. It smelled faintly of fish and sulfur.

Borri glanced over Finneas' clothing and nodded his wry approval. He gestured for Finneas to take the fourth seat at the poker table. Lou sat in the dealer's chair and introduced each of the players. There was a small group of presumed luminaries hidden in the shadows whispering to each other. They spoke in hideous, unknowable languages with clicks of the tongue and gargles of the throat. He tried to get a good look at them, but the candle light left too many shadows for them to hide their faces. "It would perhaps be better if you didn't look too closely in the shadows," Borri whispered.

Finneas felt like a Christian awaiting the lions. He watched the other players carefully during the first few rounds of the game. Jimmy "the shark" Schultz was a lean fellow with large bulbous eyes. His cheeks were sunken and his lips were wide, giving the impression of a fish. He knew that the Shark was from the east coast and stuck mostly to Massachusetts. Occasionally, the Shark won a couple of large pots in Boston and then disappeared for years at a time. He played cautiously, slowly grinding out small wins.

Dog-Eye Eric Vanhee was a swarthy, voluminous man with jet-black hair. He chewed constantly like a goat, occasionally spitting into a spittoon. Dog-Eye traveled extensively in the southern territories, occasionally making it to San Francisco. Finneas had the dubious pleasure of meeting Dog-Eye at a gambling house in Chinatown where he had a pretty girl on each arm and a jug of rice wine on the table. Finneas had been able to watch him play before leaving. He played aggressively, as though each hand meant life or death.

Samuel Kane was an old man with thin puffs of white hair upon his otherwise bald head. It was rare for a gambler to reach old age without retiring willing or via the business end of a bullet. Samuel rarely moved as it seemed that each motion stirred pain in his joints. As his own hands had started to creak in the mornings, Finneas very much sympathized. Samuel seemed content to play each hand and take a measure of his opponents. Although he had never heard of this man, Finneas pegged him as the potential threat.

The game progressed slowly. Schultz played conservatively while Vanhee raised the pot several times. It was easy enough to push Dog-Eye Vanhee out of the game. Aside from keeping count of the various cards in play, Finneas noted that Vanhee counted his chips every time he had a good hand. His body would tense as though preparing to fight. Finneas, Schultz, and Samuel took turns draining Vanhee's chips.

Two hours into the game, Finneas won a hand with three of kind. Vanhee growled. His cheeks flushed and he slammed his fists down upon the table. His fingers became clawlike, ferrous, and monstrous. Tiny bone horns peeked out from his thick hair. Worried, Finneas started to reach subtly for his pistol. A deep voice from the shadows silenced Vanhee; it chilled Finneas. "Do not shame me further."

Vanhee's shoulders slumped and then he stood and left the table. Finneas and Samuel had piles of chips roughly the same size. Schultz trailed them by half, but he had been slowly adding to his pile. Finneas changed his strategy and started betting less and letting Schultz win a few hands. Samuel matched his attack, which worried him. Meanwhile, Schultz started getting more aggressive. Each win of five dollars became a loss of ten dollars in his mind. As he started winning more hands, Schultz started betting more. Finneas and Samuel fed him just a little and then pulled the chair out from under him. Schultz started losing in larger and larger quantities. Once his nerve was rattled, Schultz was desperate to win big. An hour later, he'd lost his last hand. He bowed to the table, and left.

"Time for a break, gentlemen," Lou announced.

Borri handed Finneas a martini with olives. "Thank you, kind sir. How ever did you manage to find olives?"

Borri shrugged shyly, but didn't answer the question. "You seem to be doing quite well."

Finneas scowled. "Perhaps not, sir."

"Explain."

"Mr. Kane is a complete conundrum. I cannot fathom his tells." Finneas sipped the martini. "And he is good. He's playing off me as though he knows everything."

Borri took a drink of coffee. "That he is, but then he has been playing for many a year."

"Surely, I would have heard of him," Finneas protested. He knew all of the best sharps in the country.

"That man has had many names. I wouldn't be surprised if you did know of some. He is the reason I sought you. I couldn't gamble against him." Borri wiped his brow, sweating.

"Perhaps, if you told me his story, I could play better against him."

"He is my third son."

Finneas glanced over to Samuel Kane and took note of his advanced years and thin gray hair. "Of course, he is."

"My appearance is quite deceiving. I am a master of the alchemical arts. I have lived quite well for far longer than you can imagine possible, Mr. Bagley."

"Why do you want your son to lose so badly?" Finneas asked.

Borri grimaced. "If he wins, he shall face a doom hither fore unknown to this world."

"He's dying, isn't he?" Finneas asked, suspicious.

"Enemies of mine poisoned all of my children. I was able to counteract the toxin, but at a price. My art can no longer prolong his life. He was condemned to a single lifetime. And now, he seeks to win the approval of the Black Man."

"His immortal soul for his life?"

"Save my son, and that which I cannot give onto him shall be yours."

Finneas began the next round slowly. He wanted to prolong each hand, hoping that Samuel would become impatient. His opponent remained calm. They played for several hours, neither side taking a decisive victory. It had turned into an endurance game.

Finneas drew the *Queen of Hearts* and the *Queen of Diamonds* for his two face-up cards. Samuel drew the *Ace of Spades* and the *Eight of Clubs*. Finneas started the bet at five dollars. Samuel matched it, raising ten. Finneas called, and then Lou dealt each of them the remaining cards.

Finneas glanced at his hand, pleased to see three Queens and a

Jack of Diamonds. Samuel checked his cards and visibly blanched. Finneas raised the bet by fifty. Sweating, Samuel matched and bet an additional five hundred. It was all of his chips. Finneas barely had enough to match it. It was a risky move, but it wasn't his money and he had to try to win at all costs. "Call."

Samuel sighed. He flipped over his hand; *Ace of Spades, Ace of Clubs, Eight of Spades, Eight of Clubs* and *six of Clubs*. The crowd gasped; it was the Dead Man's Hand.

Finneas glanced at Borri. He had the cards to win, but wasn't sure that Borri would still want it. The alchemist nodded sadly. The room was as silent as death. Finneas showed his hand.

Samuel clutched his chest as the black mist rose from the cards, burning his fingers. Finneas dropped the cards, trying to see Samuel through the haze. He imagined Samuel's heart beating, struggling to burst through the chest. His own heart burned, his chest barely able to contain the fear. A hand formed in the mist and reached for Samuel. "Father! Help me!"

Finneas drew his pistol, aimed at Samuel's heart, and fired twice. Samuel slumped into his seat. Black blood seeped from the wound. A heinous howl erupted from the mist as it began to fade. "Tell my father, I understand."

Borri stood behind his son. He leaned over, and whispered, "I am very proud of you, son."

Samuel struggled to make his last few raspy breaths. He tried to reach for his father. Borri grabbed his son's hand and watched him die. "I'm very sorry, Doctor Borri," Finneas whispered. "I couldn't stand to let the Black Man take him."

Borri reached into his pocket and produced a small vial. "Drink this within the hour and all I promised shall come true."

Finneas accepted the vial gratefully and turned to scoop up the remaining cards in Tituba's Deck. "Thank you, Doctor Borri."

"I would run now, if I were you." Borri cradled his dead son in his arms. "It has already started."

Finneas sniffed the air. There was smoke somewhere near by. He had not noticed it previously. "We should leave the building."

Borri scoffed. "I will remain here. I suggest you leave now, Mr. Bagley."

Finneas slipped Tituba's Deck into his pocket, grabbed Lou by the arm, and made his way to the door. The black smoke was thick on the city streets. "Do you have a fire department?"

"Only a bunch of drunken volunteers!" Lou yelled.

As the fire swept up the street consuming building after building, they treaded up the steep slope hoping to escape the city limits. An explosion rocked the area as the liquor store caught fire. Exhausted, they stood on the hill, watching the city burn. Finneas thought of Tituba's Deck and wondered if it had caused this as punishment for denying the Black Man his rightful prey. He pulled out the small vial and flipped the stopper off with his thumb. Finneas gulped the foul smelling liquid and fell back upon his rear.

"I'm ruined!" Lou cried.

"So are we all, Miss Lou. So are we all."

Jedediah Smith and the Undying Chinaman

By Charles P. Zaglanis

August 24, 1895

I languished in the saloon of a no-name town near the Nevada border in a foul mood. The whisky was thin, the beer was worse, and the Chinaman's trail was cold. I lit a fine Cuban cigar to cover the reek of a festering spittoon next to me. I'd been standing at the bar most of the day, doing my best to keep the proprietor of that wonderful establishment in the black and to assuage my lingering guilt over letting the Chinaman escape with the disk in the first place. At least my ribs had finally healed.

A room for the night to sleep off the swill was starting to sound like a good idea, but as my gaze focused on the filthy mirror behind the barkeep, I noticed a dirty miner talking to his buddy between gulps of what passed for "liquid courage." He steadied himself against a stool, and then meandered my way. His friend was either too smart or too cowardly to leave their table; most likely the latter. I didn't need the hush of the one-eyed whore hawking her wares or the creak of the floorboards to announce his presence. A stone drunk could smell him at ten paces: a sour stench that screamed to anyone interested that the greasy bastard only bathed when the Almighty saw fit to catch him in the rain.

I wish that what was about to happen was an uncommon occurrence.

People like me tend to stick their noses in places where big men like to throw their weight around, and I'm not a big man. I have lived a hard life, and underneath the denim pants and light blue shirt, I'm iron—or "wiry," as an Irish friend of mine once observed. If this fella could have seen my eyes, he'd have known I wasn't the sort to trifle with. My momma always said I had mean eyes, and my hard drinkin' daddy made sure there was plenty of viciousness inside to back them up.

I hooked my right thumb in my belt and then looked over my shoulder askance, favoring him with a one-eyed appraisal. I'm not the type to back down from a bully in the best of times, and once I get my fill of the hard stuff, I'll even spit in the eye of Old Scratch himself. The miner was a big sonofabitch; he looked to be about six-four, beefy, bold, and none too smart looking from the neck up. I figured him for a man in his early twenties, but it was hard to tell through all the dirt.

"What's yer name gramps?" he slurred and grinned.

What teeth he had were black and jagged. I'd be doing him a favor if I knocked him on the jaw and finished what hard living had started. But I didn't want to risk losing my hand to gangrene.

"Why?"

There wasn't any steel in my words; I knew Hoss was past the point of no return. I did keep my back to him, partly to let him know I wasn't afraid, but mostly because I wanted to show him a little trick I'd picked up over the years. He'd really managed to get my dander up. The last time I remembered having a birthday, I was thirty-two. Now, I've seen my share of sun in foreign lands and had some narrow escapes that probably contributed to my white hair, but I didn't think I looked like anyone's grandfather.

"'Cause I like ta know the name of the feller whose ass I'm about ta stomp."

Hoss had the audacity to stand behind me and bray like a mule. There's little I hate more than a man who laughs at his own slack-jawed humor. I slipped my hand snake-quick over the worn handle of the Colt Peacemaker I kept crotched. My arm swung up in an arch as I skinned the cannon and then smashed the butt against the bridge of Mr. Joker's beak. *Crack.* He staggered back, a scarlet stream running from his noise, painting the floor red. I kicked him in "the sweets," sending him down. And, because I was feeling ornery, I upended that damned spittoon over his face.

I shook my head at Fate or Lady Luck or whatever the hell guides our lives. I could have been just like him, if it weren't for my uncle. He'd taken me in and paid for my education after the consumption killed my momma.

I took a long pull on my cigar and let the smoke ooze slow and evil out of my mouth as I said to anyone listening. "My *name* is Jedediah Smith. Does anyone *else* want to ask me a question?"

This time I threw some of that steel in my voice mentioned earlier. Hoss's buddy jumped up with his hands in the air, knocking over their table as he did so. I hadn't realized I still had my gun out. A glass pipe caked with tarry residue rolled along the floor with the shot glasses and beer bottles. My eyes widened for a second as a bolt of inspiration struck me full on and a gnarled finger pointed in the direction of Hoss's friend.

"You!"

"Me?" he squeaked, pointing to himself, but looking around for a more promising target. The whore scurried behind the bar while the other patrons ducked beneath their tables.

"Yes, *you*. Where can I find some opium around here, lots of it?"

He looked puzzled, which was only slightly different from his usual idiotic stare. "Why do you . . . ?"

I cocked the Peacemaker, interrupting him. "It sounds like you're asking me a *question*, and you've seen how I cotton to *questions*." I kicked Hoss once in the gut—hard—for emphasis. The poor bastard gurgled and curled up like a dying bug while his buddy turned wedding dress white.

"No . . . no . . . I . . . There's a bunch'a chinks workin' outta that old ghost town about two days ride due east. That's where Wade got his stuff. Oh God, please don't kill me, mister!"

I shook my head in disgust, holstered my pistol, kicked Wade in the chest out of spite, and strolled outside to my horse Aztec. As I rode east, my spirits brightened.

My quarry had been known to stop and satisfy his unsavory habits in the past, so this was my best chance of picking up his trail. I looked forward to making camp later and digging into my battered copy of the new H. G. Wells novel *War of the Worlds* while I had a few hours of sunlight.

⁂ ⁂ ⁂

The sound of Aztec munching on scrub grass was about the only comfort to be found as I used my saddle for a pillow. An Indian moon cast its sanguine glare upon me while coyotes sang their nightly dirge. I contemplated the pinpricks of light in the sky, wondering what cold, calculating intellect even now plotted the doom of mankind. Some might think it was my choice of literature of late that drove me to such thoughts, but they couldn't know that during my wanderings and excavations as an archeologist, I'd come across evidence that we were neither the most intelligent nor most malign critters on Earth or beyond. There have been visitations of the foulest sort to our planet and on occasion things have stayed that shouldn't be allowed to taint our clean air.

I banished those thoughts from my mind, since ruminating upon such things could lead to madness. Instead, I walked through the more mundane events that led me to this sour patch of land.

Jackson Park hadn't seen my face since the end of July 1893. The deaths and insanity surrounding the arrival of "The Raven" to the World Exhibition left a bitter place in my heart for my home in Illinois. At my insistence, my superiors at the Columbian Museum of Chicago sent me to a dig as far from the western world as they could muster.

In Northern Persia I found the solace I needed amongst the ruins of an ancient nameless necropolis. I did good work out there with nothing but the howling of lost djinn and a few brave workers to keep me company. Eventually we earned the trust of the local tribes, despite their fear of that shadow-haunted place. In my zeal to learn all there was to know of the tombs, I awoke some *thing* that should have passed on from this mortal coil aeons ago. The will to live and a wagonload of luck allowed the tribesmen and me to carry the day. I even managed to keep the pitted wavy dagger of meteoric metal that came in so handy that dreadful night.

My arrival home was bittersweet. Much of the darkness I'd carried in my heart had dispersed, and I soon began the pleasant task of cataloguing the myriad items sent back from the dig. Scars still ached in my soul however, manifested as an acute trepidation whenever wandering through the Egyptian exhibit.

Perhaps for the best, the whisky in my gut finally lulled me down the halls of deeper slumber and away from my dark reverie. I'm sure my snores were frightful enough to quench the curiosity of any wild critters interested in giving me a poke or a pinch.

※ ※ ※

A black bottle fly on my nose served as well as a cockcrow to rouse me from my sleep.

"G'morning Beelzebub. Hot as hell this mornin'."

Aztec whinnied in greeting when offered water from one of the canteens, then I used the rest to cook some beans. Mr. Wells's novel was finished and put away while breakfast roiled in the pot.

We were maybe five miles from camp when I found the first corpse. He'd been a man of Chinese descent once, but now he was just a half-melted slab of festering meat. The eye-watering bite of ammonia that lingered on the body was unbreathable; even the flies weren't settling down for a bite. Swallowing my bile, I hunkered down next to the corpse to get a closer look when his eyes snapped open and his mouth started working like a salmon on a sandbar. There was nothing to be done for him, too much was broken or melted away, so I drew my Peacemaker and put a bullet between his eyes. One more sin my quarry would have to account for—and I meant to collect the Reaper's toll.

As I rode on, I passed several more bodies in a similar state. Some were burnt; others sported queer symbols carved deep in their flesh; and a few were crushed as if they'd fallen from a great height. Whatever perpetrated this massacre didn't have a preference as to whom it killed; there were men, women, and children of all races littering the ground.

I knew where to find the town before it ever revealed itself. A storm cloud of buzzards circled about, teased and tempted by the tang of blood in the air, yet frightened of the other, less natural smells they sensed. About a mile out, Aztec would approach no closer. His eyes rolled and he snorted frightfully, so I left him unhobbled and munching on sweet grass, finishing the trek alone.

If the settlement didn't look like Hell's abattoir, I would've been hard pressed to know it used to be a ghost town. The walls were freshly painted, the buildings in good repair— or at least they *were.* Now the walls bore strange symbols painted in blood that defied my eyes' attempt to trace them and gave me a headache if I considered them overlong. Several buildings looked to have been crushed by drunken giants at a hoedown gone awry.

And then there were all the bodies. In my time I've seen terrible things done to people; hell, I've been the one *who's done* those things on occasion, but this place left me shaken. I knew there'd be a lot of nightmares and sleepless nights before I worked the taint of such carnage out of my system.

The cries of frustrated vultures echoed from above as I walked through a pestilent stench. I saw movement to my right and drew my Peacemaker on it, but it was only the flitting shadow of an Indian skewered on a slowly turning weather vane anchored to the roof of the general store.

The place they peddled their opium from had seen better days. It'd been a saloon or a brothel once, I reckoned, but all the cushions and pipes sort of gave away the vice of choice for its most recent patrons. I'd never tried the lotus personally; I've enough personal demons yammering around in my head to give pause before partaking of anything that's going to make them worse. Most of the walls had blown outward, but there weren't any scorch marks indicating dynamite had been used. I started looking around for any sign of my quarry when a melodious Asian woman's voice spoke up behind me.

"This was my uncle's place; I hope you're not here to steal anything."

I'll admit I nearly jumped out of skin. I could be church mouse quiet when necessary, and sneaky folks usually have a hell of a time trying to get the drop on me, but I had no idea she'd come up behind me. So I spun around, pulling my gun out of habit. She kicked it from my hand just as easy as you please and nearly broke my finger in the trigger guard. She was right pretty, I must say. Long, straight black hair set off her almond eyes and petite features. I could tell that someone had broken her nose in the past. I also knew she kicked like a damn mule.

"Do you make a habit of sneaking up on armed strangers young lady?"

"Only when they're busy nosing through my property."

Her tone and the smile she flashed said she was relaxed and willing to talk, but I noticed her right leg was drawn a couple inches further back then her left—a scorpion's tail waiting to strike. I was trying to think of a clever retort when I noticed something . . . something different in the air. The vultures had gone quiet.

I looked to the sky and the vultures were gone, but in their place—barreling out of the sun toward us—was a winged nightmare. Shoving the girl aside, I was rewarded by a swift knee to the ribs. There wasn't even time to wonder if anything was broken before pain and that all too familiar stench of ammonia beset me. I found myself carried above the town by a creature black as the Pit.

Words fail to describe the *wrongness* of the monster. It was larger than a man and its form shifted from moment to moment. Oddly, it never made a sound, though mouths formed and tried to take my face off. Noxious winds buffeted and choked me as I beat at the creature with everything I had but it didn't seem to notice. As I flailed about, claws dug deeper into my shoulders. The beast soared and dived until I lost all sense of orientation. One of its six mouths spit something green and fetid smelling at my face, but I managed to duck away and barely drew my wavy bladed dagger from its sheath in the back of my britches.

I reckoned I was a dead man, one way or another, but there was no way I was going to Hell alone. "Die you rancid bastard!" I screamed as I plunged the dagger into its chest. The thing's rubbery flesh sizzled around the blade and, while it didn't cry out, it changed colors in a mad fashion. I dragged the dagger down as much of its body as I could until ropy things fell out; then it let go and I followed the viscera to the ground.

The sensation of falling was a familiar one for me unfortunately, but until then I'd yet to have the pleasure of crashing through a roof onto an overstuffed down mattress. Pieces of wood bit and tore as the legs of my savior shot out in four directions. The room filled with beauteous white feathers. I lay there for a mite bit trying to get my wind back and figure out if I would ever walk again. I heard someone taking the stairs two at a time before the door was kicked open.

She looked like an angel in black silk wearing the midday sun like a beautifully gilded raiment. The expression on her face was almost worth the couple of re-broken ribs; her eyes were wide and her mouth formed a little "O" with shock at my survival. Though it pained me something fierce, I couldn't help but laugh. She joined me soon thereafter and had to sit to keep from falling over.

When the hilarity of my near-demise subsided I introduced myself, "I'd like to try this again. My name is Jedediah Smith. Is the thing dead?"

Her eyes—such lovely eyes—twinkled as she said, "Do you honestly think I'd be up here if it wasn't? It was never really alive anyway; it was more the manifestation of its caller's will than anything else. After you gutted it, it lost too much of its corporeal integrity and began to decompose."

She handed me the dagger I'd dropped as I plummeted.

"You're lucky you had this. Star-born metal can have a strong reaction to such things, and I'll bet there's been a blessing laid on it by someone skilled in magickal workings."

"Who in the hell are you?" I asked, impressed. She had better diction then any cow poke or school marm I'd dealt with in weeks.

She flushed a little, quite fetchingly really, and said, "Oh, I'm Mai Ling. My uncle owned the opium trade in this town. He was a powerful seer; he foresaw the coming of the priest and yourself."

"What priest?"

"The man you seek is a priest of a dead god. The disk he stole from you will allow him to speak directly to his god instead of merely getting glimpses of the being's dreams."

※ ※ ※

Memories of the night the priest broke into the museum danced before my mind's eye like a stage play. I was working late, trying in vain to decipher the writings on a metallic disk found in the temple. The script was like nothing I'd encountered previously. Looking up as I stretched revealed an Asian man standing in the circle of light created by my lamp. He wasn't very impressive looking, but his eyes seemed too black somehow, provoking the feeling that I was seeing a man with no soul.

"It is most unfortunate that you are awake at this late hour, Dr. Smith. I had hoped to remove the disk without anyone being the wiser."

"You've got a lot of sand coming in here like this, but you'll get the disk over my dead body." I said as I stood.

"Yes, I will."

I snatched up the pencil I'd been making notes with and buried it in one of his crazy eyes. He cried out, more from surprise than pain I think, and pulled the wood from his eyeball. Instead of the blood and jelly I expected to see, dark frothy syrup oozed out and covered the orb. Two blinks later and his eye was whole again.

"Aww, shit!" I said. Even if I had my trusty gun, I reckoned it wouldn't have done any good.

He grinned at me then, but it was more of a facial twitch that held no humor. "I was going to do you the honor of making your death look like a heart attack. Now you will suffer instead. It will be hours before the guards downstairs awaken. There is much I will do to you until then."

The thief lashed at me with the palm of his hand. I tasted blood as ribs snapped. I snatched up the disk to use as a shield but he started making sweeping kicks at my legs, driving me back toward the night-darkened windows.

He punched me in the gut and dinner came up to discuss the situation with me. I swallowed steak and potatoes again as I smashed the disk on my assailant's crown. He staggered back momentarily. I think I truly angered him for the first time because his face screwed up all kinds of ugly, then he snatched the disk away and did a spinning kick that launched me out the window.

I wish I could say that was the first time I'd been thrown out of a building, but I'd be a liar if I did. I landed on a fresh pile of compost three stories below my office. The mound was warm and inviting. Despite efforts to stay conscious, a dark abyss yawned wide and swallowed me up.

I woke in a hospital the next day. The groundskeeper had found me and went screaming to the guards that there was a dead man in his compost. I'd suffered a concussion—which explained the headache—and some cuts along with my four broken ribs. After explaining the situation to my superiors, I tracked the priest for the better part of a month and a half.

Looking up from my thoughts at the prettiest set of eyes I'd seen lately—they contrasted so well with my glacial blues—I wondered what the hell I'd gotten myself into.

※ ※ ※

"What the hell have I gotten myself into?" I tried to get out of bed and winced at the pain. "And why are you still alive?"

"I felt some ribs give when I kicked you," she said, "let's cut some bandages off of this bed sheet." I eased myself over the side of the bed and removed my shirt while she cut long strips off the linen with a knife of her own.

"My uncle was a warlord in China. He raised me from a child, but I have reason to believe he'd had my parents killed. He was a truly terrible man and a powerful wizard. He would make me watch as he tortured men to death and then raised up their souls so that he could continue torturing them. The screams of dying men were the lullaby that lured me to sleep as a girl."

She looked ashen as she remembered the man and began wrapping the makeshift bandages tight around my chest. "I've seen him call up creatures similar to the one you fought and send them after rival wizards or warlords. He hired teachers from foreign lands to educate me. If I didn't perform to his standards, he beat me—badly. He trained me in the martial arts himself in our family's style and a little in his wizardry; he even used me as an assassin. We left home in a hurry one night, taking as much of his wealth and as many of his most trusted followers as we could. He'd had a vision that the other warlords were plotting against him and knew that even he could not defeat them all. So, when I was twenty, we came to these shores. I'd always wanted to come and my uncle needed an interpreter he could trust, because he refused to learn English."

"I can't believe you've managed to keep your wits about you all this time."

"Don't think me soft because I'm a woman, Dr. Smith. I've killed men and worse for my uncle and, depending on the victim, sometimes I've *enjoyed* it." She tightened the last of the bandages a little too snug for my taste and continued, "We've been here about five years now. My uncle's contacts brought in drugs and girls for the whorehouse. I've done what I can for any innocents involved but I couldn't leave or he'd hunt me down like a dog. The I Ching told my uncle of a great calamity about to descend on his house, and a lotus dream revealed the priest and yourself to him. When the priest came, I went against Uncle's orders and warned people with families, but they were so deep in Uncle's pocket, they refused to leave. The priest proceeded to smoke an unbelievable amount of opium. He cannot die you see. His god has put something of himself where the priest's humanity used to be and only the mightiest of magick may bring him down."

I raised an eyebrow at this. "Seriously? He can't die?"

"No weapon of Earth can kill him, no. His god can; or the spawn of his god; and wizards of sufficient power might, but nothing as mundane as a gun. It is a spawn of his god that he seeks here, buried beneath time and rock as it waits for the heavens to align themselves the way they used to be and allow its kind to live again. The priest needs the creature close to create the link between the god and himself. When the priest entered deep into the lotus-trance he whispered horrible things and words of power. Uncle sent me to the cave where we keep our gold. He told me when to come out and look for you here. He knew that he would die here and made me swear that I would avenge him."

Now, for any other man, this may have been too much to take in all at once. But with all I'd seen in my life, and the irrefutable facts around me, I had to accept what she said as gospel truth. "Well, I reckon we aren't doing any good here sitting on our laurels, best if we scrounge up some supplies and start looking for his trail."

"Don't worry about that, I know exactly where he's going." She shivered then, and I started to worry.

※ ※ ※

We found some jerky, water, and other things I thought we'd need and threw them in a carpetbag. Mai set off at a brisk pace north, and after an hour I was wishing I had Aztec with me. As we approached some hills, I noticed a distinct lack of vegetation and pointed it out to Mai.

She nodded and said, "This land is tainted by what lurks below. It is an immense thing whose roots have flung wide. Dead, it still gnaws at the lifeforce of everything around it. If we could hear the Earth, she would be sobbing here. Notice that you can't hear any bugs or birds? It's as if they're afraid to make their presence known to what lies beneath us. It is not the only one of its kind on the continent. Sometimes you hear of a whole town gone missing? These creatures are known to stir in their deathless slumber."

I stopped short for a second. "This is madness you know. We're trying to kill an undying priest before he has a pow-wow with his monstrously huge dead god who has a propensity for waking up and eating people?" She nodded and a crooked grin spread across her face. "Fair enough," I continued, "I just wanted to make sure I got everything."

Mai found the mouth of the cave we were looking for easily. Signs written in Chinese warning people not to enter had been thrown to the ground. We made some nasty preparations to aid our escape if we made it that far and sparked up a lantern before we entered. I crossed myself, although my faith was steadily becoming a shriveled, wretched thing in light of recent events. I noticed Mai making weird gestures with her fingers as well.

Further in, we found sporadic green fungus on the walls that gave off a sickly green luminescence like torchlight through slime, so I turned the lamp down low. "See, there *are* things growing down here."

"This place is a temple to evil men and things that wear the skins of men like clothes if they feel like bothering to walk amongst us. If you cared to investigate further, I'm sure you'd find that this fungus isn't native to Earth."

"Oh."

We continued further in and deeper down and came across cave drawings sporadically. Not only was the subject matter grotesque and often incomprehensible, I could discern that they were made by different peoples over great epochs of time. One drawing made by some ancient cave-dweller took up most of a wall. It showed an immense creature towering over mountains. At the very bottom, barely recognizable people looked to be sacrificing one of their own to it.

"Dreamers, poets, those who see beyond the veil of commonality most people blind themselves with are drawn to places such as this. The dreams of the gods mesh with their own, showing them grand vistas and new perspectives. Such sensitives are moths to the flame and often wander below to their deaths. You've seen the destructive power the priest wields with only an occasional dream-fragment to guide himself and his fellow clergy. Consider if he were to learn directly from the Dreamer in R'lyeh."

"Are you saying there are more like him?" I asked.

"Yes. Ageless and insane, they rule a worldwide cult of assassins dedicated to suppressing knowledge of themselves and preparing the world for their master's arrival. Even if we survive this day, we may very well find ourselves marked for death."

"Peachy."

Down innumerable passageways we searched. When the way became convoluted I made notes on the walls with chalk so we wouldn't get lost. We spoke in hushed tones as we went, in case our common enemy was lying in wait, though we should have known better. You only ambush a target you think can hurt you.

Screams echoed from somewhere in the darkness ahead and we ran toward it. Mai and I turned a corner and witnessed a hellish sight—a broken, battered, Chinese man lay on an altar of bones. Standing near his head, the priest had slit the man's throat and his blood was drawn *upward* to cover the disk floating above his body. Beyond the altar lay a crevice about the size of Texas and probably cut clean through to the other side of the planet. Within seconds, the metal softened and took on an organic look.

"The man on the altar is my uncle." Mai whispered.

The priest intoned strange words that sounded like he lacked the proper apparatus to speak properly and . . . something answered from deep down in the crevice, something that taught us what the words were supposed to sound like. We heard—we *felt*—rocks begin to shift and tumble and we knew it was act now or lie down and die if we were lucky.

Mai lunged forward with a shout and kicked the priest in the back—this was no time for honor—then quickly backpedaled and set herself up in some sort of defensive stance. The priest spun around snarling, so I threw the lantern at him. With a crash, the Chinaman was half covered in burning oil. Mai swept in low and broke one of his legs at the knee, but it just realigned itself with an audible *POP*. She kept at it as he slowly unbuttoned his flaming shirt and wiped his face and hair with it.

"Idiots," he screamed, "this is holy ground you sully! I will feast on your hearts and death will be a salvation forever denied you!"

He snatched Mai up by the front of her shirt and shook her until her eyes rolled. A breeze came from the crevice as the tip of a colossal tentacle nestled against the back of the disk. In the darkness beyond writhed a shadow-play of movement—the fissure filled with undulating tendrils. Then a fold of flesh opened in the center of the living disk and a voice thrummed over me like a pronouncement of doom.

This was the voice of the Dead Dreamer! This was the voice of a god who answered when prayed to, for whom faith was an outmoded and idiotic concept! I wanted to run screaming from this unnamable horror, but I also wanted to bow down and worship before it. Mai was lying with her face in the dirt, crying and rocking as images invaded our minds. We saw the god's plans for us, the wars it would wage with others like itself using us as raw material. Its need for worshipers was a temporary inconvenience; none would be spared from its unutterable urges when it finally strode triumphantly from its corpse city.

The priest was in ecstatic glory, rapturous from the mental torrents of his god. I used Mai Ling as my anchor because my mind was in danger of being subverted to a vast alien will. Perhaps it helped that I wasn't one of those sensitives she talked about. I'd never had much use for painting or poetry and when I've encountered weirdness in the past, I tried not to give it more thought than how to kill it. Even so, there was a bloodlust building in me, as much a "gift" from my pa as that great dead thing beneath the waters I reckon. In someone unused to it, such a primitive need to kill would have made them unable to do ought but follow their new instincts, but I had built up a resistance to such feelings through the years. I . . . just . . . needed . . . a . . . target . . . there! I pulled out my dagger and drove it with both hands into the living disk.

Vile frothy fluids gushed over me by the bucket load as the voice of the dead god fell mercifully silent. Instead, the thing in the pit roared and shook in his stead. The Chinaman glared at me with murder and worse in his eyes.

"You ignorant savage," the priest wailed, "I may never get another chance at this!"

He came at me then, his hands wreathed in bright burning flames. I couldn't pull my dagger free of the disk; it had already turned back to metal. Before the priest could strike, a thrashing pseudopod wrapped around him and carried him aloft, crushing him to pulp as it did so. Mai wrapped her arms around my waist and pulled me toward the exit. I looked back and saw her haggard face, then glanced at my dagger and ran for freedom.

I soon learned we weren't out of it yet. Rocks continued to fall on and around us while, from behind, something smashed aside all obstacles as it searched for the two humans that had caused so much trouble. My chalk markings served us in good stead and we were able to make it out of the cave just before the creature finished us. As we burst into the light I threw myself onto the plunger we'd left outside.

BOOM!

The dynamite I had planted in the cave went off without a hitch, burying whatever was coming under a ton of rock.

※ ※ ※

The first decent looking stream I came to, I stripped down and leaped in. Water never felt so good; it was a balm for the soul. Mai looked down at me with that quirky grin of hers.

"So, how does it feel to be baptized by a god?"

"Honestly?" I said. "I'd rather bathe in a spittoon."

I looked at the gunk—was it really the blood of a god?— and watched it wash down the river. For the first time in a long while I felt really clean. I heard a splash and watched Mai wade in with her clothes in one hand and undergarments in the other. So much for introspection.

"I hope you don't mind Jed, it looked so inviting and I'd like to get these clean." Her eyes held a profound mystery to me, a beautiful thing more priceless than gold. I edged a little closer.

"I don't mind at all Mai. With your uncle dead, you may want to consider moving to Illinois, I could find you a job at the museum, you might even want to go on a dig with me, and at least you'd have someone to call a friend."

I edged a little closer still.

She threw her clothes back onto the shore and slid in close to me. I could feel her warm skin through the water.

"I suppose I could live with that. Too bad though; I was hoping to find someone more than a friend. I'm thinking we can get a wagon at the nearest town and load up all of my uncle's gold. I don't think he'll need it anytime soon"

I kissed her on the neck and my voice grew a little husky as I whispered, "Once we get done 'bathing' I'll let you ride Aztec to town next to me." She splashed me then and wrapped her arms around my chest. I only winced a little.

"Silly man, I'd rather *walk* next to you."

SNAKE OIL

BY MATTHEW BAUGH

"The Devil thus Irritated, immediately try'd all sorts of Methods to over-turn this poor Plantation: and so much of the Church, as was Fled into this Wilderness, immediately found, The Serpent cast out of his Mouth a Flood for the carrying of it away."

—Cotton Mather

There was a man in the middle of the desert. He sat on a flat-topped rock as the morning sun gave a silvery sheen to the sea of prairie grass all around. The sky above was clear but there were thunderheads over a line of bluffs far to the west.

Of the places I've been, the northern part of New Mexico Territory is the most beautiful I know. I'd volunteered to run a prisoner down to Santa Fe for the chance to be out in it for a few days.

For all that, it was a desert and a man alone and on foot wouldn't last long. I turned my horse and trotted toward him. As I drew near I could see that he was an Indian, maybe a Navajo or an Apache.

Up close I realized that I knew him. He was a Crow who had left his people's lands long ago. His name was Billy Nine-Fingers and he had worked as a scout for me back in my buffalo hunting days.

I remembered some other things about Billy that prompted me to pull my Winchester from its scabbard and lay it across my lap.

He looked up at me as I drew nearer.

"Billy," I said.

"Dave," he returned my greeting.

"What are you doing sitting out here?"

"Snakebit," he answered. "Figured it was best not to walk around."

"No horse?"

He shook his head.

"Died on me a ways back."

He was sweating and trembling. I could see a poultice he had tied to his leg. I decided he was telling me the truth. For Billy Nine-Fingers that was a rarity.

"You going to shoot me, Dave?" he asked.

"I probably ought to," I replied. "You near got me and my brother Sy killed the last time I saw you."

He didn't answer. He just sat there watching me and shivering. As he did I noticed something odd.

"Hold out your hands, Billy."

He did. They were pale and trembling, but otherwise whole.

"I guess they don't call you Nine-Fingers anymore," I said. "How in Perdition did you manage that?"

Billy reached into his shirt and, very slowly, brought out a bottle of patent medicine. I stepped down and took it. The label read *Professor Galen's Ophidian Elixir*.

"Good for what ails you," Billy said.

I pulled out the cork and sniffed the stuff. It had a light fishy smell overlaid with spices.

"What is it?"

"Snake oil," he answered. "Got it from a medicine seller in *Ojo del Cerdo*."

"And it grew your finger back?"

He nodded.

"I figured it would cure anything, but it don't seem to be much good against snakebite."

"Can you sit on a horse?"

He looked surprised.

"You ain't gonna shoot me?"

I shook my head. He probably deserved to die but I'm not much for shooting sick men. Besides, the business of his regrown finger needed looking into.

I put Billy on my horse and led it. We could have ridden double, but that would have given him the opportunity to grab my knife or one of my pistols. Sick or not, I didn't trust Billy Full-Set-of-Fingers enough to chance that.

※ ※ ※

It was noon when the horse spooked. We had come down into a dry *arroyo* to take advantage of the bit of shade it offered. As we crossed into shadow a buzzing surrounded us. There were rattlesnakes all around.

I wasted a moment trying to calm the horse, then the snakes started striking and I let him go. One snake lodged its fangs in my boot and several others bit at the horse's rear legs. I pulled both pistols and began shooting.

When it was done, I checked my boot. The rattler's fangs had failed to pierce the tough leather. Billy lay twenty feet away. He had fallen when the horse bolted. There was no sign of the animal, but its tracks shouldn't be hard to follow.

"How many snakes was it?" he muttered.

"I killed eight," I replied. "I don't see more, but we're getting out of this gully just the same."

He was strong enough to walk with me supporting him. I left him sitting against a rock and went after the horse.

※ ※ ※

I found the animal about a mile away, fallen and suffering from the poison. I shot him, and felt a touch of regret doing so. He had been a good horse.

I walked back with the saddlebags across my shoulder. As I approached, I saw a cluster of half a dozen horsemen where I'd left Billy. They were armed but only one of them looked like a fighter. They had tied a rope into a hangman's noose.

"Who are you stranger?" one of the men asked. He was a big fellow with the look of a shopkeeper about him.

"My name's Mather," I answered. "I'm deputy marshal up in Las Vegas."

"Mysterious Dave Mather?" the man's eyes widened and the others traded glances. I was pleased to see they had heard of me. It could make things simpler.

"Who are you men?" I asked.

"My name's Rance Collins," the big man answered. "This is Frank

Laribee, Bill and Johnny Rourke, Quint Ames and Pete Martin. We're a posse out of *Ojo del Cerdo*. We've been on the trail of this redskin all day."

"Looks like you're fixing to lynch him."

"We were just trying to figure the best way," Quint said. He wore his gun tied down on his thigh. The look in his eye made me think he was burning to show someone just how quick he could draw it.

"There's no trees out here to hang him from," he continued. "We thought it would work to hitch the rope to a saddle and let one of the horses drag him till he strangled."

The other men shifted uneasily. I guessed there hadn't been total agreement about the plan.

"What did he do?" I asked.

"Don't matter what he done," Quint growled. "If we want to kill a damned thieving redskin that's our concern."

"He stole something vary valuable," Collins interjected.

"What?"

"Mister," Quint cut in. "It ain't none of your business! You've got no authority out here. You ought to head back to Las Vegas and leave this to us."

He was right about me not having jurisdiction, though I don't often let such details bother me.

"What did he steal?" I repeated.

"I warned you!" Quint cried and pulled his gun.

He was blindingly fast, but a man who tries to draw a pistol on one who has a rifle ready is fighting too great an advantage. My shot took him high in the chest and he pitched over backward.

The others moved to tend Quint. He wasn't dead but probably would be soon.

"You all saw him draw," I said, keeping the rifle leveled.

"We saw," Collins admitted. "Quint's a hothead, Deputy Mather. We aren't looking for a fight. If you want the Indian, he's yours. We just want what he took."

"We need to get Quint back to town," Frank Larribee said.

"Bandage him up the best you can," Collins ordered. He moved to Billy's pack and rummaged around for a moment. His hand came out with a clear gemstone twice the size of a man's thumb. The afternoon sun struck bright flashes of every color off of it.

"Here's what he stole," he said.

There were several flaws in the stone, blood red streaks of an impurity that passed through it like veins. It was cut in an oval with so many facets that it made me dizzy. I had an odd sense that there was an intelligene hidden in those glittering depths.

"That can't be a diamond," I murmured. "Is it quartz crystal?"

"The professor says it's a diamond," Collins answered. "In any case, it's his and this Indian had no business taking it."

I nodded. Billy had a liking for pretty things that belonged to other people. More exactly, he fancied objects of supposed magical power that belonged to other people.

"How far to *Ojo del Cerdo*?" I asked.

"Twenty miles," Collins answered. "Maybe twenty-five."

"I'll come with you," I said. "We can get Billy and your man doctored up, then I can take them on to Las Vegas for trial."

The posse members didn't look too happy with that suggestion, but Collins nodded.

"We were wrong to think of lynching this redskin," he said. "We don't have a lawman or a judge so we've gotten too used to taking care of things ourselves. We'll do as you say."

※ ※ ※

We rode into *Ojo de Cerdo* late morning of the next day. It was a flyspeck of a town built on a natural hot spring. Collins said the name came from a big herd of javelina that used to water there.

The town didn't have a jail so we took Billy and Quint to the church and laid them out on the pews. I looked around while Larribee went to fetch help. It was about what you would expect for a small town church, except for one detail. The back wall sported a "T" shaped cross rather than the usual kind, and there was a fierce-looking brass snake coiled around it.

After a few moments Laribee returned with a gaunt man dressed in fancy clothes.

"You found the rascal?" the man's voice was as resonant as a stage actor's.

"Yes Professor," Collins said. "Deputy Mather here found him for us."

"Ah?" the professor looked me over. Something in his glittery black eyes reminded me of the gleam in the diamond.

"I am most grateful to you, Deputy. I am Professor Galen." He paused. "Do you have my property?"

Collins fished the stone out of his pocket and handed it over.

That's a fancy gem, Professor," I said.

"It's more than an ordinary gemstone, Deputy," he replied. "This diamond is the sacred *ulun'suti* of the Cherokee people. It is an essential tool in my healing work."

He moved to each of the men and gave them a dose of the same patent medicine that Billy had carried. Then he placed the diamond on their wounds, each time muttering some sort of prayer or charm under his breath. Finally he rose with a satisfied look on his face.

"Both will recover," he announced. He started to slip the gemstone back into his pocket but I stopped him.

"I'm sorry, Professor," I said. "But that diamond is evidence. I have to hold onto it until after Billy's trial."

"I don't understand," the gaunt man protested. "Surely there's no doubt that it is mine? The whole town can attest to that."

"I understand," I said. "But it has to stay with me till the trial. That's the law."

"But I need it in my healing ministrations!"

I'll be happy to let you use it anytime you're working on someone," I replied. "The rest of the time it stays with me."

The professor gave me a cold look.

"This is most inconvenient!" he hissed. Without another word he turned and marched out.

"You'll have to excuse the professor," Collins said. "He's a good man but he's none too patient with rules and regulations."

In the professor's place I might have felt the same. As I was not in his place, I didn't see any point discussing it.

"Who's the preacher for your church?" I asked.

"I am," Collins answered. "I also run the general store."

"I'd never heard of a preacher leading a lynching posse before."

He flushed.

"I'm president of the citizen's vigilance committee," he said. "I confess that we were overzealous with that Indian. I'm grateful that you stopped us."

I nodded then looked up at the back wall.

"Never seen a big snake decorating a church," I said.

"It's unusual, I know," Collins answered. "It is a Christian symbol."

He picked up a Bible and opened it. "Here in Numbers 21 it tells about a time when the Hebrew people came to a place where they were afflicted by poisonous serpents."

" . . . *the Lord spake unto Moses*" he read, "*and sayeth, 'Make thee a fiery serpent, and set it upon a pole: and it shall come to pass that whomsoever is bitten, when he looketh upon it, shall live.'*"

He closed the Bible.

"The symbol of the snake on the pole is called the *Nehush'tan*. In John's Gospel we learn that this is the same as the image of Christ on the cross. It is a sign of healing and redemption."

"I am not much of a church-goer," I said. "However I am descended from preachers. I think they might disagree with you."

"Mather," he said thoughtfully. "You're not kin to Cotton Mather, are you? That old Puritan who presided at the Salem Witch Trials?"

It wasn't a very accurate description. Old Cotton had only been called on to give testimony, and he had admonished the judges not to convict without certain proof. Still, his involvement was what had made him famous.

"I'm kin to him," I said.

"Perhaps he wouldn't care for it," Collins said. "Cotton Mather was famous for being joyless and narrow-minded in his faith. If you come to services tomorrow evening I can guarantee you'll see truer worship than anything he led."

"Maybe I will," I answered.

❋ ❋ ❋

The town had a small hotel that served a decent steak. I ate and went up to my room where I laid an old book out on the table.

The book bore the title: *The Secrets of the Invisible World: Observations As well Historical as Theological, upon the Nature, the Number, and the Operations of the Devils, Witches, and all their Kith and Kin, Including Methods for the Recognizing and Combating Thereof*, by Cotton Mather. It was my legacy from old Cotton, handed down through generations of Mathers.

The Witch Trials had been mostly superstitious panic, but my ancestor had found that a few accusations had some merit. There really are dark beings in the world, and humans who align themselves with them can gain terrible powers. I suspected that was exactly what I was dealing with in *Ojo de Cerdo*.

Cotton had a fair piece to say about snake worship. He mentioned the *Nehush'tan* and the African snake gods, Set and Damballa.

He had written, " ... *in the Times of Moses the Devil, that Old Serpent, was mightily Constrained by the Hand of the Almighty and made to give Succor to his People Israel. Yet as the People did turn from God to worship the Brazen Image in his stead, So the Lord did raise up King Hezekiah to cast down the False God. That which Acts the Angel when serving Man is Always revealed as the Very Devil when Man turns to Serve it.*"

That made some sense to me. Unfortunately, it didn't give me much clue what was going on. I took the diamond from my pocket and gazed into it. The angles on the facets came together in a way that shouldn't have worked, and there were colors in those depths I couldn't name. It wasn't any natural stone. Examining it gave me a sick headache. I wrapped it in a kerchief and tucked it away in the toe of my boot.

I blew out the lamp, but sleep was a difficult matter. Around midnight I rose to relieve my bladder. I touched a bare foot to the ground but some impulse prompted me to pull it back. A slender red and black form streaked past, barely missing my heel.

I pulled my knife from under the pillow and flung it. The Arkansas toothpick caught the creature in mid-body and fixed it in place. I watched as the snake writhed and lashed until it finally lay still.

I re-lit the lamp and saw that the serpent was nearly three feet long. Its red and black stripes were interspersed with slender yellow bands. I had seen coral snakes in the wet parts of east Texas, but never in the desert. They were usually shy creatures, and were ten times as poisonous as a rattler.

I gave up on the idea of sleep and kept the lamp lit the rest of the night.

※ ※ ※

Professor Galen's medicine wagon was well made. Painted on the side, under the professor's name, was a picture of a bearded man wrapped in a sheet and holding a heavy stick with a serpent wound around it.

The lettering below the painting touted the virtues of the professor's elixir, calling it: "*That miraculous unguent whose powers are known so well to the celestial physicians of far Cathay. It can cure rheumatism, dropsy, gallstones, fever and ague, and consumption. It is the best possible guard against smallpox, typhoid, measles and every shade of fever from scarlet to yellow. It will improve your appetite, put the spring back in your step, and enhance your native manliness.*"

"Deputy Mather," Galen's tone was pleasant. "I apologize for my brusqueness last night. You were clearly only executing your bounden duty."

"Thanks, Professor," I said. "This is a fancy rig you've got."

"I noticed you looking over my painting of Asclepius."

"The fellow with the snake-on-a-stick?"

The professor chuckled.

"Asclepius is the Greek god of medicine," he explained. "His rod is the universal symbol of all who practice the noble art of healing."

"I guess I have seen such on doctor's signs," I admitted. "Though I thought it was two snakes on the staff, and little wings at the top."

Professor Galen chuckled again. "You're thinking of the caduceus. Many physicians use that in the mistaken belief that it is a symbol of healing. Actually, it is the sigil of Mercury, the god of thieves. It's a common error, but a very appropriate one I have always thought."

"Your picture looks a lot like the big snake Mr. Collins has at his church," I commented.

He nodded sagely.

"The ancients of all lands recognized the aptness of the symbol. Seeing the snake shed his skin, they reasoned that he had the power to discard his old, sickly body and be reborn in the bloom of health.

"Occident and orient are alike in their reverence for the serpent, nor are the Americas lacking in this insight. South of the border they tell tales of the god whom they call *Quetzalcoatl*, or *Kukulkan*. In this part of the country, the Hopi call him *Bálölöokong*, and among the Pueblos he is *Avenyu*. The Caddo of Texas call him *Kika kiokahuni*."

"You used a Cherokee name before."

"That is true," he said. "In Cherokee territory he is called *Uktena*, the horned river serpent. It was while I was among them that I received the *Ulun'suti*."

"How did they come to give such a thing to a white man?" I asked.

"You don't believe that I gained their trust?"

"Most people don't pass on their sacred treasures to outsiders," I replied. "Not red people, nor white."

Galen's smile was thin, but his eyes looked genuinely amused.

"You are most perspicacious, Deputy," he said. "They would

never have given me their sacred stone."

"You stole it?"

"Hardly. I went to the great serpent and obtained my own."

※ ※ ※

Billy was manacled to a hitching ring in the stable. Johnny Rourke was sitting nearby with a shotgun. Billy looked healthier than I had ever seen him.

I relieved Rourke from his guard duty. He didn't want to go but a badge and an evil stare persuaded him.

"You feel like talking?" I asked when Rourke had gone.

Billy stared at me with a strange look in his eyes. It reminded me of the face of a trapped coyote. He didn't say anything.

"I could get you out of this place," I continued. "But I mean to know what's happening here first."

Billy only stared. I can outstare most men I've met, but this time I was the first to look away. We sat in silence until a girl of about twelve came in with a basket of food.

"I'm Maggie Collins," she said. "My Pa asked me to bring this over for you and the prisoner."

I thanked the girl and took the basket. When she had gone I poked through it. There was cold ham, some biscuits, and two wedges of apple pie. I passed it to Billy, after removing the fork and knife she had provided.

"Ain't you eating?" he asked around a mouthful of ham.

"I figured I'd watch a bit and see how your food sits with you," I answered.

A nasty smile crept onto his face.

"You're a cold one Dave," he said. "This food's good. If it had been poisoned, I'd have smelled it."

I nodded, without any real conviction.

"Do you know what these people are?" he asked between bites.

"I'd say some sort of snake worshippers."

Billy laughed harshly.

"Smarter than I remembered you," he said. "Yeah, these folks worship the old snake god. He goes by a different name among each people but his own folk call him Yig."

"That doesn't sound like an Indian name," I said.

"It ain't," he agreed. "Yig is from a language that goes back before any of the nations."

"I thought you Indians had always been here."

"This ain't the first world the human people have lived in," he answered. "The Hopis say this is the fourth world. Humans came into this world out of a hole in the ground a long time ago, but there were already other people here. There was Shonokins, who look almost human but ain't, and fish people in the sea, and sand people hidden in underground towns, and there was the snake people.

"The snake people hated the humans, being so much smarter than we are. They fought and schemed for a long time but humans beat them in the end. Maybe it was because humans can be brave and clever when they have to. Mostly, I think it's because humans breed so fast.

"The snake people mostly died out and even old Yig was driven into the deep waters. He can't come out because the thunder and lightning will strike him if he tries. But he is still powerful. With his own people gone, he had to make due with human followers. They give him a few of their own as sacrifices and he gives them good crops and heals their diseases."

"So, what's this diamond?" I asked.

"Yig is a big devil," Billy answered. "His body is as thick as a hundred year oak and he's so long that a man would have trouble seeing both ends of him at the same time. He's got two horns on his head and a diamond crest in between. A long time ago a Cherokee named Aganunitsi fought the serpent and stole his crest. It gave him all kinds of miracle-powers.

"When I came to this town I saw that the professor had a crest. I don't know how he got it, but I figured I'd take it for myself."

"You wanted all that power," I said.

Billy grinned his coyote grin.

"Better me than him."

I wasn't sure there was so much difference, but I didn't say so. I had the diamond now and it might be best for me just to slip out of town with it. The people were sure to lynch Billy once I was gone, which was too bad for him. I calculated that I could live with that on my conscience.

The problem was getting away. I wasn't too worried about a posse, but the professor seemed to have a way to send snakes after people. I thought I should leave at night, when snakes are holed up against the chill. I didn't have any more plan than that.

※ ※ ※

Young Maggie brought supper with a bright smile. Looking at her I wondered at the place of a sweet-seeming child in a town of snake worshippers. My thoughts were interrupted by a cry from outside.

"Mather! Come out front and bring the Indian."

I stepped to the stable doors and looked out. There were about a dozen men there, wielding a variety of weapons. Quint Ames was in front looking healthy and whole.

I stepped out and leveled the shotgun. Quint's hand froze by his holster.

"That's good sense," I said. "That trick didn't work against a rifle. It'll go even worse against a shotgun."

"You can't shoot us all Mather," he replied. "You've only got two shots."

"You're right Quint," I answered. "I figured I'd use both barrels on you and my six-guns on the rest."

"You can't win."

"Right again, which means all I've got left is killing enough of you to take the sweetness out of your victory."

Maggie had come up behind me, her breathing sounded frightened. I reached behind to push her back.

"Get inside child!"

I felt a stab of pain in my hand. The girl had sunk her teeth into me and was holding on for all she was worth. I slung my arm forward and back and managed to shake her off.

That was more than enough time for Quint to pull his pistol and fire. He was faster than anyone I had ever seen. It made me think of a rattler striking.

Fortunately, he was young enough and dumb enough that he put too much faith in his quickness. If he'd hesitated the smallest fraction of a second to make sure of his aim, I would have been dead. As it was, his shot missed me by a good three inches. I put a double load of buckshot into him before he could fire again.

The rest of the mob started shooting. I dropped the empty shotgun and pulled my Colt revolvers, ducking inside.

"Dave, set me free!" Billy yelled.

I tossed him the key and turned my attention to the townspeople. They had scattered for cover when I started shooting. Three of them hadn't made it.

"Saddle two horses," I cried. "We'll have to ride through them."

"You should give me a gun," Billy called back.

"Come with me or don't," I answered. "Either way, I'm not giving you a gun."

I kept shooting to keep the townsfolk from getting organized. By the time the horses were ready, my hand was throbbing where I'd been bitten, and I was starting to feel light headed.

We crashed out of the stable with Billy whooping and me firing wildly. The mob got off a few shots but didn't hit either of us. I think we would have made it, if my head hadn't been buzzing so much. A wave of nausea struck me and I felt myself slipping out of the saddle.

I hit the ground with a painful jolt. The last thing I remember was the sight of Billy galloping away.

✳ ✳ ✳

I was half conscious when they dragged me to the professor's wagon. I couldn't move, nor speak, but I could sense what was happening.

Galen dosed me with a few swallows of his elixir. It wasn't too pleasant, but it was no worse than the cod liver oil my Ma used to give me when I was a kid. He pressed the crystal against my wounded hand. I felt warmth flood into me.

My eyes opened. Through their bleariness, Professor Galen seemed different. His gaunt body was even thinner, his skin dark and scaly, his face more that of a serpent than a man. I blinked several times and the image shifted to the well-dressed sharpster again.

"Glammer," I muttered. "An illusion."

"You are a man of some parts," the professor said. "Not many of your kind understand the influence a superior mind can exert over humans. You are also quite dangerous, and have placed Quint and two others beyond even my curative powers. It seems only fitting that you replace him."

"You'd be wise to go ahead and kill me now," I growled.

"You are reasonably intelligent for one of your race," Professor Galen said. "Sadly, that's not saying much. Your people haven't even discovered the double spiral chains that give living creatures their shape and form, much less learned how to shape them at will. It is a tragedy that you have supplanted us throughout this world.

"But these dark days are drawing to a close. My experiments, coupled with the power of the *Ulun'suti,* allow me to remake the people of your brutish race in my own image."

"What do you mean?" I demanded. Then it dawned on me. "Maggie?"

He bowed his head in acknowledgment.

"The more severe the injury, the more the healing transforms a person. Maggie was badly burned and would have died. The healing transformed so much of her body that she is nearly like me. Her fangs have yet to develop, but you have felt her venom.

"It may take centuries, but our time will come again. Your people are sentimental. I heal their loved ones and they give themselves willingly into my service."

He locked eyes with me and said some words in a language I didn't know. A kind of calmness took hold, as if my mind was being locked away from my body. He left me there for a time. I was unshackled and unguarded but I didn't try to leave. I didn't even want to.

※ ※ ※

He came to collect me when it was dark. My body responded to his commands, but my mind was still remote.

We crossed to the church under a sky dark with storm clouds. The place was brightly lit and filled with the good folks of *Ojo del Cerdo* in their Sunday best. Rance Collins stood at the pulpit, preaching a fierce sermon about the Last Days. He said that only the people marked with the sign of the holy serpent would be saved.

" . . . *And these signs shall follow them that believe,*" he read. "*In my name shall they cast out devils; they shall speak with new tongues; they shall take up serpents; and if they drink any deadly thing, it shall not hurt them; they shall lay hands on the sick, and they shall recover.*"

At that the doors of the church were thrown over and dozens of snakes slithered in. The people began to cry out in strange tongues and to dance among the creatures. Many were bitten but they continued to dance as if nothing had happened.

At the professor's command I lay down in front of the altar. Snakes began to crawl onto my body. I knew that they would bite soon. I didn't have any fear of death. I understood that the professor would heal me, just as he would heal all who were bitten. The venom would not kill us; it would reshape us into poisonous creatures.

I knew that this should have upset me, but it didn't. I only found it interesting in an abstract sort of way.

As I lay there I could see the faces of the dancers. Most were lost in a kind of religious ecstasy, but Johnny Rourke looked alert and seemed to be watching the professor with a strange intensity.

I blinked my eyes and the face shifted. For an instant, it was Billy Nine-Fingers instead of Rourke. I wondered if the Indian had his own sort of glammer.

Professor Galen was moving from one person to another, touching the diamond to their wounds. The disguised Billy palmed a knife and moved closer to him. He caught the professor's wrist with one hand and stabbed him with the other. The snake-oil man sank to the ground with a shocked expression.

Billy's face was his own again, coyote grin and all. He backed away from the congregation. He had drawn a pistol, and I could see the diamond in his other hand. The revels of the dancers continued as though nothing had happened.

With great care, Billy picked a snake-free path to the open door and bolted into the night. Professor Galen's face had hardened into a look of fury. He began to chant in his strange language. Despite his wounds, the words held a power that seemed to shake the air.

The heavy sky opened. It was what the Navajos call "male rain," a sudden, pounding downpour. The roar of it was deafening, but I could still hear another sound. This came from the direction of the hot springs. It was a rubbing noise, as if something colossal was slithering across the wet ground. The noise increased until it seemed to be right outside. I heard a cry of fear and pistol shots and realized the unseen horror must have found Billy.

Then there was a flash of lightning that lit the world with impossible brilliance. For a second I saw the creature, huge beyond belief with two great horns curving from the sides of its head.

I saw this for only a fraction of a second before the thunderclap hit. It shattered windows and threw people to the floor. Then there was silence and darkness.

※ ※ ※

When I woke it was light outside. The rain had ended and the snakes were gone. The church was filled with the bodies of those who had been bitten in the ceremony. A reptilian body in Professor Galen's clothing lay nearby. Billy's knife was still lodged in its chest.

Rance Collins was kneeling by the altar. He held the badly burned body of his daughter in his arms.

"He has abandoned us," the preacher said quietly. "The Lord has withdrawn his blessing from this place."

I didn't answer. I went out onto the street to look for any trace of Billy, or the diamond, or the giant serpent I had glimpsed last night. It was hopeless; the rain had washed away all tracks. All that remained was a pit of fused glass in the center of the street where the lightning had struck.

I stayed in town long enough to help Collins bury his daughter. I surely didn't owe it to him, but it seemed the right thing to do somehow. The human thing.

CEMETERY, NEVADA

BY TIM CURRAN

HE FOLLOWING IS AN un-posted letter found among the personal effects of the late Daniel J. McHenry:

Daniel McHenry
C/O Elm Creek Hotel
Medicine Lodge, Kansas
April 14, 1912

Foley's Frontier Sideshow
and Wild West Museum
Clovis, New Mexico

Dear Sirs,

Am I to understand that within your museum of curiosities and oddities you claim to have the body of the notorious outlaw and pistolman "Nevada" Jack McCall? Perhaps I have been misled, if not . . . well, sir, I find that particular claim not only unlikely but more than a little disturbing. For the last I saw of Nevada Jack he was tucked away dry and bloodless like something wrapped up in a spider's web. Yes, sir, I speak the truth. The truth that not only took the lives of Nevada Jack, but some very good friends of mine.

But allow me to explain.

In the fall of 1892 I was one of a group of hard-riders and pistol-fighters that history often refers to as regulators. Well, we didn't see ourselves as regulators. Mercenaries, maybe. Soldiers of fortune. Opportunists is what we were. Men baked hard by a hard, unforgiving country, worked like clay and oiled like saddle leather until we were only good at spitting lead and catching it. Men who came out of the War Between the States with nothing but a talent for killing and shooting and riding. We were a tough, callus bunch to be sure. Our leader was "Doc" Piper. And it was Doc who'd thrown us together as regulators for the Union Pacific railroad. We were all war vets—me and Jessie Brock, Kevin Macon, Big Mike and Johnny Q. Starkweather—good with guns and knives, bad with holding anything remotely like a decent job. Drifters to the man. Under Doc Piper it was our job to hunt down gangs that were preying on the Union Pacific's interests, that mainly being express and mail cars.

We'd made a pretty good show of ourselves on more than one occasion, raiding against outlaw bands and gunning down thieves and road agents and all manner of trash that walked on two legs and robbed for a living.

Then Doc put us on the trail of Nevada Jack and his crew of cutthroats and renegades.

We hounded them from the Painted Desert in Arizona Territory, across the Colorado into Nevada and brought them finally to ground in the wild gold town of Pine Grove. A dusty, violent hamlet known for the money being pulled out of the ground and the rough clientele it attracted. Well, on a September evening we walked into the Gold Eagle Saloon, into that nest of vipers and gamblers, painted ladies and hardrock miners. All six of us came in, Doc first, the rest of us spreading out behind him in a rigid line wearing identical khaki dusters and carrying Colt sixes and sawed-off Greener shotguns. We were all rough as unfinished planks, our eyes shining like chips of flint and all that life-taking hardware straining in our fists. Sharks swimming in that stinking, sweaty sea of cheap perfume and spilled whiskey, grubby poker hands and pungent cigar smoke. That's what we were. Christ, yes. And to a man, we were showing our teeth.

Doc said, "Looking for Nevada Jack McCall. Any of you folks know his whereabouts, you'd best tell and tell right now."

What happened then? Pandemonium. A half dozen men went for their irons and we opened up, lead flying like pissed-off hornets. When it was over, there was pain and blood, shattered glass and bodies, spilled liquor and a haze of gun smoke, more than one man begging for Jesus and the Holy Mother. Among the dead were Johnny Starkweather and Big Mike. Poor bastards. Ventilated like sprinkling cans. Of the five other bullet-ridden corpses, only two of them were members of Nevada Jack's gang.

Like a jailhouse privy, we caught some shit over that.

But a week later, a prostitute friend of Doc's down in Marietta told him that Nevada Jack and his confederates had slipped out of Pine Grove as we rode in, made for Death Valley, just as slick as a snake into a rabbit hole.

The hunt was on again.

And this time it led us straight into the far side of the Devil's asshole. A sun-blasted, scorched lick of hell called Death Valley and with good goddamn reason. It was the sort of place that boiled animals in their own skins, drove men mad as their brains bubbled in their skulls like hot tar. But you know the place, I'm sure. About as inviting as a three-dollar whore with a straight razor gleaming up her money hole.

Doc Piper said we had business with those animals what put down Johnny Starkweather and Big Mike and he didn't get no interference on that point. The six of us had been tighter than a spinster's corset and to a man we wanted payback. We wanted to heel and hide that pack of mother-raping hyenas. Johnny and Big Mike had gone up to Heaven or down to the Bad Place and either way, we wanted to send some company their way.

So, on we went. Just the four of us. Like I said, we were all veterans of the War Between the States and only the Grim Reaper himself had taken more lives than us.

Doc was a veteran of Hood's Texas Brigade. Had lost a leg at Sharpsburg and walked with a wooden replacement. I myself served the Union cause in the 5th Kansas Volunteer Cavalry. I was with Colonel Clayton at Pine Bluff when we slammed the door shut on Marmaduke's graybellies. War does funny things to a man. Pulls all the good things deep into him and drags out all the bad ones until you get to hate a man just for the uniform on his back. Crazy business, war. Doc and I might have fought against each other back in those days, who can say?

But for all that, I will say that Doc Piper was the finest man I have ever known. Certainly, he was a rebel and a fine one at that for Hood's army was a notorious spur in the ass of the Union. But Yankee and Reb, Doc and I got on just fine. And then there were Kevin Macon and Jessie Brock, they were a pair of lowdown, murdering Missouri guerrillas. Ugly-tempered, vicious devils they were—but good people to have riding at your side.

Anyway, a few days later we were in the shadows of the High Sierras up above Furnace Creek, broiling like game hens in a roaster, meandering our way across that salt pan desert. It was desolate and lonely country. Narrow canyons and sheer gullies, flat-topped mesas and craggy sandstone buttes. Crumbled rock and blowing sand jutting with the gleaming white bones of critters that had just laid down and given up. Nothing much else save scattered clumps of arrowweed and blackbrush, greasewood and mesquite. An occasional alien-looking Joshua Tree to break up the monotony that itched in our brains like nits. We saw a few coachwhip snakes and collared lizards, a roadrunner or two and some turkey vultures high above . . . but that was about it.

I hadn't seen such godless, forbidding territory since the Staked Plains of Texas.

Well, the second day out in that wind-haunted graveyard of bones and rocks and sand dunes, we came over a rise and below us nestled on a flat between the hills was the town.

Cemetery, Nevada.

It was well named, for from our vantage point it looked dead as a curled-up snake. Just a collection of weathered saltbox buildings, frame houses, and stone cabins squeezed together along a winding dirt road that was more dirt than road. We could see brick-fronted shops, a church, a livery, and a few barns all just blasted gray by the wind and sand. The four of us watched for the better part of ten minutes and not a damn thing so much as twitched down there.

"Hell of a name for a town," Jessie Brock said, sliding a .44 Evans out of its boot, just staring with those narrow knife-slit eyes of his. "Seen Devil's Hole and Purgatory, Bone Ridge and Funeral Creek . . . but never once a place called Cemetery."

Doc said, "Well now you have."

Kevin Macon slowly rolled himself a cigarette. "Name like that, nobody's gonna wanna live there."

"Son," Doc said to him, fingering that sharp mustache of his. "I get the feeling no one does anyhow."

I didn't care for what I was seeing. I'll readily admit to that. All those tall, empty buildings and deserted houses squatting below us, coveting shadow and memory and the Lord knew what else. It gave you a funny feeling in the pit of your belly. Made you want to ride straight on out without a second look, hope you were long gone come sundown.

Macon and Brock were skittish. I could see that. Both had their rifles out and both looked like they'd rather be riding straight through the Comanche Nation than Cemetery, Nevada, that grim collection of tombstones and monuments waiting down there for us.

Doc just kept nodding, like he'd expected as much, said, "Well, boys, let's go take in the local color."

He led us on down and I rode at his flank, Macon and Brock bringing up the rear. All you could hear was the wind moaning through those buildings and the sound of our horse's hoofs ringing out, the creak of leather. The road edged off to the left around an outcropping of red rock and as we came around we saw what looked to be scarecrows nailed up on wooden crosses, crosses that were leaning this way and that, ready to fall right over.

"Hell is this?" Macon said.

Doc and I dismounted.

Sure, they were scarecrows *now*—all six of 'em—but when they'd been nailed up there they'd been men. Browned by that unforgiving sun and leeched dry by the climate, they'd gone to burnished leather like Huron chiefs laid out on funeral scaffolds. Birds had pecked their eyes into black, staring holes and their hands were skeletal claws withered-up like petrified spiders.

"What kind of heathen shit is that?" I said, my Henry rifle in my hands now.

"Devil's work," Brock said, spitting tobacco juice into the dirt. "That's what it is."

"Don't concern us one way or the other," Doc said, sliding back into leather.

We rode on in then, nothing but yucca and saltbush to either side, a few parched smoke trees. Then the town itself, tall and shadowy and crowded. Empty windows looking out at us, porch swings and weather vanes creaking in the wind. Cemetery had been a mining town at one time. You could see the borax workings up in those rippling, yellow mudstone hills. Lots of holes channeled into the rock. White trails of borax on brown bluffs, quartz and gypsum and colemanite winking in the sunlight. And above them, the Sierras themselves rising high and craggy, pinyon and bristlecone pine just beneath the snowline on the higher elevations.

We dismounted and tethered our horses to a hitch rail out front of a saloon called the Yellow Sign and just stood there, rifles in hand, waiting for word from Doc on how we were going to do this. But maybe each secretly hoping Doc would just say, piss on this circus, boys, let's ride.

But nobody was saying a thing.

Just looking and watching and trying not to breathe real loud. I was spooked and they were, too. Whatever was in Cemetery—or not there—had crawled under our skins like fever ticks, decided to stay awhile, breed maybe. The silence in that sullen town was heavy, ominous, but expectant. The wind began to pick-up a bit, dust devils twisting down the road. Signs creaked on posts. Somewhere, a loose rain gutter was rattling.

I stood there, smelling something and not quite knowing what. A pungent stink like sun-dried cornhusks stored in a dusty, forgotten silo. Something like that. I found it disturbing.

"Smells funny," Brock said, pushing his flat-brimmed hat farther up his brow. "Old leaves and brittle straw, I'm thinking, all locked-up in an old barn."

But Doc told us it was just age and time settling in, magnified by the harsh desert climate. But it was more than that and I think we all knew it. This was a bigger, meaner odor like maybe the whole town had only just recently been yanked from some airless, cobwebbed crypt and the wind hadn't yet blown the stink of dry decay off it.

"There's a couple horses tied down yonder," Macon said, indicating a roan and a paint down the way, standing still and proud and patient before what might have been a dry goods store.

"I see 'em, all right," Doc said, sliding his big bore Sharps out of the saddle scabbard. "What I don't see are any folks to ride 'em and that's sitting on me wrong. You stay out here, keep your eyes wide, Kevin. We're going to have us a look see."

We followed Doc through the batwings and Macon looked at me, looked like he didn't particularly care for the idea of being left alone out there. I dropped him a wink, let him know there wasn't a thing to be worried about. But he didn't believe me. You could see that.

And what did we find inside the Yellow Sign?

Not a goddamned thing. A bar and some tables and a fine player piano netted with cobwebs. Bottles full of liquor and a big mirror just as grimy as an old camp stove. There were some glasses set out, an uncorked bottle, but not much else. Less you wanted to count the mouse droppings in the corners and that thick, undisturbed layer of dust hanging over everything like silt. It was so thick we left bootprints in it.

"Ain't been no one here in years," Doc said.

"What the hell happened?"

"Mine played out most likely," Doc told us. "Been known to happen. Folk all moved away."

"And left all this liquor? The piano? The mirror? Jesus H. Christ, Doc, I been in towns like this before, folks strip 'em right to the bone," Brock said, eyes darting about in that swarthy face. "And if'n they don't, others come by and do it for 'em."

"Don't read too much into this, boy."

Brock chuckled. "Yeah, shit, I'm funny like that. A town's god-damned empty and I got questions. Hell of a thing." He cut himself a chew and worked it into his cheek. "Maybe you're right, Doc, maybe it ain't nothing but what you say. But that don't explain the smell. Stinks like a wagon load of scalps and you know it."

He was right, but Doc didn't comment on it.

Outside, Macon was looking a little pale. "Anything?" he asked.

"Just ghosts," Brock told him.

Macon said, "Funny sort of place, ain't it? I been watching them horses and you know what? Sonsofbitches haven't so much as moved an inch."

We started on down that street toward the horses to see what there was to see. The wind was picking up for real by then, those dust devils kicking up their heels. Tumbleweeds were racing down the road. Boards were groaning and roofing timbers creaking. Somewhere, an unlatched door knocked against its frame. I didn't care for that wind. Not in the least. A good blow could get born up in the valleys and lonely canyons of the High Sierras, twist in upon itself, gain momentum until it was a regular tempest, then come sweeping down the mountain sucking up grit and turn the desert into a whipping barrage of sand that you couldn't see four feet in.

We kept going, all those empty buildings rattling and moaning and sighing and what those sounds were saying was that we were dead alone there. But we walked on, fanned out like maybe we expected trouble and couldn't make up our minds from which direction it might be coming. Yeah, we were a pretty lot, the four of us. I could've popped us easy from atop those crowded roofs. Took us down real quick before we knew from which direction the lead was flying.

And I was no Nevada Jack McCall.

That boy could've blown the cock off a stuffed monkey from three hundred yards, give or take.

We got up to that first horse, a blue roan. It just stood there. It did not move. It did not swish its tail. It did not even blink. Brock went right up to it, jabbed it with his Evans and still it did not move.

"Sumbitch's dead, Doc. Gotta be. Dead or–"

"Stuffed," Macon said.

He went right up to it, unsheathed his big Bowie knife and sank it right into the roan's flank. Nothing. Something like powder trickled out, that was about it. "Stuffed," he said.

"You think so?" Doc said, moving past him. He whipped out his own blade, a long skinning knife and cut a deep slash across the animal's withers. Dug in there, examined the powdery residue on his fingers.

"Stuffed full of sand," Macon said.

But Doc just shook his head. "Ain't sand. It's horse. All that's left when you suck the juice right out."

And that made sense. It explained the shrunken, slat-boned look of the roan. It explained that, sure, but left a mystery, a hole in our midst you could've dropped West Texas through.

"Why?" I said. "What in the hell stuff or bleed a horse dry for?"

Macon nodded. "Yeah, what fer?"

But Doc had no answers, he just looked sort of thoughtful and maybe a little scared. Though it was hard to tell with Doc Piper. His face was hard like something chiseled out of granite, just that sharp nose and stiff mustache, eyes gray as a stormy sky.

He led us on down to the paint and it was worse. Dried-out, shrunken down to the size of a pony, it seemed. Its bones jutted like the rungs of a ladder. But that paint wasn't what was bothering me, I tell you. It was the windows of a hotel looking out at us.

They were so dirty they looked like they'd been whitewashed, just flyspecked and squalid. But on each one there was a cross painted in black. Faded now, but you could see it just fine.

"Look yonder," I said.

There was a big old barn, leaning hard to the right like it wanted to crush the one-room schoolhouse next door. It was gray and splintered, but you could plainly see all the crosses carved into it. Crude things, it looked like they'd been done in a real hurry. We walked over there, examining them. There were other symbols scratched into the double-doors, too, but I'd never seen the likes of 'em before. Kind of like witch-sign or some of that pagan shit Injuns would paint on rocks and cut into cave walls. There was a word carved there, too, amongst them: KROAT, it said.

"What the hell's a 'Kroat?'" I asked.

Doc just shrugged. "Probably some foreign word. Mining towns get people from all over the world. Probably Russian or Polish, means 'Hello' or some such business."

But Macon wasn't buying it. "I don't think it means 'hello.' I don't think that's what it means at all."

And that pretty much said it for all of us. That word . . . we didn't in Christ know what it meant right then . . . but just the sound of it echoing through our brains was enough to fill us with shadows and crawling things. Whatever it was, it was not a good thing.

"C'mon," Doc said.

We looked in a laundry and a general store. Both were empty and neither had been touched. Almost like their owners had just stepped out for a smoke, forgot to hang the BACK IN FIVE MINUTES sign up. Then we came to the barbershop. It was bad, what we saw. Real goddamn bad. It was just a little place, two chairs and a rack of soaps and strops and what have you, but it wasn't empty. No, sir. There was a fellow sitting in the chair and another standing behind him with a razor in his hand.

But they were both dead as rocks.

Their clothing was soiled and dusty as old lumber and their faces brown and dried like Texas jerky. Dehydrated, they were, stiff and dead and crumbling like sideshow mummies. Seeing them staring out at us with those empty eye sockets . . . I could barely swallow.

Brock stormed right in there, jabbed the one in the chair with the butt of his Evans and shoved the standing one backward. He . . . or it . . . tipped straight over like a lodge pole, fell against the shelf of scissors and toilet water, but did not go down. The hand holding the razor and the arm it was connected to snapped clean off and hit the floor with a breath of dust like a stepped on puffball. It hadn't just dropped. It had pretty much fallen apart, shattered into a heap of calcified flesh and bone.

"Hot damn," Brock said. "Y'all think this is just a normal little town now, Doc?"

We went back outside, the wind making our dusters flap around our legs and snap like flags in the breeze. A storm was coming and we all knew it, just like we all knew we should've been riding hell for leather out the back door, but we weren't. Weren't doing a thing but standing there. As always, we were pretty much letting Doc do the thinking for us. Which was just fine with me under the circumstances, because I was just plain white and shivering inside and I was so confused and scared I don't think I could've found my dick if I had to piss or figured out which end to point.

That deserted town of mummies just brooded around us, the moaning wind becoming its voice. A voice that haunted all those old buildings and houses and a voice that was the shrilling cry of a wraith cutting lose in a graveyard at midnight. We stood there, taking it all in, the lot of us thinking many things and not one of 'em concerning Nevada Jack McCall.

"All right," Doc said firmly, with authority. When he talked like that, snapped in that military tone, it always made me straighten-up, made me wish somehow that I'd fought for the South just so I could have served under a man like that. Because Doc was really something. "All right now. Here's how this slices up, boys. Don't know what happened here and honestly don't care to. We're here to track down Nevada Jack and his ilk and that's what we're going to do. To hell with all this. Jessie? You and Kevin light out, poke around, see what you can see. Me and Danny'll do the same."

Macon just shook his head. "Don't like that. Don't like that at all."

"Hell you say?"

But Brock stepped between them. "He's saying we should stick together."

"You calling the shots in this outfit, Jessie?"

"No, sir. But whatever's happened here, I don't want it happening again with us. I don't plan on becoming a window dummy and neither does Kevin."

Doc sighed. "Listen now. One hour. We look for one hour, canvas the town. We don't see nothing, we meet back by the horses and we ride out."

"But—"

"No buts, goddamn you. The Union Pacific Railroad is paying us to do a job, and I mean to see that we do it. If you boys are missing your mama's tits, they're back in Missouri, so you best start humping. You gotta a long walk. So either git and suckle mama or stand with me like a man and do a man's job. Which is it gonna be?"

Macon checked his pocket watch. "An hour, that's it."

They wandered off grumbling, and I wanted to do some grumbling myself, but I was afraid that Doc would simply slap me around on general principles. Sure, there was something awfully wrong in that town, but I wasn't quite sure at that point if it was worse than Doc's temper.

We began by checking the town store by store, house by house. Most of them places were empty and filled with funny echoes like ghosts were moving about us, but we did manage to find no less than a dozen more mummies. Sitting at the dinner table. Lying in bed. Chopping wood. Even one taking a bath in a foam of dust and cobweb.

But the worst place by far was one of them little stone cabins that we saw everywhere, squeezed into any little lot or opening that could be found. Doc said they were company houses. Well, we searched three in a row without finding a damn thing, but the fourth . . . well, we found a cozy little family scene, all right. A mother in her rocking chair, her face and hands baked saffron and next to her, a little bassinet with an infant in it smoked and cured like Chicago beef. Its flesh was thin as lace, holes eaten right through it, nothing but a lot of tiny, pathetic bones on display. I accidentally bumped the bassinet and it began to rock back and forth, casting lurching shadows, and that sent my skin to crawling.

We backed out of there, wide-eyed and shaking—even Doc—and I don't think we started to breathe until we were out in the streets and the wind was blowing sand in our faces. Maybe we were afraid that the woman and baby would wake up if we didn't get out. But it was just nerves, because driftwood never wakes up. The only thing awake in Cemetery, Nevada was us.

Only thing human, that was.

"How long, Doc?" I said, my voice just a whisper. "How long you think this town has been like this?"

"A year. Maybe ten. In this climate, hard to say. Things tan-up quick."

That wind breathing hot and foul and gritty about us, we crossed the road to the congregational church set there. Like everything else in that mausoleum of blowing dust it was weathered a flat gray. The doors were warped in their frame, so it took a little doing to get in there.

But we did.

God help us, but we did.

Now I'm going to tell you what we saw. And it's no easy thing for me. For what was in that church has stayed in my brain all these years, very often showing itself when I close my eyes at night or wake sweating. Well, here goes.

We breezed in there, into that dusty corrupt coffin and the atmosphere was so heavy and wicked it sucked the wind clean out of us. It stank like a tannery in there, of heaped hides and pelts and skin shined to leather. Of salt and spices and advanced age. To this day I can smell it. I know what it must have stank like in an Egyptian embalming parlor. For it was like a violated tomb in that church. The air was thin and clotted with dust, great flakes of it drifting in the pale sunlight that broke through the dirty windows.

But it wasn't just motes of dust I was seeing, it was motes of something else.

For the church was not empty.

There were no less than thirty parishioners packed into those narrow pews, all done up in their Sunday finery—lace and bows, fine suits and boiled shirts. But they'd all been mummified. Their faces were fissured like peach pits, their skin fossilized and flaking like old birch bark. Just thirty hollow-eyed skulls with varnish-brown skin thin as parchment stretched over what lay beneath. Men, women, children. Shriveled fingers clutching prayer books and holding other spidery hands. There were cobwebs all over them. Ropes and nets and fans of web. Cauls of web covered their faces and matted their necks, spread down to their hands like fine filigree. And so thick were those webs, you would've needed a knife to saw through them. Yep, thirty cadavers salted dry and spun with webs like blown cotton.

They were flaking apart, bits of them floating in the air like feathers.

It was hideous. Appalling.

I felt like I was trapped in a haunted house. Just me and Doc and all those mummies looking out at us, the atmosphere in there making me think of graveyards and crypts. I was terrified, filled with cracking white ice. I think if one of them had moved—be it from gravity or resurrection—I would have screamed myself insane. Or maybe just put the barrel of the Henry under my chin and blown my brains to sauce.

Doc must have seen how it was for me. He grabbed me by the arm, dragged me away toward the pulpit. "They've been dead a long time, Danny. They can't hurt anyone."

I followed Doc up onto the pulpit—noticing with some concern that there were no Christian artifacts to be had—and to a little door back there. It led into a little house connected to the rear of the church. Vestry, I supposed it would have been called in a more civilized locale. Regardless, it wasn't much. A bedroom, a little kitchen with a potbellied stove, and something like a study with lots of books and the like in it.

It was dusty in there. Dusty, dirty, mildew-smelling. But it beat the shit out of that church. I was still smelling all those mummies. Their stink was on me like it had been sprayed on with a hose.

Doc sat at the desk pushed up in the corner. "Sit down and take a rest," he told me, sorting through the heaped papers on the blotter. "Let's see what the hell happened here . . . if we can."

He shuffled papers and I sat on a little red velvet window seat, watching that storm coming. Watching the sand brewing and boiling out there. I knew if we didn't get gone and get gone right now, we'd never leave. The idea of a night spent in that town . . . well, I'd have sooner scratched out my own eyes or chewed off my own dick.

I rolled a cigarette, but did not set my rifle down.

Doc said, "Got a diary or journal or something here. Written by a fellow name of Flood . . . first entries are dated fifteen years ago." He stared at me as if this should have special significance, but whatever he was inferring went right over my head like a low-flying buzzard.

Doc put his feet up. Sat there reading and reading and I sat by the window, worrying and worrying and thinking I was seeing something out there in that blowing sand. Something . . . well, something big. But only now and again, like the sun had to be reflected at a particular angle for it to be visible. I figured it was my imagination, but I didn't like it none.

"Apparently," Doc said, "this Flood was some sort of minister, come to Cemetery to save himself some souls. The church here was abandoned six, seven years before he arrived. The other minister killed himself, I gather. Lost his mind."

Doc read some more, explained it all to me. Flood had come to Cemetery on the urging of a few Christian families, being that there was no true church or place of Christian-type worship in town. Most of the folks in Cemetery were immigrants who couldn't speak a lick of English. They had some sort of religion going, some secretive thing that was led by a town elder name of Blake. But outsiders weren't invited in. They were firmly, yet politely told to mind their own. Well, Flood, he popped a hard-on about that, was of the opinion there was something funny about it all. Was hearing things about midnight masses and moonlight services and "sacred groves in the hills." Smelled to Flood like Satanism or witchcraft. He was figuring it was some sort of pagan religion imported from the old country, what with all them foreigners, Slavs mostly.

"Interesting stuff," Doc said. "This Blake fellow was no foreigner. He was from New England, Flood says. He'd been a trapper and mountain man, had been living with a Paiute tribe up in the Sierras, living as them, had been real tight with some big deal hoodoo medicine man name of Ghost Wolf . . ."

When the borax workings opened up, Blake came to town, settled right in, started getting real friendly with them foreigners, had injuns with him more than not. This is what Flood learned from those who would talk to him. Anyhow, Flood wasn't too hot on this Blake. Blake seemed to be in charge of the town and nobody so much as took a piss without him telling them first. Blake walked around wearing some weird outfit that was part puritan, part Paiute. He wore one of them black, square-cornered puritan hats, animal hides and leggings, a blanket coat with a leather belt and brass buckle, tall shiny black boots. He had some power over the townsfolk and was involved in every facet of their lives. He delivered the babies and made the rules. He also indulged in what my mama used to call "witch-lore"—reading fortunes and divining the future by sorting through the bowels of stillborn calves, making with the herb-cures and practicing folk magic.

Doc told me he wanted me to read some of it, see what I thought. I didn't take much away from Cemetery, Nevada but my life, but I did take Flood's journal—at Doc's urging—so I won't have to quote any of this from memory. Here's the entries Doc was most interested in:

July 12, 1877

Blake came to see me to-day. It was just I and Robert Lowry and his two fine sons in the church. God bless the Lowry's! Along with the Hodgkins and Smiths, they are the only true Christian families in Cemetery, shining pearls in a vile, pestiferous stew. At any rate, Robert and his sons were assisting me in planking the pulpit as the old wood had gone quite to rot before my arrival. Just after noon, Blake showed. He stood there for some time, merely staring at us, grinning as is his way with that full set of narrow rodent's teeth. Ug! What a man! Robert and his sons were very apprehensive and I must admit, even in God's house, I was a bit unnerved by that unblinking, soulless stare Blake affects. It is somehow quite unpleasant, makes one's skin actually crawl!

Before I go on, a word about Blake. Ezra is his Christian name ... if anything so positively loathsome as Blake can be called by such an epithet. He is tall and thin, pale as fresh cream, his hair long and white. His face has no more meat on it than a skull, and is lorded over by those greasy, colorless eyes. His face is long and sharp, nose hooked like that of a storybook crone. Striking, yes, but certainly not handsome nor dignified ... merely appalling. Although quite wizened—he could be sixty or eighty or a hundred years of age for all I know. He possesses a sprightliness and lightness of step that is most disconcerting.

Well, Blake took me aside, decided we would have an impromptu chat. Basically—out of earshot of the good Mr. Lowry—he told me that it would be in my best interest to move the church and my religious viewpoints to a different town. That "my kind" of worship was neither wanted, nor needed. That I would only bring trouble down upon myself and my flock, that preaching "your rubbish" (his words) would anger "those who could devour the known world." I sent him away, firmly stating I would not be intimidated, that Jesus Christ was my master. To which he flashed me the fork-fingered evil eye, saying, "Aye, preacher, you'll soon be having commerce with my master and you won't care for it."

Through Robert Lowry and a few others, I have learned much of Mr. Blake. Most of which I have written of in earlier entries, but new information has arisen of a most shocking nature. Rumors are abounding of Blake and his "congregation" worshipping some pagan devil in the hills. That he has fathered no less than thirty children in Cemetery and—dare I say—lain with all of the town's women, married and otherwise. And this with the complete approval of fathers and husbands! Revolting, to say the least. Lowry has told me that incest is commonly practiced here and has been for years, resulting in the most obscene examples of miscegenation one would care to imagine. Yes, Cemetery is a veritable boiling kettle of heresy, sin, and madness. I can think of no other town that could possibly match the iniquity of this terrible place.

Something must be done . . . but what?

July 28, 1877
Events have not improved here.

More stories are filtering back to me of such a horrifying nature, I find that I cannot write of them. Cemetery has certainly degenerated beyond spiritual redemption. I fear that the town and its inhabitants—save the few brave, struggling Christian families—have given themselves over to a blasphemous pagan religion spawned in part by the heathen Paiute and in whole by Ezra Blake. The moon has been of a most unnatural orange of late and seems to hang above the town, unmoving. Flocks of whippoorwills have descended on us, shrilling from dusk to dawn and with such volume sleep is near impossible. Rumors continue to reach me of profane, godless services in the hills. I find that my faith is severely challenged. My small flock looks to me for guidance, but I have none to give.

Lowry tells me that when the borax mines first opened there were no less than 700 inhabitants in Cemetery. Many left after Blake arrived, but many more stayed. And that is the worst possible of all things. I fear that a malignant evil is being openly practiced here. Black mass and Satanism, but not in the form generally understood. Whatever it may be, it is even more debased than one can imagine.

August 2, 1877
Trouble, surely. Last night, the Lowry's witnessed a most repulsive, sacrilegious act. By the light of the moon, Blake stood before their house drawing symbols in the dirt with a stick and chanting what Robert tells me was "a most unholy rubbish" in a language that was most fearsome to hear. In the morning, Robert tells me he

saw what looked to be some sort of pentagram scratched into the earth. He rubbed it out with his boot. I would like to have seen it. The Hodgkins and Smiths have been similarly menaced. In a rage, I went to Blake and he laughed at me, told me that his god was old when the good earth was nothing but a vortex of gas. He mumbled what seemed to be nonsense concerning something called "Kroat" and "The Slitherer in Charnel Darkness" and "He Who Crawls in Cosmic Wastes." I asked him what this Kroat was. He told me simply that Kroat was "The Dark Lord of the Tomb-Herd. The Eldritch God of Embalming and Mortuaries."

I believe him to be mad or maybe it is I who is mad.

I've written to a Dr. Crowden at Brown University in Providence, an expert in occult and folkloric matters. Perhaps he can better explain these things. This town is in the grip of something ancient and venomous, but I do not know how to fight it.

October 5, 1877

The letter from Dr. Crowden arrived not two days ago and my mind is filled with lurid, impossible thoughts. All that the esteemed Dr. Crowden—himself the ancestor of a confessed and executed Arkham witch—told me has stolen not only my sleep, but jangled my nerves most severely, leaving me dangling helplessly at the edge of some void of utter lunacy. You'll excuse my emotional, colorful outbursts, but things have reached such a deplorable state, that I find my outlook decidedly melancholy and bleak.

Dr. Crowden claims to be very familiar with the name of "Kroat." This creature or being forms part of a great tapestry of ancient, pre-Christian gods that Crowden assures me are of the most malevolent and noxious variety. Though the sects that revere these evil ones date back to the farthest antiquity, his research has shown him that it is quite possible—and even likely—that these cults still exist in many inaccessible backwaters. On this, I can certainly concur. Crowden also tells me that these "Outer Ones" (his words) are much more pestilent and loathsome than any ten Christian demons sewn together.

Kroat or "Krotis" is a deity that has been mentioned in Sumerian, Babylonian, and even Assyrian sources. He is most usually associated with graveyards and tombs, mummification and the like. The Mayan embalmers gave sacrifice to him (or "it"). In ancient Persia, huge altars constructed entirely of human bones and flesh were erected to this abomination. Crowden says that Egyptian Anubis was but a harmless, sterilized version of this horror. Crowden believes that Kroat may be actively worshipped by such far-flung Indian tribes as the Crow, Ute, and Ojibwa. Many of the world's great banned books, so-called hellbooks and witches' cookbooks, pay homage to Kroat. Crowden says that Kroat has appeared—in some detail—in forbidden, foul tomes such as the dread *Cultus Vermis* and sinister *Liber Ivonis,* as well as in Augustus Verdin's grim unnatural history, *Unspeakable Survivals.* He mentioned another rare book of Medieval vintage, the infamous, demented *Morbidus Pestis de Resurrectus* by the deranged Austrian nobelman—and warlock—Jozef Graf Regula . . . a name which still inspires terror in Central and Eastern Europe. Crowden has done a great deal of research into these "Outer Ones," believing their origin not to be of this Earth. He has written a privately-published pamphlet on the matter, believing these cults to be not only active but incalculably dangerous to the human race. And on the subject of Kroat, he had this to say in particular: "It is my firm belief after no less than thirty years spent researching these obscure, nameless sects that Kroat and his followers may quite possibly be responsible for mass disappearances around the globe. The vanished populations of the Etruscan city Varqua in the Po valley circa 510 AD, and the Medieval Czech city of Stradyko in 1377. As well as the Aleutian Indian villages of Ejiikul and Korjja in 1823. And need I make reference to the numerous empty Incan villages encountered by Cortez in the 16th century? In our own country, we need look no further than the missing colonists of Roanoke Island in 1590—the most elusive, yet grisly of clues being the following words scratched into a tree: CRO. Those three letters have given me nightmares of the sort I will not relate to you . . ."

Crowden's letter ran at some length, but his closing words told me in no uncertain terms that I should get out of Cemetery while I still could. That Kroat and his followers were not to be taken lightly . . .

October 13, 1877
The Lowry's are no more. Something beyond belief attacked their cabin during the night, actually tearing through the roof to get at them. I could find no remains. The Hodgkins and Smiths have vanished as well. Blake is behind it. Dear God, what will I do now?

October 29, 1877

My time on Earth grows nigh and soon, I am certain, I will be in the bosom of the Lord. Tried to leave town three days ago, but was turned back by Blake's people. Blake has told me it is too late, far too late. The eldritch, unnamable services in the hills grow nightly into a frenzy. The moon has gone to the color of blood. At night there is a most loathsome chittering sound coming from the sky above the town, a smell of spices, salts, and corruption. What can it mean? The whippoorwills scream from dusk to dawn with rabid intensity. This morning just before sunrise the church was assailed by what I thought was a rain of gravel. Outside, I discovered literally thousands of dead whippoorwills. They were frozen as if they had fallen from some impossible height. Of further interesting note, the sky has gone opaque and poorly transmits light so that it is dim and shadowy here even at full-noon. Day by day, there seems to be less activity in Cemetery. I fear that with each nightly sabbat, more townsfolk are offered up to some blasphemous monstrosity from beyond time and space.

October 31, 1877

Made a most damnable discovery during a secretive jaunt into the hills not two hours ago. A huge, smoldering pit filled with the cremated remains of what could only be hundreds of townspeople. The stench was hideous. Blake tells me that those in the pit have been offered to Kroat as burnt offerings, that they were not deemed worthy to receive his "sacred touch." Blake also tells me this Kroat is closer each night, scratching nearer and nearer, rending some ethereal void to join the faithful, to claim what Blake calls "the master's crop" as if all those unfortunates were merely corn to be harvested. And maybe they are. A cataclysmic horror approaches. I do not doubt this.

Not sure what day it is.

I will fight this evil to the last. That nebulous, grotesque malignancy that now hangs over the town like a collection of writhing viscera will not take me. Not without a fight.

Dear Christ.

It's coming

Coming

God help us all

✳ ✳ ✳

After I finished reading those passages, it felt like something wet and clinging had grown up the back of my throat. The day was warm and positively stuffy in old Flood's study, but I swear to you I shivered like a kitty in a wet bag.

"You . . . you believe this shit, Doc?" I put to him.

Doc looked at me for a long time, those eyes unreadable and flat. "I don't know," he finally said. "I just don't know."

"C'mon, Doc . . . I mean, something funny happened here . . . but that, that business, I just can't accept it."

Doc didn't say anymore on the subject. All I'm going to say about his reaction to that diary of Flood's was that old Doc, dear old Doc Piper, looked like he'd aged ten years. His face was sallow, hanging low and sloppy like a hound dog's jowls. There was a tic in the corner of his mouth and it almost looked like he was just done in, like he wanted to curl up and die like a snake crushed in a wagon wheel rut. I didn't feel much better myself, no sir. Everything inside me had gone gray and brittle and a good swift kick in the ass would have shattered my innards to powder.

Well, the blow outside was kicking up. It was throwing sand up against the windows like a snowstorm in January. It was getting nasty out there. You couldn't see much but sand whipping and everything was sort of dim and obscured. I didn't like it at all. About that time we heard something that froze us up tight. It was a sort of low, thrumming roar like a tornado slamming through a train tunnel. It picked up its intensity until the whole goddamn church shook and swayed.

Me and Doc just stood there staring at each other.

Then we heard gunshots, heard some screaming that the wind splintered in a hundred different directions. Doc and I came charging out of that little vestry like we had hot coals shoved up our asses. We came out into that pounding, screeching tempest of blowing sand and moaning wind. A blizzard of sand. We had to tie our neckerchiefs around our faces and squint our eyes and that sand nearly slapped us down. You couldn't see but five feet in any direction and that sand ground into our faces like powdered glass.

We heard shots again, raced in what we thought was the right direction. We found Macon with his bolt-action Springfield crying out about Mary and Jesus and shooting straight up in the air. The sand was shrouding the whole town, so we couldn't see what it was he thought he might hit up there. He just kept working that bolt and spitting brass. It took both me and Doc to get him under control, to drag him out of that gale and into the barn with KROAT written on it. He was hysterical. Just straight plumb out of his gourd, fighting and spitting like a mountain cat with its balls in a beaver trap.

Doc finally had to slap him across the face and feed him whiskey.

But you should've seen that poor Missouri killer—face all corded-up and tight like he was on the verge of a stroke, shaking and whimpering and crying, his eyes bulging right out of his head. It took him some time to get it out, but finally—tears rolling down his cheeks and leaving clean trails in his grimy face—he did.

It'd take too goddamn long to put down the words of a man who was spitting and drooling and beating the dirt with his fists, so I'll give you the short version. What happened was, they'd found Nevada Jack McCall and his murder-happy half-breed friend Cherokee Billy DeBride. Found 'em both at the jailhouse, both of 'em salted and tanned like the others, looking more like withered pork rinds than men. They were worse than the others, Macon told us, because Brock said they looked to him like they'd been embalmed real recently, blood sucked out of 'em like a fly in a black widow's web. What was different was that they still had their peepers . . . and from what Macon said, he'd never seen such terror in a man's eyes before. It drew the life right out of you. Brock slit Cherokee Billy wide open, said he was stuffed full of straw and dry leaves . . . but it wasn't that at all, just his insides gone dry as cane.

Well, Brock and Macon had been making their way back through the streets looking for Doc and me, then the storm came up, right out of nowhere. From a gust to a real blow and then they heard that thrumming, roaring sound.

". . . right then, Doc, right then . . . oh sweet mother of Jesus . . . Brock's standing off to my side and he gets yanked right up into the air," Macon told us, drooling and gibbering. *"Right up off his feet like he was one of them marionettes or a noose had been thrown around his neck . . . I heard . . . I heard him screaming, Doc . . ."*

That's what Macon said.

Brock was yanked up into the storm and for one quick second, the sand overhead thinned and he saw what had taken Brock. Something gigantic and quivering, something like a living, writhing net of tentacles hanging over the roofs and blotting out the sky. Like an immense transparent jellyfish full of burning eyes and feelers and squirming entrails. Part liquid and part gas and part solid, all boiling and churning up there, fluttering and swelling and flapping in the wind.

Doc looked at me and neither of us said "Kroat," but you could be goddamn sure it was in our minds.

Maybe we would've told Macon about it, given time, but I doubt it. Regardless, that roaring rose up outside and the wind was wailing to some awful crescendo and the barn sounded like it was going to fly apart around us. It began to creak and groan and it sounded . . . well, it sounded like something huge had just leaned up against it.

"Let's get the hell out of here," Doc said.

I thought he meant right out of town, but not Doc. Brock was one of us and Doc would not leave without his corpse or pieces thereof. So the three of us started down that howling, sand-blizzarding street, rifles up, ready to kill the first thing that moved. The town—what we could see of it—was dim and crawling with shadows, tumbleweeds bouncing around us, pebbles and tree branches whipping down the road. All the buildings and houses were shaking and swaying and groaning like they were being torn up from their foundations. The sand was still piling up, still whipping in the air. Currents of it moved down the street like rivers, sculpted into dunes and banks along storefronts. It was hot and dusty like Satan himself was exhaling, the sand peeling us raw. We could barely stay standing in that driving wind.

But we did.

We trod forward, leaning into that screaming, lashing maelstrom, squinting as that grit peppered our faces. It was more than sand, had to be more than just sand. Like being pummeled by finely-ground gravel and stones and you name it. I think the entire town was eroding around us, buildings and houses and barns being weathered right down to fragments that the wind took hold of, swallowed down deep, and spat right back into our faces. It was so murky by that point that it was like being trapped in a bank of fog, only this fog had force and bite and anger. At times, Macon and Doc both disappeared as the storm ingested them, only to re-appear three, four feet from the last place I had seen them.

We were looking for Brock, yes, but we were also looking for our horses. Though I was pretty certain they'd either broke their tethers and ran or were stripped to bone by that point.

The effect of that storm was like some crazy hallucination and my brain was filled with weird sounds and sights. I'm not sure what was real. The town seemed to be in motion, jumping and lurching and shaking in that blow and from time to time you'd catch a glimpse of a doorway or filthy window, maybe a boardwalk, but then they vanished in a blast of sand. We guided ourselves finally by taking hold of the hitch rail that ran straight down the main road in front of the shops.

I kept hearing things echoing around me—above, behind, to the left and right. I was certain every time I looked I'd see something that would turn my hair white or, at the very least, would see that I was alone, completely alone. But even had Doc and Macon took a powder, I knew I wouldn't have been alone.

Because there was something out there.

Something huge and shapeless moving in the storm.

I never got a clear look at it, but from time to time the flying murk around us got just that much murkier like someone had pulled down a shade. So, yeah, it was there, all right. Something of colossal proportions dipping in and out, slipping by, circling and drifting. Now and again I got a brief, horrible glimpse of something like gray jelly, something maybe part mist and part flesh. Something shiny and wet and quivering. Whatever it was, it made everything inside me wither and droop like it had been kissed by a killing frost. Doc was ahead of me, straining forward almost horizontal, dragging himself into that pissing, shrieking cyclone handhold by handhold. His duster was flapping around him like a cape. My hat had been blown clean off, Macon's, too . . . but Doc's Texas flat-top was snapped on his head tight as the lid on a pickle jar.

Macon was swearing behind me and I was cursing Jesus and his Mother and only Doc had retained a shred of composure.

But finally, he stopped, clinging to the hitch rail. "No . . . good," I heard his voice shout in that raging tempest. "Should've . . . horses . . . by now . . ."

He was right.

The sand sea came up to our knees in spots and I thought we were going to drown in it, sink beneath its grainy waters. And when those waters receded one day, wouldn't be nothing but three sets of white polished bones left to commemorate our passing.

Macon started hollering and swearing and I tried to hang onto him, but he broke free, trying to run. But the wind found him, decided it liked his feel, and spun him around like a top. Poor bastard. He could barely stay on his feet out there, that wind tossing him around like a bedsheet in a hurricane. About that time, the sandstorm went dark as pitch. Something glistened like running oil and . . . I can't be sure what I saw.

Not really.

That darkness moved in, surged, roiled like there was a whale swimming through it, dropping down on us like a spider on a thread from some great height. One minute, Macon was trying to find his feet and put them to use and the next, something came slashing out of the sand, coiled around him like a jungle python and pulled him right up and out of sight. It happened in less than five seconds.

I don't know if Doc saw it, but I think he did.

All I know is that he had me by the arm, dragging me out of that blow and through the first doorway he found which was into one of those squat stone cabins. I was half out of my head. I think I fought and struggled like a brat, but he overpowered me and tossed me through the doorway. I came to rest on a cool flagstone floor. Doc was some crazy silhouette behind me, wrestling the door shut. It took some doing.

"It's out there," I said while Doc found a tin matchbox and scratched some light into that shadowy cabin. He lit a kerosene lantern and the cabin was flooded with a warm, orange glow.

My throat was dry and scratchy and my skin ached like it had been blasted with rocksalt. We shed our coats and about five pounds of sand and dust and our faces were red as sunburn. We found some tepid water in a tin jug and washed our faces, had a drink. It was metallic and awful-tasting, but it was the best bet going.

"It's that thing," I said to Doc, wanting to be hysterical, needing to be in fact, but I bit down, forced it away. I tried to be strong like Doc. "That thing, that Kroat or Krotis that sucked away them other towns and this one, too. It's out there, Doc, and . . . it knows where we are."

Doc rolled us cigarettes, calm and unhurried. And that was simply testament to his fine Southern breeding. Inbred, backwoods Yankee that I was, I wanted to scream and blubber and stamp my feet. But there was something about Doc. Something soothing about him. Wherever he was or whoever he was with, he was in charge.

The reigns were in his hands and if you needed to start wailing or pissing your diddies, he'd let you know when the time came.

"Danny," he said, lighting me a cigarette and handing it to me. "Whatever is happening out there, it'll blow over. We just have to sit tight and wait it out. I'm willing to bet by morning we can be on our way."

"You think so?" I said, deflating now, happily so.

"Certainly, son. You trust me, don't you?"

"With my life."

He nodded, dropped me a wink. "You're like kin to me, Danny. I think you know that. I apologize for involving you in any of this. Sometimes . . . sometimes I'm not exactly as smart as I'd like to think."

For Doc—stoic, stern Doc—to say things like that was practically like you or me breaking down at our mother's laps. I suddenly felt ashamed. Terribly ashamed for my weakness, my spongy backbone, that set of BB's I liked to proudly proclaim were my balls. And recognizing the fact that I was acting like something that needed a spanking and a nap, I felt better. Not calm exactly, but ready.

"Doc, this ain't none of your fault. I trust you all the way. I don't know what's gonna happen here, but if the Lord has decided to punch my ticket after all these years, I'll go with a grin on my face and smoking pistols in my hands. Next to the finest man I have ever known."

It choked me up saying it. Doc, too. Something passed between us and that something was solid and forever and all-encompassing like a favorite blanket. Whatever that lick of vomit outside decided was our fate, so be it. We'd go down, Doc and I, but we'd go down hard and pissed-off and what we had between us, that thing could never hope to so much as scratch.

We were quiet for a time. We smoked and listened to the squall do its thing out in the streets, mainly just whipping and wailing and pounding dust out of the rafters overhead, but now and again toppling a barn or building in a crash of flying lumber.

Our dusters over on the floor were not just sprayed and pitted with sand, but all gray and smeared-looking. I examined them and they were covered with gray ash.

I started remembering that body pit Flood had written about, knowing that the storm was not just sand and dirt, but ash and bone fragments and what have you launched in a cloud of waste like something from a crematorium.

I looked at Doc and he just nodded. We didn't bother discussing the obvious.

I pulled fresh water from the pump in the little kitchen, splashing my face and back and hands, figuring it would take about twenty good, long hot baths to clean the grit out of my pores. Doc went up and checked the loft, checked out a room at the back. When he came back, his face was all mottled and gray and he was breathing hard.

"Brock's in there," he said to me with some effort.

"Brock?" I said, making to push past him, but he stopped me with an outstretched hand, just shaking his head forlornly.

"No, Danny. He's been . . . he's just a mummy like the others. Let him rest in peace. He's gone, just gone."

But I had to look being the idiot I was. I took the lantern and there he was, just sitting on the bed with his rifle in his lap. But small and thin and shiny, like a joint of beef smoked over a cherrywood fire. I closed the door.

Doc and I sat there, smoking and chewing jerky that Doc had in his coat and waiting for dawn. There were sounds outside, terrible sounds for the next few hours. Sounds like some enormous bulk dragging itself along the outside walls of the cabin. And soft, slithery noises like snakes trying to find their way in. But they weren't snakes. Not exactly.

Doc and I kept vigil, but we were sleepy, just plain worn out, so that when we heard that knocking at the door, I think we both jumped. And for one crazy, lilting moment, maybe we thought we were both dreaming. But we weren't dreaming, because it came again.

Thud, thud, thud.

Just the sound of it out there in that blizzard of sand and wind wailing like banshees set my skin to creeping. Someone was out there. Someone just patiently knocking. Not rapping on the door quick and hard like I would be, saying, let me in, let me in, you dumb sumbitch!, but just biding their time. No hurry in the world. And that's what got me to trembling. Like maybe it wasn't a man out there, but some machine knocking, some haunt born of wind and sand and ash paying us a call.

"Danny," Doc said, getting up. "Take up your rifle. I'm going to open that bolt. If you see something that has come to do us a hurt, blast its asshole out through its throat."

I crouched down with my Henry, eased my finger against the trigger.

Doc stood by the bolt, removed it and pulled the door wide open. It came slamming in, throwing him up against the wall, sand and debris and wind blowing in in a wave of hot, stagnant heat, glancing off the walls like birdshot.

I saw a form standing there.

A man.

There was something wrong with him and I knew it. He stepped forward with a jerky, heavy gait and I saw it was Macon. Poor Macon, grinning and staring and moving like some wind-up soldier, no more alive than a handful of grave dirt. Just a husk sucked dry and set in motion by some diabolic cancer that owned Cemetery, Nevada.

I couldn't bring myself to shoot him.

He shambled in with an unpleasant, grim relentlessness. His face was fissured like pine bark, the skin gauzy and flaking, stuck to that skull beneath like wet paper. He got within three feet of me, seized up, and fell straight over, sand pouring from his mouth.

I helped Doc get the door closed again, seeing something moving out there ... something with too many moving parts and shining things like marbles that might have been eyes in some toxic plane of existence.

We dragged Macon's corpse into the corner, covered it with a blanket.

Outside, something was pressing itself up against the walls, slinking over the roof and rattling the shutters. It was on to us, whatever in Christ's name it was. Tired of playing, it had come to claim what it considered to be its own: Doc and I.

"Be ready," Doc said, chambering a shell into his Sharps, growing pale and old, lines spreading out over his face like crevices in granite.

I was ready as I could be, just staring up at the ceiling, listening to those stout, smoke-blackened timbers shift and moan and shake. The sounds were everywhere and whatever hell that Kroat had been vomited from, it had now engulfed the cabin like a shroud of cloth. The walls shook. My guts hung in cold, loose spirals. Something was sliding and slipping and oozing out there, desperate to find a way in ... which I knew it would. The lantern light began to spit and sputter, casting great twisting and leaping shadows. The air grew heavy, leaden, became thick and clotted and hard to breathe.

I smelled something hot and acrid and nauseating like burning hair.

And that's when it happened. The wall behind Doc became fluid, seemed to run like wax as if it was not stone at all, but liquid or gas or maybe both and neither. A tentacle came right through the wall. Then another and another and another. They tapered from the point of a pencil to the thickness of a man's thigh where they wriggled through the wall. They took hold of Doc and wrapped him up and there wasn't a goddamn thing I could do about it. They poured through the wall and undulated down from the ceiling, shiny and wet and stinking, glistening with snot or bile. They were perfectly smooth and unlined, not like the tentacles of a squid or octopus at all, just smooth, rubbery things that were whipping and coiling and perfectly transparent.

I could see Doc right through that living web of them.

Viscid, gelatinous things pissing a foul steam, translucent and oddly artificial-looking. Macon was right: they were exactly like the tentacles of a jellyfish.

I let out a wild scream and my Henry rifle dropped from my greasy fingers.

The tentacles pulled Doc up and squeezed him tight and his mouth peeled open in a silent cry of agony . . . and then he shrank, deflated like the air had been bled out of him. And as he did so, the tentacles went from that transparency to a pulsing, ruby-red. They were filling with Doc's blood and you could see it go streaming through that network of tendrils. At the same time, Doc went black as sin.

I didn't understand what happened then, but I do now.

You see, that horror had leeched the blood from him like the embalmer it was and injected him with some inky fluid to preserve him. And this in the span of about ten seconds.

With a hissing, slithering noise, the tentacles retreated back through the wall and out the ceiling, made of some insubstantial ether whose atoms were not like ours and could breach solid stone like you or I can breach smoke or mist.

But Doc was solid.

He slammed against the wall and stayed there.

Stiff as a plank and mottled gray and brown and yellow, his eyes staring and ebon, bubbling with that fluid. I went to my knees, chattering my teeth and pissing my pants and crying out. I don't recall much of that. But suddenly, suddenly Doc leaned forward, walked stiffly and painfully to his seat by the fire and sat down. His eyes were on me, fathomless and dark and glimmering, portals into some dead-end, godless tract of space.

The corner of his lips pulled into a crooked half-smile.

But that was it. Doc never moved again. He was a mummy, a manikin, a straw- and leaf-stuffed dummy. But I think, I truly believe that part of him was still there, but fading fast. And though that smile was the rictus of a cadaver, it was his only way of reaching out to me.

I watched Doc all night, but he did not move.

Part of me hoped he would and part of me was terrified at the idea.

The tentacles came and went several times, but they never got me. They'd slither and glide across the floor, up the walls, tangle in the beams, but I always avoided them. Just before dawn, the storm abated. I don't think by that point I was strictly sane.

I had to tunnel my way out. The cabin pretty much buried in a drift. I was white from head to toe, powdered down with ash and sand that had blown in through the door, funneled through cracks in the walls and corners. I walked out of town or the wreckage of it—great drifts and walls of sand had pretty much obliterated it, not much standing but a few buildings and cabins and spires of chimneys—and wandered out into the desert. Cemetery, Nevada was submerged in a series of rolling sand dunes and the church was just plain gone. Yes, I walked out, feverish and hallucinating and dizzy with heatstroke and exposure. Behind me, the town looked like the masts of sunken ships breaking through some dead, muddy sea.

My memory pretty much ends there.

A friendly group of Shoshone Indians found me lying in the desert, near-dead and brought me to a mission hospital in Reno. God bless them. And whites have the audacity to call them savages. How many whites would have done the same for a Shoshone?

Well, gentlemen, so ends my disturbing narrative which you will no doubt quantify as horseshit. So be it. All I have said is the truth. I swear this in the name of Jesus. It happened. As to Cemetery, Nevada? Well, I suppose it's been borne under the sands by now.

But maybe not.

If you do indeed have the body of Nevada Jack McCall, then perhaps it's still out there, that town. If I were you, I might investigate into the method by which Nevada Jack was mummified. You may be in for a shock that our science cannot hope to explain.

In conclusion, sir, let me say this. If you have Nevada Jack's body, for the love of God burn it to ashes. For if you do not, you might discover that its owner may come looking for it one dark, windy night. And may God have mercy upon your souls if that ever comes to pass . . . though I doubt that any Christian god will protect you.

Signed,
Daniel McHenry
Medicine Lodge, Kansas

THE RIDER OF THE DARK

BY DARRELL SCHWEITZER

I see by your outfit, that you are a cowboy.

—*The Streets of Laredo.*

I met him in a steakhouse in Denver in 1927 while waiting for a train, on my way home from college at Christmas break.

He slammed a silver dollar on the counter and said, "Give me a whiskey!"

As this was a steakhouse, and Prohibition was in effect, the man behind the counter could only gape and fumble with a towel and try to explain that they didn't serve alcohol on the premises.

"When I say I want a whiskey, I want a whiskey!"

I could see that this guy was what you'd call a "character." He was old, maybe seventy, a little hunched over, his face like old, gnarled tree-bark, his beard a bristly white. His clothes were an unsavory mix of leather and denim so worn it was shiny. Quite out of fashion.

As I drew closer, I noticed that he didn't smell too nice either.

"A whiskey!"

"Sir," said the cook behind the counter, "If you don't quiet down I shall have to call–"

Nevertheless my instincts were aroused. Here was source material, a *story*.

The old man looked at me, hard, then his look softened when I opened my jacket and showed him the silver flask in my inside pocket. Though a freshman, I had begun to move in sophisticated circles.

"It's all right," I said to the man behind the counter. "My grandfather is here to meet me. It's okay."

We sat down. I ordered steaks for both of us. The old man snatched the flask out of my hand before I could offer it to him.

"The name's Rufus T. Harris, and I ain't your grandpappy—"

"I know, but I had to tell him something. You were making a *scene*, Mr. Harris."

He took a long swig from my flask.

"Don't I have the right to? I can't find a decent saloon in this here town—"

"It's called the 18th Amendment to the Constitution, Sir—"

"Well, *my* constitution needs a good snort now an' then—" He drank some more. "Damn, boy, that's good hootch you got there! You shouldn't be drinkin' such stuff till you got whiskers on your chin, though surely this'll raise hair if anything will, uh—"

"Yes. Is there a problem?"

"You got a name, don't you, boy?"

"Oh," I stood up and extended my hand. "I'm so sorry. I have been impolite. My name's Blake, Robert Blake—"

He didn't take my hand, but finished my liquor and dropped the flask to the table-top, then belched. I sat down again.

"I got you pegged, Bobby Blake. You're one of them writer fellows, ain't you, wantin' to meet a real older-timer who can tell you what it's like livin' life in the raw, back when the West was really wild? Ain't that so?"

"Kind of . . ." This was not the time to explain that I really wanted to be the successor to Poe and Baudelaire, rather than Jack London. "I *am* a journalism student," I hastily added.

"Well, ain't that grand? So here's your story, Bobby Blake. No! Put that stupid notebook away! If it ain't worth rememberin' it ain't worth hearin.'"

Just then our steaks arrived. As we chowed down, he began to tell me his story.

"It was a long time ago," he said, pointing at me with his fork. "I was about your age, which means I was so wet behind the ears I didn't know a longhair from a longhorn, but I was like you in a way,

Bobby Blake. I wanted to experience the whole big, wide world. I wanted manly adventure, just like in the dime novels."

The first rule of journalism, even if you're not really intending to be a journalist, is knowing when to say nothing. Don't argue. Let him think what he wanted of me. Let him get on with his tale.

"So I joined a cattle drive, back in the old days, when the railroads only came to Kansas City, and we had to drive the cattle north. My uncle Joshua convinced the trail boss, one Samuel Quintus Knight—now you remember that name, Bobby Blake, because Big Sam Q. Knight was the biggest, bravest, toughest cowboy there ever was. Why, the other cowboys told me he once shot the tip off the crescent moon with his six-shooter, and he split a man's skull at fifty paces by spittin' a chaw of tobacco–"

He waited to see if I would react. I didn't. I just let him think I believed every word he said.

He went on with his story.

※ ※ ※

Yep, [Harris said] I was just like you, Bobby, I was. I looked up to that man like he was God. I thought he could catch the lightnin' in his bare hands. He was everything I ever wanted to be. I was terrible, terrible grateful to Uncle Josh for getting me this job, and I stuck real close to Sam Knight, because I wanted to learn everything I could from him, and I wanted him to know I'd learned everything I could *from him*. So I worked mighty hard. And, I tell you, it was the thrill of my life to be ridin' and ropin' beside him, and to sit near him around the campfire at night when he an' the boys would get out the harmonicas and guitars and make soft music to keep the cattle quiet.

I suppose that's how I come to notice the signs, then. I mean, there was something in the way Big Sam looked out into the darkness, how he watched a cloud pass over the moon and then turned his eyes away suddenly, how he made strange emblems like five-pointed stars in the sand around the edge of the camp each night, and muttered something I couldn't make out. And one night his voice faltered as he strummed a guitar and sang, *"Git along little shoggoth, it's your misfortune and none of my own."*

Almost asleep, I rolled over in my sleeping bag and asked,"What's a shoggoth, Sam?"

He stopped playing. "You don't want to know, son," was all he said. "You just don't want to know."

And that morning two men were missing, the tall cowboy named Shorty and the right-handed one named Lefty. Their horses was still there, but no sign of them. There was nothing we could do.

I could tell Big Sam had somethin' on his mind. The way he looked up at them vultures circling. The time, in broad daylight, something *dark* and huge that the eye couldn't quite wrap itself around blotted out the sun for several minutes. There weren't no Injun smoke signals atop the mesas. Nothing like that. It was quiet, too quiet, all the way, and if I knew, what more must Sam be knowing, that's what I wanted to know.

Bad signs. Of course it was the place for it. We'd passed through the Superstition River Valley, near Hanged Man's Gulch, betwixt the Screamin' Skulls Mountains, just past Great Old Ones Canyon—and you don't have to know precisely where any of those places is. Let's say west of the Pecos and north of the Rio Grande.

That's enough. Bad place. Not where you want to be caught at nightfall with ten thousand head of cattle, but night falls when it does, and there we was.

I had a bad feeling about this.

But we made camp, there in the dark. There wasn't no moon that night, and not because Big Sam had shot it neither. Just no moon, and precious few stars, though it wasn't *cloudy* exactly. There was just somethin' funny about the air, like the air itself was thicker than usual and you couldn't see much farther than you could spit. Not countin' that Big Sam had once kilt a man with a chaw at fifty paces—no I mean as far as any other ordinary feller could spit.

Nobody felt like singin' much that night, though the cattle was mighty restless.

So we was sittin' in the dark, just a-waitin' for something, for the sun to come up we hoped, but for something real bad to happen, we was all afraid—then something real bad happened.

There was a man a hollerin' out there in the dark somewhere. That's a real bad thing on a cattle drive, because the herd was already nervous, and anything that starts a stampede can get us all kilt real fast.

"Help me, fellas! Help me!"

We all got up. We reached for our guns. Somebody lit a lantern and shined it out into the darkness, where the cattle's eyes seemed to shine back at us like the eyes of wolves. It weren't natural. It was another sign. It was wrong. Now, sudden-like, the herd was quiet, too quiet, and then there came staggering into the firelight none other than Tex Weinstein, the scruffiest, mangiest owlhoot in the outfit, with a beard like a tumbleweed and a little cloud of horseflies that seemed to follow him everywhere. But he'd always been good enough at cowboy work, even though he was just a bit of a moron, who would sometimes talk gibberish and just stare at you and say "I don't know how" till you whapped him on the head with the handle of your six-shooter to snap him out of it . . . but that wasn't gonna do no good now because, we couldn't help but notice as he come moseyin' into the firelight, his eyes was all rolled till only the whites showed, and the top of his head was chawed clean off.

He spoke in a weird, gurgly voice. "It's too late. You didn't help me."

Big Sam just drawed out his pearl-handled six-shooter and plugged Weinstein right through both of them blank eyes. *But he kept on comin'!* I tell you, it was the most god-awful thing I ever seen in my life. Sam shot him again and it took off most of his head, till there was just his jaws a'flappin' and slobberin.' *But he kept on comin'!*

So we all backed away as he came into the firelight, his hands out to grab us like they was claws, black ooze sputterin' from out of where his brain used to be.

Real quick Sam drawed one of them five-pointed signs in the dust—*sigils* he called 'em—and when Tex Weinstein stepped in that he was caught somehow, and just blundered around, gropin' at the air, and Sam shot him one more time through the heart and he dropped down to the ground, stone dead.

Only it was obvious he'd been dead all along, living dead. I got out my own gun, just to be sure he was *dead* dead. But Sam pushed the barrel aside and said, "Don't waste your ammo, Rufus. You're gonna need it."

I looked down at the *dead* dead man who seemed content to stay that way.

"What happened to him, Sam?" was all I could say and what we all wanted to know.

"He be a *zombie*," said Louisiana Louie. "I seen things like that down in the swamps outside New Orleans. Them black folks can raise up a dead man like that with their African magic–"

"It wasn't African magic," said Big Sam, holsterin' his pistol. "It was a whole lot worse." And he told us then, what nobody could believe if they hadn't seen it and what nobody could forget in all their born days if they had, how we just happened to be, at the worst time of the year in the worst place, because Great Old Ones Canyon wasn't called that fer nothin'. *Millions* and *millions* of years ago the Old Ones, monsters or devils or something, come down from the stars on a dark night like this, when there wasn't no moon and the darkness was, *thicker* somehow, like the air opened up and there was something even darker behind it. And these Old Ones was sleepin' in that canyon, waitin' for something like Judgment Day, when they could come up out of the ground and take over the whole world. But meantime, when the stars was *just right*, they could sometimes walk through the desert night in dreams—I didn't quite know what that meant, but that's what Big Sam said—and if you ran into a dream-ghost of a Great Old One, and you happened to be dead, that would turn you into a zombie, it stood to reason.

"But it *don't* stand to reason," I said, amazed and terrified that I would actually say something against the trail boss at a time like this, but it didn't, and I said so. "It *don't* stand to no reason because Tex *wasn't dead.* I mean sometimes with him, when he gets funny, maybe you ain't so sure, but he ate his grub tonight, so I *don't think* he was dead–"

"The boy's right," said Coyote Jim the Halfbreed. "He wasn't dead, so he musta got turned into a zombie some other way."

"There is only one way," said Louisiana Louie. "For a living man to get turned into a zombie, he has to get bit by a zombie."

Some of the other cowboys joined in.

"That's why the top of his head was chawed off then?"

"Stands to reason."

It took them a while to work out the implications.

"That means there's *another zombie out there!*"

"Among the herd!"

"My God! We gotta protect the herd!"

Now what I wanted to know, and didn't have time to ask about, was why the whole top of Tex Weinstein's head was chawed off, because, well, a man's mouth ain't big enough to take a bite like that.

Just then a strange and eerie *mooing* came out of the darkness, like a long, lonesome wind, but with a voice, saying things you'd rather not hear.

I didn't have time to ask anything more because Big Sam shined the lantern out at the herd again, and we saw that every last one of them longhorn steers had its eyes rolled up all white, and them white eyes was *glowin'* like a million evil stars.

"It's too late to save the cattle," Big Sam said.

All of a sudden Louisiana Louie let out a shriek, because a zombie-eyed steer had lunged out of the darkness and caught his head in its foaming mouth. He wriggled a bit, but it wasn't no use. The critter chawed off the top of his skull and sucked out his brain as we watched. Then he came at us, hands out like claws, all a'slobberin' and most of us together shot out his eyes—which distracted him long enough for big Sam to make another of them *sigils* in the sand. When Louie—or what used to be Louie—stepped into it, we plugged him in the heart and that was the end of him.

"How did you learn to do that?" I asked Sam, pointing at the *sigil.*

"When you're trail boss long enough, son," he said, "you learn all sorts of things that come in handy."

Again, my heart swelled up with sheer hero-worship. "Jeepers—"

But there was no time for that.

All of us high-tailed it after that. We couldn't even get to our horses, because we heard the horses screamin' and we knowed that the cattle got to them first. It ain't a smart idea to ride a zombie horse. So we ran on foot, the cattle closin' in, until we reached the base of a rocky hill.

There we made our stand, shootin' out the eyes of the zombie longhorns, which continued to distract them a mite, but didn't kill them.

And among the rocks, there was no place to draw a *sigil.*

And we was runnin' out of bullets.

Up we climbed, up, and up, the cattle comin' after us. Somehow a dead steer can climb a lot better'n a live one. Don't ask me why. Maybe it's just more determined to catch up with a living man and chaw out his brain.

Another scream, and one of 'em got Coyote Jim the Halfbreed.

Up. There wasn't much of any place to go. Fortunately we came to an open, sandy spot, where Big Sam could make another *sigil*, so we was able to plug what used to be the Halfbreed and a dozen of the cattle, but there was too many of 'em, and our ammo, and our numbers was runnin' out, as the zombie cattle zombified one more cowboy after another.

At last it was only me and Big Sam at the top of the hill, back to back. I can tell you I was scairt. Who wouldn't be? As far as we could see, in every direction, zombie longhorns with eyes like glowing coals was coming at us, up, up to chaw out our brains.

But that wasn't the worst of it. Maybe I was plumb crazy already, but I swear as I looked up into the sky, I seen *behind* what few stars there were, enormous shapes, faces, the dreaming ghosts of the Great Old Ones walking above Great Old One Canyon, and some of them had faces full of feelers like squids, and some had wings, and burning eyes, and none of them was like anything you ever seen on Earth; and I knew that they *hated* us more than words could express, and were just lookin' for the chance to wipe us all out like some goddamn vermin they think we are.

I had only one bullet left. I put the muzzle of my gun under my chin and said, "Well, Sam, I wanted to grow up to be just like you, 'cause you're my hero, but I guess I ain't gonna get the chance." I was sobbin' then, I am not ashamed to say.

But Sam he took the gun away from my chin and he said, gently, like a daddy would to his boy, "There is another way, Rufus. But only for one of us." He pressed what felt like a piece of smooth, cold stone into my hand. "This is something else I picked up 'cause it might come in handy someday. It's called a shining trapezohedron. Stare into it like you is looking far, far away. You'll see something movin' in there. Call it to you. Ask it for help. There will be a price you have to pay. But it is the only way. Do it. Now give me your gun, and I'll try to distract them a bit more so you have a chance."

He took my gun, and put his last six bullets into his own, yelled "Yippie ki-yi-yo!" and charged down into the zombie herd, blastin' away. I don't think he got very far.

Then it was up to me. I held the shining trapezohedron in both of my hands and stared into it hard, and, yes, it was shining somehow, with light of its own, and then it seemed that a million stars flowed *out* of it like water out of a geyser, and I was *falling down* but into the sky at the same time, and the wind was howlin' all around me like the worst winter blizzard you ever heard with a hundred tornados joined in as chorus, and then I was lookin' out on *someplace else*, a different world, that was like a desert of blue ice, with three or four blue suns in the sky that didn't give off no heat at all.

And I saw, ridin' across that blue desert, a man all in black, but for his *silk mask,* which was yellow, and very strange because the bulges behind it didn't suggest a *human* face at all, not like he had a nose or a chin or anything . . . but Big Sam had told me what to do, and I done it. I called out to the rider of the dark, in something other than words, because when I opened my mouth there was only more howlin' of the wind, but somehow my *thought* was sent to him, and he heard me, and he turned in his course and came ridin' right at me, closer and closer, and I thought he was gonna ride me down, but at the last minute he grabbed me up like I was a little child and swung me up behind him in the saddle, and I clung to him as he rode down the rocky hillside. He didn't use his reins. His horse didn't need guiding. He had *black,* shiny six-guns in both hands, blazing away, and even after he'd shot a thousand times, he didn't run out of bullets, and somehow when he did it, as if *he himself was the sigil,* he kilt them zombies and zombie cattle, every last one of them. We rode on for hours, blastin' away, up and down the hill, all across the plain, into Great Old One Canyon and out again, shootin' and shootin' until there was nothin' left movin' anywheres, and then the sun come up, and the masked rider seemed to just fade away like mist, and I landed on the ground with a bump, and I didn't have no six-gun (because Sam had took mine), just the shining trapezo-hedron in my hand, and there was thousands of dead zombie cattle and dead zombie cowboys as far as the eye could see.

Then all I could do was walk, for days and nights without stoppin', without eatin' or drinkin', until I had become completely crazed, and it was all like a terrible dream that never, never ended. And I don't think it ever did end, even when I come to a farmhouse and fell down fainted on the floor. I remember thinkin', *Who was that masked man anyway?* and I remembered answerin' myself that he'd said his name was Nigel, Nigel R. Lathotep . . . some kinda Irish name, I think. And I laughed and laughed at that like I didn't have no brain left at all, and the folks that took me in thought I was just delirious, but what did they know? They had not *seen* what I had *seen,* now, had they?

※ ※ ※

Old Rufus Harris was still laughing over the table in the steakhouse when he finished this. "Now what do ya think of my story, Bobby Blake?" he said. "What do ya think? Did I give you the *real stuff?*" And he went on cackling and wheezing and cackling some more, so much that I was acutely aware that people were beginning to stare.

"Please, Sir," I said desperately.

He paused for just a moment to gaze longingly into my empty silver flask.

"I don't suppose you got any more of this fine concoction —?"

He started cackling again, louder and louder.

I had no choice. I got out the spare I carried in my boot. I had hoped to save that one for the holidays.

He snatched it from me and drained it.

"So, Bobby Blake, what'cha think?"

I measured my words carefully. I refrained from saying that, yes, he had given me the *real stuff*, because, having planned a career of writing about grotesquerie, horror, and the insane, it was helpful to make the acquaintance of a genuine, raving lunatic.

Instead I merely asked him about the *price* Big Sam had mentioned.

"Oh, that," he said. He got out what looked like a shiny black stone, perhaps a piece of obsidian, cut strangely, with many angles, so the eye could not quite grasp its shape. It was, of course the shining trapezohedron. He began to explain, in a voice that faded away as the wind roared louder and louder, how he had exchanged death for deathless bondage, how he was now an eternal servant of the Rider of the Dark, whose name was, more properly *Nyarlathotep*, and it was his task to recruit more such slaves like himself, whether willing or unwilling, it did not matter. "Ain't no use fightin', boy," he said. "You can't get away nohow."

Then I heard nothing more, and, staring into the shining trapezohedron, I seemed to be falling *down* into the starry sky, and gazing, or floating, over the frigid blue desert beneath the cold blue suns, as the rider in the silken mask drew ever closer to me.

It was only with the greatest strength of will that I broke away. I pushed the black stone back at the old man, then ran screaming from the room, out into the street and across to the train station, where, I discovered, I had missed my train.

Then I fell down faint, into a delirium, and I heard a voice whispering in my mind, the voice which inspires all my nightmare visions, all the hideous and terrible and strangely beautiful writings for which I have since become famous.

We shall meet again, Robert Blake, it says. *Though you flee to the ends of the Earth, it is no distance. We shall meet again.*

About the Contributors

JASON ANDREW lives in Seattle, Washington with his wife Lisa. As a child, Jason spent his Saturdays watching the Creature Feature classics and furiously scribbling down stories; his first short story, written at age six, titled "The Wolfman Eats Perry Mason" was rejected and caused his grandmother to watch him very closely for a few years.

MATTHEW BAUGH was born in Arizona and raised in New Mexico where he developed a great love for the cultures and landscape of the Southwest. Ironically he currently lives in the greater Chicago area where he is the pastor of a church. He is married to a lovely woman named Mary and is the obedient servant of their two cats.

TIM CURRAN lives in Michigan and is the author of the novels *Hive* and *Dead Sea* from Elder Signs Press. ESP will also be publishing the next two volumes of the *Hive* trilogy. His short stories have appeared in such magazines as *City Slab*, *Book of Dark Wisdom*, and *Inhuman*, as well as anthologies such as *Horrors Beyond*, *Shivers IV*, and *Hardboiled Cthulhu*.

STEVEN GILBERTS began displaying his work at science fiction and fantasy conventions in 1995. In 2003 he made the leap into the publishing field starting with *Space and Time* magazine. Now, living in a small Dunwich-esque southern Indiana town with his devoted wife Becky and an assortment of furry critters that run the household, Steve produces work for publications such as *Space and Time* magazine, *Dark Wisdom* magazine, and *Cemetery Dance*.

DURANT HAIRE lives in North Carolina and works full time as a technical writer. He's been published in *Horror Between the Sheets*, *Darkness Rising 6*, *Decadence 2*, and *Dark Lurkers*.

ANGELINE HAWKES has been appointed 2007 Texas A&M Alumni Ambassador for the Department of Literature. Her collection, *The Commandments*, received a Bram Stoker Award nomination. *Tales of the Barbarian Kabar of El Hazzar* is her latest series. *Blood Coven*, co-written with Christopher Fulbright, was just released from Dead Letter Press. Angeline has work in 30+ anthologies, novels, novellas, and short fiction.

WILLIAM JONES is a writer and editor who works in the fiction and hobby industries. His work spans mystery, horror, SF, historical, and fantasy. Some of his writings include *The Strange Cases of Rudolph Pearson* and *Frontier Cthulhu*, and a few of the anthologies he appears in are *Blood and Devotion*, and *Thou Shalt Not*. William is the editor of *Dark Wisdom* magazine, and he teaches English at a university in Michigan. www.williamjoneswriter.com.

SCOTT LETTE is a former communications consultant and post-graduate from Queensland University of Technology specialising in creative writing and media production. As an author he has worked on various role-playing titles before turning full-time to his craft, writing for the small screen, theatre and the printed word. This is his second Mythos outing in print.

PAUL MELNICZEK is the author of *Restless Shades, Frightful October, and A Halloween Harvest,* and has sold work to over 100 markets.

LON PRATER is the lucky father of two great girls, a stunt kite flyer and a writer of odd little tales. His dark fiction can be found in *Writers of the Future XXI*, the Stoker-winning anthology *Borderlands 5*, and many other venues. Find out more at www.LonPrater.com.

STEPHEN MARK RAINEY is author of the novels *Balak, The Lebo Coven, Dark Shadows: Dreams of the Dark* (with Elizabeth Massie), *The Nightmare Frontier*, and *Blue Devil Island*; three short story collections; and over 90 published works of short fiction. For ten years, he edited *Deathrealm* magazine and has edited the anthologies *Deathrealms, Song of Cthulhu*, and *Evermore* (with James Robert Smith). Mark lives in Greensboro, NC, with his wife Peggy. Visit him on the Web at http://www.stephenmarkrainey.com.

ROBERT J. SANTA has written speculative fiction for more than twenty years. His work has appeared in *Paradox, On Spec* (to include a radio play of the same story), Artemis and Horror Garage. Robert lives in Rhode Island with his beautiful wife and two, equally beautiful daughters. When not writing, he is editor and publisher of Ricasso Press.

DARRELL SCHWEITZER is the author of *The Mask of the Sorcerer, The White Isle,* and *The Shattered Goddess,* plus about 275 stories. He was co-editor of *Weird Tales* for 19 years and has published books about H.P. Lovecraft. He also rhymed "Cthulhu" in a limerick. He has been nominated for the World Fantasy Award 4 times. He recently edited *The Secret History of Vampires* (with Martin H. Greenberg) for DAW.

RON SHIFLET was born in Ft. Worth, Texas and currently resides in Crowley. He is an admirer of Robert E. Howard and H.P. Lovecraft and first contemplated writing after reading their work. His stories have appeared in *Dark Wisdom, Seasons in the Night,* and *Dark Legacy.* They have also been selected for anthologies such as *Eldritch Blue, Maelstrom, Travel a Time Historic* and *Goremet Cuisine.*

STEWART STERNBERG is a writer, educator who still sleeps with the lights on, and believes there are things scratching at the windows that are best ignored. He lives with his wife and three dogs, teaching alternative education in a rural school district. Interests include gaming, politics and American History. He also serves as a deacon at the *Church of the Starry Wisdom,* reformed.

CHARLES P. ZAGLANIS was able to claw his way to the Associate Editor position at *Dark Wisdom* Magazine through Machiavellian machinations and pure dumb luck. Pointed in Lovecraft's direction at a tender age by an Iron Maiden cover, Charles published RPG material with Chaosium and then moved on to fiction. His skewed vision of reality can be read in his short stories and anthologies. Visit him at: http://deep1hybrid.blogspot.com/.

LEE CLARK ZUMPE joined Tampa Bay Newspapers as proofreader and staff writer shortly after earning a B.A. in English at the University of South Florida. His nights are consumed with the invocation of ancient nightmares, dutifully bound in fiction and poetry. His work has appeared in *Weird Tales, Dark Wisdom, Horrors Beyond, Corpse Blossoms* and *Arkham Tales.* Visit www.freewebs.com/leeclarkzumpe.

CPSIA information can be obtained at www.ICGtesting.com
Printed in the USA
LVOW080016041211

257684LV00001B/6/A